The Wolf's Cub

Forge Books by Richard Parry

The Winter Wolf
The Wolf's Cub

The Wolf's Cub

Richard Parry

A TOM DOHERTY ASSOCIATES BOOK

NEW YORK

THE WOLF'S CUB

Copyright © 1997 by Richard Parry

This book is printed on acid-free paper.

A Forge Book
Published by Tom Doherty Associates, Inc.
175 Fifth Avenue
New York, NY 10010

Forge® is a registered trademark of Tom Doherty Associates, Inc.

Map by Ellisa Mitchell

Library of Congress Cataloging-in-Publication Data

Parry, Richard, date
    The wolf's cub / Richard Parry.
        p.   cm.
    Sequel to: The winter wolf.
    "A Tom Doherty Associates book."
    ISBN 0–312–86018–8
        1. Frontier and pioneer life—Alaska—Fiction. 2. Fathers and sons —Alaska—Fiction. 3. Wolves—Alaska—Fiction.
    4. Alaska—Fiction. I. Title.
    PS3566.A764W6   1997
    813'.54—dc21   97–13268

First edition: November 1997

Printed in the United States of America

0 9 8 7 6 5 4 3 2 1

To Faith Peck,
for putting a roof over our heads,
and
to Kathie,
for sheltering my heart

★ ★ ACKNOWLEDGMENTS ★ ★

I am deeply indebted to Tom Doherty for his faith in publishing this work and to Doug Grad, my editor, for his expert guidance. Annie De Santis at Tor and Adam Goldberger deserve a special thanks for their careful editing. Richard Cowley and Peter Lutjen must be congratulated for their wonderful art work and cover design that grace this book as well as the cover of *The Winter Wolf*. David Hale Smith of DHS Literary, Inc., is an agent that writers dream about. His encouragement and business acumen made this series possible.

Many thanks to Sharon Coulter and Sarah Kavorkian for running the office while I typed away.

Words cannot express my gratitude to my lovely wife, Kathie, for her constant encouragement and support.

⋆ ⋆ AUTHOR'S NOTE ⋆ ⋆

In creating historical fiction, the writer has the enjoyable task of weaving through the forest of a plot that has many real elements. Some of those forest trees are fictional and some represent actual historical fact. Care must be taken in handling them both. Fortunately, Alaska's history is replete with colorful characters and actual dramatic events that would tax the mind of even the most imaginative novelist. That has made my task so much easier.

Nathan Blaylock, Jim Riley, Doc Hennison, the spy Dickinson, and Marta Kelly are fictional characters. But Captain Abercrombie, Bishop Rowe, and Sam Steele of the Mounties were real and heroic men who played important roles in the opening of the Interior of Alaska.

E. T. Barnette and his whole riverboat crew also existed, and his chance grounding on the banks of the Chena River did lead to the founding of Fairbanks. His fortunes soared when gold was discovered and fell just as quickly when his unscrupulous nature finally ruined him—but that and his battles with Nathan Blaylock are the woods of the next book in this series.

—RGP

Arctic Ocean

Pt. Barrow

Icy Cape

Cape Lisburne
Pt. Hope

Manning Pt.
Demarcation Point

RUSSIA
East Cape

Kotzebue Sound

Romanzoff Mts.

Arctic Circle

Mackenzie

Bering Strait

Cape Prince of Wales
Hooknut

Koyukak R

Yukon Mts

Yukon River

Ft. Yukon

ROCKY

BRITISH
NORTH AMERICA

St. Lawrence Island

Norton Sound

Nulata

Eagle

Ft. Reliance

Cape Romanzoff

Anvik

KAIYUH MTS

Yukon River

Ft. Selkirk

Ikogmute

ALASKAN MOUNTAINS

Susitna R.

Copper R.

Nunivak Island

Kuskoquim R.

Valdez

Mt. St. Elias

Fort Alexander
Bristol Bay

Coos Inlet
KENAI

Port Etches
Pt. William Sound

ALASKA PENINSULA

Kodiak Island

Pacific Ocean

Baranof Island
Sitka

Coalfish Banks

Shumagin Island

Pedro's Dome

North

Site of the ✠ Moose Kill

Chena River

CHENA POST

Cap. BARNETTE'S TRADING POST

0   1   2 miles

Tanana River

Bates Rapids

Elisa Mitchell

Eagle ○

Yukon River

CAP. BARNETTE'S
TRADING POST

Tanana   Volkmar

Dawson ○

40-Mile R.

60-Mile River

ALASKA RANGE

River

TANANA
CROSSING

Delta River

White River

Tok R.

Shana

MENTASTA
PASS

Tetlin R.

Nabesna R.

Gulkana R.

the
WINTER
SLED
ROUTE

Snag Cr.

Lake
Louise

Taslina R.

Copper River

WRANGELL MTS.

SKOLAI
PASS

tanuska R.

the
GLACIER

Tonsina R.

ALASKA   CANADA

Valdez

CHUGACH

Tasnuna

Chitina River

owe

MOUNTAINS

Mt.
Logan

Prince William
Sound

Mt. St.
Elias

Pacific Ocean

0   25   50 miles

The Wolf's Cub

By the summer of 1901 the great stampede to the Klondike had slowed to a trickle. The fabulous golden sands of Nome lay covered with tents and enmeshed in webs of mining claims. Giant mining cartels and commercial companies controlled all the richest mines. Only the raw plains of the Alaskan Interior offered an unfettered chance at the next El Dorado.

But the Interior was far more hostile than all the other strikes. Its streams and rivers, mostly uncharted, trapped the unwary with their treacherous sandbars and countless braided courses. Worse still, these icy waters, milky white with powdered rock, flowed out from the Interior, away from the gold. So travel on the waterways was constantly a struggle upstream. What gold was found in streambeds lay deep beneath the surface, clenched in the relentless grip of the frozen land.

Yet, singly, and in groups of twos and threes, desperate men moved into the silent plains and mountains in search of that yellow metal that drove them to forsake all else. Scratching and searching each rock, each stream as they ventured deeper into the unknown, they marked their endeavor with camps and trails, and with their bones—which the land soon swallowed.

Two men traveled this wilderness for a different reason than seeking gold. They came simply to view the next unknown valley, to taste the water from a stream unsampled by white men, to breathe air unsoiled by coal fires, and to listen to the silence in the cold of night. The rattle of sluice boxes and the rumble of stamp mills insulted their ears, and gold held no lure for them other than to buy the bare necessities for their next trek. In short, they came for the freedom that the land presented.

The travel was hard, but to both men, the young one as well as his older companion, life had always been hard. Events had cruelly robbed them of their childhood through no fault of their own.

The older man, Jim Riley, had been on the run since he killed five men in a saloon shoot-out in the cattle town of Newton Station, Kansas, in 1871. As a seventeen-year-old youth he had avenged the killing of his trail boss. His success made him a legend and forever doomed him to a life on the run.

His youthful companion, Nathan Blaylock, had suffered equally in less than two years. Torn from an orphanage in Colorado, he discovered he was the bastard son of Wyatt Earp, the legendary gunfighter. Chasing a deadly request for revenge and fortune from his dead mother, he and Riley had pursued his father across half the Pacific Coast to the wide-open town of Nome. Their encounter left both Blaylock and Earp unexpectedly changed.

The death of his Chinese lover in Dawson while giving birth to his own son further fired Nathan in life's crucible, ending his youth forever.

Forged together by their trials into a tough and self-reliant team, the young and the old wandered the wilderness.

ONE

TANANA VALLEY, ALASKA.
AUGUST 26, 1901.

The bull moose loitered just inside the stand of birch trees that had been his home for most of the summer and swung his massive head to sample the cool breeze rising from the valley floor. His eyes swept the undulating folds of forest rolling carelessly down to the braided bed of the Tanana River. Though far away, the course of the Tanana stood starkly as a reminder of the force and mastery of the rivers over this land. While the distant water glinted brightly, its bed flashed white as if the bones of the earth had been scoured clean by the river's passage.

Already the birch were turning, spattering the verdant hills and surrounding the somber green spruce with islands of golden leaves that burned brightly in the low morning sun. The bull grunted, and his breath steamed in the air. The last remnant of the evening frost crackled beneath his hooves. All his instincts pointed to one thing: winter was coming.

His nose caught the smell of a new animal in his realm, one especially rancid smelling. But he was unconcerned. In the sixth year of his life, he had no real enemies, except perhaps a desperate grizzly. Heavy shouldered and with massive antlers, he presented a formidable target to all but the largest of bears. Only a broken leg or a wound from the coming rut would see him dragged down and torn apart by winter wolves.

What he smelled was no bear, so he returned to eating and to his task of stripping the velvet from his horns. By rasping his brow tines and wide palms against the trees and brush, he had transformed his antlers from soft brown to bone white to a now willow-stained mahogany. With his darkening coat and thick-timbered headgear, he could look forward to dominating the mating season. Soon his neck would swell and he would cease eating, devoting all energy to sparring with rival males while the cows watched and waited.

The brush crackled, and he swiveled his ears in that direction. The pungent odor came from there as well.

A tongue of flame leapt from the underbrush, followed closely by a crack that rolled into the valley to reverberate off the surrounding domes. The moose staggered and started to run. Instinctively he sought water, where his long legs gave him an advantage. Ahead lay a creek, dammed by an industrious beaver where it flowed in the crotch of the hill. He pitched forward into the beaver pond and sank. Only his dark, glistening back and the tops of his antlers remained above the surface. He sighed once and his last set of bubbles blew to the surface.

"Damn, he sure don't drop like no buffalo I ever saw," Jim Riley swore as he rose from a clump of alder. He pulled his tattered slouch hat from his head, waved it at a few mosquitoes, and wiped his forehead on his sleeve. "You drilled him square through the heart, Nat, an' he still was contrary enough to go and sink hisself."

Beside him emerged Nathan Blaylock, still holding his smoking .45-70 rifle. He frowned at the rifle in his hands. "Maybe I need a bigger gun, Jim."

"They don't make no bigger gun, boy. 'Less you use a Sharps .50, and I ain't lugging that shoulder cannon all over this creation unless I have to. Your rifle is damned heavy enough as it is. Or do I have to remind you we are afoot."

Riley sidled down to the water and squinted at the steaming hump. "This sure ain't gonna be no fun," he said flatly. "If I weren't hungry enough to eat my cartridge belt, I'd have half a mind to leave him. No self-respecting buffalo would ever do such a mean thing as this. No sirree. They'd set down right proper so's you could dress 'em out with nary a fuss." He slumped onto the bank and let his ruined boots slide into the water. "Well, you're the one with all the sea experience, so you gits to be the deep-sea diver, Nat."

Nathan strode past his friend to wade into the pond. Submerged to his waist, he groped about in the water until his fingers touched the velvety soft muzzle of the animal. Gently, he lifted the enormous head and propped it against the bank. For several moments he studied the baleful brown eyes of the creature he had just killed. Then he broke a willow branch and placed it carefully in the animal's mouth.

"Doing that Indian thing again, I see," Riley commented.

Blaylock nodded. "Food for his trip to the spirit world. I don't want his *inua* angry at me."

Riley pulled off his boot and studied the remaining remnants of his sock. More foot than fabric presented itself. "How come we don't do that to all the men we killed? Maybe they'd have appreciated munching on a potato or two while they tramped down the road to hell, eh?" His stomach growled loudly at the thought of food. "But do you have to shoot the potato, too, to turn it into a spirit potato? How else are they gonna be able to eat it?"

Nathan smiled at his companion. More father and mentor to him than Wyatt Earp, his real father, Riley still tried hard to hide his soft side with a prickly facade. But the youth refused to take the bait. "Well, Jim, you just might have a point there. Maybe we ought to carry a can of beans for just such an occasion."

Riley chuckled. "Hell, we'd need to carry a crate of beans at the rate we're going." He removed his gun belt and pulled a bowie knife from the top of his boot and slipped into the water.

Riley was right. It was no fun. The animal lay atop his legs, making it impossible to turn him, and with no tackle, the two men could not pull him from the pond. Eventually, Nathan resigned himself to quartering the moose where he lay.

Four hours later, the two men sat panting on the bank. Riley rolled onto his back and raised his head to look down at his blood-soaked rags as he wiped his greasy hands on his shirt.

"I'd say us and this moose are even now," he sighed. "You may have killed him, but he just put us through plain hell."

Nearby, the four quarters of the moose and its ribs rested on the clean, out-turned hide. The rich meat gleamed at them, filling the air with its sweet smell, while brash camp-robber jays boldly stole chunks of suet from the piles. Overhead, three ravens circled the kill and showered the two men with raucous insults in hopes of driving them away.

Alongside the meat, a small bed of coals alternately glowed and faded as the wind fanned its embers. Skewers of backstrap muscle roasted patiently over the fire. Riley crawled on his knees to the fire and sniffed the aroma of the sizzling meat. His mouth watered at the thought of the first meat they'd eaten in over two weeks. Hunger got the better of him, and he juggled a slab of hot meat from hand to hand until it cooled enough for him to wolf it down.

Nathan waded over to the rivulet pouring over the beaver's dam and washed the blood and grease from his arms. He stripped off his reddened shirt and scrubbed it with a handful of spruce needles. The sunlight rippled across his muscles as he washed.

He had come a long way since leaving the Catholic orphanage in Denver as an awkward youth. Now twenty, he stood well over six feet, and his body was iron hard from crisscrossing the rugged Alaskan Interior. In their wanderings since leaving

Nome, Nathan and Riley had explored lands never seen by white men. While they hiked or rafted or rode the land, it molded the youth into one of its own. The Great Land did that to all who came, considering them trespassers until it could test them. Those who passed its exams were forever changed; those who failed died, or left as broken men.

Nathan Blaylock had passed with flying colors. Now his limbs and muscles were hard as the rocks lining the hidden mountain passes, and his gray eyes were clear and cold as the glacial streams. But inside, a part of him still yearned for the lost love of his China girl.

"Do you ever regret not collecting that twenty thousand dollars, Jim?" Nathan asked. "I mean not killing Wyatt for that bounty money?"

Riley stopped gnawing on a charred hunk of meat and wiped the dripping juices from his chin. He started to reply, but an unchewed morsel wedged itself in his throat, causing him to cough and choke violently.

"Damn! That moose is trying to kill me again!" he sputtered. His finger dug about in his mouth until he extracted the offending wad of gristle. He inspected the culprit before flinging it into the brush. Instantly, a camp robber retrieved it and flew off. "Maybe you ought to stuff more sticks in its mouth or something." He eyed the moose's head suspiciously.

"Do you regret it, Jim? We could be sitting in a grand hotel in San Francisco right now, sipping champagne and eating caviar."

"Nah." Riley rolled his tongue over his front teeth. "They'd make me take a bath afore they'd let me into one of those fancy places. And listen to yerself talk, boy. You ain't never had no caviar. It's somethin' you read about in a book. Nothing but fish eggs."

Nathan laughed. "Well, you just took a bath with that moose."

"Yeah, and we both needed it."

Nathan stopped laughing, and his face turned somber. "Seriously? No regrets? That was a lot of money."

Riley flung his skewer away and watched the birds dive after it. He sighed loudly. Nathan had a melancholy streak in him a mile long at times. Riley recognized it because he had one, too. Fortunately, their streaks had not yet surfaced at the same time.

"I reckon it's time again for my Uncle Jim talk. How many times have I told you that no good ever comes of bad money? That reward yer mama put on yer daddy was for revenge. That makes it bad money, plain and simple. Bad money leads to bad luck, no matter how much it is. Besides, it don't take no expert to see Wyatt Earp weren't none of the things we was led to believe he was. He did the best thing for you he could."

Nathan nodded. "I think so. I just feel bad for you at times. . . ."

The old gunfighter exploded. He jumped to his feet and began stomping about the campfire in his holey stockings. "Listen here, don't never feel sorry for me, Nat. When we met in Pinal, I was a stone's throw from freezing to death—a broken old saddle bum with nothin' to his name but a played-out saddle blanket. And you gave me a new life. You gave me the two things I wanted most. You taught me to read like I promised my mother, and you gave me a true friend."

"Why, Jim." Nathan grinned lopsidedly up at his emotional friend. This was a tender side that the thorny gunman rarely exposed. "That's the sweetest thing you ever said to me. But you're my family, Jim, and I hope you think the same of me."

Riley wiped his eyes on his sleeve and blew his nose on the corner of his shirt. "Damned moose must've got up my nose as well," he muttered defensively.

Nathan hugged his knees and gazed across the rolling valley. They'd traveled the last ten days without a single sign of another living soul. But Wei-Li was always beside him, blowing on the back of his neck in the evening breeze, laughing softly in the chatter of the leaves, and waiting for him in the shadows. When he got that faraway look, Riley knew he was remembering her.

"You know, Jim, life loves to play sour tricks on us. Here I was intending to kill Wyatt for leaving me in that orphanage, and all the time he never knew I existed. Yet I *know* I have a son, and I left him in Dawson. Does that make me a worse father than my own?"

"Now don't go sitting on yer spurs about that. You did the best you could at the time. You ran away when your girl died. I would have done the same. Yer babe got—well, sort of overlooked in the process. Hell, when they're small like that they're easy to miss."

"Do you think he might grow up wanting to kill me?"

Riley sighed. That thought troubled him as well. "Nat, we did all we could. We went back to Dawson when most sensible folks were holing up for the coming winter. But they was gone. Doc and yer babe vanished without a trace. And we've been all over this godforsaken land looking for them. Why, I never heard tell of no other white man's been where we've tromped, like over that canyon route from Valdez to here for instance. We done checked every dang place big enough to have a tin-roofed outhouse looking for yer boy. I swear, my feet are plumb worn out. The next blacksmith we run across, I'm gonna get myself shod. But I ain't complaining, mind you. Being with you has give my life a whole new direction—mainly north. It's just no self-respecting drover would give hisself over to so much footwork as we have."

Nathan studied the piles of meat. "What do you suggest we do with all this meat? We can't pack it."

Riley brightened as he removed another skewer and sucked a cube of meat into his mouth. "Best to hole up here and eat away until the pile is carryable," he suggested help-fully. "We got enough to eat now and that makes me real happy."

"If you're happy, Jim, well, then so am I."

"Happy? You bet I'm happy. Jus' look about you." Riley sat up and swept his arms in a wide circle. "If this ain't God's coun-try, I don't know what is. Cold clear water, sweet-smelling air, and room to stretch out without bumping elbows with some yahoo. Not like Frisco, where you couldn't walk a straight line without running into some swell and his dandified horse, and especially not like that hellhole Dawson."

Nathan winced at the mention of the city that held so many painful memories for him, and Riley immediately tried to cover his unfortunate slip.

"Nat, that place weren't natural. Forcing men to live and work in holes in the earth like prairie dogs was plain sinful." He scratched the back of his head and poked a grubby finger at his eyes. "Jus' look what it did to me. My peepers were turning into beady little things like a mole for lack of sunlight. Oooh"—he quivered—"it makes me shiver even now, thinking about it."

Nathan stood slowly and stared past his friend at the silver fishhook of the river far below them. But Riley continued his sermon.

"Yes sirree, this is the place, boy. Just us. Not another per-son in a thousand miles to tromp on yer toes. No one to—" Riley stopped in midsentence and turned to follow Nathan's gaze.

A black wisp of smoke rose from the distant river, standing out starkly against the painfully blue sky before trailing off downstream. The wind shredded this smudge until it vanished, but more fumes belched from the tiny craft that threaded its way among the braided channels and sandbars of the upper

Tanana. The two men watched in silence as the vessel struggled without success to find a passage. Then it doubled back, leaving a sooty black cloud as the only marker of its failure.

Nathan glanced at his friend. "Looks like company. We're not alone anymore. . . ."

★ ★ TWO ★ ★

Elbridge Truman Barnette stood feet apart on the high riverbank and glared up at Charles Adams, captain of the steamer *Lavelle Young*. His right hand rested on the butt of his pistol, and his fingers tapped the bone grips menacingly. In turn, Captain Adams kept half his body hidden behind a wooden support to the upper deck. His deck crew eyed the confrontation warily and waited for orders. Both men had quick tempers fitted to their pigheaded natures.

"Damn it, Adams, you can't unload my supplies here!" Barnette swore. "We're in the middle of nowhere!"

"That was the contract, Captain Barnette, and you agreed to it back in Saint Michael. The *Lavelle Young* was to proceed up the Tanana as far as the mouth of the Chena River. And I've done that. We can't get past those channels in the Tanana. We grounded three times trying."

"Goddamn it, Adams, be reasonable! We're no more than halfway to Tanana Crossing."

"You agreed if I could get no farther beyond the Chena Slough you would get off with all your goods *no matter where that happened to be!*"

"Look, Adams, I've talked to an Indian who says this Rock River joins up again with the Tanana above Bates Rapids. If we just—"

Adams waved his hand abruptly, chopping the air. "We

tried that E. T., and look what happened. We ran out of water eight miles upstream! And we got stuck up there, too! Lord, they didn't name the Chena the Rock River for no good reason. Chena means rock, and we hit a hundred of them coming and going."

"But—"

"No buts, Captain Barnette. The *Lavelle* has no steam winch or deck gear to pull us off a bar if we really get stuck. Now, I took a chance as it was backing downstream to put you off here. It's the best place I could find. It's high ground with plenty of trees to build your camp."

"For God's sake, Adams. At least take me back down the Tanana to the telegraph outpost or Chena City. This is wild country here. I've got my wife to think about!"

Adams flushed a deep crimson at that remark. He had urged Barnette not to bring his wife, but to no avail. Now he resented having her thrown in his face. *I can't do that, you pig-headed fool!* I would if I could, but I can't. Running downriver with your load would kill us all if we struck a sandbar. The force of the Tanana would rip the bottom out of an overloaded boat for sure. Even if it didn't, we'd never get her unstuck. This is the best I can do for you. And it's in the contract, fair and square. We both agreed to that."

"To hell with your damned contract, and to hell with you," Barnette said, and stomped off.

Adams turned to his first mate. "Start unloading and make it quick. The sooner Barnette's supplies are ashore, the faster we can get out of here. There's frost in the air, and the water's dropping. I don't want the *Lavelle* stranded here for the winter." The mate touched his cap in a salute and hurried down to the main deck, where crates and supplies wrapped in canvas lay lashed to the cleats. Adams dug into his pocket for the key to unlock the firearms in his day cabin, and headed in that direction. Barnette might make a fight of it.

Ashore, Captain Barnette thrust his hands deep into his pockets and stomped around the bluff with his shoulders hunched. Dark black spruce covered the site, casting a gloomy pall on his blackening mood. His plans to reach Tanana Crossing had failed. The river was too low. And he had agreed to be put off if they couldn't get any farther upstream. But to be marooned here in the middle of nowhere, facing a bitter winter and hostile Indians, was a bitter pill.

He toyed with the idea of seizing the *Lavelle Young*. A handful of men remained loyal to him: Big Ben Atwater, Jim Eagle, Shorty Robinson, and Wada the Jap. But he'd not had time to arm them. The return of Captain Adams to the bridge quashed that idea. Adams emerged from his cabin looking like a river pirate, with a brace of pistols thrust into his waistband and a Winchester nestled in the crook of his arm. Worse still, his first mate and two other men also sported rifles.

The hysterical sobbing of his wife, Isabelle, diverted his thoughts. He walked to where she huddled on a chest surrounded by threatening spruce. The splintered lower limbs seemed to stab at her like spikes from an iron maiden. She met his gaze with frightened eyes.

"E. T., they can't abandon us here!" she cried. "We'll die out here."

"Now, Belle, don't fret. Everything will work out, you'll see." He patted her shoulder, but she only intensified her wailing.

Barnette grimaced. He'd married Isabelle Cleary in Montana for her beauty and her money. Having a powerful brother didn't hurt either, but since coming to Alaska she'd turned more and more demanding, clinging to him at the drop of a hat and falling into jealous fits. Lord knew what she'd do if she learned of his dalliances.

"Where do you want us to start, Captain?" Jim Eagle interrupted his thoughts. Eagle was an old Indian fighter who'd missed the Klondike stampede, but his gray head held useful experience. "This is the best ground as I see it. We can clear it and use the trees to build a trading post and a stockade in case the natives prove uppity."

Barnette nodded. "Captain Adams, will your men help us clear this site?" he shouted to the grim-faced Adams.

Adams dissolved in relief at the thought of avoiding a fight. "Be happy to, Captain Barnette!" he answered.

Within minutes the silty bluff overlooking the surly river rang with the sound of axes and falling trees. All day long Barnette's men and the crew of the *Lavelle Young* labored to clear a site for the winter. Tents were erected to cover the stores and provide for Mrs. Barnette as the men worked on into the night. A crisp evening kept the mosquitoes at bay as the work continued under the flickering glow of pitch-soaked torches and kerosene lamps. All the while Adams anxiously watched the level of the river drop.

By the next morning an eight-by-twelve-foot cabin for the captain and his lady rubbed shoulders with a log trading post fifty-four feet long and twenty-six feet wide. Half the weary men struggled to roof the structure with sod and tin sheeting while the rest anxiously completed the six-foot-high walls that encircled the stockade. Canvas wall tents sprawled about inside the protective walls, adding to the impression that a careless giant had stomped the hill flat while emptying the contents of his pockets onto the ground. But Captain E. T. Barnette had his trading post.

His wife emerged from her tent in a silk dressing gown, but her rouge did little to hide the anxious look on her face as the *Lavelle Young* fired up her boilers in a cloud of black soot.

Adams emerged from the wheelhouse and climbed down to the main deck. He noted with satisfaction his ship was riding higher without the 130 tons of Barnette's trade goods. He walked ashore and extended his hand to E. T., but the man refused to shake. Instead he thrust a packet of letters into the startled skipper's hand.

"I'm sending an urgent letter to my brother-in-law, Frank Cleary, to catch the first steamer to Valdez. I trust you'll deliver my mail for me?"

Adams nodded. "I'll do that."

"Dan McCarty here will head south over the mountains to meet Cleary in Valdez and bring him back," Barnette continued, half speaking out loud to himself as he formed his plans.

"What for, man? They'll have to cross the Valdez Glacier in the dead of winter. Why risk their lives on such a dangerous passage?" Adams asked.

"None of your damned business," Barnette snapped. He now regarded Adams as no friend, possibly even an enemy. Cleary was the only one he could trust to guard his supplies while he left to find a flat-bottomed craft that could cross the braided channels above Bates Rapids. Reaching Tanana Crossing to build his trading post at that strategic site all but consumed his entire thoughts.

"Well, then to hell with you, Captain Barnette," Adams snarled as he touched his cap in a mock salute. "And I'll be taking my leave of you and your nasty nature." He retreated up the gangplank, taking care not to turn his back on Barnette, and disappeared into his wheelhouse. Instantly, the steam whistle shrieked twice, shattering the silence, and causing the crew to scramble aboard.

Isabelle Barnette wailed in alarm as the captain and his handful of men gathered on the bank to watch the *Lavelle* pull her prow off the mud bank and edge down the river. Like a wary prizefighter retreating to his corner at the bell, the battered ship backed away, feeling her way into deeper water before executing a turn. With another cloud of smoke, the paddle wheel churned the water into mud and the *Lavelle* disappeared around a tree-shrouded bend.

The group watched until the trail of smoke vanished and all sound of the thrashing paddle blades ceased. Then each man returned to his work. No help was coming. They were cut off from civilization. Their survival now depended on their own skills.

"Captain Barnette! Captain Barnette!" Ben Atwater's voice broke across the clearing. "Over here, quick, Captain!"

Isabelle clutched her husband's arm as he turned to search for Atwater over the field of tree stumps. "Indians!" she cried. "Coming to scalp us!"

Barnette broke free from her grasp, snatched a rifle, and strode to the far end of the compound. An amazing sight greeted him. Here in the middle of the wilderness, his unfinished store already had customers.

Two ragged miners stood outside the stockade and gawked at the place. One, a frail-looking swarthy man, was staring at Jujiro Wada, the Japanese cook. The captain waved the men through the gate and waited.

"I'm Tom Gilmore," the one prospector said as he extended his hand. "And this is my sidekick, Felix Pedro. We saw your steamer yesterday from that dome over there." He pointed to a rounded mountain off to the northeast. "Saw you turn back, so we started down to meet you. Where's your boat?"

"He left us here," Barnette said flatly. "I aim to establish a trading post here for the winter until I can move further up the Tanana to Tanana Crossing."

"You should stay here, mister," Pedro advised in heavily accented English. "This place gonna be a bigger strike than the Klondike. Bigger than Nome, I bet ya."

Barnette's ears perked up at the mention of gold. He ushered the two miners out of earshot while he waved his crew back to work. Gilmore and Pedro followed him, stopping at times like children in a candy store to look at the piles of flour sacks, tins of beans, and jars of coffee. For the last month the two had been boiling spruce and willow bark with Labrador tea leaves as a poor substitute for coffee, and gnawing on dried moose jerky until their teeth hurt at the thought of eating.

"Sit down and fill your bellies, men. You look like you could use a good meal." He waved at the bubbling pot of beans and pork that Jujiro was stirring beside the boiling coffee. E. T. watched the two salivate as he piled food onto their tin plates. As the men wolfed down the food, he studied them craftily. When they began to slow the shoveling process, Barnette asked offhandedly, trying hard to keep the excitement from his voice, "What's this about a strike?"

Gilmore started to shrug, but his excitable partner spilled his beans as well as their secret.

"We found a big strike. Nuggets like goose eggs just laying in the creek bed. You couldn't step without standing on a million dollars. A big strike!" His hands, still clutching a slab of Wada's sourdough bread, spread wide as his shoulders.

"Where?" E. T. asked.

"Out there." Felix's finger jabbed the air in the direction of their dome. "Somewhere up there."

"Somewhere?" Barnette's eyebrows arched.

Gilmore shuffled his feet in disgust. "That's just it, Captain. We found the damn creek in ninety-eight. We call it Lost Creek 'cause we ain't been able to find it since. That's what we're doing now, searching for our Lost Creek. We run out of supplies and was planning on heading back to Circle City for another grubstake when we saw your steamboat. Buying supplies from you'd save us a three-hundred-mile walk to Circle and back."

"Our Lost Creek is a rich strike!" Felix protested. "Someday, you'll see. We'll find it, and then this place is gonna be twice the size of Dawson."

E. T. shook his head. Next, they'd ask him for credit. They must take him for a fool with their lost creek story. "I think you boys have been out in the bush for too long." He started to return to supervising his stockade when Pedro grasped his shoulder.

"Maybe you think different about these, eh?" He grinned as he withdrew a filthy red bandana from his trousers and unfolded it.

Captain Barnette's eyes widened as the morning sun cast its light on three thick nuggets, each larger than a silver dollar. Exposed to the sunlight, the gold nuggets gleamed sullenly, as if they resented being wrenched from the dark earth where they had hidden since the world was formed. *There was a lost creek.*

★ ★ THREE ★ ★

Isabelle Cleary Barnette busied herself with arranging the things in her new cabin. There was plenty to do, unpacking her traveling chests, fitting curtains to the one window of her home, and covering the dirt floor with throw rugs. But her mind kept returning to the marked change in her status since coming ashore. In Montana and Seattle, she was the captain's lady, wined and dined and fussed over. Here on this ugly mud rise with its somber spruce, she felt more like one of her husband's precious goods.

E. T.'s overwhelming obsession with reaching Tanacross, as the natives called it, had filled his every waking moment up to this point. Now his trading post obsessed him. That left little time for her, and Isabelle was feeling neglected.

But E. T. had changed as well. Here he no longer was the charming man who had courted her in Montana. So dashing, so reckless then with his buckskin coat and pants, he had fitted her girlish notions of the true adventurer she so cherished. Born and raised in a strict Catholic family, Isabelle sported a romantic nature far different from her parents. Her only escape from their close watch had lain in reading. James Fenimore Cooper and his Leatherstocking Tales had transported her from the dullness of her life and had filled her nights with romantic dreams.

Her heart skipped at thoughts of the strong, silent woodsman snatching her from danger and carrying her off. E. T., she thought, was that cavalier when she married him, but now she knew differently.

Isabelle blushed as she realized how the threat of Indian attack and abandonment had given way to something else, how it had left her aroused. But her husband was too preoccupied to notice. Damn him and his silly fort.

She pouted as she looked out her cabin door at Barnette. He took more interest in those unkempt prospectors then he did in her. There he was outfitting them when he should be tending to her needs, she thought.

Hands on her hips, Isabelle paced about the confining cabin until she thought she would scream. The walls threatened to smother her. She needed to get out. The idea of looking for cranberries sprang to mind. The ground back from the river seemed ideal for them, so with basket in hand, she slipped outside.

Isabelle toyed with the idea of asking her husband for an escort, but the scathing look he had given her when she screamed at those miners cast a chill on that idea. He'd only call her hysterical. Sullenly, she reckoned her husband and the others would never miss her. Besides, she'd overheard those miners telling the captain that the Indians were friendly, so there was nothing to fear.

Once past the log stockade, the spruce forest opened onto gentle folding rises crowned with gold-leafed birch and carpeted with scarlet fireweed and highbush cranberry. The air smelled fresh and clean after the smoke-stained steamship, and bore the licorice scent of meadow mushrooms. A light breeze rustled the branches overhead, and Isabelle skipped among the aureate shafts of sunlight and falling flaxen leaves, feeling all the while like a princess in a magical forest.

Soon all sight of the compound vanished, and only the sounds of axes and hammering served to orient her to the location of the stockade. A dense patch of cranberries filled a sunlit clearing ahead. Humming happily to herself, the captain's lady spread her crinolines among the colors and began to fill her basket.

In no time her basket brimmed with dark red cranberries, and she rose to return to the camp. But a stirring in the thicket to her left piqued her curiosity. Several plump spruce hens had waddled unafraid across her path as she walked, and once she saw a soft-eyed rabbit watching her with equal unconcern. Wouldn't E. T. be impressed if she caught one for a pet, she thought. Maybe then he'd pay more attention to her. With a giggle she crept to the bushes and parted them.

Isabelle started in terror. Inches from her face a black bear lurched upward onto his hind feet, cranberries, branches, and leaves dropping from his mouth. The bear snorted as Isabelle screamed. She spun, scattering her basket's contents in all directions. Stumbling blindly through the brush, she kept looking over her shoulder, indifferent to the branches that snatched at her dress. Any minute the bear would be upon her, she feared.

Isabelle Cleary Barnette crashed headlong into the arms of Nathan Blaylock. Colliding with his muscled chest all but knocked the wind out of her, but his sinewy arms caught her before she could fall. There he held her, breathless, while she gazed into his iron gray eyes. His lean face, framed by shoulder-length raven hair, seemed to swim before her startled vision. To make matters worse, Nathan had stripped his shirt off and the sun now backlit his windblown hair and muscled frame. In an instant, Isabelle knew *he* was the woodsman of her dreams.

"The bear! Save me, please!" she gasped, wide-eyed. But her eyes never left his face. Already she felt her body responding to his. Her reaction filled her with shame . . . and with a delicious thrill.

Nathan looked past her to the forest beyond. Swatches of sunlight leaked through the screen of spruces, and the light breeze rustled the falling birch leaves. But no other movement caught his eye. He frowned. No bear was forthcoming. He tried to free himself, but she clung steadfastly.

"I don't see any bear," he said.

"There was one. . . ." Her voice trailed off, and she felt foolish. The captain would laugh at her, maybe even slap her like he'd done on the trip to Saint Michael.

But Nathan simply smiled down at her. "I believe you. But he's not coming. I suspect you scared that bear as much as he did you," he said gently.

"Them bears ain't the most dangerous thing in this here forest," Jim Riley muttered as he stepped from behind a tree and watched the girl entwined with his friend. The old gunfighter studied them with narrowed gaze, and his old eyes saw trouble. A white woman in the middle of nowhere, all gussied up in crinolines and ribbons, meant grief for sure. This lady obviously belonged to some powerful man, and Jim knew those types of men didn't take kindly to others messing with their females. Sort of like a bull elk in perpetual rut, he surmised. Doing so was a good way to get gored.

Isabelle looked at Riley, then back at Nathan. She chose to ignore the older man's flinty words, but she caught his meaning. Surprisingly, she didn't care. Her eyes lighted upon the green carved dragon hanging from his neck; but before she could speak, the sound of a rifle being cocked reached her.

"Unhand my wife," E. T. commanded. He stood, chest heaving from exertion, with a Winchester clasped in his hands. Behind him stood Wada, Jim Eagle, and a third man. All held rifles.

"Now hold on, mister," Nathan protested.

"Shut up!" Barnette snapped. "I know what you men were

planning. And we hang men for rape." He nodded to one man, who stepped forward and drove the butt of his rifle viciously at Nathan's head.

But Nathan did the unexpected. He pushed the startled Isabelle into Barnette and ducked under the rifle's swing. Using the man's own weight, Nathan swung his assailant around as a shield and stripped the rifle from his hands. Concurrently, Jim Riley vanished behind a tree.

That split second turned the tables. Barnette struggled to regain his balance, entangled in his wife's dress, while the others stood helplessly by. Nathan held his attacker by the throat while his Colt .45 pointed at the captain. Riley popped up unexpectedly behind a clump of trees four yards away with his own Winchester covering the others.

"Ain't gonna be no hanging for somethin' we ain't done!" Riley called out. "Not by no cheechako Johnnies like you jokers."

Isabelle sprang to her feet, her face burning in humiliation, and launched a tirade at her astonished husband. "These men saved my life, E. T.!" she shrieked. "They helped me, and you . . . you want to hang them? Oh, I'm so embarrassed! What were you thinking, Captain Barnette?"

"What . . . ?" Barnette stuttered.

"*There was a bear!* Chasing me!" she continued while she straightened her dress, trying to avoid the stare from Nat.

Old Jim Eagle stared at the trees that held Riley. "Damnation," he grinned. "I ain't seen that trick but once before, and it was down in the Powder River country. A gunman named Jim Riley pulled it on some rustlers."

"Well, you lived long enough to see it pulled again by the same Jim Riley," came Riley's growl. "But you ain't living beyond today, 'less'n you drop them lever actions, now!"

Barnette watched his men drop their rifles, and he followed suit. He stepped away from his fuming wife and set his own rifle down. "We made a mistake, mister," he addressed Nathan. "I'm sorry, but—"

"Sorry don't mean much to the wrong man you done hung," Riley spit. "I seen too much of that in my time."

"Don't shoot Soapy." Barnette softened his tone as he addressed the youth. He'd noticed the young man had said little but done much in the last few seconds. A man of action, E. T. noted. "Let him go."

"Soapy?" Nathan cast a quizzical look at Barnette as he released his shield.

"Soapy Smith the second, I call myself," the man retorted. "Give me back my rifle."

Nathan studied the speaker. He wore a checkered waistcoat and tan breeches tucked into the tops of his boots. With a wide-brimmed hat set on the back of his head, and his close-cropped beard, he bore a passable resemblance to the notorious con man from Skagway. "Strange that you'd call yourself after a cheat and scoundrel who was shot down on the streets of Skagway. I'd have thought there were better names available," he said.

"Like what?" the man simmered. His eyes glinted sharply like two chips of obsidian.

"Like Natty Bumppo or Ivanhoe, for one," Nathan drawled as he grinned. But his smile carried no warmth. He sensed this man was vermin, perhaps a killer as well, and not one who'd face you in a fair fight. His smarmy looks reminded Nathan of a weasel or a marten trying to steal the meat from a fresh moose kill. The youth made a note to watch his back around this second Soapy. "And I'll keep your rifle for the time being," he added.

Isabelle's heart soared at his words. Her rescuer was literate. He had a mind to match his magnificent body. Truly, she had met a kindred soul.

"Well." Barnette shrugged. "A man's past is a man's past.

Up here we all can make a fresh start whatever you decide to call yourself. The two of you know how to handle weapons. I know that much about you." He'd caught the look Isabelle gave this young man, and he didn't like it one bit. "Did you work for Soapy Smith, the first one?"

"No," Nathan said. "But we saw him get killed. He was planning an ambush, but it backfired on him." Nathan gave Smith the second a meaningful look.

Riley stepped forward and extended his hand to Jim Eagle. "Crossed a few rivers since I seed you last, Eagle."

The old frontiersman grinned widely, exposing two remaining teeth standing guard at opposite corners of his lower jaw. "Yup. Thought you went under years ago."

"Hell." Riley shuffled his boot in the moss. "I'm too ornery to die. I'll jus' probably ossify one day and freeze in my tracks. And there I'll be, standing like a signpost as a warning to those who aspire to this vanishing way of life."

"Them's mighty fancy words, Riley," Eagle said with a frown. "Coming from a range rider. Ossify? What do that mean?"

"It means to get all stiff and bony like."

Eagle rubbed the old arrow wound in his left hip. "That's a good word. I believe I'm on the road to ossifying myself. Where you learn it from?"

"I've been reading," Riley replied proudly. "Got it from books."

"Well, I'll be damned," Eagle exclaimed in awe. "If that don't beat all."

Barnette avoided his wife's glaring looks and changed the subject. "What are you boys doing out here? You don't strike me as prospectors."

"Just traveling about," Nathan said with a shrug. "Hunting, doing a little trapping, and seeking the other side of the next hill." He noticed how the captain's wife was now devouring him with her eyes like a starved lynx eyeing a lame rabbit. "We'll be moving on soon," he added for her benefit.

"Hunters, eh," Barnette said. "You wouldn't have any fresh meat to sell, would you? Wada here is a great cook, but we're all tired of eating his salt pork."

"We've got most of a moose hanging in the trees on that hill over there. Send some men with us, and we can pack in the quarters." Nathan pointed to another dome rising above the wooded hills north from the one the miners had indicated. His response surprised him. All his instincts warned him to leave, but the scent of Isabelle's perfume lingered, and he wanted to stay.

"Better yet"—E. T. forced a strained laugh—"I'll send our horse along. Tonight we'll have a feast to celebrate our new trading post."

His men cheered and turned back to the stockade. Barnette shepherded his wife ahead of him while Nathan and Riley purposefully drew up the rear. Dropping out of earshot, Riley gave his friend a meaningful stare.

"You know that bull moose we just kilt got careless 'cause he was thinking about the lady folks. Going into rut and all. And now you're starting to act just like him."

"If you see me scraping the velvet off my antlers, you can shoot me, Jim," Nathan said. He tried to make light of it, but his actions worried him, too. He felt like a moth spiraling into a candle flame.

"Barnette will save me the trouble," Riley said. "So I hope you know what you're doing, son."

"So do I," Nathan replied.

FOUR

By eight o'clock that evening the roof over the trading post was completed, and all Barnette's precious goods were safely stacked inside. The lingering summer sun dawdled behind the hills, igniting the dappled clouds into glowing shades of purple, gold, and crimson, while harbingers of the coming winter crept from the shadows to cast a chill over the open ground. At this time the summer's warmth and the impending cold seemed content to hold an uneasy truce. The days were still longer than the nights, so the Interior was blessed with long-drawn evenings and equally spectacular sunrises. Neither would last for long.

A light mist rose from the riverbed, but few in the new settlement noticed. Secure behind their stockade, they clustered around roaring bonfires and watched the moose roasts sizzling on their spits. The tightfisted captain had even opened a keg of rum, so spirits soared higher with each twist of the bung.

E. T. made the rounds of his men with Isabelle on his arm. The captain's wife looked radiant with a dark velvet dress and matching ribbons in her hair. A lace shawl, worn either for modesty or against the cold, did little to conceal the daring cut of her gown. Part of Barnette reveled in parading his gorgeous piece of property, for he had always considered Isabelle to be just that. But a growing uneasiness touched him whenever he pondered the fact that she was the only white woman within a thousand square miles. The way she looked at Nathan Blaylock heightened his concern.

Approaching the farthest fire, the couple encountered the two wanderers talking to the prospectors, Gilmore and Pedro, while Jujiro Wada and Jim Eagle carved a smoldering roast. Riley was hungrily chasing the remnants inside a can of beans with his spoon while Eagle popped a dripping slice of meat into his mouth. Both men struggled to carry on a rapid-fire conversation with their mouths full.

"How can you prefer beans to fresh meat?" Eagle asked while his tongue fended off the burning food.

"I ain't saying I *prefer* beans," Riley replied. "It's jus' that I ain't et them in a passable long time. Moose and caribou we had every day. To me this canned stuff is a real treat."

Eagle shook his head in disbelief.

"Well," the gunfighter explained, "when you gits used to something on a regular basis, it don't hold its appeal. That's when something different becomes real special, almost exotic." He looked up from the shower of sparks to see the Barnettes. Isabelle's breast was rising and falling like a storm-whipped surf line as she watched Nathan out of the corner of her eye. Instantly Riley regretted his words.

"Gold is real special," Felix Pedro interjected. "Just like our Lost Creek." He flashed his nuggets for emphasis.

"Heck." Riley discounted the nuggets with a wave. Four gills of Barnette's rum had warmed his stomach and loosened his tongue. "We had us a strike, too. In Dawson. Didn't we, Nat?"

Nathan looked at Isabelle as he shook his head. "It brought us no luck at all."

"Gold? Bad luck? I can't believe that," E. T. snorted. His eyes remained fixed on Pedro's gold, so he missed the intensity of the youth's stare.

"Why do you say that?" Isabelle asked, but Nathan had already turned away to disappear into the gloom. She looked to Riley for an answer.

He emptied his cup and held it out to be refilled. "The boy and me made a big strike in Dawson, but his wife died there. She got burned up in a fire. Now we're looking for his baby son, but he ain't nowhere to be found."

"Oh, how sad." Isabelle sighed—the tragic hero searching for his lost child. She wanted to rush after Nathan to hold him and comfort him, but the firm grasp on her arm by her husband restrained her.

"He gits a mite moody when the moon is full," Riley slurred his words. "But he don't care nothing for gold because of that. He ain't interested in being rich."

Jujiro Wada straightened over the smoky fire and turned his sweaty face to Riley. He tapped his chest drunkenly with the carving knife and tossed his head. Droplets of sweat scattered into the night. "I was rich once," he boasted. "Rich and powerful. I was the great medicine man of Icy Cape."

Riley thrust his face closer to Wada's. "You ain't no Eskimo, are you?"

"No!" Wada shouted. "Japanese! But I was the great shaman to the tribes of Icy Cape."

"Here we go again," Jim Eagle grunted. "He tells that derned story at the drop of a hat. So excuse me. . . ." He staggered off to the next circle of light.

"Japanese?" Riley screwed up his face as he recalled a map from one of his books. "That's an island on the other side of the world. How the devil'd you git here?"

"Whaling ship," Wada said, nodding solemnly. "I jump ship at Icy Cape. Lived with Eskimos there. White traders thought I one of them." He erupted in gales of raucous laughter.

"Well, I believe that," Riley mumbled. "You look like one to me. So what happened to bring you here?"

Wada slumped onto a tree stump. His head hung dejectedly. "Too much drink. The Icy Cape tribes thought I powerful magician. Once I bring chief out of a trance. They give me all their ivory and furs to trade. But . . . too much drink! After trade I got drunk. In the morning everything gone. Furs, ivory, trade goods. Only Jujiro Wada . . ." His voice trailed off as he searched for the answer in his tin cup.

Riley drew a deep breath. "I reckon you didn't figure on explaining to them savages you got hornswoggled. So you lit out, eh? Sounds familiar. Well, don't feel bad. There's a chief down in the Copper River valley who's gonna lose his shirt the same way. He's telling everyone he meets about his mountain of copper."

"Copper?" E. T.'s eyes narrowed. "What's this about copper?" His planned outpost at Tanana Crossing bisected the shortest All-American route to the goldfields, but copper was almost worth its weight in gold. Could this outpost here command a copper strike?

"Nat!" Jim called into the darkness. "Come back here. Captain Barnette wants to know about that mountain of copper we seen."

Now Barnette waited as breathlessly as his wife while Nathan emerged from the darkness. The young man thrust his hands into his leather pockets and faced the captain.

"What do you want to know, Captain?" he asked.

"Is there really a mountain of copper out there?"

In reply, Nathan removed his right hand from his pocket and held his closed fist out to Isabelle Barnette. She responded with upturned palm. He opened his fingers and dropped eight copper bullets into her hand, but not before Isabelle had used the opportunity to touch his fingers. The feathery caress electrified her beyond her wildest expectations.

Instantly, E. T. snatched the bullets and scrutinized them

in the firelight. He bit one, then studied his teeth marks in the dented slug. "Pure copper!" he exclaimed. "And you've seen a *mountain* of this?"

Nathan shrugged his shoulders. "It belongs to Chief Nicolai of the Taral Village. He's the big tyone, the supreme chief of the Copper River tribes. He controls the Woods Canyon, a narrow gorge on the river. No one can trade up or down the Copper River without paying him a tariff."

"An' he's one haughty cuss," Riley added. "Thinks the world of hisself."

Barnette seemed lost in thought. "You two know those trails fairly well, do you?"

Riley bobbed his head. "We've been up and down the Copper River and the trail to Valdez more'n any other white man, I suppose. Why, we even found a secret cut through this canyon that takes you into Valdez without crossing that damn . . . durn glacier." He corrected his speech in front of Mrs. Barnette. "What'd we call it, Nat?"

"Keystone Canyon. It's a steep cut alongside the river Lieutenant Lowe named after himself about fourteen miles outside Valdez."

Isabelle summoned her courage and asked Nathan directly, "What was Valdez like, Mr. Blaylock?"

"A terrible place, ma'am," he answered. "Many miners landed in Valdez and tried to cross the glacier to the Klondike. Most never made it. Scores died on the glacier, and those who returned to Valdez suffered from starvation and scurvy."

"And yet you made it," she said.

"I guess we were lucky, ma'am. And we weren't carrying much."

"Perhaps it was skill," she said, watching him from beneath her lowered lashes.

Barnette lifted a jug and refilled their cups. "Would you two take on a job for me?"

"Depends on what it is," Nathan responded before his companion could say yes. In his lubricated state Riley might agree to anything.

"Well, I sent Dan McCarty south to Valdez to meet my brother-in-law, Frank Cleary, in Valdez. They are to return here overland. John Jerome Healy has given me his word he'll build a railroad from Valdez straight to Eagle. From there it's only a short ride up the Yukon to Dawson and the goldfields. That's why I was headed upriver to Tanana Crossing until that craven coward Captain Adams panicked and unloaded my supplies here. Tanana Crossing will be the middle of the railroad from Valdez. My trading post there will make me a fortune."

Nathan had heard this talk before, and it all sounded dangerously similar. "J. J. Healy, the fellow who calls himself the Buffalo Bill of Alaska?" he asked.

"The same man."

"Captain"—Nathan looked down and edged the end of a burning log further into the fire with the toe of his boot—"I don't think Healy or anyone else will be able to build that railroad, not in the next twenty years. The mountain range between there is shaped like a fishhook, and it's just as sharp."

Barnette's face smarted at this boy questioning his judgment. Healy had pledged his word. But he pressed his plan. "They said that about White Pass in the Yukon, but Big Mike Heney built the White Pass and Yukon Railroad—ahead of schedule. Healy plans on using Heney. And your knowledge of this Keystone Canyon might make all the difference. McCarty left this afternoon before you came into camp. He doesn't know about your canyon route. I'd pay you well to catch up with him and show him that route. What do you say?"

Nathan rubbed his chin. "Let me sleep on it, Captain."

"Your friend strikes me as a mite overcautious," E. T. remarked to Riley. "Especially for one so young."

"He's jus' careful," Riley replied. "He's had some hard

knocks for all his short years. Heck, we've tramped up and down those trails for nothing. Being paid to do it sounds like a mighty sweet deal."

"Well, Mr. Riley?" E. T. pressed. "Do you need this young-ster's say-so?"

Riley grinned slowly. For all his drinking, his head re-mained clear enough to realize he was being goaded. "We're partners, Captain Barnette. Maybe you've had lots of them, being as how yer a powerful man. But this here youngster's saved my life more'n once, and he's the only honest to God friend I've ever had."

An awkward silence followed while the men studied each other. Isabelle burned with chagrin for the shameful way her husband spoke to Nat. But she somehow felt this, too, was a test for him to pass. His response surpassed her expectations. Nathan simply smiled.

"I'm still going to think it over first, Captain. I've had too much to drink tonight to make a clear decision," he said. Set-ting his tin cup on a freshly sawed stump, Nathan tipped his hat to Mrs. Barnette and walked away.

Riley watched his friend vanish into the shadows. "Well, to answer yer question, Captain," he chuckled. "Yeah, Nathan speaks for me. . . ."

Four hours passed unnoticed by most of the camp before the moon rose to its apogee. Another keg was opened, and Bar-nette drank heavily with the rest of his company. The day's fail-ures and limited success irked him, but the rum and whiskey dulled his frustrations. Isabelle retired to her new cabin, leav-ing her husband to his drink. By the time the moon began its descent, the entire camp was decently drunk. All but Nathan.

Close contact with these people left him confused, with mixed feelings coursing through his mind. More than a year had passed since Wei-Li's death, and he'd spent that time, with few exceptions, wandering in the wilderness. Away from all human contact except for Riley, Nathan found he missed her the least. Short trading trips to native villages and the sparse white outposts had been their only contact with others. Now he was thrust beside this woman against his choosing. Worse still, she fanned feelings in him he had hoped were long-burned-out coals.

To clear his head, he rose from his blankets and crept into the forest to a spot he recalled. There, about a quarter mile from the camp, a spring bubbled over granite boulders to fill a quiet pool with clear, sun-warmed water in a hidden clearing. The heat retained in the rocks kept the pool slightly warmer than the icy current of the nearby Chena, and the surrounding birch hid the spot.

Stripping in the moonlight, Nathan slipped into the pool and waded up to his chest. He caught his breath, but the water's chill cleared his head. He bent his knees and slid beneath the black water, enjoying the icy needles that pricked his skin and heightened his senses.

He surfaced and exhaled a cloud of steam into the frosty night. He wiped his hair from his eyes and froze.

Standing on the bank, watching him, was Isabelle Barnette. For an eternity their eyes remained locked. The glen admitted no sounds to break the spell, the sole movement being the birch leaves spiraling into the pool and the rise and fall of the woman's chest.

Slowly she undid the ribbons holding her dressing gown closed and let it slide to her feet. A toss of her head spilled a flood of red hair over her bare shoulders. She stood by the pool and let his eyes feast on her. The moonlight shone across her breasts, caressing her flat stomach before running down her thighs to coat the water's surface in ivory tones. All Nathan could do was blink.

Holding him fixed in her gaze, Isabelle stepped into the

pool. The cold scarcely fazed her as she moved to his side and pressed her body against him. His body heat, a fiery island in the icy sea, burned away all restraint, and she fixed her lips on his. Her pounding heart beat against his chest as he crushed her in his arms.

A torrent of emotions, too long pent up in them both, burst forth. Isabelle moaned as Nathan covered her neck, her breasts, her stomach with his kisses, and her hands urgently explored his taut body.

Rolling in the pool, their bodies entwined and smoldering like two burning stars in a frigid universe, they made love with the hopeless abandonment of those who realize they have no future, only the present they find in each other's passions.

At last, spent, they dragged themselves onto the leaf-carpeted moss to lie panting in each other's arms. Yet neither slept. Both struggled to sort the myriad emotions that flooded their minds. For Isabelle, this mad indiscretion surpassed the wildest dreams and romantic notions she held so dear, while Nathan struggled with the realization that love and passion need not always be both sides of a single coin. This was new to him, for Wei-Li had always commanded both, but for Isabelle he felt no love.

Before he could speak, she rose to her knees and gazed down at him with widened eyes. She bent forward and kissed his lips. He started to say something, but her kiss smothered his words. Gathering her dressing gown in her arms, Isabelle fled back to her cabin.

In her flight she failed to notice a figure standing in the shadows of a clump of alders. Soapy Smith the second stepped from behind the bushes to watch the fleeing girl. Even though whiskey blurred his weasel eyes, his mind remained alert and plotting.

"Where you been, missy, all naked like that?" he asked himself. "Sporting with that smart-alecky young buck, I'd bet. Won't the captain be interested to find that out."

Smith crept back in the direction Isabelle had come from, drawing his pistol. His other hand slipped a stained bowie knife from the top of his boot. "First I'll find him, and then I'll bring the captain the boy's scalp. Then I'll just slip my blade nice and quiet between his drunken partner's ribs. We'll say they had a fight while drunk and killed each other."

Smith paused beside a gnarled cottonwood and twisted his head like a serpent seeking the scent. Unexpectedly, the tree's lowest limb wavered in the air. Smith looked up in astonishment as the branch circled in the air like a soaring hawk, then crashed down heavily upon his head. The would-be assassin crumpled unconscious onto a patch of cranberries, with his hat, sporting a neat cleft, driven down over his eyes.

The cottonwood's silhouette parted into two shapes. Jim Riley emerged from the shadows to poke the inert body with the stout branch he held. "Bad habit, talking to yerself," Riley whispered. "Makes you easy to spot. That and tromping about like a moose with his head up his ass."

Riley drove the toe of his boot into the man's ribs. "You ain't killing nobody tonight. Not my pard, not me, 'cause I ain't never as drunk as I pretend to be. . . ."

★ ★ FIVE ★ ★

Riley pretended to be sleeping when Nathan slipped beneath his blankets and fell fast asleep. The gunfighter lay awake the rest of the night with his Colt drawn and cocked beneath his own blanket. Any minute he expected a torch-carrying mob to emerge from the stockade with the cuckolded Barnette at its head. But no one came.

Morning dawned colder than usual, and the forest floor sported a silvery carpet of frost. The sharp air carried the sounds of movement from the camp shortly after sunrise. From the muted noise, Riley surmised most men were suffering from the previous night's revelry. The hammering and chopping sounded halfhearted, fading away when the cook, Wada, finished boiling his coffee.

The smell wafted to where the two wanderers hunched over their small collection of embers and gnawed on strips of moose meat. Riley's stomach growled loudly at the thought of coffee.

Nathan looked amusedly at his friend when his stomach rumbled again. "That coffee sure smells good, eh Jim?"

Riley made a last valiant attempt to swallow the mix of spruce bark, willow, and birch leaves they had substituted for coffee for most of a year. His stomach answered Nathan with another upheaval, and Riley upended his cup. He watched with disgust while the greenish black water attacked the frosted leaves.

"It do," he agreed. "This Indian java just don't cut it."

"Well, why don't we pay the captain's trading post a visit and get you a cup of the real thing?" Nathan asked brightly.

Riley studied his friend. Last night's activity seemed to agree with him. His eyes were bright and clear, and an easy smile decorated his face. "We ain't got nothing to trade for the coffee," Riley stalled.

"The captain owes us for our moose meat."

"Okay," Riley sighed. He got to his feet slowly, working the kinks out of his joints. He ignored Nathan's questioning looks while he strapped on his gun belt and slipped his knife into his boot.

"What are you packing all that iron for, Jim? We're not going to rob them, are we?"

Riley leaned close to his friend and sniffed. "We might need these when the captain catches a whiff of his wife's perfume that you're wearing," he said darkly.

Nathan blushed. "I . . . she came to me," he blurted.

Riley held up his hand to cap the conversation. "I ain't passing judgment, or nothin' like that, Nat. You're a growed man, and you was scratching an itch. I'm just saying the captain didn't strike me as no generous kind, leastways not where his wife is concerned."

Riley paused to let his words set in. He handed Nathan his belt and holster with his pistol. "So let's git us some real coffee. After what I drank last night, I'm ornery enough to plug any fool dumb enough to stand between me and that coffeepot."

Nathan followed his friend down to the clearing with its field of knee-high stumps standing guard. Following the threadbare back of Riley, Nathan felt grateful to have so loyal and understanding a friend. Impulsively, he leaned forward and whispered in Riley's ear, "Good thing she didn't find *you* in that pool, Jim. She'd still be hanging around you like a love-struck moose cow, and we'd have a war on our hands for certain," he joked.

Riley bristled. "Don't even joke about such a thing. My pipe ain't been used in so long a time, I suspect it's all rusted out."

Just outside the stockade, both men tightened their gun belts, and Riley warned, "Watch that weasel Soapy the second. He was sniffing along yer trail last night afore I coldcocked him. I dragged him over to the wall and jammed his head against a stump. He smelled like a Saint Louie beer hall, so with luck he won't remember a thing 'cept he tripped and hit his head."

Cautiously the two stepped inside to the friendly greetings of the others. Smith sat propped against a crate of canned tomatoes with his head wrapped in a dripping rag. Clearly, he was still hungover and recovering from Riley's cudgeling. He studied them for a lengthy span, as if trying to remember something, before turning back to nurse his cup of coffee. By his side a plate of bacon and beans remained untouched except by those hardy flies surviving the night's frost.

Wada emerged from the smoke of his cook fires to thrust a steaming tin cup of coffee into Riley's fist. Wada jerked his head contemptuously at Smith. "Too much whiskey!" he roared. He stomped around his kettles, adding a glop of beans, bacon, potatoes, and moose steak to each of the men's plates.

Riley juggled the hot tin cup while he inhaled the coffee's aroma like a sommelier judging the world's finest wine. "Mr. Jujiro, you just made my day." He grinned as he sipped the tarry brew. He rolled his eyes back in ecstasy. "If you can cook as well as you make coffee, I'm gonna marry you."

Wada erupted in laughter. He nodded happily as Riley scoffed down the heaping plate. "You too ugly for me," he chortled. "But you need this!" In his ham-sized fist he waved a cigar. Then he stood back to watch with amusement as Riley tried to drink, eat, and smoke all at the same time.

Nathan's big surprise came when Isabelle emerged from her cabin. Wrapped in a fur-collared coat, she stepped outside and looked around. Seeing Nathan, she paused to adjust the hair piled atop her head, while Nathan recalled those long red locks cascading down her bare shoulders. Then she walked over to where they stood, gliding through the smoke of the campfires like a fairy princess.

Nathan flashed his warmest smile as she accepted a cup of coffee from Wada. Their eyes met, and the youth winced as he beheld nothing but the coldest of recognitions. With no more than a curt nod of her head, Isabelle strode past them to her husband's side. Nathan watched crestfallen as she kissed her husband and shared her coffee with him.

Riley cocked his head and eyed his friend's bewilderment with mild jocundity. "Ain't women nothin' but confusing?" he quipped out of the side of his mouth. "Guess she was jus' scratching an itch of her own."

SIX

That morning, September 6, while Nathan puzzled over the vagaries of Isabelle Barnette, two events still to take place would alter his life and direct him on a quest that would test the very mettle of his nature. While he sipped his coffee and warmed his hands on the tin cup, the waning autumn sun, withdrawing from the skies of Alaska, was still sharing its bounty on a narrow strip of steaming jungle far to the south.

Snow, ice, and winter were foreign concepts to the Isthmus of Panama, where the muddy Chagres River sawed its way through this band of earth belonging to Colombia that separated the Pacific Ocean from the Caribbean. Both the Chagres and the Tanana, leagues to the north, carried silted water. But where the Tanana carried the dust of glacial flour from rocks crushed and powdered by tons of ice, the Chagres moved only soil washed from the mountains by the warming rains. In this respect the Chagres could be called a gentler river than the Tanana, but danger and death followed both rivers that day.

The midday sun filtered through the cacao trees, turning the morning's rain into steamy geysers spiraling skyward from the sawgrass and the small patches of potatoes and banana trees that encircled the village. The fishing village of Santo Ignacio near Gatun Lake boasted no more than a dozen thatched roofs, raised stilt hovels, and dugout canoes—nothing grandiose enough to justify its fine name.

Eking a bare existence from the muddy river and the ever-encroaching jungle, finding food for the day, and worrying about the salvation of their souls consumed all of the inhabitants' thoughts. And now the bone-weary residents slept. Siesta afforded the one release from their hard life that required no payment in return. So the citizens of Santo Ignacio slept.

All, but one. Marta Cristobal Kelly opened her eyes and looked at her parents snoring at the far end of the one-room hut. Quietly she rose from her straw mat and slipped the reading primer from beneath the woven rug. The tattered and stained booklet was her most precious possession, a gift from nuns in the town twenty miles to the west. With its help, Marta was learning to read.

Her father disapproved in public, imploring her to find a husband like the other girls in the village, but secretly he marveled that this eighteen-year-old beauty had come from his loins. She was fated to be different from the start. Her father, an Irish sailor who jumped ship, had traded his life at sea for one of equal hardship. One woman, Marta's mother, had changed him into a fisherman and farmer. From their love came Marta, a wondrous mix who spoke both Spanish, her mother's tongue, and English, the language of her father.

Taller than the other girls, Marta's lush body drew admiring stares from all the young men. But her father knew none were good enough for her. In his prayers he asked that Marta find a man worthy of her looks and her mind. Perhaps, he suggested gently to the Blessed Virgin, a foreman from one of the rich haciendas or a wealthy *gringo pensionare* like those who seemed to be pouring down from the north with pesos falling from their pockets. Every day he prayed harder, for at eighteen Marta was getting old.

With book in hand the girl glided without a sound down the steps and across the hard-packed red earth to the secret clearing by the river where she studied. Her feet knew the way by feel, treading on the hot soil before entering the moist, cool grass at the edge of the trees. So Marta read and reread the faded letters in her primer while her feet guided her. Eagerly, her mind snatched the simple phrases from the pages. Soon she would be ready for the next lesson.

Suddenly a dark shadow loomed before her, one alien to the friendly trees that marked her path. Her eyes darted upward and she opened her mouth to scream. But filthy fingers clamped over her mouth before her cry was completed. Other hands brutally pinned her arms behind her back.

The hard eyes of the *federale* officer studied her from beneath the shadow of his cap. Rivulets of sweat painted channels in the dust and grime coating his face. Tobacco stains tinted the underside of his thick mustache and his days-old beard. His gaze lingered over her thin dress, seeming to undress her, so that Marta struggled while her face burned with shame. His hand reached out to caress her throat, then wandered down her front, covering her breast and her stomach, before it snatched the booklet from her hand.

"What have we here my little bird?" he chuckled.

She fought to answer, but the hand still gagged her.

The officer studied the primer, turning the pages with great deliberation. He waved it at his sergeant. "What do you think, Tomaso? Is this that rebel propaganda?"

The sergeant, a thin man with watery eyes, winced at the question. "You know I cannot read, jefe," he said.

"I know that, imbecile!" his superior snapped. "And neither can I! But what does it *look like*?"

The sergeant nodded quickly. "It must be! Yes, it's that trash from the rebels calling for revolution. What else could it be? For what other reason would these dirty peasants have a pamphlet like this in their village?"

"So, my pretty one, you are a revolutionary, are you?"

Marta shook her head and moaned, but the fingers

clamped tighter until she felt she would suffocate. The acrid stench of the *federale's* sweat made her gag.

"No?" the officer teased, rolling his eyes in mock innocence. A crooked smile crossed his fat lips as he nuzzled her neck. "Then why don't you show us how loyal you are? How grateful you are to your country's soldiers." His hands tore open her shift, his nails scratching deep cuts into her shoulders in doing so.

Marta kicked out, driving her knee hard into the groin of her tormentor. His face turned a dark purple as the wind rushed from his lungs and he crumpled forward. In doing that she unwittingly saved the man's life.

Her father leapt from the undergrowth like a tiger directly into the startled company. His machete transcribed a silvery arc against the verdant backdrop, and the closest leaves splashed bright crimson with the blood of the sergeant. His head, still holding its astonished look, toppled from his shoulders. But the old man missed his target, the officer.

Her father recovered his balance, whirling around to slice a deep cut into the shoulder of another soldier before the others overpowered him by sheer weight of numbers and battered him to the ground with their rifle butts. Marta turned her head away, but the sounds of the rifles thudding down on her father bored into her brain, driving her to the brink of madness.

The officer rose shakily to his feet and vomited. He wiped the bile from his mustache with the back of his hand. Then that hand cracked across the side of Marta's forehead. Her head spun even faster, but her struggling ceased. A chilling numbness grew in her stomach to spread through her limbs until she no longer could stand but sagged against the legs of the man holding her. She and her father were doomed, she realized. Silently she began to pray.

The *federale* chief stumbled back from the girl and looked

down at the still-twitching body of his sergeant. His bleary gaze hardened to a venomous glare as he peered down at the battered attacker. "Who are you, old man?" he croaked.

"Let my daughter go, you pig!" came his reply.

The officer tenderly groped his groin. "You killed my sergeant, and your whore of a daughter tried to ruin my manhood. And you ask for clemency?" He stood over the old man and dug his fingers into the gray hair. He jerked the bruised face close to his. "Thanks to your daughter, I cannot pleasure her today. But we will watch together what my men can do!"

When the men were finished with Marta, they dumped her in a crumpled heap in front of her father. Like a wounded animal she crept to his side and lay her head against his knee. Turning to look up at him, she forced her eyes to meet his, expecting to see the accusation and revulsion that she'd witnessed in the faces of the other village fathers whose daughters had been despoiled.

Instead she saw only tenderness and love in her father's tear-streaked face. He struggled against the manila ropes that cut deeply into his flesh and freed his right hand enough to gently smooth her disheveled hair.

"Forgive me, Father," she sobbed.

"You have done nothing to forgive," he whispered. "God always favors the innocent. I pray with my dying breath that he protects you."

Again the shadow of the officer loomed above them like the silhouette of the condors circling overhead. Marta watched as the man slowly withdrew his revolver and placed the barrel against the back of her father's head. Her father never flinched, but his face hardened to the familiar set he wore as he battled the ever-pressing jungle, carving out his pitiful farmland. All his life he had asked for nothing more than to be allowed to grow enough food to feed his family. His resolve strengthened Marta, and she clutched his hand.

"Avenge us, Marta!" were his last words to her.

The pistol crack shattered the drone of the jungle, sending a flock of brightly colored macaws protesting into the air. That shot also sundered the life that Marta Cristobal knew and changed her forever.

At that very instant, that very same day, September 6, 1901, thousands of miles to the north, the former governor of Ohio stood shaking the hands of well-wishers in the train station of Buffalo, New York. While his face carried a public smile, inwardly his heart ached for his wife, now reclusive and an invalid since the death of their two daughters. The Major, as his close friends called him because of his exploits in the Civil War, extended his hand to the next man in line. This poor fellow's right hand is hurt and bandaged, the Major noted. Thoughtfully, he shifted to clasp the man's uninjured left hand.

A shot shattered the air. William McKinley, twenty-fifth president of the United States, fell mortally wounded from that bullet. Instantly, the assassin, Leon Czolgosz, was battered to the ground and held for the police. A shocked and sorrowful crowd clustered around the stricken president or milled about in dazed disbelief. First President Lincoln and now their popular Major. His actions had fixed the gold standard, raised tariffs, and returned prosperity to a struggling country. Women sobbed and men wept openly at this tragedy.

But one man, a Mr. Dickinson, drew back from the crowd. Unlike the others, his mind was clear, crystallized by that fatal shot that dazed all others. While pretending to be shocked like the rest, he ordered his thoughts. Already he was weighing the consequences of this anarchist's deed, and how it might impact the narrow strip of jungle where Marta Cristobal Kelly knelt beside her dead father.

Two shots leaving two men dead, one the most powerful man in the United States, the other a humble farmer, would cause reverberations around the world, linking two world powers, linking Dickinson, Marta Cristobal Kelly, and—far into the north—Nathan Blaylock.

SEVEN

Nathan Blaylock hunched against a fallen aspen and munched a handful of snow. Thoughtfully, he studied the change that had transformed the Tanana Valley. Only a month had passed since he and Riley watched the *Lavelle Young* retreat downriver, yet in that time great changes had overtaken the valley. The brief fall had fled, replaced by ever-biting winds from the north that moaned among the naked branches and cut to the bone. Each morning found the river lower than the day before, so that now scoured sides of glacial mud and silt marked the banks for a good ten feet from the frozen grass line. Silted bars emerged from hiding in the milky waters like monstrous prehistoric reptiles lying in wait. Now the land turned hard, bracing itself for the heavy cold to come, and life seemed to stop, simply waiting and hiding its secrets for the return of the warming spring.

Two days before, the sky had turned gunmetal gray while an advancing wall of whiteness rolled in from the flats to wash over the expectant hills. Large white flakes crashed straight to earth to die in splashes of moisture until their ever-increasing numbers covered the frozen ground. The snow continued for those two days, and now an ivory mantle stretched as far as the eye could see to the broken mountains rimming the south. Only the still-flowing river glowed molten silver as it absorbed light from the roof of clouds. All else turned white.

Abruptly, the snow stopped, and an intense blue filled the sky. The sunlight's dazzle burned the eye as it reflected off pristine drifts and miles of branches bent with hoarfrost. Winter had closed the door.

Nathan viewed these changes philosophically. No stranger to the seasons in Alaska, each with its unique hardships, he simply adapted. Not to do so was to die or go mad. Nathan had long ago learned to let the strength of the land carry him where he wanted to go, rather than fight against its might. More like a leaf blown in the wind, he let the flow of the country carry him.

He munched thoughtfully. Alaska he could understand, but not women. More and more he felt like the rut-dazed bulls who staggered about half-starved and confused. Since that fervent night in the pool, Isabelle Barnette had regarded him with icy disdain, seemingly going out of her way to demean him. She appeared to take a perverse pleasure in his discomfort, even dreaming up dangerous hardships for him. It was Isabelle who was responsible for the two men being on this hillside. She had all but forced her husband to send them far into the hills in search of caribou meat, even though Nathan's Sharps kept the camp amply supplied with moose meat. And yet, Nathan sensed she still wanted him.

"Now don't be thinking about Mrs. Barnette, or you'll do somethin' stupid like step into a beaver pond and break your leg. Then I'll have to shoot you," Riley said. He shifted his weight on his half of the log and thrust his legs out into a snow-tufted willow. He could always tell when his friend was thinking about women. Silently, Riley exulted in the fact that his only contact with females came with the exchange of gold coin. And since he had no money and no soiled doves were available, he was unencumbered.

"It's that obvious, is it, Jim?"

"To me it is, but you better hope it ain't to her husband. I reckon he thinks that sour look on yer puss comes from bad gas, otherwise we'd be shooting our way outta his camp right now."

Nathan scooped a handful of snow and scrubbed his face and neck, but the icy tingle did little to order his thoughts. "I just can't figure what I did wrong, Jim."

"Boy, she sure got a nose twister on you. Can't you get it through yer thick skull? You probably gave her a better time than her husband ever did, an' now she's dead scared of you."

When Nathan's puzzled look remained, Riley elaborated. "Look at it this way, son. Here this filly got herself hitched to a powerful tycoon, thinking she'd be all set up for the easy life. He's gonna build a city the size of San Francisco and run railroads to here and back. Suddenly she finds herself plunked down a hundred miles from the middle of nowhere, and he's all the security she's got." He paused for effect.

"Now along comes this strapping buck called Nat, and next thing she knows she's learning things from him she never even dreamed of. Well . . . look at you. You ain't no millionaire. You ain't got nothing to offer her but yer socks with holes in 'em and a good time! And we both know you can't eat a good time. . . .

"This gal's not stupid. She's gonna avoid you like the pox; 'cause if she slips up and gits caught, her husband'll give her the boot."

Nathan drove his fist lightly into the sleeve of his friend. "Here I was fussing because I hurt her. Jim, where'd you learn to be so smart?"

"Trial and error, son, trial and error. And mostly error." Riley rose to his feet and brushed the snow off his Henry rifle. The army was going to the new Kraig bolt-action rifles, but the old man still trusted his lever-action. "Well," he sighed. "Ain't no durned caribou within this poor child's sight. Best we limp on back to Captain Barnette's grand palace and take the ribbing we gonna git like growed men."

Trudging along through the snow, they crossed the backbone of a ridge when Nathan held out his arm. Riley stopped and followed his friend's look. Down below, where the trail ran against the sharp face of a rock cliff, a handful of ravens hopped about, pecking at a pile of rags propped against a spruce. No movement came from the collection as a bird tore off a strip of flesh and flew away. Nathan felt the hairs rise on the back of his neck.

Riley confirmed his feelings. "Yup, looks like some poor devil went under. Don't see no other tracks about. Let's have a look-see."

Working their way down took little time, and soon the two men bent over the body. Dressed in rags, the frozen man appeared to be sleeping except for his pale blue color and the bullet hole in the side of his head. Frozen chips of blood and brain covered his left shoulder while the butt of a Remington revolver jutted from the snow where it had fallen from the lifeless right hand. Nathan studied the glazed face that seemed to look through him. Ravens had stolen one eye, but the other regarded the youth with bitter indifference.

Nathan shivered but not from the cold. "It must be terrible to die out here all alone," he said.

"Boy, every man dies alone," Riley counseled. "No matter if'n it's here in the snow or smack-dab in the middle of the busiest whorehouse in Skagway. It's something nobody else can do fer ya. But more'n a few men wished they could git a substitute." Satisfied with his sermon, the gunfighter sat down alongside the corpse.

Nathan started visibly when Riley settled himself beside the corpse. The two seemed matched in size and appearance, almost identical for an instant. "God, you look like twins!" Nathan shuddered.

"Not hardly," Riley replied with a shrug. He spit a stream of tobacco juice off to one side. "I'm the live one in case you gits confused over which one to walk back with." He reached down and pried a crumpled piece of paper from the stiffened fingers. "What's this? I hope it weren't no map this poor sod were following to safety, 'cause it done him no good. No good at all."

Nathan stole another look at the body. The grayed features looked resigned while at the same time utterly worn out. The face managed to appear placid in spite of the cruel shredding given it by the birds. Behind them the ravens warbled in protest at this interruption of their meal and hopped about impatiently. A wave of anger surged through Nat, causing him to draw his pistol. With one shot he blasted the closest bird into a cloud of black feathers. The others fled to the tops of the trees, where they loudly protested this harsh treatment.

Riley looked up from the paper. "The foxes will appreciate yer cutting down on their competition fer them," he said sanguinely. Then he read the words scribbled on the paper in large, shaky letters. "I . . . am . . . done for. Tell . . . my cousin . . . George DeWolf in . . . Portland. Signed . . . Tom . . . Pender."

Riley got to his feet and looked down at the body with pity. "Poor bastard, give up never knowing the captain's stockade is jus' over the next rise, not more'n a mile or two from here." Riley waved the scrap of paper at Nat. "Let that be a lesson to you, boy. Don't never, never give up!"

Young Blaylock watched the paper waving inches from his face. Besides being tattered it was yellowed with age. Obviously, the dead man had safeguarded it for some time. "That paper must have been important for him to keep it. He sure doesn't have anything else." He glanced at the pile of rags that once was a human being. "Maybe it will tell us something about him."

"It's yours." Riley stuffed the scrap into his hand. "We'd best be making tracks before dark."

Nathan stared at his hand. The note was written on the page of a newspaper. He studied it for a second, then stopped. Somehow reading this man's newspaper clipping without regard for the man's rotting body struck the youth as obscene—as if he were a voyeur. "Wait, Jim. We have to bury him."

Riley kicked the frozen ground impatiently. This man brought to mind the time in Pinal when he was freezing and was contemplating the very same action to end his plight. Strangely, he felt ashamed of his weakness, and this corpse made it worse. "I ain't brought no dynamite, and this ground is froze solid as a parson's virtue."

"We'll find a way," Nathan responded. He tucked the paper inside his jacket and stooped to break a rock free from its icy cement.

An hour later a mound of rocks covered the man's body, and his two rough-cut gravediggers were trudging over the rise in the direction of the smoke and fires from Captain E. T. Barnette's metropolis. Another hour passed before the weary men slipped within the stockade walls and made their way to Jujiro Wada's cook fire. Sunset was long past; so the fires cast eerie shadows against the timbers and off the canvas tents, turning the trading post into a frightening scene of dancing black shapes and eerie white snow. All this served to heighten the sense of isolation that pervaded the camp. Now in the grip of winter, Barnette's riverside fortress was more sequestered than ever.

Nathan and Jim ate in silence while Wada scoured the dirty dishes with an equally filthy rag before dunking them in boiling water. Engulfed by billowing clouds of smoke and steam, the Japanese looked every bit the powerful shaman the Eskimos mistook him for, except for his greasy apron and the cigar glowing in his mouth.

The ribbing Riley had expected failed to materialize. Most of the camp had rushed off up the Chena to Pyne Creek, where two prospectors claimed a rich strike. Only Wada and Mrs. Barnette remained in camp.

Wada watched them clean their plates. As the snow had increased, the men's tempers had flared, and his cooking had come increasingly under fire. The cook appreciated these men's appetites and their lack of criticism. Wada produced a half-full bottle of whiskey from his cook shack and waggled the flask at them. Riley beamed appreciatively and held out his tin cup, but Nathan shook his head.

"I'll pass on that drink, Jujiro," Nathan said. "I think I'll just turn in. Tomorrow, I'll try heading east for that caribou herd, so I'll need an early start. I'm sure Jim will do right by both of us."

Riley emptied his cup and held it out for a refill. "That I will, lad. Have no fear of that."

Nathan shuffled to his tent and cracked open the frost-stiffened flap. Inside, hoarfrost encrusted everything, turning the canvas walls into a fairyland of feathery crystals that flashed red and purple in the glare of his lantern. He swept the rime off his caribou-robe bed with his hand, then turned his attention to kindling a fire in the cast-iron Yukon stove at the back of the tent. Soon the stove was puffing and shuddering as the dry spruce blazed. More split wood brought the stove to a steady roar, turning its sides a cherry red and filling the air with the aroma of burning spruce.

Standing before this source of warmth, Nathan stripped off his soaking clothes and bathed. Through the sounds of the busy stove, Nathan still heard the singing and happy babble of Riley and Wada. Obviously, they'd found another bottle that needed protecting. Then Nathan slid into bed, falling fast asleep.

In his dreams he rested on the side of a grassy knoll, watching Wei-Li, his lost love, climbing to his side. The sunlight glinted off her ebony hair and shone through her diaphanous dress as the wind played with her long tresses. Smiling, she reached his side and slid down beside him. Her lips found his neck while her fingers caressed his body and aroused him. Unexpectedly, she bit him.

". . . God!" Nathan awoke from the pain in his neck.

But slim fingers clamped across his mouth as the kissing continued. "Shh!" Isabelle Barnette commanded as she draped her leg over his stomach.

Nathan focused on the shape wriggling beside him. The light from the stove showed a cloak lying in a heap beside his cot, and the woman's skin burning against him left little doubt that all she wore was in that pile.

"Mrs. Barnette!" he protested. "This isn't right. . . . What about the captain?"

She stopped her activities to cast a feral look at him. "All he's interested in making is his precious fortune, not love. That thought occupies him entirely. He has time for nothing else. *He has no time for me anymore!*" The bitterness seeped through though her words were whispered.

"But . . ."

She watched him catlike while her fingers played across his chest and crept down his stomach. She cast her hair across his face. "Are you afraid of the captain?" she taunted. "Is that it?"

"No," Nathan protested out of foolish pride. "I'm not afraid of him." But the instant he uttered them he realized his words would trap him.

"What is it then? Don't you find me attractive?" Isabelle asked coyly.

"No, no, I think you're beautiful," Nathan blurted out, unwittingly avoiding her deadly trap.

"Good," she purred. "I think you're beautiful, too. Much more handsome than the captain." Her lips returned to nuzzling his neck. "And so much more . . . more experienced. Where did you learn all those things you do?

"But we just shouldn't . . ." Nathan felt his face burning. Even in the darkness he imagined it matched the glow of the

Yukon stove. He could feel the presence of the Sisters of Charity who raised him in the orphanage shaking their heads, could see the fires of hell beckoning. Fornicating with another man's wife was a heinous sin.

"You liked me before," Isabelle teased.

"It's just that I work for Captain Barnette, and that makes this wrong." He tried another argument, knowing full well it fell on disinterested ears, for her fingers were busy exploring him again. Disturbingly, that part of his body was also ignoring all reason.

"Well, you work for me, too," Isabelle stated. She was tired of talk as she shifted under the covers to sit atop him. "So get to work. . . ."

Shortly before dawn a bleary-eyed Jim Riley lifted the flap to the tent he shared with Nathan and stared at the two figures beneath the caribou robes. The velvet dressing robe on the ground drew his vision sharply into focus. He backed out the entrance, cursing his clumsiness, and hoping the girl had not awakened.

But Isabelle Barnette lay frozen in terror. Would this bumpkin blab his findings to the cook or to her husband when he returned? She forced her body to relax and her breathing to slow down. Riley was Nathan's friend and would do nothing to harm him, she reasoned. Still, he might let his tongue slip, especially while drinking. Beside her Nathan slept soundly, resigned to his fate and worn out by her demands.

Stealthily, she slipped from the bed and dressed. The predawn light illuminated the tent and all its contents. Nathan's coat lay tossed across a frosted crate. A tattered piece of paper jutting from its pocket attracted her attention. Isabelle withdrew the scrap and studied it in the meager light. She read the man's suicide scrawl, then turned the paper over. The note was written on a portion of a newspaper. The scrap belonged to the *Morning Oregonian,* dated 1887. What could possess someone to safeguard part of a newspaper for fourteen years, she wondered. Isabelle focused on the side without the written note.

Her eyes widened in shock. With trembling hands she read and reread the clipping, her lips silently forming the words. When she finished, her limbs were trembling so hard the paper seemed to flutter with a will of its own.

The headline read: A SWINDLER CONVICTED. The article described the conviction of E. T. Barnette for stealing $2,300 dollars from a George DeWolf.

Isabelle clutched the side of the tent to keep from fainting. Her husband, the captain, had been sentenced to four years in the Oregon State Penitentiary! She knew her husband's line of credit and his debts for these supplies depended upon his partners trusting him. If this got out he was ruined. And she would be, too!

Isabelle tried not to picture the result, but ugly images of her stranded on this riverbank, without escape, without social connections, and without funds flooded her thoughts. She never realized the scrap belonged to the cousin of George De-Wolf and that man had killed himself. Nor did she realize Nathan had not read the side condemning her husband as a thief.

Mrs. Barnette caught hold of herself. She needed a plan. Now two dangers imperiled her: her indiscretions with Nathan and this paper that threatened to expose her husband.

In a panic she rushed back to her cabin, clutching the damning article to her breast. Stumbling over unearthed roots and tree stumps in the near dark, Isabelle at last reached her log cabin. No one saw her as she bolted through the door and slammed it behind her, shivering from fright. She leaned her back against the rough-hewn planks and gulped air into her protesting lungs. The keen air cleared her head; so encouraged by her focusing mind, she splashed equally frigid water on her face and neck. Then she sat down to study the clipping.

There was no doubt about it. The paper, while old, was authentic. Her husband was indeed a convicted felon! But how had Nathan come by this injurious information, and what were his motives? She could only guess.

For three hours Isabelle struggled with alternating waves of doom and fear until the barest outlines of a defense materialized in her mind. Over the next hour she shaped the scheme, rehearsing her actions down to the smallest details. As the morning sun ignited the narrow pane of glass that constituted her only window and cast its slanting rays into her room, Mrs. Barnette added the final touches. She mussed her hair, pulling a handful of curls across her face, and tore the sleeve of her dressing gown. Then, bracing herself, she slapped her own face hard with her hand until a trickle of blood oozed from her lip and angry red welts rose from her right cheek. After checking the results in the tiny polished metal mirror on her dressing stand, she sat back to wait.

Her vigil was not long. The sound of voices, growing stronger with each second, reached her ears, so she steeled herself anew for her role. Her husband was returning with the rest of his crew. His feet rasped outside the steps as he scraped the snow and mud from his boots, and then the door swung open.

"God, what a damned waste of time!" E. T. grumbled as he stepped inside and slammed the door. "There's more gold in my pocket watch than on Pyne Creek. Blast those idiot miners up there. They wasted my time." He clomped to the woodstove and threw off his gloves while rubbing his hands briskly before the stove. But the cast-iron heater was cold.

"Damnation, woman," he swore. "You could at least keep a fire in the goddamned stove. Is that too much to ask, Isabelle?"

His wife nodded abjectly and hugged herself in the shadows of her bed.

"Well, Isabelle? Is it? Isabelle?" Barnette turned at the sound of his wife's sniffling. "Now don't cry, for God's sake."

With timing to rival Sarah Bernhardt's finest performance in Victor Hugo's *Adrienne Lecouvreur,* Isabelle turned just enough to expose a part of her bloodied and bruised face. The movement appeared to happen as if by accident. Bravely, she stifled her sobs and tried to hide herself. Painfully she moved to the stove like an obedient wife and endeavored to fill it.

"Good God, woman!" Barnette grasped her elbow and turned her to face him. "What happened?"

Isabelle sank to her knees and clasped her husband's legs. "Don't hate me, Elbridge, please don't hate me," she pleaded. "He hit me. He, he forced me to . . . to . . ." Her voice dissolved into sobs.

"What? Who?" E. T. backed away from his wife's clutches. His suspicious mind was already filling with doubts. How often had his wife taunted him with the fact that she felt neglected and had but to snap her fingers to bring anyone in his company running to her side.

"Name the man!"

"Nathan Blaylock."

She followed him on her knees across the floor, head bowed while her hand held up the newspaper clipping. "I would die first before I'd dishonor you," she added melodramatically. "But he said he'd expose you if I didn't let him have his way with me. He showed me this!"

Barnette's qualms concerning Isabelle's overacting evaporated when he snatched the scrap of paper and read it. Isabelle watched his face blanch, and the muscles of his jaw knot spasmodically. So it really was true, she realized.

Carefully, E. T. walked over to the stove and dropped the paper onto the glowing coals. He watched it flare into flames, wishing he could dispose of his past as easily as this ruinous reminder. Turning back to Isabelle, the inhospitable look she saw frightened her far more than anything he'd done to her before. She'd always characterized their relationship in her mind as the sparring of a cat with a dog, her being the wily cat outwitting the other by guile. But this was a far more brutal side of her husband than she'd known. Captain Barnette carried the look of a cornered rat.

"Who else knows about this paper?" he demanded, his voice a glacial calm.

"I . . . I don't know," she stammered. Suddenly and unexpectedly Isabelle found herself on the defensive, all her well-rehearsed lines forgotten.

"Think carefully, woman. Who else might have seen that clipping? Did you show it to anyone?"

"No, he doesn't know I saw it. I took it from his pocket while he was sleeping," she blurted out.

Barnette's backhand caught her unexpectedly. His blow was far more vicious than hers, and this one sent her reeling into the corner and definitely split her lip. She struggled to look up at him from the spinning floor. A single thought flooded her mind, obliterating all others: This man would kill her if she ever told.

"Well, my dear," he said softly. "Your . . . escapade appears to have uncovered a threat far more serious to me than the loss of your virtue." His lips twisted cruelly. "A modest loss, I'd imagine." He watched her blush in shame, then began pacing about the small cabin while he plotted his move.

"If news of my past gets out, I'm ruined. *We're* ruined. That includes you, my dear. My backers will call in their notes, and my plan to raise more capital will fail. As soon as your brother Frank arrives with McCarty I intend to take you with me to Valdez. There I plan to raise funds to build a shallow-bottomed steamer that will take me and another cargo to Tanana Crossing. I'll show that fool Adams it can be done. Then I'll have two trading posts."

"Travel in the winter!" Isabelle gasped. She might not be imprisoned in this dreary outpost for the winter after all. Valdez was a sizable town.

"Yes. We'll travel overland by dogsled. Wada has skills along that line. I'd hoped to use the boy and his friend, but now that's impossible. I don't know why young Blaylock carried that paper," Barnette continued to himself. "He doesn't strike me as malicious, and I'd wager you made the first move, my dear, but no matter."

Isabelle shrank back from his stare. It cut right through her. She could read his mind. He planned on killing the two.

Barnette rolled his tongue around in his mouth as he thought. "Well," he said at last. "We'll just use your deflowering as an excuse."

With that he jerked her to her feet and half dragged her out the door of the cabin. The captain drew his revolver and fired it into the air. The sharp reports caused Isabelle to flinch.

Five minutes later Barnette and his armed crew encircled the tent where Nathan and Riley slept. The gang bristled with rifles, and Smith and Atwater carried ropes. In spite of the cold their blood boiled at the insult to their captain's wife. Hanging the culprits was foremost on their minds. After Barnette had whipped them into a frenzy, only Wada and old Jim Eagle carried doubts, and these two prudently held their peace.

"Come on out and meet your fate!" Smith yelled. "We've got you surrounded."

Silence greeted his order.

Atwater dropped his rope and switched his rifle to a two-handed grip. He levered a round into the chamber and aimed at the tent flap. "You heard Soapy," he roared. "You'll get a fair chance to speak, and then we'll hang you."

Still no reply came from the besieged tent.

"Cover me," Atwater ordered as he crept closer. Smith, more a bushwhacker than a face-to-face fighter, took cover behind a stump. Barnette also slipped behind the front row. Cautiously, Atwater's rifle barrel lifted the tent flap.

The tent was empty.

Simultaneously, Short Robinson called out from the back of the tent. The group rushed around to stare at the two sets of tracks leading away in the snow. The trail led to the stockade wall and beyond.

"They made a run for it!" the enraged Smith shouted. "But they won't get far. After them!"

"Give them a fair chance to tell their side of what happened, men," Barnette called after the mob. But he nodded to Smith, and his signal left no doubt he wanted the two killed before they could talk. To the bloodthirsty Smith, this was his opportunity to settle with Riley and his friend.

The trail led into the forest, crossing a clearing filled with highbush cranberries, before ducking into a dense patch of alder and willow. The thought that their prey might be armed and waiting for them slowed the lynch mob's headlong rush, and half an hour passed while the men leapfrogged from cover to cover as they cleared the bushes. But the tracks continued on. First the signs appeared to head for the Chena River, but then the trail angled away from the Chena into a series of sloughs between that river and the wide braided channels of Bates Rapids. Atwater and Soapy both smiled at each other when they realized the men were fleeing toward the Tanana River.

The mob's leaders directed their men east, where the unraveled river was most shallow and divided into channels. Obviously this was where the two escapees planned to cross. Once across they could disappear into the vast morass of the Tanana Flats. By cutting east ahead of them they could trap Nathan and Riley in the swift-running oxbow of the main Tanana.

The pace quickened. Like baying hounds on the scent of a wounded bear the men shouted and bellowed as they leapt tussocks and crashed across frozen sloughs. A volley of shots broke out as the right flank flushed a group of ducks. Frazzled by their late departure, the goldeneyes exploded from the open water as the men burst upon them. In response, the gun-shy pursuers dove for cover and fired in all directions, filling the air with lead as the birds raced by on whistling wings.

Sheepishly, Atwater raised his head and followed the departing game birds with his eyes. No sign of their prey encouraged him to signal a renewed pursuit.

The broad stretch of the river eventually appeared through the thinning brush, and the crowd broke out of the willows to tumble onto the silty banks of the pewter-colored Tanana.

"Spread out!" Atwater shouted. "Look for tracks."

The men dashed up and down the riverbank, searching the powdered snow for signs. A shout brought them to a spot on the river just below a cutbank. Tracks led down to the riverbed, but here the river had deposited pebbles and smooth-washed stones for over half a mile.

Eagle, who had found the tracks, studied them intently. "Looks like they jumped off this bluff onto the riverbed," he said. His fingers traced the deep impression in the frozen gravel, then pointed to the one set of prints that scraped unevenly downriver. "One of them's limping after that jump. Might have busted his leg. They won't get far now." A tinge of regret edged into his voice. The old frontiersman liked the two. Secretly he'd hoped Jim and Nathan would beat them to Bates Rapids and escape to take their chances in the wilderness rather than with this mob. At least the two would stand a chance in the country, Eagle reasoned. The grim set on Atwater's face and Smith's rabid frothing left little doubt a hanging was imminent.

"Let's run 'em to ground!" Smith shouted. "We got them trapped between the rapids and the deep water."

He waved his rope and fired his rifle into the air to draw the others to the spot. Then baying again like hounds the men rushed downriver after the tracks. A few miles downstream at the mouth of the Chena lay an outpost for the army's new telegraph route. Euphemistically named Chena City, its handful of scattered shacks lined a shallow slough at the river's mouth. If the two got there first, they might seek sanctuary. Smith redoubled his urgings, steam and spittle spewing from his mouth into the frosty air as he shouted.

Ahead the riverbed jogged west in a dogleg of jagged rocks and snags piled against the bank. The gnawed stumps of birch trees lined the bank like gravestones, some still coated with the frozen slaver of the beavers. Within the crescent of the curving bank, a beaver dam blocked the water, creating a backwater for the rodents' houses. A single beaver house of mud and sticks rose from the center of the pond, jutting like a satellite from the earthen dam. The tracks led onto the dam.

The mob clambered across the dam, slipping and sliding on the ice-covered mud and picking their way around the snarl of logs and branches used by the animals to hold back the restless water. The footprints of their prey ran straight to the edge of the dam. And stopped.

"Where the hell did they go?" Atwater cursed. He leaned over the swirling, leaden water to peer at the rime of ice lining the patted mud. Several deep grooves ran down the face into the water.

"They must have crossed here!" someone shouted. That opinion arrived a second before the rest of the mob skidded to a halt at the water's edge. But their momentum carried them into the giant Atwater, knocking him off balance and into the river. With a screech the man lurched into empty air, then disappeared beneath the surface.

"Goddamn!" Eagle exclaimed. "It must be deep here."

Instantly, Atwater breached the surface like a sounding whale, his eyes wide in fright and his arms beating the air like twin propellers. His fingers clawed into the slippery mud until he pulled himself half out of the river. Smith, Wada, and Eagle dragged him the rest of the way onto the bank. Sputtering and cursing, Atwater flopped onto his back and shook the icy water from his sleeves.

Through chattering teeth he stuttered his analysis of this escape route. "My God! That water's colder than death itself!"

"Look over there!" Eagle interrupted. He pointed to a section of cloth dancing a jig in the river's current. About a quarter mile downstream, the fabric appeared snagged on a sweeper that bobbed with the current. A trapped bubble of air buoyed its center, giving the impression it covered a body. "Is that a jacket? Or a body?"

Smith squinted at the brown shape and cursed himself for not bringing his pocket telescope. It could be a man struggling to hold on to the sweeper. "I can't tell," he growled. "Do you think they tried to cross here and the current got 'em?"

"One way to make sure," Atwater answered. He shouldered his rifle and jacked a round into the chamber. Carefully he laid the barrel across Wada's shoulder and aligned his sights on the struggling object. Wada stuck a finger into his ear. The giant squeezed the trigger, and the Marlin .45-70 bucked off the cook's shoulder. A spout of water shot up from the center of the cloth, followed by the sound of the bullet slapping. Then the sharp report of the heavy rifle echoed back from the stony cliffs below the Chena's mouth and rolled across the Tanana Flats like thunder. The thing gave loose and drifted down the river.

"I think you just killed a blanket," Eagle opined.

"Maybe, maybe not," Atwater snapped. "But that looked like the coat the boy was wearing. I think I nailed him. I think they tried to cross the river here when we trapped them below the rapids, and they had to swim for it. One drowned on the crossing and the other was hanging on when I plugged him. That's what I think."

Eagle shrugged. "Like you say: maybe, and maybe not." He turned to pick his way off the beaver dam. A distasteful feeling saturated his stomach. Now all he wanted was to get back to camp, get warm, and try to forget this day's dirty work. One way or the other, the hunt was ended.

The lynch mob moved off the beaver dam and headed back the way they had come. A few men grumbled, but a warning scowl from Atwater silenced them. The sound of them breaking trail back through the brush lingered at the slough for several minutes until the men moved out of hearing. Then the oxbow returned to its normal sounds: the lonely wind biting through the leafless thickets, the scattered slosh of a branch dancing in the current, and the endless hiss of the glacial silt scouring the river's bed.

EIGHT

The manhunt for Nathan Blaylock and Jim Riley had ended, but another one was still in progress. Without new snow to aid their tracking, soldiers who hunted the rebels in Panama could only hack their way through the emerald jungle and hope to stumble across the path of their prey. The foliage grew fast enough to hide a trail by the next day just as another snowfall along the Tanana River would mask all traces of the conflict that had ended in that frigid land to the north. So the Colombian soldiers struggled on while E. T. Barnette's crew of cutthroats slogged back to the safety of their stockade.

Ruiz Fernando Cardoso, lieutenant in the Provincial Guard of the Republic of Colombia, stopped along the trail to light his cigar. As he blew out the blue smoke he removed his stiff-brimmed officer's cap and mopped the sweat from his forehead. His men broke ranks and fell out to seek shade under the dripping mahogany leaves. Ahead, the mountain trail wound ever upward as it disappeared into cottony patches of fog. Cardoso swore to himself. This land belonged to the devil. And the stiff-necked peasants.

Since the very moment of his transfer to this God-cursed Isthmus of Panama, Ruiz had hated the place and its people. The place was a pesthole. Worse than that, the peasants were without culture, fractious, evil-smelling, and totally lacking in refinement. He regarded them as little more than beasts to be hunted down. Rebellious vermin at that.

Presidente José Santos Zelaya had been wise to choose his officers from his own political party, Cardoso mused. Hailing from León, with its religious and cultural preeminence, Ruiz could be trusted as a member of the president's own Liberal Party. Furthermore, he was a true mestizo of mixed Spanish and Indian blood, not some mongrel mix like these insurrectionists with their tainted blood from English pirates and Miskitos, Indians from the Mosquito Coast intermarried with blacks.

Now the scum were refusing to pay the taxes and openly talking about seceding and forming their own country. The gringos were behind this, Cardoso knew. Those Americanos couldn't keep their hands off the region. In 1855, that devil William Walker had invaded from the north, even sacking Granada, and now they were at it again. Since the gringo President McKinley was shot, the trouble had returned. That fanatic Roosevelt loved making war. Rumor had it that he was helping the rebels.

Ruiz twisted the cork from his water bottle and gulped down the last drops. He sighed and picked up his cigar from the trail and continued smoking. Another month and he might request a transfer back to León. But first he had to find food and drink for his men. He searched inside his breast pocket and extracted the worn map of the district.

Just ahead the trail descended to the Chagres River. There was a fishing village beside the river although it wasn't marked on the map. What was its name? Santo Ignacio, that was what they called it. Ruiz laughed. Such a grandiose name for a pigsty and a collection of dugout canoes, he mused. His company had passed through Santo Ignacio a month before, the lieutenant recalled. That was where his sergeant had been killed by that revolutionary. Reactively, Ruiz reached for his groin, and he winced as he recalled the spitfire who kicked him before he shot her father.

Cardoso stood up and stretched his legs, avoiding the anxious stares of his men. Several climbed wearily to their feet, but he waved them back down. The rest period wasn't over even though he was on his feet. Ruiz stomped about in agitation. It was a mistake to let her go. That bitch had made a fool of him. What she was carrying turned out to be a primer from the nuns, not some radical tract. His superior had cursed him for being so stupid. If she were smart she would hide when they entered the village. If she appeared again, Cardoso vowed he would shoot her.

Suddenly, a figure appeared in the trail ahead. He was wearing the tattered white garb that all peasants wore, with a floppy braided hat. Cardoso discounted the man as another worthless local, and his soldiers turned back to their business of resting. But the peasant shouldered an ancient shotgun and fired.

The shot ignited the jungle in a frenzy of protest. Howler monkeys and macaws scattered in all directions. The dense foliage trapped the sound and hurled it back at the soldiers in a series of muffled echoes. Ruiz spun in the man's direction even as he felt some stray shot slice across his neck. In front of the officer, a soldier doubled in pain as the charge of lead shot and stones struck his stomach.

"*Viva la revolución!*" the man shouted.

Ruiz fired his pistol at the cloud of powder smoke floating in the trail just as his men loosed a volley from their rifles. But the peasant was gone.

Cardoso clapped his left hand to his neck. A thin trace of blood leaked from between his fingers, but the wound was superficial. "Get that bastard!" he shouted. "I want him alive!"

Firing in all directions, Cardoso's men rushed the narrow pass but found no sign of the man. Running up to the spot, the lieutenant found only footprints in the muddy trail leading down to the village. Obviously, the assassin had fled to the safety of his friends. This time there would be no mercy, Ruiz decided. He would burn the town to the ground as an example.

"Spread out," he commanded. "Advance on the village, men. We will drive the peasants out and burn the place as a warning."

His men cheered. Burning a village meant other things, too: looting and sport with the women. Fanning out into a skirmish line, the troops advanced with leveled rifles, moving steadily down from the road to the scattered collection of huts and shacks. A few dogs barked in warning and the chickens scattered to duck beneath the raised huts like when a condor or hawk appeared.

The men moved closer until they were among the hovels, yet no sound greeted them except for the noise of the animals. No frightened faces peered from doorways, no women ran screaming for the boats while their men pleaded for mercy.

The attack slowed and the soldiers shifted and swung their rifles about in nervous expectation. Ruiz felt the hair creeping upright on the back of his neck. The village was deserted. He paused to inspect a cooking fire that still smoldered. A battered iron pot rested atop the struggling coals. Within the vessel sat a bubbling fish stew. Cardoso thrust his hand into the pot and fished out a sweet potato. Turning the vegetable over, he crushed it between his fingers. The potato was only half done. A warning rang through his mind like an alarm bell. The village was not abandoned. The occupants had only just left. It was a trap!

As if they sensed their trap was sprung, a horde of peasants erupted from the jungle's edge, roaring and running with spears and machetes in their hands. At their head ran the farmer with the ancient shotgun.

85

"Take cover men!" Ruiz shouted as he waved his pistol. "Over there! Behind those boats!" He pointed to the riverbank, where a dozen canoes, carved from tree trunks, lay overturned and drying in the sun. With the river to their backs the boats would make a perfect barricade. Cardoso noted with satisfaction that only the one man carried a shotgun. All the others waved billhooks, hoes, and machetes.

With their repeating rifles, his soldiers would make short work of these insurrectionists. Holding together in good order, the squad backed toward the shelter of the fishing craft. A few more feet would place them behind the hard wood barriers of the boats; then they would rip the advancing mob with rifle fire. In fifteen minutes it would all be over.

To Cardoso's surprise the man to his right uttered a strangled scream and pitched forward onto the sand. His body jerked spasmodically while his legs dug furrows in the sand like a child at play. But the dark pool of blood that stained the sand was from no child's game. Ruiz stared at the dying man. A polished fish spear protruded from between his shoulder blades, quivering with the soldier's death throes. Cardoso spun around.

Twenty men leapt from hiding behind the overturned canoes and attacked. In a second the rebels were among the soldiers. Guns were useless at this close range, but the fishermen's knives were not.

Lieutenant Cardoso had learned some of his military lessons well. And he was right about one thing—in fifteen minutes it was all over. A machete bit deeply into his right side, his pistol spun from his numbed fingers, and Ruiz Fernando Cardoso slumped onto his side in the wet sand. Vaguely, the corner of his eye caught the bare feet and threadbare pant legs hurrying about. Then he heard them chanting.

"El Tigre! El Tigre!" The shouts filled the clearing and rebounded from the mountains.

"A great victory, Tigre!" someone cried.

Begrudgingly, Cardoso realized he had been defeated by this El Tigre, the tiger. This man must be a great general, the officer conceded to himself. His trap was perfect. Then he heard a woman's voice.

"We must have rifles," she said. "We cannot expect to win with spears and machetes."

"Now we have the soldiers' guns," a man replied.

"It is not enough," the woman chided. "We must have better weapons."

Cardoso frowned through the haze that muddled his thoughts. The woman's voice had a strange accent, and . . . she sounded familiar.

"You are right, el Tigre," the man said.

El Tigre? Ruiz pondered. A woman?

A callused foot rolled him rudely onto his back. The movement exploded fireballs of pain that spread from his right side into his legs. The pain filled his eyes with tears. At the same time the sharp point of a fishing spear pricked his Adam's apple, causing him to swallow against the pressure. A shadow fell across him. Cardoso blinked and looked up at the face backlit by the sunlight so that a blazing halo appeared to surround the head. The woman's face was beautiful, with large emerald eyes, and was framed in dark ringlets.

The lieutenant's eyes widened in astonishment before a bitter realization took hold. "You!" was the only word he had time to utter before Marta Cristobal Kelly leaned firmly on the shaft of the spear.

⋆ ⋆ NINE ⋆ ⋆

As blood spilled across the sands of the Chagres River in Panama, it reflected itself in a sky of matching hue above its brooding sister stream, the Tanana River. Thousands of miles to the north, the sun, hamstrung by its shortened span, bundled off with its warmth and dropped below the horizon. The layered clouds that cloaked the mountains to the east altered from bands of blue and purple to brilliant threads of crimson, rose, and fuchsia reminiscent of threads in the finest trade blanket.

These colors bled into the rolling marsh of the Tanana Flats, ten thousand square miles of bog and brush eager to suck a man into oblivion. Hostile to humans, the flats welcomed the long-legged moose, the beaver, and the black bear—all of whom could traverse the swamp where two-legged animals feared to go.

Still, the face of death can exhibit beauty, and tonight the sunset cast the swamp in its best light. Soft clouds of pink fog rolled into the lower sloughs, and tongues of ochre sunlight licked across the marsh like horizontal flames. The sunset extended to the edge of the river, but the swirling silt rejected any sign of gaiety. So the alpenglow jumped the flow and illuminated the far bank. Near the mouth of the Chena the pewter water of the Tanana bowed into the tea-colored waters of the clear flowing Chena. And just below this ceaseless struggle, a beaver pond glowed crimson.

Silently, a face broke the water beside the beaver's house. The eyes blinked away the stinging water, then glanced furtively about before slipping back beneath the surface. Abruptly two heads returned.

Nathan struggled up the side of the tamped mud house and pulled Jim Riley beside him. Both men shook from their time in the icy water, and their hands resembled stiff clubs from the cold.

"Next time you go poking the captain's wife, remind me to layer on an extra pair of long johns," Riley stuttered through chattering teeth. "I ain't never been so cold, in all my life. Not never."

Nathan bobbed his head while his club hands beat against his chest. "We'd be dead for sure if it hadn't been for that beaver's room."

The image of Riley and himself huddled on that narrow ledge above the water while a furious beaver clicked his teeth and hissed at these intruders still filled his mind. Fortunately, the beaver had built a large room inside his lodge, large enough for the two men to crawl out of the freezing water and lie upon while their lynch mob stomped about overhead. Breathing holes in the mud roof allowed Nathan an occasional glimpse of his pursuers. Once he held his breath and shrank back against the wall as Jim Eagle glanced down at the den, but the man failed to see him.

So the two had passed the day freezing instead of hanging, with the den's owner spitting and snarling at them. In time the beaver begrudgingly accepted these squatters and waddled off to slip underwater. That left the two men shivering on the damp ledge. Only when the sun set did Nathan decide it was safe to emerge.

Nathan looked around. In another two hours it would be dark, and the temperature would drop. Without shelter or fire, they stood little chance of lasting until morning. Most of all they needed dry clothing. And Barnette's stockade was the closest.

"Can you stand on that ankle, Jim?" he asked as they both studied the man's swollen foot.

Riley staggered to his feet and tested his right ankle. Standing caused pain, and he winced as he added his weight. "Well, it ain't broke, but it sure got a nasty twist on it. I can't believe I caught it in that spruce root like I did. Me, who never stepped nor rode my horse into no prairie dog hole in my entire life." He jammed his soaking Stetson down over his ears and hobbled about. His good leg crushed the frost-stiffened sticks on top of the den, making him sound like a cattle stampede. "Damn. I'm making more noise than a three-legged cat," he cursed.

"You stay here," Nathan said. "I'm going to slip back into camp and get us some dry clothes and blankets."

"I'm going, too."

"If you stomp in there like that, you'll wake the whole company."

Riley levered open the breech of his Henry rifle and blew down the barrel until no more water came. Then he slapped the action closed and lowered the hammer to half-cock. "So what. With them chasing us like we was horse thieves, I say if they poke their heads up we kill the whole damn bunch." His teeth chattered all the harder, but there was fire in his eye.

"They were just following orders, Jim."

Riley paused to reflect on his bloodthirsty scheme. "That might teach 'em some manners," he added, untroubled by his sanguinary suggestion.

Nathan studied his friend. The man's temper and his skill left little doubt they could wipe out Barnette's fort if need be. "Better you stay here and let me sneak in. I'd feel bad killing all those men just because I was in bed with a married woman. That doesn't seem right, does it, Jim? After all, what I did caused the problem."

"Okay," Jim conceded. "You're right. I reckon you learned yer lesson better'n yer own teacher. Killin' a man ought be for a good reason. But that half-assed man who calls himself a captain ought to keep a tighter rein on his filly, or she'll do just what she did—wander off into someone else's pasture. And hanging a man just for riding yer mare seems a might stiff to me. I know half a dozen husbands who'd be grateful for someone to exercise their wife. Besides, I ain't done nothin', why hang me?"

Nathan sighed in relief, but Riley held up his hand.

"I'm sneaking with you to the edge of the stockade, and I ain't taking no for an answer. The first sign of trouble, and I'm coming in shooting," the old gunfighter resolved. "Now git yerself some grass."

"Grass? What for?"

Already Riley was working his way along the tree line gathering handfuls of horsetail and cotton grass from the bluff. He looked up impatiently at his young friend. "Yer too young to remember the Blackfeet when they owned most of Montana. Lord, they was a powerful and arrogant bunch. But they knowed how to save their red skins if caught in a winter storm. Stuff that grass into yer pants and boots till you look like a scarecrow. It'll keep you warm as a banker's wallet."

Nathan filled his wet clothing until his bulging pants and jacket would hold no more. To his surprise the packing provided instant insulation, and his shivering stopped.

"How do I look, Jim?" he asked as he twirled around.

"We both look like a pair of walking sausages," Riley responded. "One thing, though. Unstuff yerself before you slip into camp. Otherwise you'll sound like a hayrack coming to call."

Working their way back to the camp took longer than their

initial flight, but they stayed warm. Darkness had long set in before Nathan slipped over the log wall. Slithering on his belly and using the shadows for cover, he soon came to the tent he once used. With knife in hand he eased himself under the canvas flap. Light from the campfires danced on the tent's wall and provided enough illumination to make out the outlines of the inside. Blankets and their clothing were heaped on one of the cots. Hastily, Nathan gathered their possessions. To his surprise the pile of clothing moved.

A startled Jujiro Wada sat upright. But the light pressure of Nathan's knife on his throat kept him from making a sound. He'd been sleeping beneath the two men's belongings to keep warm. The cook's eyes widened in fright until he saw Nathan. Then an enormous grin spread across his face. He carefully raised one wedge-shaped hand and waggled a beefy finger at the lad.

"I knew you not dead," he whispered. "You too slippery."

"I prefer smart," Nathan hissed in the cook's ear. "And I plan on staying alive. I just want my things, and then I'll be gone. So don't give me away."

"No, no," Wada replied. He cautiously bobbed his head while watching the blade under his jaw. "That's why I wait for you."

"What?"

Wada rolled his eyes to the bundle on the floor. "I pack food for you and Jim. Help with escape."

"Well, I'll be damned. . . . Thank you, Wada."

The cook blinked his eyes and waited expectantly. When Nathan remained silent, he added, "Captain say you beat his wife. I know that not true. He want you dead for some other reason."

E. T. Barnette stuffed his cap down over his ears against the evening chill as he headed for the outhouse. The route took him behind his cabin between the scattered tents where his men slept to the far corner of the stockade. While his men were savvy enough to dig the privy downstream from their water supply, that placed it at the farthest point from his wife's cabin. The mad rush to prepare for winter had left no time to dig a private outhouse for the captain.

He silently cursed his wife, Captain Adams, and his forced disembarkation on this river bluff. Barnette's porcelain chamber pot was still missing, buried in the mountains of supplies. As he shivered, Barnette made a mental note to move the second convenience up on his list of projects. Stumbling over these half-cut stumps in the dead of winter was unthinkable.

He reached the outhouse and stepped inside. Snapping down his braces and dropping his trousers, he eased himself gingerly onto the icy planks. The shocking cold jolted him. Now he was wide awake. Damn that missing chamber pot, he cursed.

The door creaked open.

"Damn it," Barnette swore. "Wait your turn. I'm in here!"

"Sorry, Captain, can't wait. I'm in sort of a hurry," came the reply.

"By God, you'll wait or else!" Barnette sputtered, half rising from his seat.

He froze in midair. The muzzle of a pistol emerged from the darkness and threaded itself through the crack in the board door to touch the tip of his nose. The door opened wider, and Nathan Blaylock slipped inside. A feral grin remained fixed on the lad's face.

"What the hell do you want?" Barnette asked. All the while his eyes focused around the barrel pressing into his face. The increased pressure forced him back down on the seat.

"I want to know why you ordered us killed, and you'd better be quick with your answer before your butt freezes to that green spruce."

"I didn't . . ."

"Yes, you did. Your boys weren't carrying those ropes out of fondness for Manila hemp."

E. T. shifted uncomfortably. "You were screwing my wife!" he hissed. "Isn't that enough?"

Nathan shook his head. His grin widened into a terrible-looking snarl. "Somehow, I don't think it is. At least not for you, Captain." He searched his mind for the reason, something that recently caused this change. Then he remembered. The dead man's newspaper clipping was missing from his pocket. Isabelle must have taken it and shown it to Barnette. That meant it was important enough to warrant his silencing them. Nathan tried a wild bluff.

"The newspaper clipping. I want it back."

Barnette stiffened. "So you can blackmail me, is that it?"

"Where is it?" Nathan demanded.

"I . . . I burned it."

What is he talking about? Nathan wondered. What was so important in that dead man's final note? Or was it what was on the other side? Before he could probe further, the outhouse door swung open, and an astonished Ben Atwater stared at the two men wedged into the tight compartment.

"What the hell is this?" the giant snorted.

"Looks kind of funny, I'll admit," Nathan replied.

Atwater's eyes widened as he recognized Nathan. He groped for his pistol. But Nathan's own gun barrel caught him squarely across the part in his hair, and the big man pitched to his knees dazed and half-blinded by the blood pouring from his split scalp. The youth spun in the close confines only to feel Barnette slip from his grasp. For an instant Nathan held Barnette's back in the sights of his pistol, but he held his fire. Shooting a man in the back was not his style. The captain fled into the darkness with one hand holding his pants. His screams for help echoed throughout the night.

Nathan hurtled over the stricken Atwater and sprinted for the wall. Getting there required weaving between a gauntlet of staggered tents. Soapy the second poked his head out with a rifle gripped in both hands. Nathan drove his shoulder into the startled Smith, knocking him back into his tent.

Another shadow appeared with a shotgun. Blaylock dove behind a pile of crates just as the night exploded with the flash and thunder of both barrels. The buckshot tore splinters from the wooden boxes, but missed Nat. Instantly he was on his feet and running again, bent close to the ground to reduce his exposure. Close behind him came more shouts as the camp organized. More bullets snapped through the cold air and whined off into the darkness. Several cut splinters from the log barricade ahead.

A small rise of uneven ground sporting two spruce stumps loomed directly ahead, and Nathan dove for that cover. Eight feet beyond lay the stockade wall and the dark freedom of the forest beyond. He readied for the last run when a series of shots plowed the path he planned on crossing. Somehow, they'd outflanked him. He was trapped.

Nathan checked his revolver out of habit although he'd not fired a round yet. His left hand drew his backup gun. Crossing that open space was suicidal, but staying was worse. In a minute they'd fan out and surround him. He crouched to spring, steeling himself for the bone-jarring bullets that would strike his back.

It was better this way than swinging from the end of a rope, he decided. His mind recalled the last lynching he'd seen, the purple face, the ghastly protruding tongue, and the bulging eyes. He wouldn't let them hang him. His legs tensed for the run.

A hail of lead erupted, the bullets passing close over his head. But the shots were coming from the barricade. Nathan peeked over a splintered stump. Barnette's men were diving for cover. The ground at their feet sputtered with the impact of bullets.

"You'd better come on now, youngster, if you've a mind to!" Riley shouted. His head popped above the logs, and he levered another salvo at the scattering group. The action of his Henry was a golden blur in the campfire, and the rifle's long barrel glowed a dull red.

Four giant strides carried Nathan to the wall and over onto the frozen ground beside Riley. Jim was just as busy laying down another barrage. Only one soul fired back, and his tardy shot clipped the tapered end of a log long after Nathan was safe beside Riley. The young man grinned. Riley had even found the pile of food and clothing he'd thrown over the wall before he went back to confront Barnette.

"Don't nobody try to follow us!" Riley bellowed over the stockade. "Or I'll come back here and burn yer shit-eating hole to the ground and kill everything that moves within five miles. You got my word on that: the promise of Newton Station's General Massacre Jim Riley! I killed half the town back there, so you turds won't take me more'n a few hours!" Then he turned to smile good-naturedly at Nat. "That broke the monotony."

"Hell, yes!" Nathan replied. His ears trained on the camp, but no sign of movement reached him. Apparently, the men were taking Jim's threat seriously.

"Well, where to, young fella? Destiny calls," Riley added with a dramatic flourish of his rifle.

"Where'd you learn that, Jim?"

"I read it on a recruiting poster for the Mounties once in Dawson. Kinda liked the way it sounds. Real fancy, don't ya think?"

"Yes. Yes, I do."

Riley squinted back at the trading post. "I can't thank you enough for teaching me to read."

"Your mother would be real proud of you."

"Yup, she would. I kept my promise to her on that. Besides, reading's opened a whole new world to me. 'Cept I'm running outta things to read. I got the labels on the bean can just about memorized. 'Sugar, molasses, flour, salt. Deluxe lima beans.' I even read that dead fella's note and the other side of his clipping where Captain Barnette was sentenced to jail for—"

"What?"

"Sure. That's what it said. That dude that shot hisself was the cousin of the man Barnette cheated out of twenty-three hundred dollars. Some English fella named DeWolf. Barnette got sent to the Oregon Penitentiary. Course, it must not be as bad as the Yuma Territorial Prison. Now that place is one hellhole deluxe."

"That's why Barnette wants us dead! He's hiding his shady past."

"Why go to all that trouble, Nat? If you ask me, Barnette got a shady present as well. So who cares about his past?"

"His creditors do! Don't you see, Jim? If they found out he's an ex-con, they'd call in their notes. He'd be ruined."

Riley scratched his beard. "Guess them fancy bankers would git a mite nervous suddenly knowing they'd handed their money over to a crook."

"If that's the case, we've made an enemy for life. And I thought he was the jealous type."

"Well, I don't think he's the generous type either, boy. And if you don't believe me, try sticking yer head up and asking the captain if he'd mind yer jumping his wife again before we hit the trail."

"Okay." Nathan started to rise to his knees, but Riley pulled him down.

"You stay away from Mrs. Barnette, boy. She can't decide which card game to lay her money on. She'll shy around like a half-broke mare with a loose pebble in her ear. That makes her nothing but trouble."

"I was going to ask the captain if you could have a ride instead of me, Jim."

Riley gave Nathan a startled look before he realized his friend was joking. Then the two of them burst out laughing. But not a sound came from the camp as they changed into dry clothing and loaded their packs.

Nathan dried the tears from his eyes before they froze on his cheeks. "What do you think about checking out Circle City?"

Riley shrugged. "I hear it's a ghost town, and it's one hundred fifty miles from here."

"I also heard it had a library with ten thousand books. I don't suppose they took all of them when the stampeders left for the Klondike strike."

Riley's eyes twinkled. "Well, why didn't you say so in the first place? Any reading beats a bean-can label. Let's head over there and scope out their library."

Nathan slapped his friend on the shoulder. "Let's go! Destiny calls. . . ."

★ ★ TEN ★ ★

Edward Dickinson stepped over a sleeping dog and walked along the pier to the pile of luggage from the steam shuttle SS *Almeda*. An icy drizzle seeped inside his thick woolen coat, and a cold drop ran down the back of his neck. He shivered involuntarily. If the sun ever broke through these gray clouds, this place might be habitable, he thought. That the place was filled with people already amazed him.

Dickinson paused to survey his new surroundings. The town of Valdez had sprung up almost overnight, like so many Alaskan towns. Two years before only a few scattered shacks had littered the shallow silt flats in the crotch of land between Glacier Creek and the Lowe River. Now a sprawling town packed the limited land that held an uneasy truce between the twenty-foot tides, while at its back waited the Valdez Glacier. What possessed men to live on this borrowed land and suffer this dreary climate, he asked himself. He knew the answer: gold. Gold, and copper, and now oil. Wherever men spat or urinated in Prince William Sound, they found riches. Finding was one thing, but prospering was another, for the land was not generous. However, gold was first to lure the unsuspecting to their deaths.

Valdez held the key to the All-American Route to the goldfields, first in the Forty Mile Region, then the Klondike. Men flocked to the spit, and the town of Valdez was born. Supplies, blankets, shovels, and beans piled along the beach waited for those hardy enough to haul them over the glacier and into the Interior.

Dickinson craned his neck to look at the ivory expanse of that body of ice that aimed at the town like a vast, frozen saber. For ten thousand years it had battled its way to the sea, carving into the knife-edged mountains surrounding the Port of Valdez like broken black glass lining a turquoise crater. Ice and time did what nothing else on earth could: it broke the mountain's back. And men planned to escape inland over that frozen wound.

But the goldfields were not Dickinson's interest. He turned away from the glacier to search along the water's arc until he spotted a jetty off the southern shore. Above the shaky trestle a series of barracks and a white-painted hospital clung to the hill. Douglas fir, Sitka spruce, and cedar encased the compound. Fort Liscum, the army's base, was as new as Valdez. A year ago trees had occupied the entire site, and the fort's namesake, Colonel E. H. Liscum, was yet to be killed in the Boxer Rebellion in China.

After arranging for his bags to be taken to the Valdez House, Dickinson found himself on a twenty-minute ride by motor launch to the army pier. The rhythmic pounding of the boat's one-cylinder steam engine helped him compose his thoughts. Within ten minutes of landing he stood before the desk of Captain W. R. Abercrombie, the post commander.

Dickinson studied the man while the officer read his letter of introduction. In his mid-thirties, Abercrombie looked twice that age. Traces of gray lined his hair and beard, and thin lines of fatigue etched permanent circles under his eyes. One of the true veterans of several expeditions into the uncharted Interior, the captain obviously had paid a high price for his knowledge.

The captain looked up at Dickinson. His eyes took in the

man's dress. There was nothing fancy that might call attention to him, yet the tailoring and fabric were first-class. The dark complexion of his face and hands caught Abercrombie's attention. The papers described him as an engineer ordered to examine the military route from Valdez to Tanana Crossing and then to Forty Mile. The papers were signed from the director of the newly formed District of Alaska and the secretary of the army. Engineer, my ass, Abercrombie thought. Dickinson looks like no engineer I ever saw. The man is a spy.

"Been in the Tropics recently, Mr. Dickinson?" Abercrombie asked as he pushed back in his chair. He pulled open the top drawer of his desk and searched about for a stale pouch of tobacco and the pack of soggy cigarette papers he kept.

Dickinson smiled easily as he withdrew a cigar case and handed the captain a cigar. He bit off the tip of one for himself and lit it. "Let's just say there's more sun south of here, Captain, and let it go at that."

Abercrombie sniffed the fresh tobacco. He closed his eyes as he savored the aroma. For over three years he'd been privy to stale, moldy tobacco at best. "You must have been in a hell of a hurry to get here, sir. Your cigars are still fresh and your suntan scarcely faded."

"Ah, shall we say, time is of the essence," Dickinson parried. "I hurried here under the strongest urgings from Washington." He paused to puff on his cigar and let his words take effect. To his satisfaction he noted a transient doubt flicker in Abercrombie's eyes. Just what Dickinson expected from a man this long in such an independent command. He blew a cloud of protective smoke, noting how its brandied bouquet contrasted with the biting smell of fresh paint, turpentine, and green cedar. "As you can read, Captain"—he pointed the smoking cigar at the officer's breast for emphasis—"you are to offer me *any and all assistance I may require.*"

Abercrombie choked in midpuff. He sprang from his chair

to the window. Outside men were still hammering despite a sudden downpour of freezing rain that cloaked the sound and Valdez in pewter mists. Four men struggled to raise a fir log with block and tackle, but the rain hid their end point and the work stopped. The heavy log seemed to swing disgustedly in midair while the men slumped onto a pile of split shingles.

"Do you see that, Mr. Dickinson or whatever your name is? My orders are to expedite the construction of Fort Liscum and to offer assistance to the civilians of Valdez. All my men are overtaxed in that endeavor. One-third are providing for the miserable devils dying in the hospital from scruvy, dysentery, and frostbite. Why, I can show you a bucket full of frozen toes and fingers that my surgeon amputated just this morning."

"That won't be necessary." Dickinson exhaled slowly.

"Another third are hacking a cut through Keystone Canyon so we can bring mules in. The work is tedious, requiring the solid stone to be cut away with picks and shovels. And the final third are struggling to finish this place before the snows come. Believe me, sir, when I tell you that the snows here can reach twenty feet in depth, so construction continues around the clock.

"Do you know what that leaves me, Mr. Dickinson? Exactly what can I provide you? I'll tell you, sir—nothing!"

"Nothing?" Dickinson repeated, unruffled. "Surely you can offer me a drink?"

Abercrombie balled his hands into fists. "This is no joking matter, Mr. Dickinson."

Now it was the tan man's turn to stand. "And I do not consider it to be one, *Captain*. I am operating under the highest authority. I repeat, the *highest authority,* and I do not take my orders lightly."

"This is Alaska. What does the secretary of the army know—"

Dickinson cut the captain off with a wave of his hand. He

reached into his coat and removed a small letter sealed in an oilskin pouch. Soberly, he passed the packet to the officer.

Abercrombie stiffened as he read the signature at the bottom of the letter. "Roosevelt, by God! I should have guessed it! It's just like him to meddle in something he knows nothing about. Teddy's still charging up San Juan Hill."

"The president must deal with the larger issues, Captain. He has more to concern himself with than some drizzly port packed with blunderers who are too weak to climb over an ice field."

The words flew out like poisoned arrows, shocking Abercrombie far beyond his initial surprise at the letter from the president of the United States which directed all authority to this mysterious man. Could it really be that this agent of the government cared nothing for that country's own people?

"If you do not cooperate, Captain, I will have you removed from your precious post," Dickinson continued.

Throughout this outburst the ash on the end of his cigar remained undisturbed, growing in length to half an inch. Abercrombie had the uneasy feeling this man's tirade was staged for his benefit and had been rehearsed far in advance. Nothing about Dickinson spoke of loose emotions. The man seemed made of lead.

But the little performance achieved its desired effect. Three expeditions into the Alaskan Interior had hopelessly addicted W. R. Abercrombie to the North. As much as the land punished him it also bound him to itself with its wild spaces and untraveled emptiness. To be relieved of command and sent elsewhere was unthinkable. Worse, it would be unbearable.

Abercrombie returned to his desk like a schoolboy sent down from the chalkboard. He removed the cigar and placed it carefully on the edge of his desk. Then his hand groped his forehead for the dull ache behind his eyes. Only the haphazard patter of the rain filled the silence. After a few moments he looked up.

"I'll do whatever you request, Mr. Dickinson," he sighed.

If he expected Dickinson to gloat, he was mistaken. There was nothing to revel about, to the agent's thinking: there had never been a contest. "Fine. I'll need five of your most experienced men and five mules. Ready to leave tomorrow at first light."

Abercrombie shuddered. Why, Dickinson might as well ask for my right arm, he thought. Instead he said: "Sergeant Sloan is the best I have. He was with me on the last expedition. At present he's in charge of the Keystone Canyon work crew. I'll send word up to him to be ready to meet you as you pass through."

"Good."

"How should I log your requisition of the mules?" Abercrombie asked. The army was still the army, whether it sweated in Manila or froze in the Arctic. Paperwork must be completed.

"The mules are to be listed as lost or stolen."

"Lost." Abercrombie grimaced. Well, they could blame the bears, again. Two animals had already been slaughtered to feed the starving miners with credit given to the region's carnivores.

"Another thing, Captain. No uniforms, just their weapons and supplies for one month."

The officer nodded, fighting back his growing sense of uneasiness. One month's supplies meant two weeks out and back, or something else. . . . "One month's provisions will get you to Klutina Lake and back," he wondered out loud.

"We're not coming back this way. Don't expect your men back until spring, when the rivers open."

"By the Yukon?" Abercrombie gasped. "But you won't have enough provisions to . . ." His words trailed off. The vague fear crystallized as he guessed Dickinson's route. "You're going into Canada!"

The spy drew heavily on his cigar. "Come now, captain. Invading our good neighbor Canada with armed troops? Surely that would be an act of war."

"We just finished with Spain and China," Abercrombie said. "I'd not put attacking Great Britain past Teddy."

"No." Dickinson waved his cigar back and forth before the captain's face. The smoke trails stacked a hazy set of rungs between them. "Washington is not that reckless. Your men are just to see me to the border. After that they are relieved of their duty. I shall cross with the mules alone and as a private citizen. Whatever happens to me will not be on the official level, rest assured."

"I'll order a detail to load the animals. I assume your supplies are in town?"

"There are no supplies, Captain. The mules are to bring something *out* of Canada." He caught himself. He'd said too much even now. So he snubbed his smoke out on the top of the commanding officer's desk and strode out.

Abercrombie moved to his window and watched the agent walking down the pier to the waiting launch. The tide was out so the pier tottered on stiltlike legs thirty feet above the water. Powdered stone from the glaciers, dissolved in the water, turned that body of water opaque. At present the setting sun conspired with the scudding clouds to change the water into a dull silver. Darkness was falling.

Empty mules, Abercrombie mused. What could they be taking out? Gold? Silver? Why go to that distance or trouble? Gold was readily found in Nome.

Abercrombie watched Dickinson climb down the ladder into the boat. He appeared to be made of the very shadows that now cloaked the spindly wharf. The officer blinked, and in that instant the spy vanished.

★ ★ ELEVEN ★ ★

Following the call of destiny proved more challenging than either Jim or Nathan expected—at least following it as far as Circle City. Because of concern Barnette might send a posse after them, the two men left the trail that followed the corkscrew path of the Chatanika River and cut north toward the White Mountains. The plan was to make for the high country, where they could watch their back trail and easily spot an ambush, then swing in a wide arc east along the valley between the Crazy Mountains to the north and the White Mountains to pick up the trail to Circle again where it met Crooked Creek. That was the plan, at least.

The reality was far different. They were on foot and without hope of a ride, so the hundred miles conspired to test the men's mettle as it did for all who trespassed. Frozen rivers, swollen with overflow coursing atop the razor-thin ice, trapped and encircled them like nests of silver serpents. Rolling hills drew them into dense thickets of willow and alder that screened them from taking bearings so that they wandered in circles and lost precious time. Breaking free of the forest's grip, the men crossed the Chatanika River and battled their way up the spiny sides of the intervening mountains.

The hostile expanse of the White Mountains afforded no shelter from the bitter winds that swept the rocky soil of all but the hardiest vegetation. Even these plants were reduced to twisted and stunted dwarves by the merciless wind. When it snowed the wind filled the valleys and narrow passes with drifts deep enough to swallow the unwary. And all the while it grew colder.

Jim Riley paused along the rise to knock the balls of ice from his snowshoes. He clapped his mittens together to restore the feeling to his fingertips. Nathan drew alongside to look at his friend. Riley's Stetson was jammed down against the wind so that only parts of his frosty eyebrows were exposed. A woolen scarf encircling the hat and snugged into a firm knot under Riley's chin bent the wide brim around the man's ears, causing him to look like a cross between a lop-eared rabbit and a Mexican saddle. Stringy icicles overburdened the man's mustache, making it droop more than usual.

"My, Jim, if you aren't a sight," Nathan said with a chuckle.

"Ain't I though," Riley grumbled. "If I look as cold as I feel, I must be some picture. Why, even my turds is frozen inside me. I can see why no horse wants to cross the White Pass, let alone step into Alaska. This ain't no place for any animal with an ounce of self-respect."

Nathan grinned, but his eyes remained somber. The image of their crossing White Pass into the Klondike filled his mind. Much had changed since then. He had fathered a child only to let the infant slip through his fingers, and his son had vanished into the vastness of the land. *I never even got a good look at him,* he thought. *All I saw was a screaming, bloody little baby.* He shook his head vigorously to wipe the scene away. The single constant was that he and Jim were still together. But that was it; everything else was different.

"We've come a long way together, Jim," he sighed.

Riley misunderstood. He thought back to their first meeting, when a green boy had handed his coat to a down-on-his-luck gunfighter. "We have? When you gave me yer coat in Pinal, Arizona, I was freezing to death. I'm still freezing."

Riley turned to discover he was talking to his friend's back. Nathan had dropped to a crouch and slipped behind an outcropping of wind-scoured rocks. Instantly, Riley slid his Henry rifle from its moosehide sheath.

Below them the trail wound to the right before dropping steeply onto a narrow trail that ran the length of the backbone of the ridge. Sharp rocks and loose, windblown scree covered the sloping sides, and snowdrifts lay scattered in pools like white quicksand waiting to swallow the unwary or inept.

"Look down there." Nathan pointed to the pass.

A handful of soldiers could hold this natural pass against an army, and someone was doing just that. Back hairs bristling in defiance and rage, a cow moose blocked the trail. Behind her stood her calf, while its smaller twin staggered about in front of the mother with its rear leg hamstrung. Facing the doomed calf, a half circle of wolves waited. Several of the wolves rolled on their backs in the snow, tails wagging, while two simply lay in the snow watching. They were in no hurry. The wounded calf was theirs for the taking.

One wolf, a black male, moved forward, but the cow launched a counterattack with hooves slashing the air. The wolf yelped as a hoof stove in his ribs and tossed him into the air. He fell to earth like a broken doll.

"She ain't gonna save that hamstrung young'un," Jim observed. "Don't those wolves jus' awaiting there give you the shivers? Sort of reminds me of a passel of bankers, don't it?"

"You got to give her credit for trying," Nathan said.

Yet as he spoke, the deadly ballet of attack and counterattack drew to a close. The moose's charges became shorter as she tired. And the injured calf lay down in the snow as if accepting his fate. Still the mother stumbled forward and stood over her calf.

"Will you look at her!" Nathan exclaimed.

His gaze was directed not at the moose but at a silver gray wolf who hurled herself onto the cow's back. The intensity of the wolf's attack implied a personal vendetta, quite different from the detached, almost mundane attitude of the rest of the pack. Snarling and biting, the wolf clung to the cow's back while the stricken animal tried desperately to shake off her attacker. The silver wolf's hold broke and she slid down the moose's side, all the while avoiding the flash of deadly hooves.

Nevertheless, the wolf's weight and charge caught the cow off balance and drove her back from her doomed offspring. Bright red blood blackened the white undercoat of her back and ran down her shoulder to streak the gray fur of her foreleg. Now separated, and suffering from the gash in her hump, the cow retreated. All she could do now was save her remaining calf. With a heartrending moan, the animal gave a last look over her shoulder and trotted off with the last of her family.

She's running away like I did, Nathan thought.

The rest of the pack casually closed in, and soon the calf was engulfed in a moving island of wolf fur. It raised its head once above the sea of wolves, eyeballs wide in terror, before a wolf grabbed its muzzle and pulled its head down. Then the animal vanished.

Riley shifted to a more comfortable spot. "Guess we'll have to wait for them gray backs to finish their morning snack. They's got the pass corked with their barbecue." He fished inside his pack for a piece of dried jerky and gnawed on one corner. He studied the scene below philosophically. "Their moose is tenderer than what I'm eating," he said.

Still Nathan continued to watch the activities. The big silver female emerged from the feeding frenzy with a hunk of meat clamped in her jaws. Amazingly, she didn't gulp it down like the others although the ribs visible beneath her sleek hide spoke of days of hunger. Instead she brought it over to where the black male lay dying and laid it before him in the snow. The male raised his head feebly, then let it drop. The silver wolf licked his muzzle before lying down beside him.

Riley followed Nathan's gaze. "Appears some females do hold to loyalty," he grunted around his mouthful of jerky.

"Yeah, but here comes her true test," Nathan answered.

The wolf pack was large, and the calf small. Over twenty animals fought to share the meager meal, and when they stepped back only the churned and bloody snow and a few strips of hide remained. The pack lived by one rule: Only the strong survive. They were still hungry, and their leader was dying. Silently, the pack closed in on the black male.

The silver wolf rose to her feet growling as the others fanned out for the attack. A long-legged male darted for her dying mate, but the silver wolf blocked his attack and fastened her jaws on his throat. With a vicious snap she flung the larger attacker away.

Riley leaned forward to study the unfolding drama. "She's taking this real personal," he muttered. "But she ain't got a chance. Best she step aside."

But the wolf wouldn't. Five times individual wolves rushed the downed male, and each time the female blocked their attack. But each fight cost her something. Now weary and dripping blood from several wounds, she stood panting beside her mate. Sensing the end was near, the entire pack rushed forward.

A rifle cracked beside Jim's ear, shattering the silence and rolling down into the pass. One of the wolves lurched to one side and fell dead in his tracks. Riley spun about to see Nathan tumbling down into the pass, half falling, half sliding in the direction of the fight. Whenever he came to rest, the lad would snap off another round, and another wolf would fall dead. But his rate of descent would deposit him in the middle of the pack before he shot them all.

Riley shook his head. "Here we go again," he grumbled. He thumbed the hammer on his Henry and squeezed off a shot that spun the wolf closest to Nathan around. The animal stiffened before tumbling over the side of the trail onto the rocks. Then the old gunfighter vaulted over the edge and slid down on his seat. Unlike Nathan, he screamed and hollered like a banshee as he fell.

Outflanked and spooked by the unexpected humans and their charge, the pack broke and fled down the trail just as Nathan reached the scene. His rifle killed the last animal as it clamped its teeth on the silver wolf's throat. An instant later Riley crashed into his friend. When they regained their feet, they covered each other's back while slowly circling. But the pack had scattered.

Riley looked bewilderedly at his friend. "Why did we jus' do that?" he asked.

"She didn't run, Jim," Nathan replied, his eyes shining. "She didn't run away."

The black male was finished, and his silver mate lay across his body more dead than alive. With her last ounce of strength she raised her head and snarled as Nathan approached. Then, too weak to fight further, she lay shivering while he wrapped his blanket around her.

That evening the men made camp by a stream walled by birch and willow. The open water gurgled musically as it washed ice-coated rocks and churned beneath the icy shelf extending from its banks. In a few more days, the creek's restless journey would cease while winter held it in its frozen grip for seven months.

The wind had granted this glen an amnesty, so hoarfrost hung from every twig and branch, turning the shelter into a masterpiece of silver lacework. Leafless birch resembled priceless Belgian lace with its inch of crystal frost, and the willow branches reached skyward with whitened fingers. As the sun retreated, its slanting rays fired the crystal lattice into thousands of exploding stars. Bursts of yellow, carmine, and violet lanced across the clearing like minuscule fireworks.

Riley settled back against their lean-to and crushed a handful of dried rose hips into his pipe. He fetched an ember from the fire and ignited his mix. Puffing thoughtfully on his pipe he cast a glance at the animal in the far corner. The wolf had been watching his every move. As they made eye contact, she emitted a low growl.

Riley smacked his lips and nodded his head. "Don't like my substitute tobacco, do you?" He tapped the mix out on the side of his outstretched boot. "Well, neither do I. It smells like horse sweat. Probably smells like that to you, too. I wish I'd snuck me a plug of the captain's tobacco afore we split the blanket with him. No matter what I mix to smoke, it ain't the same."

The wolf growled again.

"You're probably thinking the same thing yourself, Miz Wolf. Two handsome men like Nathan and me jus' ain't the same as yer mister. But we'll jus' hafta make do. 'Cause he's dead, and I ain't likely to stumble over no tobacco drummers out here."

Nathan tromped into camp with a brace of snow white ptarmigan and three snowshoe rabbits slung over his shoulder. The wolf's eyes moved to watch him. "Well, how's she doing, Jim?" he asked cheerfully.

"She ain't been too sociable. But then she ain't tried to eat me, neither."

Nathan cut one rabbit into chunks and pushed the pieces over to the wolf. Whenever his hand came too close her upper lip would curl threateningly. As he retreated from her corner, she warily ate the meat. Carefully, he returned and fed her another rabbit.

"Well, Jim, what shall we name her?"

"Don't make no sense to name something that don't belong to you. Leastways something that might try to eat us when she gits better."

Nathan leaned back against the spruce they were using as a lodgepole and studied the valley and the Tanana Flats off to his right. The sharp peaks of the Alaska Range pierced a layer of cottony clouds that filled the horizon. The knife-edged mountains stood out in sharp contrast against the darkening sky. He watched as the film advanced toward him like a great onrushing sea of white water. The clouds rolled over the foothills and spilled into the basin of the flats. Behind the mountains the sky turned a flat blue. The slanting rays of the sun hit the hoarfrost, and their entire camp burst into orange and gold colors. Suddenly the moon popped above the layer of clouds and floated on the layer like a battered iron disk. As the sky darkened, the moon changed to a creamy silver coin the size of Nathan's fist.

"This is beautiful country, Jim," Nathan said. "Cold, but beautiful. I really love it."

Riley stopped picking his teeth to watch the full moon. "Yup. It sure is pleasing to this old eye. No need to go stretching yer neck to look around them tall buildings like in Frisco just to see the moon, or the sun for that matter."

Secretly, the gunfighter rejoiced in the way Nathan was turning out. Tall, tough, and smart, but sensitive and without a mean streak to his name. Sure Wyatt Earp had supplied the seed, but he, Newton's General Massacre Jim Riley, had shaped the plant. My ma would be proud of me, Riley thought. I helped make a good man out of a green boy. That counts for plenty. Mostly what I've done is sent men to their Maker, but this counts for plenty.

But he kept his thoughts to himself. No need to embarrass the boy or fluster himself. Even hugging, like Nathan did once or twice, seemed awkward to the gunman. Better to whack him with a piece of cordwood when he done wrong than kiss him when he done right, Riley reasoned. Don't want him getting soft.

Instead he looked up at the Big Dipper overhead and said: "Looks like it'll be colder tonight."

"A small price to pay for this gorgeous sunset," Nathan replied. The presence of the she-wolf, even though hostile, buoyed his spirits.

Riley let slip a grin. Nathan had something special, something that came naturally to the lad that Riley had to work at and other men could only guess at. Nathan had an innate feeling for this land like a sailor for the sea. He realized its power, and he navigated through this wilderness taking advantage of the land's strength like a skilled seaman used the tides and currents of the ocean. And each day saw him grow more skilled and much stronger. Maybe this lad has two fathers, he thought, but Alaska is his mother.

The men rested for three days while the silver wolf mended. Each day Nathan brought her food, and each day she growled if he came too close, but she never lunged at him. And she ate the meat. Riley watched this test of these two wills: Nathan always delicately pressing his affection without threatening, and the wolf always watching, always on guard, and never relinquishing an inch of her space.

"Why do you suppose she doesn't trust me?" Nathan asked Riley one night. "I doubt she's seen more than a handful of men, so she can't be too fearful of humans."

Riley squatted to study the wolf. He looked into her yellow eyes reflecting the light of the campfire, then into Nathan's iron gray ones. Man and animal looked remarkably similar. "I suspect it's a matter of pride," he said at length.

"Pride?"

"Yup. Two great big prides bumping into each other."

"What makes you say that?"

"Well, she's been a queen in her own tribe, giving orders and never giving it a second thought. Now, she got hurt, and yer treating her like a infant don't sit right with her pride."

"Why does she eat the food, then?"

"Because she's smart enough to swallow some of that pride. You'd do well to remember that lesson."

Nathan sat back and released a long sigh. "She sure is a beautiful animal. I was hoping to make her my pet."

"Boy, that there is a wolf, an Alaskan wolf. She ain't no dog. She ain't never gonna be no dog, neither. And she ain't *never, never* gonna be nobody's pet!"

"Tripping over my own pride, eh, Jim?"

"Right, son. You can't take the wilderness out of her 'less she lets you. You can't take nothing from her, only what she's ready to give."

On the morning of the fourth day the silver wolf was gone.

Nathan awoke to find the blanket in the corner of the lean-to empty. He rose cautiously from his blankets and looked around the camp. He hoped she was nearby, but the animal's tracks led off through the willows and over the next rise into the thickest string of spruce. He tracked her half a day without catching sight of her. Then he waited the rest of the day for a sign of her, but she never returned. So the next morning Nathan and Riley packed their gear and headed off. More than once, Nathan paused to look over his shoulder only to suffer the disappointment of seeing nothing but the barren ground and their own tracks trailing behind in the snow.

Each passing day grew shorter and colder, and more snow fell in the high country until the mountain meadows they crossed became a vast, dazzling white world. The warmth seemed to have gone out of the land, leaving a cold barrenness equal to the emptiness the she-wolf's departure left in Nathan's heart. Her presence increasingly reminded the lad of his lost love, Wei-Li. Perhaps it was the wolf's combination of softness and beauty that belied a steely ruthlessness—that mix of danger and dazzle. Or perhaps it was the fact that the animal had faced her fate squarely and refused to run. Whatever the reason, the wolf's disappearance reopened old wounds, and added to the heaviness the youth carried in his heart.

Riley sensed this and tried his best to distract his friend. Both men pushed harder along the trail with hopes that Circle City would offer a needed diversion. The deepening cold helped to spur their efforts. The clear mornings and inky black nights foretold of a coming hard cold.

One starlit night Nathan lay beneath his caribou robes and stared at the myriad flawless diamonds that flashed red, green, and purple overhead. The waning moon had not shown her battered face, so the stars ruled the night. Nathan and Riley had learned from the Athabascans the value of caribou hair that most white men overlooked. The hairs were hollow, providing a warmth and insulation far exceeding that of wool blankets.

Now Nathan lay studying the stars in the relative warmth of his robes. Both he and Riley had split the coals from their campfire and placed them beneath a bed of green spruce boughs for added warmth. Only his nose and face remained exposed to the stinging cold.

Without warning a pale blue wisp materialized directly overhead to flutter like a tuft of cotton grass. The light vanished only to be followed by two separate spirals of similar color that started in opposite ends of the sky. The circling lights rolled rapidly across the heavens as they changed from blue to green, then back again to blue. The spirals uncoiled to form a band that filled the night with its intensity and undulated like a snake across the sky.

Nathan sat upright to watch this display of the Northern Lights. Riley, too, shifted in his bed to watch.

"The natives say those lights are the lamps guiding souls that took their own lives or died violent deaths," Nathan whispered.

"Why don't them Indians name it after something more cheery like a snake or something?" Riley snorted. Superstitions of any sort made him uneasy.

"They've never seen a snake, Jim. You forget there aren't any snakes this far north."

"If they weren't so ignorant, they'd know about snakes. I'd take more kindly to them being snakes rather than ghosts."

"I wonder if anyone we know is up there?" Nathan said suddenly after an awkward moment of silence.

Riley studied the display. "Is it limited only to Alaskans?" he questioned. " 'Cause if it ain't, we may have contributed to some of them spirits."

As if in reply, the Northern Lights exploded in a burst of light, splitting the sky with a ruffled band that raced back and forth even as it changed colors. A red hue fringed the base as it demonstrated two separate types of motion. While the giant band undulated as a whole across the night like an enormous serpent, slowly waving to and fro, the light itself roiled briskly within the band like the rolling of a rogue wave against the uniform motion of the sea. A low hissing sound accompanied the display.

"Look at that!" Nathan pointed to the metal tip of a fish spear they used to spear whitefish and grayling. The tines protruded from a pack. An eerie green light encased the metal points.

Riley poked his Henry rifle out from his robes and held it overhead. The end of the rifle barrel attracted a similar phosphorescence that leaked down along the entire metal barrel.

"Hold up yer knife blade," he commanded.

Nathan did so and was rewarded with the same glow coating his blade. "What is it, Jim?" he asked.

"I seen it in Arizona once or twice on a cattle drive. Happens before a storm, usually. Sailors see it at sea. They calls it Saint Elmer's fire. No, that ain't right. There ain't no Saint Elmer. It's Saint Elmo's fire."

Nathan extinguished the glow when he thrust his knife back into its sheath. In doing so he turned his head to one side.

A pair of eyes glowed at him from the dark.

"Jim," he hissed. "Look over there. I think it's the wolf." But the twin lights vanished, and the young man was left with the uncertain feeling he had imagined the whole thing. With a great sigh he lay back in his bed to watch the rest of the Northern Lights.

TWELVE

Dickinson balanced on the rising stern of the army's steam launch as it rose to meet the darkened shape of the Valdez pier. In the twenty minutes it took to cross the bay, darkness had fallen. Now only the shadowed crossbeams supporting the wharf loomed out of the night and the patchy fog. The coxswain, an army corporal with minimal boating skills, shouted a warning as the skiff crashed sideways into the pilings. Riding the crest of a wave, the boat scraped barnacles and mussels from the posts as it grated against the pier.

Dickinson jumped for the rungs of the ladder. His fingers locked on the slime-coated rungs, and he clambered up to the rough plank decking.

"Hand up my cane, if you please," he shouted down at the boat.

The corporal muttered something that passed unheard by the agent, but he stretched his arm up with the stick. Dickinson tipped his bowler and turned to survey the platform.

As he stood in the dim light, the antiseptic smell of creosote from his tarred hands and soiled pants assaulted his nose, along with the stench of rotting kelp. Below him the irregular thump of the steam engine signaled the retreat of the launch.

The agent cursed his ill fate for being sent to Valdez. He angrily wiped his hands on a linen handkerchief. The cloth, now soiled beyond repair, was balled into a wad and tossed over the side of the planks. He squared his shoulders, adjusted his coat collar against the cold rain, and began the walk to town.

The pier itself trailed off toward the town like a spent arrow to vanish into the mist of icy drizzle. Ten minutes of slipping and sliding on the wetted timbers found Dickinson on the front street. Tin-roofed shacks and wall tents stood shoulder to shoulder with two-story frame hotels and saloons. Oil lamps lit several windows, acting in place of streetlights. The reek of stale beer, tobacco, and sweaty bodies flavored the freezing mist.

Dickinson plodded through the muddy street. Endless feet had churned the glacial silt into a leaden morass that threatened to pull the boots from his feet. Each step produced an annoying sucking sound. In vain he searched ahead in the dim light for an intact boardwalk, but none existed. Scattered planks protruded from the exteriors of the more posh places, but no attempt had been made to link them into a coherent sidewalk. This disjointed path along with the low-hanging fog that cloaked the town like a clammy blanket and shut off all view of the surrounding mountains gave the town the aura of being abandoned in spite of the scattered lights and human voices.

The agent saw his destination ahead, the Grand Hotel, marked by a row of lighted windows that illuminated its sign. The building sat on the near corner of the next block. The thought of a warm meal and a hot bath spurred him on, and he redoubled his efforts to wade down the street.

Off to the right of the Grand ran a dark alley, as the side of the hotel had no windows. Glass panes had to be shipped from Seattle or San Francisco at outrageous cost, so most hotels sported windows facing only the main street. Irregular shadows filled the narrow lane, shifting in the flickering light from across the street. Dickinson's alarm lowered as he identified the specters as pushcarts and wagons rested against the side of the hotel. Shrugging off his fears, the agent angled for the boardwalk in front of the hotel. His course took him across the darkened mouth of the alley.

Two shadows separated from the pile of carts and blocked his way. A third moved behind him. In the darkness Dickinson caught the flicker of a knife blade. His eyes darted from one figure to the next as they edged him closer to the alley.

"What do you men want?" he demanded.

"Care to stake us to a beer, gov'nor?" the closest figure replied with a thick English accent. "We could use one."

"Are you actually begging drinks from me?" Dickinson answered, his voice thick with derision. "Why don't you get a job. I suspect there's plenty of work for your kind at the docks."

"Our kind, gov'nor?" the man replied. "What would that be?" He moved closer, holding his right hand hidden behind his back.

"Slackers," Dickinson replied indignantly. "I've no time for the likes of you." He went to adjust his bowler, but the nervous movement of his hand knocked the hat from his head, and it sailed into the mud at his feet. "Damn! Now look what you've made me do, you sot!" he complained. "My hat is ruined!"

Turning his back on the two men in front of him, the agent bent over to retrieve his hat. In the process, he shifted his walking stick to his left hand.

Seeing his unprotected back, both men rushed forward with knives drawn. They had been waiting for him for over an hour, and the thought of the potbellied stove and a drink in the saloon on the next street made them eager to complete this night's work.

But Dickinson spun around with unexpected catlike quickness to meet their charge. Still bent low, his right hand now held a narrow sword extracted from his cane. Remaining crouched, he thrust directly at the closest attacker. That man, the one who spoke, desperately twisted to avoid the blade. But his feet skidded in the slick road, and his momentum carried him onto the sword. With a surprised gasp, he watched the blade pierce the breast pocket of his jacket. Run through the heart, he crumpled into the mud.

Already Dickinson had withdrawn his blade to parry the second man's attack. The blades clashed once, and the agent sprang to one side while he whipped the heavy sheath across the side of his assailant's head. Now off balance, the man staggered onto his left knee. Dickinson drove home his attack and skewered the man through his side.

But his blade stuck in bone. The man fell, jerking the sword from the spy's hand. The third attacker rushed at Dickinson, and his knife skittered along the agent's ribs. Desperately, Dickinson grappled with the flashing blade, and the two men fell to the ground.

To the sound of clinking beer glasses and the tinny plink of an upright piano, the two men rolled grunting in the mud outside the row of saloons while they struggled for control of the knife. Dickinson smelled his attacker's rank sweat mixing with his cologne and the musty odor of the dirt while they fought. Finally, the agent twisted his left hand free and grasped a four-barreled derringer from his waistcoat. Jamming the pistol against the other's chest, he pulled the trigger to all four barrels. The flash momentarily blinded him while the cloud of smoke burned his face, but their bodies muffled the report. The man flopped back, dead.

Gasping for air, Dickinson rolled away from the body and struggled to his knees. He glanced about, sword cane at the ready. The normal nighttime sounds continued unabated. His deadly struggle had gone unnoticed. He got to his feet and kicked some mud on the burning coat of the man he'd just killed. The wet silt smothered the cloth ignited by the powder charge and turned it into a smoldering hole. A quick inspection of the man's pockets revealed nothing. Moving to the others, the agent turned their pockets out. The leader had eighty dollars in double eagles and a crumpled scrap of paper. Dickinson held the paper up but it was too dark to read its message. He pocketed the coins and the note and slapped the soil caked on his suit.

Dickinson snapped to attention and brought his blade up. He bobbed his head in salute and waved the sword with a flourish.

"Épée champion. Harvard, class of eighty-nine," he said.

Then he dragged the bodies into the alley and hid them behind the pile of carts. It would be midday before they were discovered, he judged. The gash in his side burned as he completed his labor, so he wrapped his coat over the wound and moved toward the hotel's entrance.

Another voice called out from the shadows, mockingly: "Care to stake us to a beer, governor?" This one sounded Irish, but carried the agreeable inflection of a Spanish accent.

Dickinson stiffened. He turned toward the voice and glared into the shadows. "Damn you!" he swore. "You could have at least helped. That last oaf nearly killed me."

"You looked in control, señor," the shadow replied.

"Well, it was a damned close thing. . . ."

"Believe me, I did not travel all this way only to watch you cut down by assassins. I would not have let that big one harm you."

"Oh? Thank you so very much for late assurances," Dickinson quipped. He flicked at the mud covering his sleeve in a fit of pique. "I could have used your help earlier. It might have kept me out of the mud."

The figure separated from the shadows behind a pile of barrels on the opposite side of the street and crossed the road. The person's movements were quick and catlike.

The spy watched as the other approached. Despite his

anger, Dickinson found his doubts about this affair fading. A Schofield revolver resided in the right hand of his contact, held at the ready with the hammer cocked. Both paused and turned as a slight movement far down the alley caught their eyes. A man had stepped from the shadows to tip his hat in a grand salute to Dickinson before vanishing into the gloom. The agent watched the spot where this man vanished for several seconds before turning to greet his contact.

"You were supposed to meet me tomorrow," he grumbled.

Marta Cristobal Kelly stepped from the darkness to inspect the cut in Dickinson's side. Her gloved finger probed the wound, causing him to wince. "I have learned the hard way never to be where I am supposed to be," she said. "You should be grateful I was here should you have needed me."

Dickinson's voice caught as her fingers pressed harder. He suspected her last poke was deliberate. He diverted his attention by inspecting his contact. She seemed to have grown taller since their meeting months ago in the jungles of Panama. Perhaps it was the knee-length leather boots and the trapper's hat on her head. The silver-tipped lynx fur framed her face in the lamplight, adding a softness to her beauty that he had not noticed before, and the leather breeches did nothing to hide her curves. But her eyes still smoldered dangerously like blazing emeralds.

"You should wear a dress," he said.

The eyes bored into him. "A dress, señor? A dress would interfere with my pistol."

The spy pushed all romantic notions from his head. He had seen her kill a man in the jungles for touching her. That the rebel had been drunk was no matter. What shocked Dickinson was the speed and efficiency of her reprisal. It reminded him of the fer-de-lance, the deadly viper of the rain forest.

Even here, thousands of miles north of her steamy little strip of land separating the world's two great oceans, Marta

Kelly seemed to fit. She had adapted to changing climates and terrain without difficulty. That thought intrigued Dickinson and appealed to his romanticism. It was that quixotic streak in him that caused him to become a secret agent for that other hopeless romantic, Teddy Roosevelt. It was Teddy's hare-brained scheme to aid the rebellion in the Isthmus of Panama to further his grand plans for a canal linking the oceans. And that led the two of them to be standing in the muddy streets of Valdez, Alaska.

Dickinson also recalled stories whispered in his ear of what the *federales* had done to this girl, to her father, to her whole family. And he believed every word. Only the most terrible events could have turned such a lovely creature to a life of hate. She was wild and deadly and beautiful. Truly, she fit her name, the one the frightened *federales* gave to her: El Tigre.

★ ★ THIRTEEN ★ ★

Nathan and Jim's progress in the direction of Crooked Creek slowed to a crawl over the next three days. The morning after, the Saint Elmo's fire broke with a severe storm. Whirling clouds of blowing snow obscured the trail and hid the mountaintops they used for landmarks. That day they wandered into a box canyon with steep ice-coated sides and spent the entire day backtracking.

Exhausted, the men barely made camp in a protected hollow before night fell. Jim dug into the snow to find enough kindling to make their meager fire. Huddled together in their robes, they ate their dried moose jerky in silence, slowly chewing the cold meat, too tired for conversation. A few handfuls of snow yielded enough water for tepid coffee. The swirling snow engulfed the limited illumination of their fire until yellow and gold flashing snowflakes spiraling within arm's reach were the only thing visible in an otherwise indigo night.

" 'Tain't a night fit for man nor beast," Riley muttered as he struggled to light his pipe. Whatever size ember he took from the fire, the cold wind conspired to extinguish it before he could ignite his pipe. At length he gave up and replaced the pipe in his pocket. He looked over to Nathan, but the youth was fast asleep.

Nathan dreamed of the silver wolf, and her yellow eyes watching him from beyond the light of the campfire. The dream was so clear that he awoke with a start, expecting to see a pair of golden spots watching him. But he saw nothing.

The storm's rage broke the next morning, and the men awoke to find the land as far as the eye could see shimmering in the fiery glow of the rising sun. To the east the horizon simmered a bright orange with a curious powder blue where the sky spilled through a hole in the clouds. Overhead, the sky danced as the sun ignited the underbellies of the low clouds.

Nathan shook the layer of snow from his covers and sat upright. Jim followed suit, rising like a corpse from a snowy grave. His mashed Stetson, folded and lashed about his ears with his scarf, bore little resemblance to his once broad-brimmed hat. Nathan stirred the coals and added fuel to the struggling fire. He shaded his eyes as he studied the vast expanse of white. The moods of this land constantly amazed him. That a land this size could change its essence so rapidly was enthralling as well as frightening. The country could be as variable and unpredictable as the sea, he thought. Only weeks before these hills and valleys blazed with the golden hues of the changing birch and cottonwood. Then the wind stripped these colors and left the land a tawdry brown. Now, everything was white.

"I guess we can forget about a hot bath today, Jim," Nathan joked as he fixed breakfast.

But he was wrong. About five miles down the side of the foothills, they both stopped and sniffed the wind blowing up the canyon.

Jim wrinkled his nose in distaste. He looked suspiciously at his friend. "If yer gonna do that, do it downwind," he complained. "It ain't proper for you to break wind in my face when you got a million acres at yer disposal."

"I didn't," Nathan replied. "But it smells like rotten eggs."

Riley sampled the air again. "Sulfur," he announced. "Hey, we might git yer hot bath after all. That's the smell that comes from hot springs like down on the Yellowstone."

The men followed the smell to a fantastic scene at the base of a series of tumbled boulders. Billowing clouds of steam rose from a succession of natural hot springs bubbling forth from the snow-covered ground. A handful of birch trees surrounded the pools, and the steam had coated every branch with lacy ice crystals. The sulfur smell grew almost smothering, and weird reddish and yellow scum lined the sides of the springs like freakish clouds. Bubbles of hot gases rose to the surface of each pool.

The hot spring mixed with the cooler water of an adjacent spring so that pools of varying temperatures resulted. By sampling, the men soon found one to suit their taste. Ignoring the biting cold, both men stripped off their clothes and sank into the hot water until only the tops of their heads showed through the steam.

"Bring me a cigar and a bottle of whiskey, and I'd be fixed for life," Riley sighed. "And twice as contented as a hog in a wallow."

Nathan stared through the mist as a cow moose and her calf emerged from the steam-glazed willows and approached the cold spring. An angry red gash covered the cow's shoulder.

"Look, Jim! It's the moose that we helped back at the pass. She made it clear with her one calf."

Riley eyed his rifle atop the pile of his clothing. "I hope she remembers we helped her and doesn't decide to stomp us instead." He sank lower into the steaming water so that only his eyes and nose protruded.

But the cow merely looked at the two occupants of the springs and led her calf past them to nibble on the green plants growing under the protection of the warm water. The better part of an hour was spent with the men soaking while the two moose fed. Then the animals shuffled off as silently as they had come, making noise only when their hooves broke through the thin ice that lined the clear spring. They approached the willows and vanished.

"What do you suppose happened to that she-wolf, Jim?" Nathan asked.

"Well, my guess is she weren't accepted back into her pack. She's a loner now if they didn't hunt her down and eat her after she left our camp."

"How do you figure that?"

"Well, that black male was the leader I guess, and she was his mate. With him gone under, the pack'll have to pick another head wolf. So she ain't the queen no more, and the new queen won't want her nowhere near."

Nathan nodded his head. "And she defended him against the rest. . . ."

"Yup. She fought them off. Turned against her own pack to save her mate. Killed a couple, too. They ain't gonna forget that. And I don't reckon wolves is the forgiving kind, them not being baptized or nothing. Turning the other cheek don't mean beans to them. The meek don't inherit nothing in a wolf's world but a passel of grief. You saw the way they butchered this mama moose's other calf."

"I wish she'd stayed with us."

"You remember what I said about naming her, Nat? You can't name something that don't belong to you."

"I know she was wild and all that, but the look in her eyes. . . . I don't know how to describe it. It was almost as if she could understand us."

Riley nodded sagely, setting off a succession of waves in the mineral water. "I knowed horses like that. And a few mules I swear was plotting for days to bite me."

"Well, I hope she's happy."

"She'll be alone, that's for sure, unless she can hook up with another wolf pack—one that'll accept her. For a social critter like a wolf, being solitary ain't a happy thing."

He saw the glum effect his words had on his friend and tried to cheer him up. "You know, us sitting in this mineral bath reminds me of the time I come across a hat smack-dab in the middle of the street when we was in Dawson. Did I ever tell you about that, Nat?"

He had, but Nathan never minded his friend's attempts to bolster his feelings. "No, not that I recall, Jim. What was it doing there in the street?"

"I figured it flew off someone's head and they might miss it. And maybe they'd put their name in it. Well, it had been raining for most of the week, and you know how that mud got churned up something terrible in the streets."

"Yup. It was terrible."

"Right. So I waded over to the hat and picked it up. And do you know what I found?"

"No. What?"

"By God there was a man's head underneath it!"

"Really?"

"It's the gospel. I said: 'What the hell are you doing hiding in this mud?' "

"And he said: 'Sshh, don't give me away! I'm sneaking a ride out of town on the stage!' "

The two men burst into fits of laughter, for different reasons.

Eventually, Riley poked one toe above the steaming surface and squinted at it. "Time for me to git out. First time I've been warm in a cow's age, but I'm getting a mite wrinkled."

Both men emerged, their warm bodies steaming great clouds in the cold air. They dressed, washed what few articles of clothing they weren't wearing, and started a fire to dry them out. Riley smoked his battered pipe while they filled their packs. Here in this frost-covered glen the harsh sounds of life were muted, and both found time to reflect.

Riley brought out his worn reading primer to study, his lips moving silently to form new and unfamiliar words. Somewhere ahead lay Circle City with its fabled library, and Riley wanted to be ready. Nathan cleaned and oiled his weapons. He recalled the softness of the wolf's fur as he waxed the walnut handle of his Colt.

Ahead lay an immense plain filled with snow. The crossing would be hard, and neither man was in a hurry to face that task. The sun was well up before they said good-bye to their private spa and trudged away.

Crossing the low tree line, they passed a handful of scattered and stunted alders clinging to the rocks, before emerging onto a high mountain plateau. The wind had swept the snow covering the plain smooth as white glass. Nothing protruded from the snowy surface to blemish the effect. A rare roll in the cover suggested an outcropping of rock, but neither tree nor bush marred the uniform surface.

Upon this pristine anvil the sun beat down like a fiery hammer. Just to look at the field hurt the eyes. And the plain stretched for miles.

At first the men enjoyed the warmth of the sun. Shining from an intense blue sky, its rays warmed their backs and brightened their spirits. Soon both men were walking with their hats removed and coats unbuttoned. By midday they'd traveled well into the white expanse so that only the shadows of the mountains to both sides shimmered on the shapeless horizon.

Riley squinted up at the cloudless sky, then down at the snow before he wiped a tear from his eye. "Whew, that sun is bright," he said. "Better put on our snow goggles."

Riley found his first, wooden blinders carved by Athabascans with a narrow slit cut to admit the powerful light and block the reflection from the snow. He pulled them over his eyes and turned to find Nathan still searching. After ten minutes of turning his pockets and pack inside out, the lad looked hopelessly at his friend.

"I can't find my goggles, Jim. I know I had them when we left. They must have fallen out of my pack when I rescued the wolf."

Riley scratched his head. "This is trouble," he said solemnly. "We can't just camp here. It's too exposed. We got to cross this snowfield, and you're gonna need something lest you come up snow-blind. Let's share mine."

"No, Jim, that's a bad idea. If we miscalculate we'll both end up blind. Better you keep the blinders. That way you can lead me across. Otherwise the two of us will be floundering about in the snow until we fall into a crevasse or freeze to death. I'll smear some soot from the bottom of the cooking pot on my cheeks. I heard that sometimes works."

Riley fought back a growing dread while Nathan blackened his face. He and the boy even exchanged hats so the gunman's wide-brimmed Stetson could shelter the young man from the blazing sun. But nothing could stop the fierce reflection from the unblemished snow. So the two descended into the featureless plain while the sun beat down on them.

By midday tears were flowing freely from Nathan's eyes to wash streaks in his sooty marks and freeze to his cheeks. His eyes themselves felt as if blasted by sand, although not a grain of dust lay exposed for miles. An hour later he thankfully noted the sun was beginning to set, but several hours of torment remained.

His plight had not gone unnoticed by Riley. Every time the boy scooped a handful of snow to soothe the fire in his eyes, the old man's heart ached. But there was nothing he could do but press onward as fast as they could. The sooner they crossed this frozen hell, the better were Nathan's chances.

Late in the day, Riley spotted a break in the monotonous skyline, a shimmering smudge ahead. As they slogged on, the smudge separated into the tops of three spindly spruce trees. The end of the snowfield was in sight.

"Nat, boy, we're almost through," he cried while his gloved hand pointed to the growing patch of trees.

Nathan raised his head and looked in that direction. His watering eyes beheld only swimming shadows. But his feet struck rock with increasing frequency until the two men slumped against the first of an endless row of spruce and bare birch. Willow and alder thickets also stood in uneven rows between the clumps of trees like uncertain squires following their knights. They had survived the great snow plain.

Exhausted, both men stripped off their packs and started a fire from dry spruce limbs. As Nathan stirred their strange version of coffee and soaked strips of dried moose pemmican in a fry pan bubbling with beans, the sun dropped below the mountains. Before it vanished a lingering alpenglow turned the white plain behind them into a crimson sea.

"Ain't that a beautiful sight for such a damned hellhole?" Riley asked as he gnawed on an unsoftened strip of meat. "I wish it'd been half as pretty when we was walking across it."

Nathan nodded his head, but the rose-colored plain was just a blur now, and even the feeble glow of the campfire hurt his eyes. Added to this, his head throbbed as if a thousand hammers beat behind his eyes. He served Jim his plate and coffee mainly by feel, then retreated to the comforting darkness outside the firelight. He ate little before crawling into his blankets.

Riley watched all this with a worried frown. He finished his meal in silence, scouring the plates with fresh snow before wrapping his caribou robe about his shoulders. He banked the coals to keep them going until morning and leaned back against a spruce. There he spent the night watching his friend while he hugged his Henry rifle.

Morning broke clear and cold with patchy ropes of clouds gathering in the west. The cloud cover thickened, robbing the dawn of its light until the morning slipped back into the eerie

133

predawn. Riley stirred first, shifting under his robes, and shaking off the thin cover of frost that coated him.

Nathan sat bolt upright, blinking his bloodshot eyes in disbelief. He stretched an opened hand in front of his face while he concentrated on it. Over and over he turned his hand. Riley rose to his feet, and the sound of movement caused Nathan to turn his head toward his partner.

Riley suppressed a gasp. The youth's eyelids were swollen twice their normal size, and the gap in the lids revealed a steamy whitish color where once were sharp gray irises.

Nathan grimaced while a terrible sigh issued from him.

"Jim, I'm blind!" he sobbed. "I can't see a thing. I can't even see my hand!"

Riley rushed to his side and cradled the sobbing youth. "Easy, Nat. You got snow-blind, that's all. I've heard about this happening. It ain't a permanent thing."

"It's not? Tell me the truth, Jim! Don't lie to me. Will it get better?"

"Sure, kid. It just takes a few days, and you'll be good as new."

"I will? Please, don't lie to me." Nathan's hand went to his revolver. "I don't want to live like this, Jim. I'll finish myself right now if it won't get better."

Riley's hand clamped down on Nathan's hand, keeping the Colt in its holster. "Easy, lad. Don't get spooked on me. We've been in worse spots than this. You're acting as green as a cook's little Mary on his first cattle drive. Yer lamps is gonna be just fine, believe me."

Nathan relaxed his grip on his pistol and withdrew his hand. But his body quivered with fright. "I . . . I couldn't live without seeing, Jim. I just couldn't. . . ."

"I know, son." Riley patted his shoulder. "It's just swelling from the sun. It'll go down." He took Nathan's head in his hands and turned his face to examine the swollen eyes. "You'll just be blessed with not having to look at my ugly mug for a couple days. Now let me have a look. Can you see my fingers?"

"It's all blurry, Jim."

Riley waved his fingers in wide circles. "But you can see me moving?"

"Yes . . ."

"Good. I don't think no nerves are damaged. Everything's just swollen. Best we put some cold bandages on yer peepers to lower the swelling."

"What do you think, Jim?" Nathan asked as Riley applied the compresses. His friend's steady voice and the pressure of his hands had a reassuring effect.

"Well, you ain't gonna attract no pretty gals with them peepers just yet. Lucky for you there ain't none around. I figure we'll just hole up here until you're better. I could use the time to catch up on sewing the holes in my socks. We got wood for fire, plenty of food, and shelter. This is as good a place as any to camp."

"I could follow you with one hand on your shoulder."

"Now, that would be stupid. What if I fall in a durned hole? You'd either lose me or fall in, too. Best we rest up until you're fit. Circle City ain't going nowhere. You keep those wet dressings on yer eyes, and I'll find a suitable piece of wood and carve you a new set of snow goggles—one that you won't lose next time you tumble down some hill."

"Better make them big."

"I just might. I might whittle a pair so big you'll need a mule to pack it."

Riley stirred the coals and added more dry spruce and soon the air was filled with the smells of coffee and smoking strips of meat. The familiar sounds and smells aided the return of Nathan's confidence. His friend placed a steaming cup of coffee in his hand and a plate in his lap. Despite this headache,

Nathan ate, knowing he needed to keep up his strength. However, this sudden calamity erased all enthusiasm for food.

Two days passed with little improvement. While the swelling decreased, light—any light—terrorized Nathan's eyes with stabbing pain. This forced him to keep his lids clamped tightly together.

"Maybe you ought to go on ahead," Nathan mentioned that evening as he forced himself to peer into the darkness. Even then his vision consisted of little more than blurred shadows alternating with lightning flashes although none were there. "You could get to Circle City and send back help."

"What? And leave you alone? Not likely. We're pards, and pards don't pull out on one another. I taught you better than that."

"I just thought . . ."

"You wouldn't leave me here if I was the one hurt, would you?"

"No."

"I didn't think so, and I ain't leaving you, neither. So shake them harebrained schemes right out of yer mind. You had me worried for a moment, talking like that."

Nathan grinned in spite of his discomfort. He'd always enjoyed the way they chafed each other. Either of them would die before professing kind feelings for the other, yet each man owed the other his life.

"Maybe they have a doctor in Circle that could look at my eyes?"

"Eeeah." Riley shivered. "I'd sooner take my chances with a Tlingit shaman than let some quack lay hands on me. Why with all their bloody training on chopping things, you'd be lucky if he didn't cut off your leg."

"My leg? But it's my eyes that are the problem!"

"Don't make no never mind. All them surgeons know is

lopping off limbs. They apply that to whatever ails you. Get shot in the belly, off comes yer leg. Got a bad case of piles, off goes yer other leg. Pretty soon you ain't got nothing more to whack off, so they declare you hopeless and leave you alone to go south. Best not think on it." Riley tried his best to make light of his friend's illness, hoping to ease Nathan's fears.

But all their talk made Nathan's head throb, so he said good night and rolled back into his robes. He wished he were better, but he knew his eyes needed time. He struggled with his thoughts until he fell asleep.

Nathan awoke as the dawn announced itself by causing him more discomfort. But he took heart that the shapes were not as ill-defined as the previous day. He groped around until he found the rag he was using. Adding a fresh handful of snow to the cloth, he tied it over his eyes and waited for Jim to make breakfast.

After the meal, Nathan helped as best he could by cleaning up. His ears and the smell of gun oil told him Riley was cleaning his rifle.

"Why don't you look for some fresh game, Jim?" he suggested. "No sense hanging around camp just to keep me company. We could use some fresh meat for a change."

"You sure you'd be all right? I don't want no bear dragging you off while I'm gone."

"I'll be fine. The bears are all denned up, and no wolves will bother me while I've got this fire going."

"You sure?"

"Yup. This jerky is getting tiresome. Just don't shoot a moose. I can't help you pack it back here."

"Well, I've been watching a flock of ptarmigan for the last few days. They seem to be hanging around over that far ridge. I suspect I could mosey over there, bag five or six, and be back before nightfall."

"You shoot them with your Henry, and all we'll have is a few feathers to eat."

"Heck, I'll just clip off the tops of their little white noggins, nice and neat like."

"Sounds like a plan."

Riley studied his friend suspiciously. "You ain't thinking of tricking this old pilgrim into getting out of camp jus' so's you could put a bullet in yer brainpan, are you? 'Cause yer gonna get better, I know it for sure."

Nathan shook his head vigorously and instantly regretted the pain it caused. "No, Jim. I am getting better. I can see shapes better than yesterday. I promise I won't shoot myself. I'll be waiting for you when you get back with those birds."

After an awkward moment of silence, Nathan added, "Take my pistol with you—then you won't have to worry."

"I don't want to leave you unarmed."

"Look, I've got my Winchester. Nobody shoots themself with their rifle. For one thing, my arm isn't long enough to reach the trigger with the muzzle pointed at me." He located his pistol by feel and handed it to Riley. "Take the pistol."

"Okay. I won't be long." Riley thrust the revolver into his belt. "If you need me just fire your rifle three times, and I'll come running back."

"Okay."

Riley packed a few essentials and shouldered his rifle. Watching his friend suffer had been harder on him than he expected. Must be getting soft, he mused. A short hunting trip would settle him.

But before he left, he pulled his own caribou robe over Nathan and covered him like a father would do for his sick son. Then with a gruff good-bye, he hiked off. Nathan didn't see him pause on the first rise to check his friend one more time before vanishing into the white wilderness.

Several hours passed as Nathan leaned against a trunk and changed his compresses. To occupy his mind he listened to the sounds that reached their frozen oasis. Once he heard a red squirrel scolding off to the right in the spruce forest. The animal had probably ventured from his sleeping den to retrieve a meal of white spruce cones from his buried midden and gotten surprised by a porcupine. Lucky for the squirrel it wasn't a fox or a lynx, or his chatter would have died abruptly.

More sounds reached his ears, and Nathan realized what he'd been told about the other senses taking over for a lost one was true. His hearing had become sharper. Behind him a cluster of chickadees fanned the air and sang their characteristic song. Far in the distance a raven warbled raucously, secure in the knowledge that life was just one big, obscene joke.

In time he heard approaching footsteps crunching on the wind-packed crust. Nathan shifted comfortably in his robes. Riley would fill his head with grandiose tales of his hunt, the stalk, and all. But he couldn't remember hearing any shots.

"Back so soon, Jim?" he joked. "I didn't hear you shoot. Did you forget your cartridges or fall in the creek? Or did all those ptarmigan see you coming?"

The footsteps stopped for a second before resuming. To Nathan's ear they sounded as if Jim was stalking him, no doubt to play a trick on him.

"I can hear you a mile away, Jim, even if I can't see you," Nathan laughed. "You make more noise than a herd of buffalo." He turned his head in the direction of the sound and lifted a corner of his dressing, but all he saw were blurred images.

"I ain't your Jim," a voice rasped like a file. "But we are acquainted, Blaylock. . . ."

"Soapy Smith!" Nathan gasped.

His Winchester leapt into his hands, but he had no target.

Nathan jumped to his knees and swiveled at a footfall. An instant later a vicious kick caused his rifle to fly from his grasp, and the cold barrel of another gun cracked across the side of his face. Shooting stars and flashing lights exploded inside his head before he dropped into total darkness.

FOURTEEN

Nathan awoke with a start. His head pounded like it resided inside a bass drum, and he was unable to move his arms or cry out. For an instant he thought he was paralyzed until he tasted the foul gag stuffed in his mouth. It stunk of rancid sweat and tobacco as well. Try as he would he could not spit it out, although it caused him to retch. As his senses cleared he felt the ropes biting into his arms and legs and the rough bark gouging his back. He was tied to a tree, he realized.

A rough hand ripped the bandage from his eyes, and he forced himself to focus on the dark shadow standing before him. Slowly his thoughts returned: the second Soapy Smith had captured him. The shadow shimmered and bent closer. A cloud of rank breath assailed his nostrils.

"Blind as a bat, are you," Smith giggled. "Done something stupid and got yourself snow-blinded, eh? Ain't that something, the big frontiersman got hisself struck blind. What have you got to say about that, mister gunfighter?" He ripped the gag from Nathan's mouth.

"Let me loose, Smith," Nathan snarled. "We've got no quarrel with you. We cut out and left the camp, so it's all over."

"No it ain't, my fancy man."

"Why not? We're over a hundred miles from Barnette's trading post, and we don't plan on ever going back there."

"It ain't done, not yet. I got a score to settle with you, and the captain's promised me a reward."

"A reward?"

"Yup. You didn't think I trailed you two all the way out into this godforsaken land just to have tea, did you? I almost lost your track a dozen times, 'cept when you camped a while back near that moose kill. Why you did that still puzzles me, but I know why you're laid up here. You got blinded and had to hole up. I been watching the two of you since this morning."

"Then you know Riley's within earshot."

"No he ain't, neither. I watched him for a good while. He's long gone, off hunting I suspect. That's a rich one: him off hunting and all the while here I am a-hunting you. Don't you think that's a laugh?"

"What do you want, Smith?"

"Well, I wants just what I got . . . you, boy. That's what I want." The gloating sound in his voice was evident even to Nathan, with no vision.

"You mean to take me back to Captain Barnette, is that it?" Nathan stalled for time, time to let his head clear, time to formulate a plan. He cursed himself for being so naive to think Barnette's anger would stop at a hundred miles. This was a big land with room for big hatreds. He'd grown careless, and this was the result.

"Hell, no. I ain't taking you all the way back to the trading post. You'd get free at the drop of a hat and slit my throat. Besides, I'd have to be looking over my shoulder for your saddle-bum friend every second. No sirree. I'm too smart for that. That's why I suggested what I did to the captain. And, do you know, he was all for it."

"You're not going to take me back?" Nathan asked.

"I'm taking *part* of you back. That way I can collect the reward. The captain's promised me three hundred dollars in gold for fixing you."

142

Nathan's jaw tightened at the suggestion, but he had to ask. "What part of me?"

"Ha-ha. Your privates. Ain't that rich? The captain thought it was funny, too. He plans on presenting 'em to his wife. Figures she'd be able to recognize 'em as the genuine article. Then he joked about making a tobacco pouch out of 'em."

"Goddamn you!"

Smith rewarded his outcry with the back of his hand.

Nathan tasted blood from his split lip before Soapy jammed the foul gag back into his mouth. He twisted his bonds until the leather bit into his wrists and blood slicked his hands, but it was no use—Soapy knew how to lash a captive. He cursed out loud at being so helpless. He was trussed like a pig for the slaughter. His helplessness aggravated him as much as anything else. Again, he rued his foolishness. His outcry had caused Smith to stopper his mouth. Now there was no way he could call to Jim for help. He realized his blindness had dulled his fighting edge. He resolved to be more cautious next time. But would there be a next time?

Soapy sat back on his heels and enjoyed the hatred blazing from Nathan's face. He smiled like a lynx. "Don't be looking at me like that. I won't leave you all gelded. Nope. I ain't that dumb. You'd follow me to the ends of the earth for revenge if I cut off your stones and let you live. Hell, I would if someone did it to me."

Nathan's muffled malediction rang in his ear.

"What's that you say, my rutting little friend? Why should I be so spiteful to you? Truth is I kinda fancied a turn with the captain's wife myself. But you scotched that for me. Now Barnette has her watched like a hawk. That makes me feel real bad, so I'm going to take my soreness out on you. Best of all, I'm getting paid for it."

Soapy cast a glance at the coals, glowing in the fire like rubies set in an ermine robe. He backed away from Nathan to shovel a handful of spruce branches onto the fire. The boughs burst into flame, and the carmine light reflected in Smith's evil face seemed to Nathan to personify the devil himself. Soapy withdrew a fearful-looking bowie knife and tested its edge. Satisfied with its sharpness, he thrust it into the bed of coals. Then he extracted a branch and blew on its blazing end until it burst into flames. Turning to Nathan he waved the fiery end close to the youth's face. Nathan sensed the movement and felt the heat scorch his skin.

"First I'm gonna make you hurt," Smith hissed.

Nathan started as the brand rasped along his neck. He smelled the burning flesh, his flesh, an instant before the pain rocked him. It started at the angle of his jaw and raced after the slowly moving stick until it seemed to leap beyond the burn itself. So sharp in feeling it could have been a knife cut, the pain spread over his neck and chest and transmuted itself into a burning that brought colors to Nathan's injured eyes.

Smith stepped back and surveyed his handiwork. A blackened streak ran across Nathan's neck. Already an angry redness rose on both sides of the burn. Soapy ripped open Nathan's shirt, exposing the white skin of his chest below the tanned skin of his neck.

"Like that, did you?" Soapy gloated. "There's more coming. I'm gonna cook you, starting at the neck and working down. When I get to your toes, I doubt you'll care what happens next."

He selected another spruce branch and added another line to the other side of Nathan's neck. The youth tried to grit his teeth at the next bout of pain. His tightly closed eyelids squeezed tears from his damaged eyes. After two dozen fiery lashes, he passed out.

Smith flopped back on his heels, panting at the exertion. "Damn, this is harder work than I figured," he gasped. He drove his boot into the side of his captive, but no movement rewarded his effort. Kicking snow onto Nathan's burned neck and his face caused the boy to stir. With greater effort Smith revived his victim. Soapy retrieved a pint flask of whiskey from his pocket and swilled the contents. He eased the gag from Nathan's mouth.

"Want a drink to ease your suffering, boy?" he teased. He held the flask an inch from Nathan's lips and poured a few drops onto the burns. But the boy didn't even flinch.

"I don't need whiskey to bolster my courage, you son of a bitch!" Nathan snarled. He spat directly in his tormentor's face. "Cut me free, and I'll tear you apart with my bare hands. What's the matter? Afraid to face me with your damned knife, even though I'm blind!"

Smith wiped the spittle from his face and grinned fiercely. "I told you, I ain't stupid."

He poked a firebrand at the lad's chest, stubbing it out like a cigarette butt on the pale skin. To his annoyance Nathan refused to cry out, even with the gag removed.

Smith got to his feet and walked around his bound captive in agitation. He emptied the last of his liquor and threw the bottle into the bushes. One of his greasy hands wiped his nose and kneaded his chin while he thought. His face twisted into a depraved mask as an evil idea struck him. He moved to the tree where Nathan was tied and began to scrape balls of pitch from the scarred trunk.

"Well, this ain't working too well," he said slowly. "I suspect I'll try my hand at skinning you a mite, but first I think I'll try this. It's an old White Mountain Apache trick I heard about. They smear pitch on parts of you and set it afire. I think they start out on your limbs and work up to your face. They also like the privates, but unfortunately I don't want to damage that merchandise. It's my cash crop so to speak."

He dabbed a spot of resin the size of a silver dollar onto Nathan's chest and ignited it. While every muscle in the youth's body tensed with the agony, little showed on his face but his tightly clenched lips and eyes. More blood trickled down his wrists as he fought his bonds. In a remote corner of his brain a sterile assessment of his plight was going on. He couldn't show this pig that he hurt, his mind argued, when only his neck and chest were burned. It would not do for him to show weakness. Besides, another part of his mind formulated a plan. If he refused to show pain, Smith would become more frustrated . . . and he would become careless. Already Nathan had managed to loosen the rawhide binding his legs. He would endure whatever Smith planned until the end. Then he would fake unconsciousness. When Smith came closer to castrate him, he would scissor his head with his legs and break his neck. Inwardly, Nathan smiled at the grim assessment that, while he would die, so would his tormentor.

Soapy's voice intruded on his thoughts. "My, my, boy, you're beginning to look like pinto pony with all them spots. I think I'll try burning off your ears first, then your eyes, even though they is puny. Wouldn't want them sensitive peepers to be giving any more gals the roving eye, would we now?"

Nathan inhaled the clean scent of the spruce pitch, and he filled his lungs with its pure essence to steel himself for this coming ordeal. He focused his mind on that corner that felt no pain and waited.

The burning twig loomed before him, its light glowing through his clenched lids as it grew larger and larger. Any minute it would touch him. . . .

A black shadow leapt into his vision, merging with Soapy Smith's. It came suddenly, silently—only the air rustled, as if charged with static electricity. The torch stopped, hovered in midair momentarily, only to drop from view. Nathan open his eyes, but blurred images raced before his eyes. His ears, however, told a different story.

A low swishing sound reached his tarred ears, something familiar, yet he couldn't place where he'd heard it before. The specter separated from Smith's shadow and dropped to one side, leaving the other jerking about erratically while wet, gurgling sounds came from it. His torturer's outline crumpled to its knees before flopping backward. The gurgling continued while what Nathan guessed were Smith's limbs flailed helplessly at the air. His rescuing phantom closed again with Smith. Their images locked together for an instant before again parting. Smith issued a strangled croak; his body arched, then went limp.

What had happened? Nathan strained his ears, but only silence reached even his sensitized hearing. He wondered if Riley had returned, had fired a single desperate shot from afar, and luckily hit Smith. But he had heard no shot. Nathan raised his head and turned his face in all directions, searching for the answer.

The same blurred specter moved from Smith's dead body to edge toward Nathan. Noiselessly, the shadow grew in his half-blind field of vision until it blotted all else, but still it made no noise. Nathan tensed, waiting for the unexpected. And then it came.

A warm, wet tongue licked his face.

FIFTEEN

"Sweet Jesus! What in God's name happened here?" Jim Riley swore softly. He stood atop the shallow bench that hid the hollow of their camp and stared down. A string of six freshly killed ptarmigan, tied by their feet with braided grass, slipped from his fingers.

"Good God Almighty," he gasped as he reviewed the carnage. He reflexively jacked a round into his Henry rifle and dropped to one knee, the rifle held at the ready.

Hours before, he'd strode out of an orderly camp where his snow-blind partner rested beneath piles of caribou robes and a slow fire simmered. He expected to return to the same. Instead, he found Nathan tied to a tree and stripped half-naked. Alternating burn stripes and angry red blisters crisscrossed his friend's neck and upper body. The camp looked as if a cyclone had touched down in its center. Pots and packs were overturned and scattered in random piles. Trampled and torn snow exposed the brown, winter-killed grass. And spread-eagled before Nathan lay a man, back arched and rigid in death, with great gouts of frozen blood scattered about his body.

Riley advanced on this hellish scene with all the care used to enter a den of rattlesnakes. He kept low with his rifle pressed to his shoulder, pausing to look down at the startled grimace stamped forever on the dead man's face. Riley frowned as he recognized the face.

"Soapy Smith the second," he hissed. "But it looks like he was first when it come to gitting kilt." Jim studied the gaping hole and torn flesh that once was Smith's neck. The whitish gristle of his windpipe shone through the blackening edge of torn muscle.

Then he heard a low growl as the side of Nathan's caribou robe rose with fur bristling.

"Easy, girl," Nathan said as he reached out with his arm as far as the ropes allowed to stroke the furry back. "That's Jim. You remember him." The animal stopped growling and lay back beside him. Nathan smiled in spite of the pain he felt.

A slow grin snaked from one ear to the other on Riley's face. "Well, I'll be damned. It's that silver she-wolf. By God, if that don't beat all!"

The young man grinned. "She came back, Jim. She came back to me."

Riley squatted on his heels as he read the signs. "Looks like this whore's son of a bitch was playing Apache with you, son." He smacked his fist into his palm in anger. The movement caused the wolf to tense her shoulders, but she made no move to spring. "Damn! I never should have left you alone. I never should have."

"Who'd have figured Barnette would send Smith to find us?" Nathan answered.

"Barnette was it, eh? Soon as you can see, I'm going back there and kill every mother's son in his stinking trading post. Then I'll pass his goods out to the Tanana tribes and burn the rest to ashes!" Riley swore. "He wanted to build a city to rival San Francisco! Ha! When I finish with him even the ravens won't remember what he built."

"I hope Smith is the end of this," Nathan said philosophically. "But we'd best watch our backs for a while." He shivered.

Riley sprang to his feet and the wolf did the same. "Damn! Here I'm jawing like we was having tea at the Empress Hotel, and you're half burned and froze all together. Will yer she-devil let me near you without going for my windpipe like she did to Soapy?"

"I'll hold her, Jim. She lets me do that now."

Warily, Riley eased over to his friend while Nathan stroked and talked to the wolf. Her yellow eyes watched every move the gunman made. Riley cut the ropes and boiled some fresh snow to bathe Nathan's wounds.

"Ain't she something," he remarked. "Not the least bit scared of fire. Hell, I thought fire was supposed to keep wolves away. There goes another of my foolish notions."

"No. Soapy was burning me a stick when she jumped him. The fire didn't stop her or nothing."

"That don't give me no comfort knowing these here meat eaters ain't spooked by it. Ain't that what separates us from the animals?" Riley paused to look back at the corpse of Soapy Smith. "Though ain't many animals would sink to torture. I reckon the Good Lord made 'em a step up on us in that regard."

Riley washed his friend's wounds and smeared bear grease on the blisters before wrapping them with strips torn from his only Sunday-go-to-meeting shirt. He'd saved the shirt in case there was a whorehouse in Circle, but his friend's needs came first. Finished with nursing, he retrieved his ptarmigan and proceeded to pluck them beside the fire while Nathan sipped hot coffee laced with whiskey appropriated from Smith's pack, which they discovered outside the camp. Jim ground a handful of spruce needles and Labrador tea leaves into the brew. All along the Yukon and Copper Rivers, he'd seen medicine men use that mix to speed healing and ward off infection.

He threaded four birds onto willow skewers and set them over the fire. The wolf looked slantways at the other two birds lying in the snow, but made no move toward them.

"I don't suppose you'd want to gnaw yer steaks outta old

Soapy over there." Riley jerked his thumb at the body as he addressed the wolf. "No? I suppose not, then. Can't say as I blame you. Wouldn't care to eat that skunk myself. Well, share and share alike." He tossed the raw birds to the wolf. She caught the first in her jaws and swallowed it in two gulps. The second bird vanished just as quickly. Next the wolf proceeded to clean herself.

The old man placed a cooked fowl in both of Nathan's hands before sitting back to eat his. His gaze wandered over to the gaping eyes of the dead man just feet away. Riley chewed thoughtfully. "Christ, Soapy, this bitch sure got the drop on you," he said. "Yer lucky she plucked out yer gizzard before I could git my hands on you. Hell, I'd show you a thing or two about playing Apache if I'd caught you, you bastard."

"You shouldn't speak ill of the dead, Jim."

"That sounds like something them nuns in Denver taught you."

"I think so. His soul is gone to his Maker, and he'll have to account to Him for his deeds."

"Maybe so," Riley mumbled while he sucked on a leg bone. "His soul may be gone, but his carcass is still here . . . and it's turning my appetite sour looking at his frog eyes. I reckon I should have buried him first, but I'm too damned tired and too hungry to play gravedigger for the likes of him." He kicked a pile of snow over the face and grunted in satisfaction. "That's a heap better."

"Jim, did you ever think that animals might have souls?"

"Sure they do. Leastways, I credit them with having a spirit. It stands to reason if even the rottenest scum like this here Smith, pardon my description, has a soul, why, then it's only fair that a decent animal should have something, too. The natives think so, and they's pretty savvy when it comes to the spirit world. That's why we always put a handful of grass or some willow leaves in the mouths of the animals we shoot for food. I learned it from the Indians. It gives the beasts a snack to tide 'em over on their trip to the happy hunting ground. Don't want their spirits thinking I got bad manners and ain't grateful for the meat. If they was to go and tell their brothers I was an ingrate, who knows when I'd get another bite of game. I notice you doing the same thing, Nat."

Nathan watched Riley's shadow explain his eccentric philosophy. "How could it be a happy hunting ground for the animals? What kind of heaven would have you getting shot or having a lance stuck in your liver?"

"Oh, that's easy, Nat. I had an old Piegan medicine man up on the Wind River explain it to me. No one ever catches anyone in the happy hunting ground. All the fun's in the chase anyway. Once you down yer animal, it ain't nothing but work. So you spend all yer time a hooping and a hollering after them animals, and they gits a kick outta the chase 'cause they knows they won't never git caught. It's real simple."

Nathan turned away from the fire and looked at the orange rim of light resting on top of the mountain range. Even to his dimmed vision the colors were evident. Dusk was settling. But this high in the Arctic, evening moved slowly. Hours would pass before darkness. This lingering transition, with its pastel blend of purples, pinks, and mauves, would please the dullest.

Without thinking, he stroked the wolf's fur and hugged her close to him. Unaccustomed to this grasp, the she-wolf issued a throaty growl and stiffened. Immediately, Nathan released her.

Riley poked a greasy finger at the two. "You got to treat her different from a woman. Remember, she's a wolf. Although she kinda reminds me of Wei-Li. She's got that same ornery nature. More than a few of the Plains tribes think a person's spirit can enter a critter's body."

Nathan cast a hard look at the hazy image of his friend. "Do you think Wei-Li's spirit is inside this wolf?" he asked slowly. "I was wondering about that myself, but it sounds too crazy to talk about."

Riley searched about the dead body until he found what he was looking for. His eyes flashed excitedly as he held up two cigars. "Thank you kindly, Soapy. Mighty thoughtful of you to provide me with an after-dinner smoke."

He lit one with a burning stick and puffed contentedly until a dingy cloud of smoke enveloped his head.

Waving the glowing tip around at the camp, he sighed, ignoring the way the wolf watched his every move. "It don't git much better than this," he added sarcastically as he motioned to the corpse. "Pleasant company, first-class dining, and a true bitch to grace our presence with her company." He grinned crookedly at the animal.

"You didn't answer my question, Jim."

"Well, I will. Jus' give me time to collect my thoughts. No, I don't think this here critter is housing your dead girlfriend's spirit. She's got her own brand of bitchiness which I think she comes by naturally, not by no spirit infusion. I reckon you jus' got yerself entangled with another dangerous female."

Nathan smoothed the wolf's fur. "I wonder why she came back?"

"Whatever the reason, we got us another female in camp, and already I can feel the difference. But I don't suspect she'll mind if I don't change my long johns every day and wash behind my ears, do you?" With that he crawled into his blankets.

Nathan turned his face in direction of the dead Smith. The body, contorted in death, appeared only as a shadow to him. "Funny isn't it, Jim?"

"What?" came his friend's muffled reply.

"The fact that we've known two men named Soapy, and both met sudden and violent deaths."

"That should be a lesson to you. Never name none of yer kids Soapy," Riley grumbled.

"What about Soapy?" Nathan persisted after a period of silence. "Shouldn't we bury him?"

Riley raised his head. Satisfied that Smith had not moved, he dropped back onto the caribou robe. "I ain't gonna spend all night chiseling a hole for that varmint. The ground is froze solid. You'd need dynamite to blast a hole big enough for even his scrawny carcass. I say leave him be to provide a good meal for the foxes and the ravens. Probably be the only good thing he done in his entire life."

"We ought to say a prayer or something, Jim," Nathan persisted.

"Okay, okay." Riley sat upright. He waved his hand in the direction of the corpse, making an exaggerated benediction. "Tough luck, you bastard, but we forgive you," he prayed. "Now are you satisfied, Nat? I'm plumb wore out and sorely need my beauty sleep. You forget I was out hard hunting while you was jus' setting here getting tortured."

Before Nathan could reply, sounds of snoring emanated from Riley's bedroll. Instinctively his hand reached out in the direction of the wolf's breathing until it contacted the warm softness of her fur. He felt the animal roll onto her back and yawn contentedly. Nathan smiled inwardly and hunkered down against the deepening cold. I could do worse, he thought. If I'm to be blind, at least I've got two friends in this world that care about me. And what other blind man can claim to have a wolf for a guide dog?

Morning brought low clouds to mask the sun that distressed Nathan's swollen eyes. The low cover turned the world to gray and white with little distinction as to what was land and what was sky. Low-lying scud masked the mountaintops and spilled into their clefts, obscuring all landmarks as well as the sun. Travel was impossible.

Riley hunted again, but this time he kept close to camp, meandering around the low hills, always keeping an eye on their camp. Neither man knew if Barnette would send another assassin, so they took extra precautions. The wolf trotted out of camp at first light.

By noon the weather showed no signs of breaking, and a light snow began to fall. Riley returned to camp—empty-handed.

He sat on his heels and poured himself a cup of what they called coffee, although the mix of leaves and weeds bore no resemblance to an orthodox brew. Riley studied the sky, then cast a sidelong glance at the hump of pristine snow covering Soapy Smith. Above the body a pair of camp-robber jays also eyed the potential feast and waited patiently for them to move.

"Blast yer hide, Soapy," Riley griped. "You could have had the decency to outfit yerself with a pound of coffee to go with yer cigars. This here Indian brew is turning my liver."

Riley had rifled the dead man's pockets, finding little beside the cigars except a brass compass and a dozen cartridges for his pistol. Riley's irritation grew when he found Smith was carrying a Schofield revolver chambered for the .44 Russian cartridge. The extra bullets were useless for their .45 Colts. To add to his embarrassment, the silver wolf trotted into camp with a fat rabbit clamped in her jaws. She dropped her kill beside Nathan and gave Riley a sly look.

"Damn," the gunman sputtered. "Where did you find that hare? Only tracks I saw were field mice."

The animal yawned as if bored.

"This is damned humiliating," he sighed. "I'm competing with a four-legged bitch as the camp hunter—and losing out big-time. And she don't even have a rifle or one of them opposite thumbs."

"Opposite thumbs? What's that, Jim?"

"Sure, opposite thumbs. I read about 'em in a book. That's

155

what sets us above the animals, this fellow says: we're toolmak-
ers and we got two opposite thumbs."

"Oh! Opposable thumbs."

"Right, that's what I said. We can twiddle our thumbs all
whichways." He threw up his hand in disgust. "Fat lot of good
it'll do me if I can't spot nothing to hunt."

Nathan had been watching Riley's shadow swim into view.
Without the sun to blind him, he could open his lids enough
to focus on close objects. His heart sang as the images of his
friend and the wolf became sharper.

The snow continued for four days, and Nathan used every
minute to recover. His chest burns healed rapidly while the
neck took longer because of the friction from his collar. But by
the time the storm passed even his vision had returned to normal. The wolf stayed by his side except to hunt, even growing
to accept Riley as a fixture associated with her new master; so
when they pushed off, the animal trotted easily by Nathan's
side—separate and aloof, but firmly associated with him.

In their wanderings the trio finally reached Crooked Creek
just north of Medicine Lake. Keeping the mountains on their
left and the low marsh to their right, they reached the outskirts
of once thriving Circle City. Nestled in the bend of the Yukon
River, the town once boasted over ten thousand occupants, saloons, and cafés. But the gold strike upriver in the Klondike
drained the lifeblood from Circle in one massive hemorrhage.
Now the travelers looked down on an enfeebled husk that
struggled to survive. During summer, Circle was relegated to
supplying cordwood for the river steamers that once stopped
there, forced to watch forlornly as the boats vanished upstream
trailing their sooty banners behind. Cordwood and supplies
for the stubborn or stupid few that still prospected for that big
find kept the skeleton of the city from crumbling into dust. A
sprinkling of smoke snaked from a dozen chimneys, and lights

glowed in the windows of those shacks. Two larger structures showed signs of life. One clearly bore the weathered marquee of a saloon.

"Which one do you reckon is the library?" Riley asked. "My guess is it's that long sod roof over there."

"Could be, Jim. But I'm heading for the bar. I want to get some whiskey to pour over this burn on the right side of my neck. It's beginning to fester."

Riley shook his head. "Drink some, too. People here will think yer touched in the head and don't know what the real purpose of whiskey is. I'll catch up with you soon as I scout out all them books."

The two parted company at the main street. Nathan followed his ears and his nose to the yellowed windows of the beer hall. Stale sawdust, smoke, and laughter seeped from the clapboard front. The wolf wrinkled her nose in disgust before sitting down outside the door. The young man scratched behind her ears and cooed to her. She dropped her muzzle into the snow and watched as he opened the door.

A dozen heads turned in his direction. Gratefully, Nathan realized he knew none of the occupants. Most looked like prospectors.

"Welcome, stranger," the bartender greeted him. A new face meant new business.

Nathan touched the brim of his trapper's hat and smiled. "Thank you. Glad to be here."

"Well, we're always glad to see a new face—if you've got money," the barkeep replied. "If you're flat busted, I'll retract my greeting. I can't afford no more drinks on credit."

A lively retort came from his patrons, most of whom confirmed that this man's heart was hard as the bedrock they struggled to break, or that he was the most miserly human alive.

Nathan flipped one of the twenty-dollar gold pieces he'd taken from Soapy onto the bar and watched the spinning gold reflect in the piggish eyes of the proprietor. "Don't worry, I've got money. I need a bottle of whiskey and two glasses. My friend will be along shortly."

The man snatched the coin before it had time to fall and laid a bottle before Nathan. He wiped two glasses on his apron and lined them up with the bottle. He beamed appreciatively as he bit the coin with the only two teeth left in the front of his mouth.

"Like I said, welcome."

Nathan poured whiskey into the two glasses before soaking his handkerchief. He opened his collar and slapped the wet rag on his troublesome sore.

"Whew!" the bartender whistled. "I bet that hurt. Where'd you get that fearsome wound?"

"I cut myself shaving," Nathan replied levelly.

His eyes covered the men and his unbuttoned coat swung open to reveal his pistol. One look at the long revolver with its polished grips and oiled holster quashed their curiosity. This man was obviously neither prospector nor storekeeper with such a lethal-looking weapon.

"Whatever you say, mister," the man responded. He held up both hands with open palms. "Sorry if I seemed to be prying. It's just that we don't get much news in the winter."

" 'Cept about whose toes got froze off," a prospector chortled. "And who fell through the ice." His reply broke the tension and both men laughed.

The owner gestured at the wound. "If you don't mind my saying so, I'd get another razor."

"I have." As an afterthought Nathan added, "There's a wolf outside that belongs to me. Don't shoot her. She's not friendly, but she'll leave you be if you give her a wide berth."

A stocky man stood up and hooked his thumbs into his vest. "My name is Ransky. I got the best dog team in town, and

I'd like to buy your wolf if she's for sale. Breeding wolf into my team gives them stamina. What do you say?"

"You *had* the best team, Joe," someone quipped. "Now you just got the second best team."

Ransky shot the man a fiery look. "We'll have our justice tomorrow," he snapped. "Well, mister, what do you say? I'll give you a good price for her."

"Sorry, she's not for sale. Actually, she doesn't belong to me."

"But you said . . ."

"That was wrong. She belongs to herself. She chooses to be my companion. I don't own her. No one owns her."

The man acted disappointed. "You see, I just lost my first-string team. All I got left now is my second string of dogs, and I'm trying to build another one."

"What happened?"

"*This!*" The bartender reached beneath his counter and slammed a dark bottle onto the bar. A cupful of the amber contents slopped onto the polished wood, immediately turning the polish opaque.

Nathan stiffened. The familiar smell of creosote and turpentine, mixed with new odors, reached his nose and jolted his memory like a bolt of lightning. He steadied his nerves and reached for the bottle.

"Some quack came into town, touting this crap as the cure for everything," Ransky said. "I mixed a bottle in my racing dogs' water. Damned if it didn't kill every one!" His face contorted in rage, and his fists beat on the counter.

Nathan turned the bottle in his hand. His head swam as he read the label: DOCTOR HENNISON'S WONDER ELIXIR.

"Doc H . . . Hennison," he stammered.

"Yup, Doc, that's what the son of a bitch calls himself. But I doubt he's a real doctor."

Nathan forced his voice to remain level and calm. "Is this Doc Hennison still in town?" he asked. In spite of his efforts, his voice sounded high-strung.

"Yup. We got him locked up over in the old jail. To my thinking he's a murderer as sure as if he took a gun and shot my best friend. I aim to see justice done. So, we're hanging him in the morning. . . ."

★ ★ SIXTEEN ★ ★

The door separating the cells from the front office swung open. Enders, the local blacksmith, whose turn it was to guard the prisoner, thrust his head inside.

"You got a visitor, Doc. Two men who want to see you," he said to the turned back of the man lying on the cot.

"Tell them to go away," came the reply. "I'm not talking to anyone."

"Not even to us, Doc?"

Hennison spun around to face the rusted bars. "Nat! Nat, boy! Am I glad to see you!" He was on his feet in a minute with his only hand extended through the grating. But a warning look in Nathan's eyes caused him to draw up short. He looked rapidly from the lad's face to the stern countenance of Jim Riley standing behind the young man. Hennison's mouth opened wordlessly, then clamped shut.

"You know this man, Marshal?" Ransky stuck his head through the door. A suspicious look covered his face.

Riley nodded sagely. He wiped the frost off his mustache with the back of his hand to hide his nervousness. Gunfights were one thing, this masquerading was something else. "Doc Hennison, snake-oil salesman and quack. Wanted for murder in Skagway. Nathan and I've been chasing him across half the territory."

"But he knew your deputy's name," Ransky persisted.

"Sure he did. That's why Nathan came along. So's he could make a positive identification."

Hennison glanced at the U.S. marshal's shield pinned on Riley's vest. Instantly his puzzled look changed to a cagey squint. "You finally caught up with me, eh, Marshal?" he said as he played along. "Come to take me back to Skagway, are you?"

"Eh?" Enders looked all the more confused. "I thought we was going to hang him."

"I've got orders to take him back to Skagway. To hang there," Riley said. "I'd be obliged if you'd turn him over to me in the morning."

Ransky's face clouded. "Skagway's a far piece off, Marshal. This snake might slip loose. I wouldn't want that to happen." His last sentence carried an ominous note.

Nathan turned at the scuffling of boots behind him. The small confines of the front room crowded with men from the bar with added new faces. Ransky had his army.

Riley clenched his jaw. "Have you got a telegraph here?" he asked.

"Not one that works," a voice answered. "The army's been stringing a line from Dawson, but it don't work."

Secretly, Riley rejoiced. The last thing he wanted was the town checking up on his credentials. But he acted disappointed. "Damn. I was going to wire for instructions." He'd done a fast head count and found them outnumbered six to one. And that didn't take into account springing Doc from his iron cage.

"It's simple, Marshal. You want to hang this rat in Skagway, and we want to hang him here. He's here. You're here. So let's string him up in the morning—*right here!*"

Riley pursed his lips as he thought. He hoisted one boot onto a low stool and studied the scuffed leather of the toe of his boot. "Well, he is supposed to hang," he said slowly. "What would you use? I didn't see no scaffold."

"Ain't got one," Enders supplied.

"How about a horse?"

All the men shook their heads.

"We ate the last mule, too, when she give out," a reedy voice called out from the back of the mob.

"No mule or horse?" Riley shook his head.

"Well, Swede up on Quartz Creek's got a mule," Enders offered. "But that's twenty miles from town, and Swede's real fond of her. He might not like us using her to hang someone."

Riley ground his boot into the stool. "This could be a mite tricky. What did you men plan on doing, digging a hole and dropping Hennison down the well while you held on to the other end of the rope?"

"Ain't got no well to speak of, either," the voice replied. "It's froze up."

Ransky's eyes lighted. "We could use my second team! It would be . . . what do they call it? Poetic justice?"

"How in the hell do you figure to do that?" Riley snorted. "If you stood him on yer sled and pushed him off, the drop ain't enough to break his neck."

Ransky scratched his head. "Wait. Wait, I know. We'll tie one end of the rope to the hitching post out front of the saloon, put the noose on the good doctor, and toss him in my sled. When the team takes off, his neck'll snap for sure. This team can really pull. Once they nearly jerked my thumb off."

A rousing cheer rose from the crowd for Ransky's inventiveness. Men began to slap each other's backs. Any hanging was considered a prime event, and none had ever heard of hanging by dogsled. That would be an extra special occasion. After their initial enthusiasm died down, they turned their attention to the pensive marshal.

Riley scratched his head. "I suppose we'll have to make do with that arrangement," he said. "Okay. In the morning, then. But first Nathan and me need to question the prisoner."

Another roar filled the jail. It was all settled. Nothing left to do now but drink until the morning. The crowd retreated back to the bar in a noisy procession that trailed off into the evening. But Ransky and Enders remained.

"Alone," Riley emphasized as he looked the two in the eye. "He knows the whereabouts of the loot from a bank robbery. If half the townsfolk find out where he stashed that gold, it'll disappear into a dozen pockets. I'll never be able to recover the money. That's why I need to question him in private."

Ransky shook his head. "Nothing personal, Marshal, but I'd hate for one of your guns to accidentally fall into Hennison's hands and for him to escape."

"Hell," Riley snorted. "I ain't never been *that* careless. Besides, he ain't got but one arm, anyways. But I don't want you having the runs worrying about that." He unbuckled his gun belt and handed it over to the blacksmith. "And don't be dropping my pistol. If the sight gits bent I'll straighten it over yer head."

"And your deputy's," Ransky insisted.

Nathan removed his belt and watched as Ransky studied the long-barreled Colt. He bristled as the man removed the pistol and ran his dirty fingers over the patina. The musher's eyes popped at the inscription to Wyatt Earp on the polished handle.

"Wyatt Earp! Is this his pistol?"

"He gave it to me," Nathan replied icily. "It's mine now, so keep your grubby hands off it."

Ransky noted the menacing tone and suddenly realized his posse had repaired to the saloon. He mumbled an apology while backing out the door with his jail keeper.

No sooner had the door latch clicked than Hennison was on his feet with his face pressed to the bars. "Thank God you've come, fellows!" he stammered. "You've got to get me out of

164

here. These bumpkins took great offense over nothing. They actually mean to hang me . . . me! For nothing!"

"You kilt all their damned dogs with yer nonsense," Riley snorted.

Hennison recoiled in mock surprise. "Is that a hanging offense? Well, I ask you, is it?"

"It is to them."

"Uncouth miners! What do they know? I tell you it's not a hanging offense. Besides, they share the blame."

"How so?"

"I told them not to give it to pigs. . . ."

"Pigs!" Riley snorted. "They ain't got no pig team pulling their sleds."

"They should have extrapolated. Pigs are closely related to dogs . . . in my opinion."

"How in the hell do you figure that, Doc?"

"Well, both associate with humans."

Riley's face turned scarlet. "You ain't changed a whit, have you, Doc? You sure you didn't just modify yer elixir some wee bit? Something that made it *more poisonous?*"

"No! No . . . well, maybe. But I only added a handful of those white berries to give it a bit more tang."

"White berries?"

"Yes. You know the kind that grow all along the trails. They were handy. . . ." His voice trailed off.

"Baneberries!" Riley exploded. "You added baneberries to yer infernal juice! They're poisonous!"

"How was I to know?" Hennison added defensively. "It didn't bother the Indians I sold it to."

Riley leaned close to Hennison's face. "I hope you didn't kill no people."

"Absolutely not! A few got sick . . . but they recovered."

Riley snorted in disgust. He spun on his heel and walked away, wishing he had a chew of tobacco so he could spit.

All this time Hennison had been acutely aware that Nathan had not spoken but stood to one side and watched him with grave, sorrowful eyes. That look hurt him more than he cared to admit. But he turned his attention to this young man he hoped was still his friend. He stretched his only hand, the left one, imploringly through the bars.

"Nat, are you mad at me, too?" he asked.

When no answer came, he dropped his arm and shuffled back to the pile of horse blankets that was his bed. Sitting down on the pile, he lowered his head into his left arm.

"I know you don't believe me, Nat," he said hoarsely. "But I didn't kill Wei-Li. As God is my witness, she was already dead by the time I got to her bedside. There was nothing I could do. All along she'd planned to cut herself open just to save the baby. . . ." His voice dropped to a whisper, then trailed off into nothing.

Nathan moved to the bars and knelt down. He extended his hand, but the iron grate prevented his touching Hennison. "I know, Doc," he said. "I'm not mad at you. I'm the one who ran away. I'm the one who couldn't face the situation."

"Bless you, boy." Hennison looked up. He grasped the offered hand. "I knew you'd understand when you had time to think about it."

Nathan dropped his head. The next question was painful to him, for it reopened the wound he had created when he fled that fateful day. "How is my son, Doc?" he asked.

"A fine, strapping lad he is, too. He looks a lot like you, but with your lady's black eyes."

Nathan smiled. "I'm glad to hear that. It took me a year to come to my senses; but when Riley and I went back to Dawson, you'd vanished. We've spent most of another year looking for you."

"And you tracked me to Circle?"

"No. How we got here is another story. I'd sure like to see my son."

"And you shall," Doc added as a crocodile smile spread across his face. "Just as soon as you set me free."

Nathan shook his head. "Believe me, Doc, I'd love to, but I don't know how. They got you guarded like the last gold shipment out of Nome. We'd need dynamite just to free you from this jail."

Hennison straightened his ruffled collar. "I don't fancy swinging from a rope."

"You ain't going to whiskey drummer," Riley added as he shook his head in disbelief. "They plan on dragging you in a sled until her rope runs out."

Hennison straightened his shoulders. The right one, half blown off in the Civil War, looked smaller than the left, giving the impression that his neck sprang off center from his body. He played his ace card.

"I'm not telling where the boy is. I have to lead you to him *in person*. He's safe and well cared for, believe me, but you'll never find him without my help."

Riley crossed to the cell in an instant. His fingers knotted themselves in the fabric of Hennison's shirtfront, and he jerked the prisoner's face against the iron bars. "You son of a bitch! You'd go to yer grave not telling Nathan where you hid his baby?"

Doc twisted free of the grip. "Succinctly put, my illiterate friend. You have a way with words that transcends your cloddishness." He spread his hand in supplication. "Believe me, I find this kind of bargaining totally distasteful. But I find hanging, by whatever means, far worse. So I must insist."

"Time is up." Enders stuck his head through the door and yelled. "Sorry, Marshal, but I my got orders. You understand."

"Okay, Doc," Nathan said as he backed away from the cell. "We'll think of something."

The deputy-blacksmith directed Nathan and Riley to a storage shed off the saloon where the heat from the potbellied stove kept the room warm and the noise from the bar was muffled. As they walked there, the silver wolf appeared out of the darkness and fell into step at Nathan's side. At the door she stopped and lay down on the snow-covered steps. From her vantage point she watched the men enter the building.

Inside the storeroom the two spread their bedding on top of a stack of flour sacks. Neither ate, and Jim sat with his back propped against a mealie bag, lost in thought. From time to time he'd rise and check on the progress of the inhabitants of the bar.

His silence finally unnerved the youth, and Nathan asked, "Did you ever find the library, Jim?"

Riley snorted as he produced two tattered and dog-eared pamphlets. "The damned place was picked clean. No books. Nothing left but these." He waved the circulars.

"What are they?"

"*Mrs. Cumming's Manners for Young Ladies* and *Secrets to a Successful Rose Garden,*" Riley grumbled. He was surprised to hear a strange noise coming from Nathan. He turned in his bed to find Nathan trying hard to control his laughter. The result was a strange snickering sound.

"It ain't funny. We got ourselves in a pickle here."

"Yes it is." Nathan's reserve broke down. "Anything in your book of manners on how to scotch a hanging?"

"Nary a word," Riley answered. "But they got a lot on dancing. I suppose they're related." Then he began to laugh, too.

"You know, we've got to rescue Doc," Nathan said after he regained his breath. "He won't tell us where he's stashed my baby, and I believe him when he says we'll never find my son without his help."

"Yup. Besides, I'd sort of hate to see old Doc hang for poisoning a few dogs. In my opinion he ought to swing for a loftier crime than acting as an unintentional dog-control officer."

"Do you have a plan, Jim?"

"I've got the outlines. Those bravos getting soused will help. Now listen. Here's what we'll do. . . ." Riley leaned close to Nathan and whispered in his ear.

By eight in the morning the dawn was threatening the last of the night's shadows although the result was an eerie, lingering twilight that appeared uncertain as to which side of the darkness it belonged. An icy chill had slipped into Circle under cover of the evening, and hoarfrost textured everything but the biting air.

Like clockwork the sober Ransky and his blacksmith assistant manhandled the protesting Hennison into the street. Trussed like a lamb, Doc could do little more than spit and swear at his executioners. His vituperations signaled the start of the main event, so the saloon door burst open and the street filled with drunken townsfolk.

Hitched to a post lay Ransky's surviving team, hunkered against the cold and rolled into clusters of furry balls. At the first sign of activity, all eight dogs sprang to their feet and jumped against their harnesses in excitement. Soon they broke into a chorus of yips and yelps that added to the din from the boisterous mob. Reaching the sled, Ransky looked around for the two lawmen.

"Where the hell is that marshal?" he asked the bartender.

"I'm coming," Riley replied from the back of the gang as he parted the men clustered around the front door of the bar. A coiled rope hung from his shoulder.

"Well, Marshal. You're in charge here. How are we going to do this? Do we—" Ransky stopped in midsentence. "Where's your deputy?" he asked suspiciously.

Riley pointed down the trail. "I sent him down the road a piece."

"What for?" asked Enders.

"In case this fellow's head snaps off on the first pull. I don't cotton to tracking after a runaway sled with no headless corpse on it. Do you?"

Enders shook his head at the grim image. "No, I guess not."

"Me, neither. Nathan's down the trail to stop that from happening."

"That won't be necessary," Ransky added. "I plan on standing on the side runner of my sled, and you can stand on the other side if you wish, Marshal."

Riley scratched his side. "Well, I wish you'd told me that earlier. It would've have saved my deputy a cold walk. Now are you going to walk out there and tell him his trek was for naught?"

Ransky scratched his beard in disgust. "Leave him be. After the hanging, we'll call him in."

"Okay." Riley uncoiled the rope and held up the knotted end. "I put a hangman's noose in this end, all nice and legal with the required thirteen turns and all. I want this to be done proper." He handed the hangman's knot to Ransky to inspect before he slipped the noose over Hennison's head and snugged it around his neck. He threw the coiled part into Ransky's face.

"Damnit, man!" the musher swore. His hands flailed at the spinning coils, and the bitter end slapped his face.

"Tie that end to something stout," Riley commanded. "And tie a decent knot. If you don't know how, git some help. I don't want it coming loose."

In the confusion, he dumped Hennison roughly onto the sled. "Wedge yer feet into the sides of the sled and keep yer blasted neck tucked down into yer chest," he whispered.

"Christ!" was all the shaken Hennison could say before Riley cinched the noose even tighter.

The gunfighter straightened up. "Let's git this over with. I ain't freezing out here any longer than I have to."

Ransky grumbled at the hurry. He'd planned on savoring the hanging. After all, he reasoned, they were his dogs that this scoundrel poisoned, so he was owed some satisfaction. "Wait, doesn't the condemned man make a last speech?" he questioned.

"Sometimes," Riley replied flatly. "But I ain't allowing no lengthy discourse, it being this cold. If you've got a mind to say a few words, Hennison, spit them out. Make it fast."

The crowd murmured that this was harsh treatment not to let the prisoner make his final speech as long as he wished, but they were so drunk they scarcely felt the chill. The bartender secretly hoped Doc Hennison would talk for an hour; he was good for business. As long as the event proceeded, the townsfolk continued to drink.

"Have mercy, men. I beg you," Hennison bleated.

A stony silence provided his answer. No one wanted to miss the hanging.

From his position, flat on his back in the sled, and with the tight noose choking him, Doc sputtered, "Curse you all then, you filthy swine. If my hands weren't tied, I'd kick all your arses into the next century."

"Hands?" Enders snickered. "You ain't got but one anyhow, Doc."

"A figure of speech, you lardacious cretin," Doc sputtered. "All I need is one hand to whip you all."

"He ain't too repentant," Riley noted, "is he?"

Unseen, he stepped onto a sled runner as Ransky moved alongside and grasped the snow hook that kept the straining dogs in place. "What do you usually say to make these dogs run, Mr. Ransky?" he asked casually.

"Most often I say 'hike' or words to that effect. It doesn't take much to set them to running."

"And you, Ransky," Doc continued, his voice rising to a shrill pitch under the strain from the constricting hemp. "I am sincerely sorry your dogs died and not you in their place.

"And to my good friend, the marshal, I say, the whereabouts of the baby will go with me to the grave, so whatever you're planning had better work!"

Ransky spun on Riley. "What did he mean by that, Marshal?"

"Hike!" Riley yelled as a bowie knife leapt into his hand from beneath the folds of his parka. With one sweeping arc he cut the rope trailing from Hennison's neck, then the line to the snow hook. With a deft backhand the heavy pommel of the knife handle struck Ransky in the center of his forehead. Dumbstruck, the musher toppled backward like a sawed tree trunk, eyes rolling back in his head and blood gushing down his face.

The team, the sled, and its passengers shot off like a dart.

"Hike! Hike! Hike! Damn you!" Doc chirped his encouragement from the sled's basket as he realized his escape was in progress.

Riley kept low, expecting at any moment to feel the slap of a bullet between his shoulder blades. But when he looked back, the drunken crowd was standing stock-still like confused pillars of salt while Ransky lay on his back unconscious. Hennison continued to babble encouragement to the team, which raced down the trail at top speed. Circle grew smaller and smaller until only the columns of smoke from the woodstoves marked its location. A lone figure in the trail ahead waited with drawn rifle. The silver wolf stood by his side eyeing the oncoming dogs hungrily.

"Nat!" Riley hailed him. "How do I stop this damned thing?"

Blaylock had no time to answer as the team sped past. The wheel dog spotted the wolf and shied to one side. Nathan gaped as the sled swung wildly around, caught one runner on a spruce root, and flew into the air. Running after them, he found the sled on its side with Hennison half-buried in a drift, swearing and spitting snow from his mouth. Riley lay on his back paralyzed by gales of laughter. The dogs roiled, biting and snapping in a tangle of harness, while their wide eyes followed the movements of the she-wolf.

"Have mercy, men! I beg you! Mercy!" Riley chortled. "Why with that sniveling plea, I had half a mind not to cut yer rope."

"Piss off," Hennison sniffed. "I'd like to hear what you'd say with a noose on your scrawny neck. Besides, you could have *told* me what you intended. I . . . I think I've wet my pants."

Riley climbed to his knees, still laughing. "No need to worry about yer pants drying, Doc. Another minute and they'll be froze good and stiff."

Nathan jerked the doctor to his feet. "Consider yourself rescued, Doc," he said brusquely, but he made no move to cut the man's bonds. "Now where did you hide my son?"

"You're a bit harsh to your old pal, aren't you?" Hennison sniffed. "Perhaps a spot of brandy and a hot meal will refresh my memory."

"We ain't got time for niceties." Riley stopped laughing and turned dead serious. "I'd wager there are other sled dogs in Circle you ain't poisoned. They'll be after us in a minute."

Hennison straightened himself and came as close to preening as a trussed-up one-armed man can come. "Those cowards? They lack the fortitude for a fair fight. Untie me at once and give me a firearm."

"Cowards, is they?" Riley said. "They caught you once. What's to stop them from snatching you again?"

"Because they captured me while I was indisposed. In a fair fight I'd lick every man jack of them." Hennison was hopping up and down now, fired with the indignity of his arrest as well as the rush of having escaped a horizontal hanging.

173

"You mean you was drunk," Riley added for clarification.

"Ah"—Doc shrugged his one shoulder—"you have a brutal way with words, my gunfighting friend. But, yes, they ensnared me while I was *slightly* inebriated." He turned to the silent Nathan and smiled crookedly. "What'd you say, Nat? Don't you have a spot of brandy for your old friend? My tongue is so dry now that I can hardly speak."

Nathan lifted Hennison bodily and tossed him into a snowdrift beside the trail. The astonished man had little time to do anything but open his mouth in protest before he flopped onto his back. As he turned his head to look back at Nathan, his eyes started from his head. A large silver wolf growled inches from his face with bared fangs and gleaming golden eyes.

"Good God! A wolf!" he squeaked.

Nathan's head appeared framed above the animal's. "Talk, Doc! Or I'll let her use your head for a chew toy!"

"Dawson! Dawson! Your babe is safe in Dawson!" Doc shrieked. The wolf's hot breath blew across his face, loosening his tongue.

"Yer lying," Riley said. "We checked all the orphanages in Dawson. And the convent as well."

The wolf inched closer, as if enjoying her role. She licked her chops as if on cue.

"No! No! It's the gospel, Nat. Keep that beast back. He's not in an orphanage. He's with a family, the Gustafsons—a nice Swedish family. He works as a driver for the bigger mines. She's raised five of her own. They think he's my sister's child. I paid them to look after him. They . . . they don't speak much English, so they stay out of the usual stores. I . . . I thought it wise, in case anyone came asking about your baby."

Riley looked at his young friend. "I think the good doctor is telling the truth—for once. Look how white he is. He's too scared to lie, and I bet his pants is wet all over again."

"The Gustafsons," Nathan repeated. "They'd better be giving him the best care." His hand went out to stroke the wolf's fur. In response the animal ceased its snarling and sat back on its haunches. Nathan reached down and pulled Doc Hennison to his feet. His knife cut the man's ropes. Without another word, he turned and walked back down the trail to listen for their pursuers.

Hennison straightened his parka and brushed the snow from his clothes. He rearranged his battered beaver hat with mock solemnity. His gaze fell on the broad shoulders and back of his young friend. To Riley he remarked, "The boy's grown since last I saw him. Look at the width of his shoulders. I'll bet he's six foot three if he's an inch." His words carried a trace of fatherly pride. "And strong, too. Did you see the way he lifted me off my pins?"

"He ain't a boy no more, Doc," Riley replied. "His woman's death changed him, and he's done a lot of fleshing out in this last year. But he ain't a full-growed man yet, either. He's got a powerful body and a keen mind, but sometimes he goes and does something crazy—like rescuing you."

Hennison ignored that slight and puffed his chest with self-esteem. "Takes after me, then, does he? Damn, that makes me proud. I always said we'd have more influence on him than his father. Wyatt Earp may have sired him, but we've spent more on his upbringing than any other."

"Ain't you forgetting those sisters in Denver?"

"Pshaw, what do nuns know about raising a boy to be a man? No, my illiterate friend, you and I are his true fathers."

"God help him, then." Riley spat a stream of tobacco juice into the snow at Hennison's feet. "I hope yer wrong on that count. And I ain't illiterate no more. I can read jus' fine, thank you. In fact I'm presently studying the science of rose gardening." He withdrew the pamphlet from his coat and waved it before Doc's face.

Hennison opened his eyes in mock disbelief. "Will wonders never cease," he remarked. "By the way, where'd Nathan acquire that wolf? She scared me out of ten years' growth. I could use her to sell my elixir. Can you picture it? Doctor Hennison's Wonder Elixir—imbued with the spirit of the wolf! It'd sell like hotcakes."

Riley watched the animal turn slowly from them to trot after Nathan. "Her? Let's jus' say she took a notion to Nat, and he to her. And don't try getting friendly with her. She may like Nat, but she hardly tolerates me."

"Ah, a discerning lady, eh?"

"I reckon. So I expect she'll take an instant dislike to you, Doc. And she's got the claws and fangs to match her disposition."

Hennison shook his head. "Nathan always had a weakness for attracting dangerous females. Does she have a name? Something I might call her if she takes to eating me?"

"Nope, no name for certain. But I think I'll call her 'Sweetness.' "

⋆ ⋆ SEVENTEEN ⋆ ⋆

While the newly liberated dog team with Hennison, Nat, and Riley headed up the frozen Yukon toward its headwaters, another party toiled northward from the south, each unknown to the other. Dickinson's group moved on a complex mission of grave international import that would change the world if successful, while Nathan's group merely searched for a lost baby. Both parties moved closer to each other in blissful ignorance.

Marta expected to hate the trek out of Valdez, anticipating a monotonous land of cloud and rain. But the beauty of the trail surprised her. Weeks aboard a rotting steamer heading north had choked her mind with biting winds, icy sleet, and endless fog. Not once in those weeks had the sun deigned to show a cheery face. Days were marked by a general lightening of the gloom for the prescribed hours before sunset.

To Marta, gray, dreary clouds, dark water, and somber evergreens characterized these northern lands. Only the lure of riches could induce anyone sensible to come to this land without warmth, she reasoned. She steeled herself to this darkness and spent her nights dreaming of her homeland, with its turquoise seas and soft, emerald hills.

Even the birds were different from those in her country. There, brightly colored macaws and scarlet parrots filled the trees with flying splashes and hues, while here, gulls and eagles bore the nut brown and slate colors that marked their grim locale. Even the graceful arctic tern was limited to black and white.

The route Dickinson chose for his mule train led them along the customary bed of the Lowe River at first. But instead of swinging left to follow the path across the glacier, as most miners did, they continued on the coarse gravel wash beside the churning, silty waters.

Choked with powdered stone from the incessant grinding of a host of glaciers, the Lowe poured through gaps in the sheer mountain ramparts that defended the forbidden Interior from the waters of Valdez Sound.

As the train progressed, Marta noted the precipitous walls of stone close in upon them. The razor-sharp slate and granite seemed to squeeze the very breath from her as they pressed closer and closer. At every twist and turn, cascading waterfalls, masquerading as fanciful horsetails and bridal veils, would cover them with chilling mist. Worst of all, the height of the walls kept sunlight from ever reaching this place. To Marta it was a place of evil, made all the more sinister by its baneful beauty. For while it was severe, it was also magnificent in its unfettered harshness.

She glanced up at the unending heights and crossed herself.

"A grim place," Dickinson remarked. "They call it Keystone Canyon. I suppose because the optimistic hold it as the keystone to reaching the Interior." He paused to wipe the glaze from his face and study his small command.

There were five mules and four men besides Marta and himself. His fifth man had been stricken with pneumonia the day before they started. Without uniforms they looked a motley bunch, he mused. But their ramrod-straight carriages gave them away to the practiced eye. He chuckled at his secret joke. None of the soldiers knew Marta was a woman. With her thick parka and pants and the knit balaclava covering all but her smoldering eyes, she'd passed as a foreigner. Wisely, the girl held her tongue and only spoke to Dickinson in whispers and when out of earshot of the soldiers. How long that charade would last, the spy could only guess.

Ahead the trail narrowed to less than three feet of slick rock separating them from the rushing waters. One slip would mean death, Dickinson knew. No help could come quickly enough. Anyone falling into the Lowe would be whisked away to an icy drowning before the others could even blink. The chilly flow, fresh from glacial melt, would cramp even the strongest muscles, so a man would drown for want of use of his limbs.

Sergeant Sloan, a square-built man with fringes of reddish hair decorating the base of his bald head and a skewed left eye, wisely ordered the ropes stringing the mules together cut. That way, if one animal fell to its death it fell alone. The sergeant meant to protect all his troop. Dickinson had not told Sloan that he only needed three mules and three men to complete his mission.

Sloan edged his way back to Dickinson and saluted from force of habit. Twenty years in the army had left the sergeant with habits hard to break. He winced at his slip and at the withering look from Dickinson.

"Sorry, sir," Sloan drawled. The man's accent screamed of the dust-blown plains of West Texas. Twelve years in the army with tours in Peking and Manila had failed to soften it. Sloan smelled a rat, but was too good a soldier to question his orders.

"Yes, Sergeant?" The agent looked down at his map as Marta turned aside from the man's sharp eye.

"Begging your pardon, but we should be coming up on the base camp. It's around the next bend."

No sooner had Sloan spoken those words than the column snaked around a pile of scree to spot five canvas tents pitched in a semicircle on the only level patch of rock beside the river.

Behind the tents loomed a sheer face of slate black rock, marred only by fractures and fissures running down its facade. The sounds of picks and sledges cracking off rock echoed about the confines. A soldier in khaki trousers and a plaid shirt waved his hat at them and shouted, but his words were lost in the roar of the water.

"What the devil are they doing there, Sloan?" Dickinson asked.

"Cutting a wider path through this blasted Keystone Canyon, poor devils. The army wants the trail big enough for wagons to pass. There's even talk of a railroad—"

Before he could finish, a flash erupted from ahead, followed instantly by a cloud of dirty dust that billowed out of a niche in the wall and a clap of thunder that deafened them.

"Dynamite!" Sloan shouted in Dickinson's ear.

The agent nodded and made a mental note to appropriate a dozen sticks on his way out of the soldiers' camp.

"Night's coming on," the sergeant added. "Best we hold up here, and get a fresh start in the morning. No sense falling off the trail in the dark." He sighed in relief when Dickinson agreed.

Two hours later the group had eaten and lay scattered in the tents with their fellow soldiers. Dickinson and Marta took their plates to the edge of the camp and ate in silence. The agent reached inside his coat and withdrew a silver hip flask. He turned it over in his hand to inspect the filigreed engraving.

" 'To my grandson, Lowell,' " he read aloud. " 'On graduating from Harvard.' " He offered the flask to Marta, but she shook her head in refusal. So he took a lengthy swallow.

"A gift from your father?" Marta asked.

Dickinson ducked his head in response, spilling the brandy down his shirtfront. "The old man would be turning over in his grave if he saw me now. He wanted me to be a captain of industry. Not, not a . . ."

"Not a spy?" Marta completed the sentence.

"Lord, no. Especially not a spy for Roosevelt. The gov'nor hated Teddy, what with all his bombast. Besides, Teddy's got his teeth set into the seats of several captains that my dear papa adored."

"You refer to him as 'governor.' That is an English term. My father used it in referring to his father."

Dickinson regarded her shrewdly. "Yes, it is. I spent several years abroad, studying. Mostly in England. That's where I met Beaufort, the thorn in my side. We felt his prick in Valdez, and I dare say we'll see more of the man."

"Beaufort? Was he the man who saluted you back in Valdez? After you killed those others?"

"Yes." Dickinson took another swallow. "Sir Aubrey Thomas Michael Beaufort of Her Majesty's Foreign Office. The black knight in this chess game."

"And you are the white knight?"

Dickinson pursed his lips while his throat recovered from the bite of the brandy. "I would prefer to think of myself as a bishop or a rook, but, yes, I suppose I am a knight as well. It doesn't do to travel in straight lines or diagonals in this line of business. Jumping about like a knight enables one to stay alive."

Marta sat down with her back against the wall. The chill of the stone seeped through her parka. A long hand threatened to crush her revolution, the one she had already paid so dearly for with her family's death and her broken body. That hand reached even to this icy land. Somehow she was not surprised.

She studied Dickinson. His long swallow of brandy and the slight quiver in his voice spoke of increased tension.

"What is this Beaufort to you?" she asked.

"He is a devil who haunts me," Dickinson blurted out. His unexpected candor caught him by surprise, but her direct question tripped his careful defenses, allowing his emotions to pour forth.

"How so?" Marta probed.

Dickinson shrugged. "We . . . we studied together at Oxford. Sir Aubrey is a blue blood with little regard for those who cannot promote his ambition. We parted bitter enemies. He did me grievous injury then, and now he dogs my heels as we joust for international power for our countries. And you, my dear, are caught in the middle of two great nations' policy differences, and the erstwhile quarrels of their two agents. For that you have my condolences."

"It was a woman. . . ."

"How perceptive, my dear. Remind me to watch my tongue around you. You are far too insightful for my comfort."

Marta folded her long fingers and sat back. "It was not hard. You forget I have spent some time in the jungle with men who say they fight for the revolution, but who really fight for revenge. With most it is a woman. What did this Sir Beaufort do, take your woman?"

"Sir Aubrey," he corrected. "But you are to be forgiven your faux pas. Neither your country nor mine have royalty."

"You evade my question. Tell me about this matter."

"I'd rather not."

"My life and the life of my land are at stake here," she said sternly. "What weakens you in dealing with this Beaufort, threatens me."

Dickinson sighed. "There was a young lady in England. The daughter of a factory owner. She was beautiful, but beneath his station. For her part, I believe she loved us both, but his title and his fancy airs turned her pretty head."

"So she married him instead of you?"

"Heavens, no. That I could accept. No, he . . . he compromised the lady; and when she begged him to marry her, he laughed at her. Said it simply wasn't done, old chap. Couldn't have that sort of thing, marrying beneath one's station, eh what?"

"And you loved her?"

"Yes. But she hanged herself in her rooms shortly after. So that put an end to the whole affair—for her and . . . me."

"That explains why you hate him so much, but not why he hates you."

"Ah, you see, he didn't escape scot-free. I hit him where it hurt the most—his precious social standing. I saw to it that the whole sordid affair came to light. Got into the *Times* and all that. For a month it was the talk of London." Dickinson smiled grimly. "It created a scandal that reached Queen Victoria's ears. The queen was appalled. Beaufort was demoted, shuffled to obscure posts with all hope of promotion lost. Do you know, I think he aspired to a cabinet post at one time, perhaps even prime minister."

Marta watched him closely. "Why am I here?" she asked.

"No one told you? Well. I'm not surprised."

"Just that I was to receive arms for the revolution. I expected them to be in Valdez, although I was puzzled that weapons were not available closer to my country."

"That is just the point, my dear Marta—may I call you that? Yes? Good. *You have no country.* You are a rebel, fighting against your sovereign country, Colombia. Caught and you'd be hanged from the closest tree."

"My country is Panama," she said fiercely.

"Panama is simply an isthmus, a geographic freak, not a country—not yet. But you have a powerful ally. Teddy Roosevelt wants to build his canal through you precious isthmus. Colombia backed out of Teddy's treaty, so the Bull Moose himself is prepared to see that you have a new country, Panama, so he can dig his ditch connecting the two oceans. He would make a treaty with Panama to that end."

"Would such a treaty be signed?"

"Absolutely. In fact, ministers for your new country have already agreed. So now we need to birth your Panama."

"Why doesn't your president declare that we are a nation? We desperately need your help now!"

"Simply not done. That would put people like me out of business. No, Teddy will do everything he can to help, but nothing aboveboard until you have liberated your strip of steamy jungle yourselves. No American troops. No, that would make Great Britain very nervous."

"The British?"

"Indeed. England worries a great deal about American control of a canal. Especially one with fortifications. Armed American forts would threaten British interests in the Mosquito Coast and British Honduras. Believe me, Whitehall is very nervous about that possibility. What happens in Panama even reflects on British interests as far north as Vancouver and even the Yukon. We've been to war with our mother country twice already, but even Teddy would like to avoid a third time if possible. The islands north of Washington are still a bone of contention with Canada. Why, less than thirty years ago, we almost went to war over someone shooting a pig there. And with an American-controlled canal, our warships could reach the West Coast while the British were still puking around the Cape. That thought makes them *very* nervous indeed."

Marta pursed her lips as she digested his political lesson. "So I am here to receive the arms and bring them back to my people. If we are caught or fail, Mr. Roosevelt can claim with an open face that he knew nothing of this."

"Good girl. You've summarized the political nuances in a nutshell."

"But why so far? Why here in Alaska?"

"British agents are watching all ports for possible shipments to Colombia, especially the arms dealers in Europe. So simply buying you new arms is impossible. Also, we can't just give you a handful of carbines. You can imagine the flap it would cause if your people turned up with brand-new U.S. Springfield rifles.

So the president accepted my suggestion on how to arm your revolution at little cost."

"And what was that?"

"We steal the needed weapons." Dickinson beamed, flashing a smile visible even in the dim light of the campfire. "Quite ingenious really. The English aren't watching their own armories. We sneak in and, ah, appropriate them while they're busy guarding their front door."

"Do they have that many here?"

"Oh, yes, indeed. When the gold rush hit the Yukon, England feared the thousands of American prospectors might riot over their regulations, or even worse—try to annex the country to the U.S. So they shipped rifles—brand-new Lee-Metfords—by the caseload to the Mounties. They're safely crated and stored, still in their Cosmoline, in Dawson."

Dickinson cast a quick glance over his shoulder as he leaned closer to Marta and whispered gleefully. "And something else that will turn the tide for your fighters. Something the Colombian army cannot stand against."

"What? Whose weapon would that be?"

"The devil's own . . . *a Maxim gun!*"

EIGHTEEN

Marta tossed restlessly in her blankets that night as her mind raced over what Dickinson had told her. She had never heard of this Maxim gun, but the American had described it in detail to her, calling it a *machine gun,* one that operated like a machine and fired hundreds of bullets in less time than it took to reload a rifle. With such a gun they could take the fortified cities, and no army expedition would dare venture into their jungle strongholds. She struggled to picture this weapon at work, the rapid crack of the bullets, the smoke, the screams of the falling men. Truly, if it worked like Dickinson claimed, it must belong to the devil.

Marta sighed as she thought of all the men it would kill, all the widows who would wear black and cry in the night for their dead men. She had cried for her father, too, but that seemed so long ago. That pain had seeped down into the darkest recesses of her being, no longer even an ache. It was almost as if it had happened to another. Now she had only one thought: to fight. This devil's gun would make many widows, and she grieved for them, but she could not stop.

Displaced pebbles rattled in the darkness. Instantly Marta came alert. All her senses strained in the pitch-black night for the cause of that sound. The group was camped in the cleft of the pass, whose black walls shuttered even the scant starlight from reaching them. She had never experienced such a lightless night. With the campfires out, even her own hands were not visible.

Her ears caught the scraping of a boot over the loose gravel. She listened closely, relying upon her ears where her sight was useless. Another rasp reached her, faint like the first and made from a foot carefully placed—not what one would hear from a soldier stumbling through the night to relieve his bladder. Someone was stalking her!

Instantly, her hand went to the pistol by her side, but she moved a second too late. A grimy hand collided with her hair like a spider's feelers before it pounces. Like the jaguar, a heavy paw clamped across her mouth. A rank body piled on top of her, following the hand and pinning her beneath its reeking weight.

Marta struggled as the hand pressed tighter, almost suffocating her as it covered her nose as well. But her action ceased when the cold edge of a knife blade touched her neck.

"That's right, girlie. Lie real still and you won't get hurt," a voice close to her ear hissed. "I'll bet you might even enjoy it."

A face bristling with stubble rasped the side of her cheek and a wet tongue slobbered over her ear. Marta jerked away involuntarily, and the blade bit into her skin.

"Still, I said!" the voice warned. "Real still. Understand?"

Marta moved her head slowly and forced her body to relax. More kisses covered her face and neck.

"That's good," her attacker whispered. "My, ain't you a fine one. Your friend Dickinson and the sergeant must think we're all blind or stupid to pass you off as a man. I been watching the way you walk, and nothing can hide a fine body like yours, no sirree. I don't aim to hurt you, just pleasure you a mite. No noise and you won't get hurt—and not a word about this in the morning, or I'll cut you something awful. You savvy?"

Marta sighed in resignation, loud enough for the man to hear. It was the *federales* all over again. The jungle trail, the men—all flared up in her mind like the painful reminder of her broken bones. Her mind screamed at this cruel replay of her rape, yet she willed her body to lie still. Her fingers dug into the gravel bed until her nails splintered. The sweaty stench of this soldier was no different from that of those soldiers in the steaming jungle of Panama. In the blackness, her mind replayed the scream of the birds, the dripping foliage, the weight of her assailant's body. She was back in Panama, suffering her fate once more.

"Good."

His kissing resumed, and the knife hand traveled over her body, exploring her, clutching at her shirt. His breathing increased in excitement.

But the frightened girl of Santo Ignacio lived no more. She struggled to regain control of her emotions, willing her body to obey. She was El Tigre, and to touch her without permission meant death.

Marta raised her breathing to match his and moved her hips beneath him. Soon she was panting and making soft animal noises beneath his hand. Her tongue licked out at the undersurface of his palm.

"You like this, don't you?" the man gloated. "I'll bet you do."

He kept one hand firmly over her mouth, but thrust his knife into the ground beside them. The girl felt the heavy metal cold against her side. His knife hand, now free to explore, resumed fondling her in earnest. Marta ran her fingers over his hair and traced down the side of his face until she outlined the angle of his jaw. Her attacker raised himself off her to fumble with his pants.

Quick as a fer-de-lance, Marta's right hand snatched the man's knife and drove it into the base of his throat, which her fingers had located with their caress. The blade entered above his Adam's apple and pierced his spinal cord. With the efficiency of one wringing a chicken's neck, Marta gave the blade a sharp twist, and her attacker flopped soundlessly on his side—pithed like a frog in a laboratory experiment.

With barely a grimace to mark her feelings, the girl rolled the dead body off her. She straightened her clothes and felt her way to the bank of the river, guided by its ever-present sound. The handfuls of icy water stung like frozen needles, but they cleared her mind.

For a good hour Marta sat by the Lowe and listened to the hissing of the glacial silt abrading the stones in the riverbed. Her heart wished the liquefied rock could scour her body as well. Time and time again her memories of the jungle and her first attack tried to escape, and each time she willed them back into the deepest recesses of her mind. Only when she knew they would not surface did she allow her muscles to relax. She ordered her breathing and sponged more water over her face and neck, but still the dirty feeling persisted. Steady in the face of danger, now her hands trembled. Marta clasped them firmly together, squeezing them until the pain quieted the tremors. Foolish to be so affected, she rebuked herself. She'd killed before, many times, and as close as this. Why was she so troubled now? But she knew without asking. The man's hands had torn away the scab of a sore that had not healed. That day in the jungle when those *federales* had used her and killed her father still festered. She crossed herself and prayed to the Blessed Virgin to make her whole someday. A disturbing thought flickered across her mind: Could the Virgin Mary see her in this narrow canyon with its sheer rock walls? This place belonged to the old life with its taboos and evil spirits. The Christian ways faltered in this land. Marta sensed that old evil seeping from the shale, and she guessed Keystone Canyon would be a place of death again.

Morning filtered down onto the encampment when the sun rose high enough to light the low-lying clouds. The effect was once again an eerie illumination of pale pink and rose glowing across the rock facing. Men stirred and soon the sound of clanking tin plates and cups filled the cleft along with the voices of tired men. The engineers would return to scrabbling and skiving the hard stone, and Dickinson's expedition faced another day of climbing out of the pass. Neither group relished the prospects ahead. Both loitered by the warmth of the campfire and savored the scalding cup of weak coffee and wondered when a hard freeze would roll down from the Interior to turn all but the most persistent water into solid ice. Ice already rimed the river and edged the waterfalls and settling pools.

Dickinson squatted by the river and ground his shaving brush about in the silver cup he carried for shaving. He winced as the silted water grated against the metal. No doubt the surface was ruined by this polluted stream, he fretted. He ran his hand over the stubble on his chin, then to the bushy side-whiskers he sported like one of the Queen's Own Hussars. He wondered if the growth would help disguise his mission. After years in England, he could affect an aristocratic air to perfection. He counted on using that skill if needed in the Northwest Territories.

The sergeant's shadow appeared behind him and lengthened over his shoulder and onto the gray stream. Dickinson sighed in resignation. The petty adjustments needed for this group taxed his patience. He preferred to travel alone, enjoying the ease of solitary movement, but that luxury was not possible. He needed help in handling the crates of rifles. The Vickers-Maxim alone weighed over 120 pounds.

"What is it, Sloan? More of your men have diarrhea? I'm not surprised, drinking this dissolved rock."

Sloan bent close to Dickinson and kept his voice low. "No sir. One of our men went and got himself killed last night."

Instantly, Dickinson was on his feet. "What the devil?"

"Private Higgins, sir." He jerked his head in the direction of a body still wrapped in his blankets.

Already enough daylight existed to arouse the suspicions of the other men, who were casting furtive looks in that direction. The spy followed Sloan to the pile of blankets. The others edged closer when Sloan nudged the body with the toe of his boot. The stiffened form failed to move. Sloan gave a hard kick, and Private Higgins's body rolled over, exposing his ashen and astonished face. His glazed eyes stared up directly at Dickinson. Darkened blood filled his open mouth and seeped from the heavy blade embedded in his throat to stain the khaki blankets.

Dickinson studied the body carefully. "Isn't that Higgins's own knife?" he asked.

"I believe so, sir. He carried that Arkansas toothpick."

Dickinson stood up and looked around. No signs of a struggle except for the deep impression of a single body in the glacial silt. But that mark appeared beside the body, not beneath it. Furthermore, two sets of limbs marked the dirt around the impression. The agent looked at the anxious faces of the remnants of his party. Marta was missing. Then he caught sight of her washing farther down the bank, back turned to them. She was watching him from over her shoulder. One look at her defiant stare answered his unspoken question.

Dickinson addressed the men. "It appears that Private Higgins cut himself shaving," he said. The spy cocked his head in Marta's direction and raised his voice for all to hear. "Evidently he saw through my dismal efforts to disguise the fact that Miss Kelly is a woman, and he decided to spiff himself up in an attempt to impress her." He paused for effect and his eyes searched the clustered soldiers. "With fatal results . . ."

A murmur rippled through the squad. Dickinson waved his hand in dismissal. "Well, now that Miss Kelly is uncovered, let me stress that her well-being and good health are essential,

I repeat, *essential,* to the success of this operation. You will remember that at all times, and conduct yourselves accordingly. We are now two men short. We can ill afford any more shaving accidents. Do I make myself clear?"

He watched stony-faced as the men nodded in agreement. Sloan, with more experience at leading men, ordered the cook to lace the men's coffee with a liberal shot of rum and issue extra tobacco and bacon. He himself buried Higgins out of sight while his men returned to the cook fire. Higgins was not well liked so Sloan hoped the incident would pass without further trouble. Once again he proved himself a good judge of his troop. Soon the soldiers were talking and joking around the flames while the rum and bacon warmed their bellies. The sergeant sat smoking his old briar pipe for the next hour while he appraised the effect of his work. Satisfied, he ordered the mules loaded, and the group set off through the narrowest part of the canyon.

Threading through the cleft in the walls which army engineers were attempting to widen with pick and shovel, the men were forced to lead their pack animals single file. The army's good intentions only added to their risk, for piles of loose shale and scree from their work proved treacherous footing.

Each man kept a tight rein on his animal while watching the hooves of the mule in front. The first animal balked at the tight squeeze and had to be blindfolded before he would move. Scarcely more than a foot away from plunging into the rushing Lowe, each handler edged forward with his back pressed tightly against the icy rock face. Sheets of ice and frozen lichen showered down on them, adding discomfort to the ever-present danger. Here, too, the Lowe, compressed by the narrowing, doubled its flow, leaping like a river gone mad, twisting and spewing freezing mist on the beleaguered travelers. The river's roaring also rose to thundering proportions.

Dickinson craned his neck to look upward. A thin sliver of

leaden sky glowered sullenly back at him through a fracture in the towering sides. If Beaufort were to pick an ambush site, he could choose no better place. A handful of rock would seal the pass after it brushed them into the waiting torrent or crushed them to a pulp. As they crept onward, he dropped back alongside Marta. She had taken up station at the tail of the procession, walking easily with her rifle balanced on her shoulder. She watched impassively as he drew near. Dickinson suddenly realized how a male spider must feel when approaching an alluring female who might just as easily turn him into a snack.

"Are you always so harsh to those beguiled by your charms?" he asked.

She appeared puzzled by his question.

"The late Private Higgins. A beautiful flower must bear some responsibility for the insects it attracts."

"Ah." Her eyes flashed understanding like light striking polished emeralds. "That one, Higgins was his name? He was a wasp, not a butterfly. He came only to sting and to hurt."

Dickinson squinted through the mist shrouding the canyon, but he continued the conversation. "The private paid a terrible price for his intentions."

Marta pulled back her shirt collar in defiance to expose the encrusted knife cut on her neck. "A terrible price for a terrible intention," she snarled.

Any minute now Dickinson expected to see tons of rock showering down upon them. Surely, Sir Aubrey would not miss this opportunity. The fact that he had so little knowledge of the terrain unnerved Dickinson. He had gotten them into a perfect spot for an ambush by his ignorance. That fact weighed heavily on his mind and contributed more to his discomfiture than the possibility of being buried in an avalanche; nevertheless, he found that talking with this girl soothed him.

"What would it take then? For someone to sample your

charms then and not get his gullet slit," Dickinson asked, more out of curiosity than anything else. Before she could answer, he held up both hands in placation. "I'm not asking for myself, you understand."

Marta shrugged, but her attempt to seem casual failed to cover the tension in her voice. "On my terms only. I am not a stick of wood to be thrown on the fire for warmth, or someone who simply stands about waiting to be used." The anger crept into her voice, turning it husky. "I choose what I do and what I wish not to do. That is the key: *my terms, my choice.*"

Her speech had so captivated Dickinson that he just then noticed that they had passed through the narrows unscathed. He felt an icy trickle of sweat roll down his back as he sighed deeply. Behind him the pass glowered in suppressed hostility. A sudden elation hit him. Beaufort had missed his chance.

He scanned the path ahead as it snaked up an ever-increasing grade into the low clouds. Shrouded in their mists lay Thompson Pass, flanked by an alpine lake with meadows and ice fields. This vast natural bowl held the warming mists from the sound, protecting this hidden valley from the arctic winds and icy blasts that ravaged the Chugach Mountains above. The crude path leading onward encompassed several switchbacks before easing through another rock cleft at the pass. Then they would face the snow and ice of Thompson Pass, followed by a downhill trek for miles while the trail followed the gorge cut in the mountains by the Tsina and Tiekel Rivers as they rushed away from Prince William Sound to join the Copper River.

Dickinson withdrew the military map from his jacket and studied its face. Great blank spaces with the word "unknown" stenciled in the empty areas greeted his inspection. Less than ten years ago the whole Interior short of the rivers used for trading remained uncharted. Only the Indians and a few trappers knew what surprises the land held, and those lucky enough to survive its traps carried that knowledge in their heads. Dickinson refolded the chart. Somewhere ahead was a trading post.

Marta bent forward as she forced her legs to climb the path. Rolling stones, kicked loose by the mules, careened past her to splash into the river. The sharp rise as they climbed the mountains broke the force of the Lowe River, and it splayed out into its headwaters of cascading streams and freshets melting from the ice fields. The very mountain seemed to be leaking its sap down exposed beds of rock and gravel, helpless to prevent its lifeblood from rushing needlessly to the sea. To the girl, the whitened gravel gaping through lush and verdant ground cover seemed like the bones of the mountain jutting from wounds in its bushy skin. Unlike her mountains in Panama, where the hills rang with the raucous sounds of parrots and monkeys, here a gloomy silence prevailed. Far to their right a silver-tipped grizzly paused in its quest for marmots before slipping into the mists, and once she spotted a white-headed eagle soaring high above the clouds. Other than that there was nothing living.

But the very magnitude and expanse of mountain awed her, and its silence spoke eloquently of the power of this place. Nothing lived, traveled, or ended its life here easily. Marta found the sight both wondrous and frightening.

In two hours the procession climbed to the second switchback, where the trail hugged the side of a rocky bench. No standing timber grew here above the tree line, only knee-high thickets of scrub alder, clumps of blueberries, and matted willows. The path narrowed to less than three feet in width while to their right, air replaced solid ground. Marta glanced down into the valley over a mile below and inhaled the cold, clear air wafting up from the valley.

She stopped. The soles of her boots quivered. Puzzled, she shifted her stance, but the tingling persisted. The mules felt it too and broke into braying alarms. Dickinson looked about in confusion as the girl dropped to her knees and pressed her palms to the ground. The earth was shaking! The sergeant halted ahead and craned his neck as he searched for sounds in the whistling winds that swirled around them. But no noise reached them other than the moaning of the air until a low rumble rose up from the trembling rock itself.

Marta's eyes widened as a terrible realization struck her.

"What? What is it?" Dickinson shouted.

"Avalanche! Avalanche!" she screamed.

Sloan recognized the sound a split second later.

"Take cover!" he yelled. But he saw there was none to be had. "Get back! Get those mules against the side of the mountain," he croaked.

Instinctively, the men flattened themselves against the side of the track, squeezing into crevices, and driving and kicking their frightened mules against the scant protection of the cut in the side of the mountain. The lead mule balked and bucked, arching its back and kicking in terror. Its soldier dove for safety just as a dirty cloud of dust, mud, ice, and rock enveloped the animal. With a hideous scream the mule was swept over the edge in the stony maelstrom. Flailing legs beat the air for a second, and then the creature was gone, falling to its death on the jagged rocks far below.

A boulder bounced down the trail before launching into space. But it managed to strike the outstretched leg of the second soldier in line. His scream was lost in the noise.

The avalanche ended as quickly as it came. The survivors stumbled from their niches, walking stiff-legged about their ruined train while the silence deafened them. A few scattered coughs split the silence while men searched the wreckage.

Dickinson lurched about. His clothing was in disarray, spattered with mud and slime, and his silver-headed cane was gone. Sergeant Sloan appeared. His entire front half, where he had pressed into a fissure, was coated in ochre mud as if he'd been painted with a giant brush. Despite his appearance he hurried about his company, taking stock of the situation like the seasoned professional he was. Only Marta seemed unscathed. Except for a trace of mud on her cheek and coat sleeves and the slime covering her boots, she was untouched.

A movement caught her eye, and she pointed to an overhang just above the trail. The spy wiped dirt from his face with the inside of his parka and followed her hand.

Two tiny figures clambered across a snow-filled depression on their way across the ridge. One figure looked squat and sturdy, and wore a Hudson Bay blanket coat over moosehide leggings while the other was a head taller and wore knee-high hunting boots laced to willow snowshoes. The taller paused to look back. When he saw Dickinson watching him, he raised his arm and waved his rifle in mock salute. Then he calmly turned and followed his companion.

Dickinson's face blanched in anger. "Beaufort, you bastard!" he shouted, and his voice cracked so he croaked like a frog. "You haven't beaten me yet!"

Dickinson kicked the side of the trail in frustration. "Damn! Damn!" he repeated in anger. "How foolish not to realize he'd attack *beyond* Keystone Canyon when my guard was down." He looked around to see Sloan and Marta watching him. "Well, what's the damage, man?" he snapped.

"Corporal Pruzinski's leg is broke." Sloan gestured to the white-faced soldier jammed into a crevice with his ruined limb projecting out from his body at an obscene angle. A dark stain of blood seeped into the torn fabric of his upper pant leg. Sloan spit a stream of tobacco juice into the valley below. "And we lost a mule."

Marta tipped her chin at the uphill route. "Worse, the trail is blocked."

Dickinson cursed. The bend in the trail disappeared beneath a pile of rocks and ice that filled everything from the cut in the side of the mountain to the sheer drop. The spy stepped past Corporal Pruzinski and walked to the end of the path. The rubble rose above his head. He tried to climb the heap only to slip on the greasy ice and slide back to the ground. He slapped his thigh in frustration.

"How did he know where to attack us?" Dickinson asked.

Marta still watched their two attackers until they vanished over the farthest ridge. "He used an Indian," she said. "He must know every inch of this trail. Like the Miskitos in my country, no one knows the land better. When the *federales* have Miskito trackers, we are in big trouble. Fortunately, the government treats the Indians as badly as they treat us, so most Miskitos hate them as much as we do."

"Goddamn it, I'll buy a whole tribe if that's what it takes," Dickinson fumed. "Right now, Sloan, we need to clear this trail. Get your men at it."

"What about Corporal Pruzinski? He needs medical attention, sir."

Dickinson blew his breath out between his teeth in a frustrated whistle. "Oh, hell. Can't you just shoot the corporal like you'd do to a horse with a broken leg?"

Before Sloan could respond, Marta spoke up. "Best we go back, Dickinson. Your man Beaufort picked his ambush spot well. This rock pile is much too soft to dynamite, and the ledge is so narrow no more than a few men can work at one time. It will take a week to clear a route for the mules. This Beaufort is smart, very smart. He hit us up here away from the engineers' camp. No witnesses and no help. And no political repercussions. Both countries can claim nothing happened here, only an unfortunate avalanche, which is common in this region I'd guess."

Dickinson regarded her like a poison snake. "You're learning far too fast, my dear," he said.

She smiled condescendingly.

"How did he know we'd take this route?" the agent asked himself out loud. "I even had the captain run a decoy company up to the Valdez Glacier. After all, most miners take that way toward Forty Mile. By all rights Beaufort should have followed them."

Sloan cleared his throat and shuffled his feet uneasily. He was too good a soldier to hide important information—no matter whom it hurt. The rest of his men's lives might depend on his being truthful.

Marta's eyes narrowed. "You have something to tell us, Sergeant?"

"Sir, I . . . I, er, that is . . ."

"What, man?" Dickinson snapped. "Spit it out."

"Well, sir"—Sloan glanced back at his other men splinting the corporal's fractured leg—"I caught Corporal Pruzinski talking to one of the dance-hall girls the night before we left. I gather he told her we'd be taking the Keystone Canyon trail on our way into the Interior."

"He what!? The imbecile! He told some whore all about the mission? That does it. I'll shoot him myself." Dickinson's eyes nearly bulged out of his head, and his hand reached for his pistol. Only Marta stopped him. The strength of her grip stunned him. He looked in amazement at the white marks on his hand when she released her hold.

The sergeant shook his head. "No sir. Pruzinski's a good man. He just told her he was going up to the canyon and would be gone for a couple of months. His girl's got a loose mouth, though, so the devil knows how many she blabbed that information to. This Limey probably overheard and put two and two together, and it added up to the Keystone route."

Both Marta and the spy reached the same conclusion. Each looked knowingly at the other. The woman turned away in disgust while Dickinson slumped to the ground as if punched in the gut. Beaufort knew, then. He knew they were headed for Dawson. Dawson was the only place with a sufficient cache of arms worth stealing. No where else in the half million square miles had that many weapons. He could figure it out. Now all the pieces of the puzzle would fall into place for him: Dickinson planned on arming the Panamanian rebels with purloined rifles from the Northwest Mounties' armory in Dawson. That would explain Marta's presence.

"He knows your plan," Marta answered Dickinson's unspoken fears. "But your Englishman makes mistakes, too. He's not infallible, so we still have a chance."

"Why? What do you mean? What mistake?" the agent asked. His mind buzzed like a hive of angry bees.

"He failed to kill us. That was his first big mistake."

Even the veteran Sloan looked at the girl in amazement. Here their objectives were known to the enemy, the trail was blocked, their company was savaged, and this girl had a plan to attack where army generals would admit defeat. "What are you saying, Miss Kelly?" he asked. "Do you think we have a chance?"

She nodded. "Yes. Now it is quite simple. It is a race, nothing more. Whoever reaches Dawson first will win. If Beaufort arrives before us, he will alert the Mounties, and the guns will be too heavily guarded for us. If we beat him we still have a chance."

"But look at the trail. It's blocked tighter than a cork up a Scotsman's ass," Dickinson sputtered. "And Beaufort's already on the other side. He'll have a week's march on us before we clear the pass. We'll never catch him."

"Don't wait for the road to be cleared. Go around the trail."

"Impossible," Sloan answered. "A man might climb up the side of this mountain and circle around the pass, but we could never lead the mules. They're mules after all, not damned mountain goats."

Marta stood her ground. "Leave the mules. We go without them."

"What?"

"No, wait. I see her point, Sloan." Dickinson jumped to his feet. "Aubrey and his cursed Indian were on snowshoes. I didn't see any packs or animals. Obviously they expected to roll us all into the valley with their avalanche. That means they either hope we'll turn back or else they have to get outfitted. But we've got to get the jump on them right quickly. We must press on immediately."

"What do you suggest, sir?"

Dickinson looked at Marta and found he didn't even have to ask. She would go wherever he went. "Make up three packs with food and supplies to hold us to the trading post. The three of us will climb this rock face and flank the obstruction. The rest will head back to Valdez with the story that Miss Kelly, you, and I were swept into the valley by an accidental avalanche. Make a great show of it so even a deaf parson can hear you coming a mile away." He turned to look at the suffering corporal and raised his voice loud enough for all the men to hear. "That will be the official report. We will be dead, officially. And by God if anyone spills the truth without my say-so, I'll personally hang him from the nearest tree. Do I make myself perfectly clear?"

All the soldiers nodded their heads.

"Good. Let's get to work. I need one of the men to take a note back to Captain Abercrombie. We'll want Abercrombie to have a military funeral for us, full fig and all to help with our little charade. I didn't see any binoculars on my dear Aubrey, God rot his liver, so he may not know who or what went over the edge in his little surprise."

"Just the same," Marta suggested, "we should keep out of sight after the others head back and start the climb at night."

"That'll be dangerous," Sloan interjected. "Climbing these hills in the daylight is devilishly tricky, what with the ice lenses and loose shale. One slip and it's death unless you're lucky."

Marta smirked at the soldier. "I'm not afraid, Sergeant. Are you? If you are I can hold your hand. Besides, climbing in the dark will be safer than giving Beaufort a shot at us during daylight should he be waiting for us with his rifle."

Sloan blushed several shades of scarlet with embarrassment and went off to see to the packs. The premonition he'd felt when they left Valdez was justified, he realized now. And things were getting worse. He was heading into the Interior just as winter was descending on the land—with a dandified spy and a madwoman—to invade the sovereign nation of Canada.

⋆ ⋆ **NINETEEN** ⋆ ⋆

While the spy, the sergeant, and the girl picked their way up the slippery face of the Chugach Mountains and around Thompson Pass, another trio, hundreds of miles to the north and east, raced along the frozen face of the Yukon River. On both groups no moon shone, and the night descended with equal callousness. For this vast, frozen expanse cared little for the humans who aspired to cross her. Indifferent to their hopes and aspirations, the Interior chose to ignore these trespassers just as the lynx ignores the fleas that travel across its hide.

Nathan knew the land's apathy well, and he had learned to live with it. More than that, he'd learned to tap the constant flow of the Arctic, whether it be the rivers, the course of the mountains and flats, or the biting winds and killing storms. Using the natural terrain to aid his travel rather than allowing it to obstruct him, he no longer battled this enormous force like he'd done when he first entered the frozen North. Looking back on his travails with rapids, swamps, and mosquito-infested bogs on his way to the Klondike, one could find no comparison to the woodsman who now followed the flow of the land.

Without benefit of moon or stars, Nathan drove his newly acquired team unerringly along the twists and bends of the frozen river. Riley and the liberated Doc, still sporting his noose as a necktie, luxuriated in the comfort of the sled's basket, toasty warm beneath the caribou robes. Scattered snow showers covered their tracks and no sign of pursuers from Circle City developed, yet Nathan still ran the team. Bred for long distances, the dogs soared happily onward. Nathan had developed some experience with dog teams in the last year, and he knew the key lay in the team's leader.

To his joy and amazement, his she-wolf assumed control of the team. Perhaps, she needed to lead others, or she missed the pack she'd turned on. Whatever the reason she chose, only one objected—the lead dog himself, a brindled MacKenzie River husky with one blue eye. He leapt in harness, snarled, and bared his teeth at her. The wolf settled the argument by diving straight for the husky's throat and clamping her fangs on his windpipe. Then, like a lion who had brought down a wildebeest, she braced her four feet and shut off the protester's air. But the savvy bitch didn't kill her opponent. Instead, she choked him until he acquiesced rather than died. Then she let him loose. The shaken husky stood shivering and gulping air while he submitted to the wolf mouthing his muzzle with her teeth. After that there was no question who led the team.

Running free of traces, the wolf guided the team over the river, avoiding deadheads protruding from the ice like spikes and skirting areas of overflow where the team and sled might break through the thin ice. Her mind and Nathan's seemed linked as they both handled the team.

The team raced through the long night. Past Takoma Bluff with its white face glowing eerily in the darkness, they approached pinpoints of yellow light from the Woodchopper Roadhouse. Used as a stopping point for sleds in the winter and a refueling station for the riverboats on the Yukon in the summer, the roadhouse offered warm food and shelter. But Nathan and his wolf swung wide of the place and slipped silently past as laughing voices from the cabin faded into the night. The cabin lights of McGregor's and Slaven's cabins received the same fate.

They swung north with the bend of the Yukon past the sharp sides of Biederman Bluff, past the mouth of the Kandik River, until they fell beneath the dark shadow of Kathul Mountain. As silently as it arose the mountain dropped behind, and twenty miles later they crossed the braided mouth of the frozen Nation River. Upstream of the Nation, hidden in the mountains, lay Hard Luck Creek, where scores of miners watched their hopes and fortunes wash away like the worthless muck that drained from their sluice boxes.

All night long they sped. For her part, the she-wolf would run forever. But the sled dogs showed signs of tiring. Rounding Eagle Bluff, Nathan spotted the clusters of yellow lamps from Eagle piercing the velvet blackness. He whistled softly to his wolf, and she slackened her pace. The wheel dogs rolled their eyes in gratitude and let their tongues droop farther from their mouths. Silently, Nathan directed his team past the town itself to the Indian village. There he pulled up to a spruce-log-and-dirt lodge surrounded by empty salmon drying racks. Circling behind the structure, he led his team to a clump of spruce trees and set the sled's drag hook. Immediately his tired dogs dropped to the ground and curled into tight fur balls with their faces buried in their bushy tails. Another team of dogs, tied to posts fifty yards away, raised their heads to inspect the new arrivals before returning to a similar nesting position.

The lodge door opened and a stooped man with a lever-action rifle cradled in the crook of his left arm emerged to watch Nathan approach. Hennison slipped his hand inside his coat in search of the pistol he'd begged from Riley. The cold grips touched his fingers reassuringly.

"Na-Tan," the man rumbled. He raised his right hand in greeting. "I was expecting you."

The lad looked surprised at this comment. "You were, Many Hats?"

"Yes." The other nodded solemnly. "The army's iron rope that talks spoke of three bad men running from Circle City. It warned the soldiers here to look for them. I was in the office when the little hammer awoke and tapped out the words. It spoke of one being a young man with eyes like the spring ice, so I knew it must be you, Na-Tan."

"The damned telegraph," Hennison hissed. "They must have fixed it."

"Bad men, eh?"

"Yes, Na-Tan." Many Hats broke into a deep laugh which ended abruptly when he cleared his throat and hawked a glob of phlegm into the night. "Bad men, yes. When it said that about you, then I knew it lied." He shrugged. "That iron rope lies a lot. So tonight I cut the wires to silence its lying."

Nathan raised his eyebrows in concern.

"Don't worry, Na-Tan. I made it look like a moose caught his antlers in the wire. I do that a lot to spite the soldiers when they steal our beef rations. They swear much at the moose breaking their wires." Many Hats laughed again at his private joke.

"Best we move on, Many Hats, if the town's been alerted. I don't want to get you in trouble," Nathan said as he turned back to his sled.

"No, no, Na-Tan. My heart would be on the ground if you refused my hospitality. The marshal, Frank Canton, is the only one to worry about, and he is down the river at Rampart. The army does not expect you for another two days. They travel with heavy sleds the size of a small house, so it takes them many days to go to Circle. Only I guessed you'd come tonight." He stopped to look sharply at the dogs curled beside the sled. "The wire said you stole that man Ransky's dog team. I see it spoke the truth about that."

"Yes." Nathan hung his head. "It could not be helped."

"Good for you, Na-Tan. Ransky is a cheat. He deserves to have his team stolen. The dogs will fare better under your care. But I see that Son of the Winter Wolf has brought a she-wolf with him." Many Hats stopped to study the beautiful animal at Nathan's side; then he asked with complete candor, "Is she your wife?"

Nathan shook his head, embarrassed. "No, Many Hats, she's not my wife."

"Not yet, she ain't," Riley added. "But she's beginning to act like one, if you ask me."

Many Hats raised his arm in greeting to the gunman. "Finger-That-Kills, you are welcome, too."

Many Hats turned to watch Hennison struggle out of the sled's basket, and the old Indian's eyes fairly shone when he saw the battered beaver hat on the physician's head. "And who is this that travels with my friends?" the native asked. All the while his eyes kept fixed on Doc's hat.

"Many Hats, this is Doc Hennison, an old friend from the dry land, Arizona. He is a doctor, er, a medicine man much like yourself."

Many Hats' mouth dropped open as Doc staggered in front of the open lodge door, and the light from inside fell on his empty right sleeve. His hand slipped over his mouth to hide his astonishment. Carefully, he advanced to Doc's side and lightly slapped the empty sleeve with his rifle barrel.

Hennison jerked upright. "I beg your pardon, but we're not that friendly, so kindly keep your rifle to yourself."

"I know of you," Many Hats said slowly. "I missed you when last you passed through Eagle. You are One-Who-Kills-Dogs."

"I'll be damned if I'll stand here in the cold and be insulted by a savage," Hennison slurred his reply. "Listen Mr. Hats, or should I call you Dr. Hats, I distinctly told them *not* to

207

give my elixir to dogs. Surely you must have patients that don't follow instructions?"

"Not many still alive," the medicine man quipped. He held his hand out to the bottle in Hennison's hand. "Is that your magic medicine that kills dogs and makes my young men crazy in the head and climb trees like squirrels?"

Hennison thrust the bottle protectively behind his back.

"Doc, have you been selling elixir to the Indians?" Nathan questioned. "You know that's against the law."

Hennison smiled sweetly. "And stealing a man's dog team isn't? I guess we're all felons here."

"Damn you, you ingrate," Riley fumed. "We stole this team 'cause we was rescuing you. I knew we shoulda let 'em stretch yer scrawny neck."

"Well, you didn't, so that's water over the dam," Doc countered. "And in my defense, Nat, I never check a man's pedigree before I sell elixir to him. It's not the color of his skin I look at, it's the color of his money."

"Give me the drink," Many Hats demanded.

Hennison looked around for support, and finding none reluctantly placed the bottle in Many Hats' hand. All three white men expected him to empty the dangerous fluid onto the snow. But he astonished them by directing the flask to his lips and swallowing half its contents. An awkward silence fell on the group as the men studied Many Hats for ill effects. But all he did was emit a loud burp.

"Too much baneberry," he said as he smacked his lips.

Later that evening, Riley, Doc, and Many Hats lolled on the floor of the earthen lodge, smoked, and reflected in the light from the fire. The three had found another bottle of Doc's elixir in Ransky's sled, one they assumed he'd kept for evidence. But Hennison wondered out loud if the musher hadn't secretly schemed to reproduce his formula once he'd eliminated the good doctor.

"I wouldn't put it past the snake to trump up that hanging just so's he'd not have my competition," Doc expounded on his theory. "And there's the matter of the rest of my stock. Ransky stole it all, all twenty-some bottles of it. Now I ask you, what would he want with my entire supply unless he planned to sell it himself?"

Many Hats wiped the sweat from his face and reached again for the bottle. He took another lengthy swig while Riley and Doc watched in awe.

"Whoever said Indians can't hold their liquor never met this duffer," Riley said. "I'd wager he can drink the two of us under the table and still have room for more."

Doc watched his limited supply of elixir diminish. "Bet he wouldn't drink so fast if he had to pay for the stuff," he sniffed.

That comment caused Many Hats to break into uproarious laughter, and soon the three drunks were laughing and giggling together with the fervent affection that only drunks can have for each other.

Riley wrapped his arm around the Indian and said with true feeling as he studied the straight black hair held in place with a red bandana, "Damn, never thought I'd get this close to someone who looks like a Apache. I tell you this with complete honesty, Hats, if we was this close in Arizona, we'd be biting each other's ears and poking each other with our bowie knives."

Hennison clarified that statement. "He means to say you remind him of the warlike Apaches down in Arizona, Many Hats."

"I know what I mean to say, snake oil, and I said *exactly* what I meant to say. So don't go putting no words in my mouth. Maybe I ain't got no fancy education like you, but I can read now, and I always could speak my mind."

"Apaches?" Many Hats smiled. "We are related, you know."

"No?" Riley recoiled back from his newfound friend. "You are?"

"Yes. So I am told. Three summers ago a man with a camera box came to take our pictures. It was for a great place back in Washington, the Smithsonian, he said, where they study everything from the tiniest spiders to tribes from all over the world. He said it would be a great honor for us. We found that very funny. We told him the spiders might feel honored, but he would have to pay us."

Many Hats paused for another sip. He pursed his lips and stared into the shadows of the far corner with the grace of a consummate storyteller. "He said that the tribes far to the south, in Arizona—the Apaches and the Navajos—are our brothers because many of their words are the same as ours. But we already knew that. We told him only the weak ones who couldn't stand the cold journeyed south. My people, the Gwitchin, stayed here. That makes us stronger than our brothers, the Apaches."

"Try telling that to all them white folks the Mescalaro's roasted," Riley countered. "I doubt they'd agree."

Many Hats grunted. "We have no need to fight the white man. The land fights them for us. The white man wants to own the land, but this land will never allow itself to be anything other than the master. Na-Tan knows this: The land is always the master. But he is the only white man I know who is that smart. All the others are trying to cut a hole through a mountain instead of simply walking around it, or building a bridge over the river so the ice has something to play with and carry away in the spring."

Nathan smiled at the offhanded compliment from his old friend. "What else did the man say?"

"He wanted us to show him our secret ceremonies, the calling of the salmon and others, and where we put our dead."

"And did you?"

"No. That would be foolish. Suppose he got the words wrong or sang the song wrong. The salmon might not come or might even swim back to the sea in disgust. No, Na-Tan, those things are too important to trust to white men—even you, who I regard like a son."

"A most wise move, Many Hats," Hennison replied. "For that very same reason, I keep my elixir's recipe secret. Only a few can handle the power of its might."

"Bullshit," Riley burped. "Only dogs and pigs can't handle it. I don't suppose that makes 'em a notch up on people."

Doc cast a spiteful glance at Riley. "You really are tiresome at times. Do go on with your story, Hats. I find it fascinating."

The old native nodded and his eyes assumed a crafty glint. "We had heard that if you show these white men where the old chiefs are buried, they sneak back in the night and dig up their bones and take them back to Washington. The spirits of the old chiefs would be very angry if we caused their bones to live in a glass box in a faraway place instead of in their home."

"So what did you do?"

"We played a joke on them, Na-Tan. When they insisted on seeing our graves we took them up the hill to where the Christian Gwitchin are buried. 'Here is where we bury our people,' we said. We pointed to all the crosses. The study men were not amused. They couldn't tell from the Christian names on the crosses who were white and who were not, so they didn't dig up anyone. And we never showed them where the bones of the great chiefs are hidden. All the chiefs' bones are still here to watch over our people."

Nathan had only taken a small sip at the beginning, and now he rose to his feet. "I'd better check on the dogs," he said as he pulled on his parka and slipped outside. They watched his back vanish into the night. His departure sobered the men.

After a moment of silence, but without any interruption of passing the bottle, Many Hats spoke.

"A good man, Na-Tan, but his heart is not in the air," he related. "He is too serious for one so young. I believe he needs a woman."

Many Hats leaned closer, the sweat dropping from him like water from a beaver's fur. "He never speaks of his past. That is not good. A man with no past to look back upon has no trail to follow."

Riley kneaded his forehead. "I met Nathan when he was about to get cornholed by some lowlifes near Pinal. He was so green, he didn't know which end of the barrel the bullets come out of. The fool lad was off to kill his real father—Wyatt Earp—for a reward his dead mother was offering. He hired me to help."

"Me, too," Doc added.

"The hell he did," Riley snorted. "You was about to get yerself hung for the first time when we met you."

"Oh, yeah, Mr. Famous Gunfighter," Hennison retorted. "Why don't you tell the truth, then. When Nathan found you, you were freezing to death. That's what your fancy shooting got you. In truth, Many Hats, we owe our lives to the lad. He gave us a . . . a reason for going on. For want of better guidance, this broken-down gunfighter and I—unprincipled as I am—have been like the boy's true father. We may not have done right for him at all times, but we've done the best we could. We turned him into a man."

"Us and a China girl, named Wei-Li, damn her eyes," Riley swore. "She bore him a son, but to do that she killed herself. That's why we're headed back to Dawson. To find his son, the one this snake-oil salesman hid from us."

"Wait just a minute, Riley, old man. You and the boy left me with the baby, remember? You two lit out."

Riley nodded to the native. "It's the truth. But why did you hide Nathan's son with those sodbusters? What was their names again, Gunnysomes?"

"Gustafsons," Doc corrected. "As fine and loving a family as you could find in all of the Northwest Territories."

"Germans are they? Why the babe will be eating sauerkraut and sausage if we don't rescue him soon."

"They're Swedes, not Germans, you lout."

"Well." Riley crawled over to the fire and lit another cigar. Besides the bottle of elixir, Ranksy had a packet of cigars in his sled. "Why'd you have to hide the baby? Why didn't you jus' take care of him herself? We'd have been spared a whole lot of traipsing up and about this country a-looking for the two of you."

"I hid him because I thought Soapy Smith's gang or Earp or who knows what might be looking for the baby for revenge. As a way to get even with Nat. Besides, what do I look like to you . . . a goddamned nursemaid?"

Riley screwed up his face at the thought. His tongue protruded from his mouth in disgust. "I see what you mean," he said. "I guess milk is a mite scarcer for humans than for foundling calves. Okay, I guess you did the best you could."

"When you two didn't return I stashed the baby and took to the road with my elixir."

"Guess I can't blame you for not being able to change yer stripes, Doc. You'll always be a polecat."

"Gosh, that's the kindest thing you've ever said to me, Riley, but since I know it comes from a half-wit, I'll pay it no never mind. Besides, you're a fine one to talk. If you'd done your work properly when you got to Nome, we'd be splitting that twenty thousand dollars three ways. Well, I heard Earp is alive and well. Last time I was in Rampart, word was that Wyatt Earp sold his Dexter Saloon for a handsome profit—eighty thousand and change, I believe—left Nome and headed back to San Francisco. Maybe we should follow him and rob him after we shoot him. That way we'd pocket the reward plus his fortune. What do you say to that, my friend?"

"Ain't never gonna happen . . ." Riley pulled the last bottle of elixir away from Many Hats and took a long swig. "Nathan and I got to Nome, damn yer eyes, and we met up with Wyatt Earp, the old gray wolf hisself. But neither Nathan nor I are ever gonna pull down on him let alone snap a cap in his general direction."

Hennison tried to focus his bleary eyes. Even through the haze from the wood fire and the effects of his elixir, he noted the serious look on the gunman's face. "I don't follow."

"Maybe it's hard for you understand, being as how you've never lived by the gun, always watching yer shadow, and living without friends."

"I've been on the run as much as you," Hennison added defensively.

"I reckon so, but it ain't the same."

"Well, tell me what happened."

Riley shifted his back against a lodgepole and took another drink. "We met Earp like I said. Nathan's damn near the spitting image of the marshal. Most everything good they say about that shooter is true, and most all the bad things ain't. You and I may fancy that we had a hand in shaping Nat, but all the breeding stock comes from his father. That made our job a cinch."

Hennison snorted. "What is he, some sort of saint?"

"No, he ain't no saint nor sinner neither. But he's a strong-willed man and upright as a new rifle barrel. You could do no better than to have him standing by your side in a gunfight. He shoots as straight as his word."

"If he was that fast, how come you're still alive?"

"Because there weren't no shoot-out, I tell you. Wyatt and Nathan liked each other. They recognized they was father and son right from the start."

Doc shook his head in puzzlement. He looked to Many Hats for explanation, but the Indian merely smiled knowingly, which confused the physician all the more. "Well, why isn't Nathan with Wyatt now?"

" 'Cause Earp's a darn sight smarter than both of us combined. He recognized right off the boy'd stand his best chance in life outside of his shadow. Being together would be a danger to both of them. Damned if he didn't see that right off. So he gave Nathan his blessing and his long-barreled Colt, and the two parted. I tell you, Hennison, it was enough to bring tears to this poor child's eyes, the two of them standing there on that cursed sand in Nome hugging and knowing they'd never be able to own up to the other no matter how much they cared for each other. It like to broke my heart."

"Earp could have parted with some of his eighty thousand in cash for his only son," Doc sniffed.

"He didn't have no eighty thousand then, I tell you. He was up to his ass in rattlesnakes just like happened back in Tombstone in the eighties. Them Spoilers was trying to bushwhack Earp something fierce, but we filled a few of their bully boys full of lead."

"The Spoilers, eh? That was the gang that controlled Nome. I heard something about the ringleaders when I stopped over in Rampart."

"McKenzie and his crooked Judge Noyes were a pair. Between the two of them they robbed the place blind. First Noyes put all the contested mining claims into receivership and handed them over to his friend McKenzie for safekeeping. Ha, that was a laugh. McKenzie's men stripped all the gold out of the claims he was supposed to be watching. Then they tried to grab the saloons without paying for them. That's why Wyatt didn't give Nathan no money. His saloon and Lucky Baldwin's were two the Spoilers wanted. Wyatt said he'd burn the place to the ground before he'd hand it over. And you know the funny thing?"

"What?"

"McKenzie actually hired the two of us to help murder Wyatt. Us and some of Soapy Smith's old gang. But we fooled them. In the end we wiped out McKenzie's best henchmen."

Hennison's eyes lit up. "That's what I heard. The miners in Nome finally got a delegation to district court in San Francisco to complain about Judge Noyes."

"Yup. Up until we drilled those rats, any miner with gumption enough to challenge the Spoilers got himself killed. So what happened?"

"A company of U.S. marshals got off the boat in Nome and arrested McKenzie and the judge."

"Well, hallelujah. Nathan will be pleased to hear about that."

Hennison leaned closer to his old traveling partner and asked almost wistfully, "What was Nome like? Was it wonderful? Gold lying all about like they said? I heard even the sands on the beach were laced with yellow dust. All I ever got to see was that damned Dawson. The big mining companies bought out all the claims after you left, so the place got real dull. Tell me about Nome. Do you think my elixir would sell there?"

"Nah, Nome was a hellhole like the rest, Doc. I'm surprised you swallowed that hogwash. It weren't no different than Dawson, except you couldn't buy a tree to save yer life."

"No trees?" Hennison frowned. "How odd. I wonder why not."

Many Hats leaned forward in interest. "A place where no trees grow. I have heard tales of such places from the Yupiks who live far to the north. They sometimes ride the riverboats which stop for firewood to feed the fire in their hungry bellies. Those boats eat all the time, but I do not think the green wood agrees with their stomachs. The boats belch a lot and pass black smoke. My young men cut trees and pile them along the river-banks for these steamers. The white man is funny about those things. He wants the wood cut to a certain length—two arms' span or the boat will not eat it, they say. But I think that is a lie. Whoever heard of a forest with all the trees equal. But Nome has no trees? How would those boats travel the rivers up north without any trees to eat?"

"They don't," Riley answered. "The rivers around Nome are too shallow for the paddle wheelers, Many Hats. You can paddle inland, but only a fool would want to. Nothing there but mosquitoes, blackflies, and miles of muck. They don't even have moose there, only caribou."

"No gold inland?" Doc remained focused on the yellow metal.

"None to speak of. All the pay streak is in the low hills and creeks surrounding the town. That's how the gold dust got into the sands on the beach. It washed out of the hills and a place called Anvil Creek."

"Well." Doc clung to his dream of easy wealth. "Panning sand has got to be easier than grubbing in the muck down a hole like we did in Dawson."

"Ain't no easy gold, Doc. The good Lord may have made it, but he gave it to the devil to hide. And Satan chose places that would try the patience of a saint. Living in Nome was just as bad as living in Dawson, but for different reasons. Every square inch of the beach and the creeks is filed on. Claims are every-where, and if you dig down a foot or two, you're up to yer neck in salt water. The water table is just under the surface. Why, you can't even dig a respectable outhouse lest it drain into the creeks. So everyone had dysentery and typhus. I tell you, the coffee there had a spooky taste. People with the runs were dropping like flies until they built outhouses atop barrels. You had to pay a dollar just to take a crap!"

Many Hats clapped his hands together in glee. "I always

knew the white man would turn his sickness on himself after his pox killed off my people."

Hennison removed his beaver hat and wiped the brim on his sleeve. "Reminds me of my service in the Confederacy. But neither side ever learned to dig the latrines downriver of the water supply. Well, I guess Nome is out."

"You'll thank me for changing yer mind, Doc. It's a god-forsaken place at best. Nothing but low sand dunes, low brush, and fearsome, wicked storms. Every other month the whole town either gits blown away or washed into the bay by the storms."

Hennison dropped his head into his hands. "A pity."

"So what have you been doing?"

Hennison shrugged his one shoulder and the movement brought a firelike pain to his scar-woven right side. "Mostly traveling up and down the Yukon selling my elixir when I can't find a card game. But the pickings have been mighty slim. Most miners headed for Nome this fall, and those left haven't got much. So I sell a lot of elixir and dodge my adversaries."

"Adversaries? You mean the law?"

"Nope. Mainly the Episcopalians."

"Episcopalians? You blow up one of their churches or something? Why would Holy Rollers be hunting you, Doc? Surely not to seek yer conversion."

Many Hats grinned broadly and jabbed his finger at the bottle of elixir. "Bishop Rowe," he said. "He look for you."

"You got a bishop pissed at you, Doc? That must have taken some doing."

Hennison waggled his hands in front of his face as if to ward off his own personal demon. "The Right Reverend Peter Trimble Rowe," he spoke in awe. "The man is a fiend. He dogs my trail like a monster. You'd think he was the archangel Michael himself the way he pursues me."

"What's his gripe with you, Doc?"

"Oh, he can't abide my selling my elixir to the Indians. He's got it fixed in his cloistered mind it's whiskey. Rowe travels up and down the Yukon preaching the Gospel and bashing the living daylights out of anyone he suspects of selling whiskey to the natives. I tell you the man is unbelievable. He's broken more stills and whiskey bottles than all the revenue men in Tennessee ever did. He dogs my every footstep. I wouldn't be surprised if he's sniffing hot on my trail even now. I fear him far more than any posse Ransky could form or the army and U.S. marshals together."

"Hates you that much, eh? And just for selling whiskey."

"*Elixir,* my good man, elixir," Hennison sniffed indignantly.

Riley drained the last dregs of Doc's brew, and belched appreciatively. "Well, Doc, I'll tell you something. I ain't drinking this elixir of yours because of all the phenomenal axle grease, poison berries, and moose turds you got mixed in it. I'm drinking it because it's ninety percent alcohol. That's a pure fact."

"Phenomenal! That's a fancy word for a saddle bum like yourself to be using. What do you know about the sufferings of a genius like myself? Here I try to help and—"

"Bullshit!" Riley burped even louder.

In an instant Hennison was on him, swinging his left arm like a club at the man who was his bosom buddy a few minutes ago. The first blows missed, but the last flurry connected until Riley dodged to one side and pinned his companion under his knees. There they sat, Doc swearing and swinging while Riley rode atop him like a bronc buster, and all the while Many Hats rocked back and forth on his heels in laughter. He always enjoyed a good fight, and a fight between white men was the type he especially liked.

The door swung open and Nathan darted inside. The stern look on his face caused the combatants to pause. "Quick," he growled. "We got trouble. I crept into town, and the army post is buzzing like an angry hornet's nest. The detachment is tumbling out and getting ready to search the village. They've already checked the sutler's store and the saloon, and they're heading in this direction. They'll be here in half an hour at best. Funny thing, though, it looks to me like a preacher-type fellow is leading them."

"Rowe!" Hennison sputtered from beneath Riley's knees. "See! See, I told you. The man is unstoppable. Why don't you just take your Sharps and plug him through his miserable golden heart. I believe the man would actually thank you, since he believes he'll go straight to the right hand of God."

Nathan shook his head. "Best we push on. I'd prefer not to kill your preacher if I can avoid it. Beside, taking on the army is a bad idea."

He sat back on his heels to form their escape. His eyes darted around as he thought, and all but he noted the similarity of the flickering movement of his gray eyes with those of the she-wolf who now waited outside. The spirit of the wolf is strong in this man, Many Hats mused. Perhaps he can change his shape like those in the legends. He waited expectantly to see if this might happen.

But Nathan's mind was racing over the possibilities as his eyes danced about. The rich brown texture of the moose and caribou robes, glowing in the light of the fire, contrasted with the red effulgence of the split salmon hanging from racks and the dull metal of Many Hats' traps. The silver mesh of leghold traps and snares, dangling like medieval chain mail from the lodge posts, only served to distract him. So he forced himself to stare into the hypnotizing flicker of the burning coals.

"Many Hats, can we borrow your dog team? Mine is too worn-out to carry the three of us, and no one will suspect two dogsleds when they find the tracks. They're looking for one team—heavily loaded. With two teams we can split up Doc and Jim—"

Hennison shook his head in protest. "I'm no dog musher. I'll have to ride in the basket."

"And I'm too drunk to drive," Riley confessed. "I'm just liable to fall off at the first dogleg."

Many Hats rose slowly to his feet. The wobble of his head and the slurred speech were gone as he spoke. "I will drive my own sled, Cub of the Winter Wolf."

"Great," Nathan responded. "We're off then—"

"But there is a price," Many Hats added slyly. "The fine beaver hat of the One-Armed-Dog-Killer."

"*What?!*"

Before Doc could say another word Nathan had stuffed his beaver hat on Many Hats' head and pushed the doctor out into the black night.

TWENTY

Like a pair of horned owls hunting in the night, the two teams dashed along the moonlit expanse of the frozen Yukon. Silent as a vast tomb, the blue-white and black shadows watched and waited. With luck and skill these travelers would pass successfully, but one slip, whether thin ice or an overflow, would spell their doom and add their bones to the countless others that littered the bottom of the river and its forested banks.

Well aware of this, both Many Hats and Nathan kept constantly alert, studying the shadows on the ice and their reflections for signs of danger. A shiny spot might mean raw ice blown free of snow by the wind—or an open lea. Water boiling through cracks in the ice could cover the frozen river in spots like an oasis in the desert. But this oasis meant death instead of life to the unwary. To fall in meant a freezing death for both men and dogs. So the mushers' eyes darted over the path ahead—their lives depended upon it.

Nathan found himself drawn to this sullen land. He recalled this stretch of water in the summer and how different it was from the face it wore now. Green birch overwhelmed the somber spruce coating the banks then, and the Yukon was alive with boats of all descriptions. For the waters of the Yukon were the one vast highway upon which the Arctic permitted men to travel into its heartland. Pitch-tarred canoes of birch bark and thin willow ribs contested the currents with churning stern-wheelers whose belching smoke could be seen for miles above the rolling hills and limestone cliffs. The summer air carried smells of all types to those patient enough to sample it: alder-smoked salmon from the natives' fish camps, creosote, tar, and hot grease from the paddlewheel, and the pungent tang of highbush cranberries that signaled the coming close of the brief arctic summer. Somehow, Nathan felt those odors had seeped into his being just as the cold had changed his life forever. Like the metals added to iron to temper steel, the traces of things special to Alaska had tempered him.

Many Hats raised his arm as his sled slid to a halt. Nathan jammed his boot down hard to keep from overrunning the first sled and felt the ice rake under his foot dig into firm ice. He guided his team to a stop behind the first sled. The she-wolf left her position as his lead dog and circled around Many Hats' team to look them over. Most of his team cast wary looks in her direction except for the lead dog, who curled his upper lip and bristled the hair on his back.

"Come on, Sweetness," Riley shouted at the wolf. "Leave them other dogs be. You can't lead two teams."

The wolf shot him a disdainful look and squatted to urinate in front of the other lead dog. The insulted male growled in rage. Then she trotted off into the darkness.

"Guess she showed you and that husky what she thought of you," Doc called out from the native's sled. He was buried beneath a caribou hide with only the top of his head exposed. He now wore a faded red-and-black checkered lumberjack's hat with the earflaps cinched tightly under his chin. Many Hats had deigned to loan him this hat until he could purchase another. The effect of this wool hat framing Doc's face was one of a very cynical woodcutter.

The other dogs took the opportunity to relieve themselves

223

or chomp mouthfuls of snow to slake their thirst. A few curled into fur balls and covered their noses with their tails for warmth. Many Hats pointed to these animals.

"Getting much colder," he remarked.

Nathan spit into the darkness and watched his stream of saliva crackle like static electricity before it simply vanished in the frigid air. He stepped around and cocked his head to listen to the sharp sound of his mukluks crunching on the snow. "Fifty below, I'd guess," he drawled. "Good thing Many Hats let us borrow these fur outfits. Better hunker down and wait out this cold snap."

Many Hats bobbed his new beaver hat in agreement. This boy knew much, he thought. Somewhere he must have Gwitchin blood mixed in his veins.

"Stop? We can't stop," Doc bawled from his pile of furs. "What about the authorities? They might catch up if we stop."

"Rest easy, Doc," Nathan replied. "We crossed the border a few miles back. We're in Canada. You're safe unless the red-coats want you. You said they don't. I hope that's true."

"Canada, eh." Doc relaxed as he looked around. "Damned if you could prove it by me. Every time I travel this river it looks different. But, yes, I told you the truth. I'm not wanted for anything in Canada."

"You mean they ain't caught you at yer work yet," Riley added.

The dropping water level of the Yukon before freeze-up surrounded the river with vertical banks impossible for the dogs to climb. But camping on the river itself was unwise. Sudden seismic tremors and the ever present earthquakes that rocked the region might shatter even the four feet of ice beneath their feet. While the frozen surface appeared dormant, the restless land below waited like a coiled trap to spring on the careless.

Many Hats pointed to a cut in the steep riverbank where a

creek fed into the Yukon. Hoarfrosted willows lined the entrance, glowing like ghostly white tendrils in the moonlight. "We camp there," he said. "Plenty of firewood and protection from the wind." With that statement he turned his sled off the river and headed into the brush.

Nathan followed, weaving his team among the alder and willow until they stopped at a gravel bar beneath an outcropping of rock. Ahead the frozen creek disappeared between a cleft in the sharp-faced hills. The creek bank had received little snow, so building a fire on the bare ground proved easy. Piles of silt-scoured driftwood beached from last summer's high water furnished ample firewood. Soon a cheery fire crackled in the hollow of the cliff, casting its yellow lights over the splintered stone. Nathan and Many Hats set a tin kettle to boiling for tea while a slab of bacon sizzled on a cast-iron skillet. Nathan removed a wad of sourdough from inside his jacket and twisted the rubbery dough around willow sticks to make bannock bread. These he set near the fire's coals to bake. The fire's warmth and the aroma of hot food did much to counter the deepening cold.

Nathan chopped chunks of dried dogfish for the dogs until the food was cooked. His wolf curled into the snow at the camp's edge and chewed on a rabbit she had caught. When Nathan handed her a slab of fish she merely sniffed at it.

Back at the fire, the young man juggled a hot piece of bannock while he sipped the scalding tea. The irony of burning his lip on a hot tin cup while the rest of him froze in the deadly cold did not amuse him. He knew traveling in this cold was no laughing matter. More than one solitary man had lost his life to the arctic winter.

"You know, when I met that oyster robber, Jack London, back in San Francisco, he told me about the dangers of traveling alone when it gets fifty below zero. Said he planned on writing a story about it, about how easy it was to freeze to death.

I never paid it much mind until Jim and I ran into it face-to-face."

Many Hats wiped his greasy lips, then licked the drippings from his mitten. "A man alone can make no mistakes. If he falls in an overflow, he has no chance. He will freeze before he can make a fire," he said.

Hennison amused himself by spitting into the air like Nathan had done and watching his saliva vanish. Under protest he helped Riley scour the pans with river silt.

"And don't be rubbing yer greasy hands on the rifles," Riley warned him. "I don't want no porcupines chewing my rifle stocks, especially that Sharps I got stashed in the sled."

"Bugger off," Doc retorted. "That fourteen-pound rifle is just deadweight. It's the one thing of Ransky's not worth stealing. You took a chance slipping it in the sled back at Circle, and for what? All it did was slow us down. There aren't any buffalo here, and there aren't ever going to be any."

"Maybe not, but you never know when a big gun might come in handy. All these newfangled thirty-calibers give me the jitters. They might work on thin-skinned two-legged varmints; but if God had wanted us to hunt with teeny little bullets, he wouldn't have made some animals so powerful big."

Hennison snorted in derision and disappeared underneath a pile of furs.

"Well," Riley said as he stood up, "I think I'll take a look around and stretch my legs. Riding in that basket gits me all cramped up. These old bones need some straightening out. I'm going to follow this creek back a ways and see if I can't spot a stupid caribou."

He hefted his Winchester and walked toward the cleft. As he followed the twist of the solid rivulet, the security of the fire vanished abruptly, snuffed out by the cold rock walls. The loss of light caused him to stop to adjust his eyes to the darkness, and a fearful premonition swept over him. But he shrugged that off while he focused on the meager light spilling over the canyon's rim into the cleft.

A movement to his right caught his eye, and he swung in that direction while his rifle came off his shoulder. A specter rose from a thicket of willows that caused the hair to rise on the back of his neck.

Standing not twenty yards before him was an enormous grizzly bear. The bear rose on its hind feet searching for him with weak eyes while its nose sniffed the air. The moonlight glinted off the bear's fur like it was coated in metal. Each strand of thick hair stood glistening and rigid and solid white.

Riley froze. The wind from the canyon brought the pungent odor of the bear to his nose, and he thanked God he was downwind of the bear. With luck he could slip back to safety. He silently slid his left foot back behind him as he eased his Winchester back alongside his foot to steady himself on the icy creek.

A numbing shock jarred his left leg, followed by a lancinating bolt of pain running from his ankle up to his thigh. He cried out involuntarily and tried to run, but his foot was caught. The bear swung to face him directly. Its upper lip curled back in a low rumble.

Riley looked down at his leg. A large metal bear trap pinned his ankle and the butt of his Winchester in its tooth vise. He was caught by a trap intended for this animal, and his rifle was captive as well. But for the wooden stock, now splintered and cracked by the force of the powerful springs, his leg would have been crushed like the rifle. The width of the rifle butt protected his leg and bore the brunt of the trap. He and his now useless rifle were trapped.

The feckless wind chose this moment to swirl around, carrying Riley's scent to the animal. The bear roared in rage and charged.

Riley drew his pistol and fired at the charging animal. His

bullets had no effect, seeming to glance off the animal's strange coat. None of the five shots even drew blood. Riley whipped out his bowie knife and prepared to die fighting.

Instantly, the she-wolf bounded between the bear and the trapped man. Circling, snarling, and snapping at the bear's flanks, the wolf turned the bear's attack. Agile despite its size, the grizzly spun after this new annoyance. Its massive jaws snapped at the wolf's back, but she had dodged away.

Riley's three companions raced to the sound of the battle. Nathan fired his Winchester at the grizzly bear with little effect. Doc took one look at the enraged giant and ran babbling back to the camp. Only Many Hats mounted a successful defense. Wielding a stout spear in both hands he repeatedly stabbed at the animal with the thick metal point. The spearpoint glanced off the grizzly's hide, but then, with the right angle it drove home under the bear's apparent armor. Blood splattered in the air only to freeze into black droplets as the crazed bear whirled and attacked the wolf and the native. Many Hats would ground the butt of his heavy spear whenever the grizzly sought to rush the trapped Riley. The heavy shaft fended off each attack.

For what seemed an eternity, the men, the wolf, and the giant bear battled in the confines of the canyon just as their primordial ancestors had thousands of years before.

Then an explosion ripped apart the night, and the bear staggered to its knees, mortally wounded. Its hind claws gouged deep furrows in the creek's frozen surface before it emitted a sigh and died.

The dazed fighters turned behind them, where Doc Hennison lay on his back surrounded by a dense cloud of powder smoke. The heavy Sharps rifle lay tightly clutched in his one hand.

"God, that thing kicks like a mule!" he groaned. "It kills at both ends. I think it dislocated my shoulder, my only shoulder at that."

Many Hats approached the still grizzly and prodded it with his spear. "Ice bear," he stated. "Very bad."

"Ice bear?" Riley looked at the downed monster. "I thought grizzlies denned up for the winter. Damn, I never expected to see one tonight."

The native explained. "When water floods the grizzly's den, this drives him out in the winter." He pointed to the frozen ice encasing the animal's fur. "The ice covers his fur and makes it hard. Bullets bounce off and do no harm. The bear is hungry and angry that his sleep is interrupted. The ice bear is very, very dangerous. They kill many of my people."

"He nearly killed me," Riley replied. He dropped to one knee and struggled with the metal trap. "And if I ever find the fool who set this bear trap, I'll cut his ears off. The damned thing liked to break my leg. Help me get it unsprung."

Nathan squatted on his heels and studied the trap. The iron bands sported inch-thick metal teeth and ended in a thick chain that encircled a log the size of his waist. The lad searched around in the brush for jackscrews used to screw open the powerful springs.

"I don't see the jackscrews around, Jim, so we'll have to pry it apart. It's going to hurt."

"Go ahead." Riley gritted his teeth for the impending ordeal.

All three men pried, prodded, and jacked at the closed bands with poles cut from the banks. Several times the wooden levers snapped as Nathan threw his entire weight on them, but the trap never budged. After an hour all four men were sweating in the subzero weather, three of them from their exertions and Riley from the pain of twisting his injured leg.

Hennison flopped onto his back, exhausted, and mopped

the sweat steaming from his head. His lumberjack hat lay trampled in the snow around the trap. "It's no use," he groaned. "We can't open the damned thing. We're going to have to cut his leg off to free him."

Hastily, Riley reloaded his pistol, although a few cartridges spilled from his cold-numbed fingers to vanish in the churned snow. He gripped the pistol in his hand as he stared at them. "Ain't nobody hacking my leg off. I'd rather freeze to death than hobble around on one stump. I seen too many men end up that way."

"It's the only way. Listen to me," Hennison pleaded. "You'll freeze if we don't free you."

"Go to hell, you bloody butcher. All you know is lopping off limbs and brewing yer poison. Didn't you git yer fill of that in the war?" Riley pointed his pistol at Doc. "I'll shoot the first man who comes at me with an ax. If you can't help, then leave me be. I'd rather freeze or put a bullet in my brain."

"Easy, Jim," Nathan soothed his frightened friend. "No one's going to cut your leg off." He carefully approached his friend and examined the swollen ankle. "Nothing looks broken. But we've got to protect it from frostbite while we figure out a way to free you up. Many Hats, get some blankets and wrap them around his leg. Doc, fetch a cup of hot tea. We've got to keep him warm."

Many Hats kneeled beside the trapped man. His eyes narrowed as he thought. "There is a trapper's cabin up the river. About ten miles, I think. He is married to a woman from Eagle. She is related to my wife's brother."

"Does he trap bear?" Riley snarled.

"No, only beaver, lynx, and marten. He had no such traps when I stopped there this fall."

Nathan looked crestfallen. "We need those damned jackscrews. This whole rig is too heavy to drag in the sled. Look at the way they drove a staple into this log to fix the chain. We can't move it to the cabin."

Many Hats agreed. "No, it is too heavy. But he does have hacksaws. You could cut the trap."

Nathan understood immediately what the native was saying. Only the racing team had the stamina left to make the journey, and Many Hats and Hennison would be needed to keep Riley from freezing—and it was now colder than fifty below zero.

"Go ahead and say it, Many Hats," Nathan said slowly. "Say what's on your mind."

The old Athabascan looked directly into Nathan's eyes and his voice lowered as if he spoke a death sentence. "There is no other way, Son of the Winter Wolf. To get there the fastest, you must travel the river tonight . . . alone. . . ."

TWENTY-ONE

With scarcely a look back at the glow of the fire, Nathan whistled to his team. The she-wolf sprang forward, and the other dogs lunged to their feet and strained in their traces. The sled lurched onto the broad sheet of the Yukon and sped away. In minutes, the light from the camp was snuffed out, and only the moonlit landscape stretched before them.

Nathan knew he ran along a knife's thin edge as he pushed on. To proceed with all due care meant that Riley would be dead before he returned with the hacksaw needed to free him, but to rush headlong into disaster meant his death as well. He had to find that narrow line, the line that allowed him maximum speed safe from deadly blunders. Just what that pace was he could only guess.

How far was the cabin? Ten miles more or less, Many Hats had said. That might take two hours if the going was rough. Silently Nathan prayed the trapper was not away, tending some distant trapline . . . and carrying his saw with him. The wolf sensed his urgency and led the tired dogs at a blistering pace.

"Hike, girl! Hike!" Nathan called to the wolf, knowing full well that her pressure alone kept the team racing at this pace.

An hour passed like a few minutes while he clutched the sled and scanned ahead at the mesmerizing ice until his eyes burned like fire. Once, twice, a third time in that space of time his eyes caught a telltale glint of open water just seconds before the team hit it, and each time he managed to swerve so the trap was avoided. But he was beginning to tire, and he knew it.

Now his worn-down senses began to play tricks on him. He swerved to miss an overflow that wasn't there, causing his sled to skitter across the ice and flip on its side. He flew into the air to strike the hard ice with the side of his head as the sled slewed about on its side. Only his iron grip on the handle kept the sled from leaving him marooned on this frozen sea. With his head spinning, Nathan righted the sled and started again.

Another half hour passed with still no sign of the trapper's cabin. A terrible doubt now assailed the lad. Could Many Hats have been mistaken? But there was no turning back now. He whistled the sled onward.

Ahead lay a patch of snow covering the ice on the river. To its left a black molten swirl signaled a recently frozen spot of overflow, while jagged log sweepers jutted from the ice on the right like a battalion of Swiss pikemen. Nathan chose the snow-covered center.

Too late he realized his mistake. The snow had blown across a thin crust masking the center of the overflow. The massive weight of the ice had forced water up through cracks in the ice to layer the frozen surface with several feet of frigid water. Only a thin skin had frozen over this recent event, but wind had blown snow over this crust to set a well-concealed trap.

The wolf jumped sideways as if she'd been scalded. The dogs followed her alarm, but Nathan and the sled plunged headlong into the icy water. Fortunately, the momentum carried him through the water, yet he emerged soaked to the skin. He rolled into the powdery snow to blot what water remained. His team, frightened and wet as well, ran on with the over-turned sled slewing behind them before slowing to a stop somewhere downriver.

"Damn, damn, damn," Nathan swore to no one but himself

as he lurched ashore. "Big mistake. Got to start a fire, or I'm finished."

Even before he reached the bank, he felt the cold robbing him of his strength. With wooden legs he tottered into a hollow to heap kindling together. His mittens had already turned into rigid blocks of ice, and his pants legs dragged against his skin, resisting all attempts to hurry.

He beat at the ice soldered to the front of his parka. The caribou pelt struggled to hold his meager warmth within the hollow core of its hairs, but the freezing water had seeped through the neck opening and under the lower edge to soak his clothing beneath. His precious matches were in his front pocket, wrapped in oilskin, but the frozen cloth prevented his reaching them.

Nathan ripped off his useless mittens and grasped his knife to cut through the obstructing fabric. The frigid handle burned his fingers like fire, causing his hand to drop the weapon. It was a race against time, and he was losing it. More precious seconds passed as he donned his cumbersome mitten again, searched for his knife in the snow, and cut away the frozen fabric that covered his only hope of survival, his matches.

His fingers stiffened and lost feeling as he fumbled for his matches. The first matchstick broke in two. Three others slipped from his fingers to vanish in the powdery snow. By now his fingers refused to obey his mind's commands. His fifth match fell from numb fingers as he tried to strike it on the box. A instant later the box tumbled to the ground. His hands now were useless. In despair, he realized he was freezing to death, unable to start the fire that would save him.

Despondent, Nathan sank onto his haunches to await the inevitable. The intense shivering that rocked his body now stopped. The burning cold bored deeper into his body until its intense bite raked his nerves to the point of exhaustion, forcing them to give way to a diffuse throb that spread over his body like molten metal. Then the pain receded to be replaced by a pleasant warmth. Nathan felt his body giving in, his drive fading as the cold robbed him of his will to live.

A vague regret now filled his thoughts. He would die here alone in the winter's blackness, never to be found, he realized. The wolves and ravens would scatter his bones. His friend Jim Riley would die also, freezing within the iron grip of the bear trap as Nathan was freezing on this lonely cutbank. They had traveled thousands of miles together, fought and killed to get here—only so they could freeze to death.

So this was his fate. What irony. All their hardships and struggles just for this. It was hardly fair. He'd scarcely gotten out of the orphanage, and now his life was ended.

His mind drifted back to his childhood in the orphanage and the dreams he'd formed while working in the kitchen. Even a cook's helper could dream. The sunlight streaming through that back pantry kitchen carried the promise of adventures and riches, love and triumphs to the dreamy youth. With no past he was free to invent his own—and his future. He was the lost son of a Spanish grandee, the brother of a pirate waiting to be rescued from the cloying but kindly grip of the Sisters of Charity. One day they would batter down the back door or swing through the sunlit window to rescue him. Then the letter from his long-dead mother had come, and with it her legacy of hate that set him on this twisted path to reach the darkness and cold of the Yukon River. Nothing had come true as expected.

He listened to his dog team barking somewhere in the night beyond his vision, and looked up to the heavens. Mocking him in the final irony were the Northern Lights, shimmering and roiling across their inky backdrop with unbounded energy. He could almost reach up and touch the coiling curtain, it seemed so close. The bands of light carried gradations of blue, green, and pink across the night's canopy, and Nathan admitted that no head of state had ever received such regal last rites.

He thought back on his short life, on the woman he'd loved and who had sacrificed her life to bear his son, on his friends, Riley and Hennison, and on his father, Wyatt Earp. Really, he'd been lucky, Nathan realized. He met a father he had never imagined existed, one he could be proud of. And, like Wyatt, he had a son of his own to carry on his line.

Still, he wanted to see that son. All he could remember was a bloody newborn, crying and shivering in the hands of Doc Hennison. The boy would be almost two now.

Nathan made one last effort to move his limbs, but they refused to cooperate. He returned his gaze to the Northern Lights. Their dance soothed his spirit. Wei-Li hated the Northern Lights. They always frightened her. She held them to be evil spirits, dead spirits forced to wander far from home and loved ones. Strange, he thought, how a woman so strong and tough-minded could be afraid of these celestial fireworks. It was their unknown origin that alarmed her.

Perhaps Wei-Li was right. Maybe they were restless souls. Would he become one of them, wandering throughout the night? he wondered. And what of Jim Riley? Would he become a light as well?

The wind swirled the snow at his feet, seeming to sing to him—or was it laughing, he wondered. He thought he heard Wei-Li's voice. He listened again. It was her voice—singing to him. The frozen corners of his mouth worked into a stilted smile. Her song warmed him even more. He was quite comfortable now, contented to relax in the shadows, to watch the light display, and to listen to Wei-Li's singing. She was waiting for him somewhere out in the darkness, somewhere out there in the warmth, waiting to embrace him, and rest her raven black hair on his shoulder. He raised his head and looked in the direction of her singing. She was out there he knew. He could feel her.

He smiled as he saw her coming for him. She was carrying a light. It flickered through the blue-blackness just ahead where the spruce lined the river bend. He blinked. Why would a spirit need a light? The idea of a night-blind ghost amused him. Still, the light persisted like a yellow pinprick in the velvety fabric that blanketed this world. He shook his head to clear his sluggish mind. *There was a light ahead.* Then the realization struck home.

Just ahead was the trapper's cabin.

TWENTY-TWO

Marta awoke with a start. She had been dreaming, she realized, about a young man with eyes like pale gray water. His eyes pierced her very soul, and he was looking directly into her heart. He was lying by a frozen river. . . . She could feel the arctic cold sapping his strength as if it were happening to her. She shivered, raised her head, and looked about. It was an hour before sunrise.

She rolled on her side and savored the warmth of the caribou robes, but the gray eyes came back to haunt her. She sat upright and watched the birth of another day.

Never had Marta known a country to change so quickly. Valdez had been a place of freezing drizzle, ice-dripped, black slate canyons hemmed in by silent glaciers and white-capped mountains with always the gray waters of the sound at one's back. But here beyond Thompson Pass another world existed, one of clear, eye-burning blue skies, painfully contrasting with white-tipped, knife-edged mountains and vast rolling basins many times the size of Panama. Thousands of trees, black spruce and winter-bare birch, filled these valleys, bristling in close-packed arrays like battalions of spearmen. The land extended forever.

It was almost as if the Chugach Mountains purposefully conspired to hide the Interior from prying eyes. Whereas

Valdez had been more green, more soft, this side of the land was white and brown and hard.

The sun ignited the sky into a pale pink behind the powder blue Wrangell Mountains until orange bled into the pink, and a fiery line rimmed the crags, blazing and shimmering like the rivers of molten lava she'd seen spill from volcanoes in her own land. She crossed her legs and watched the light emerge. Another day of hard traveling lay ahead, yet she found herself looking forward to the trek. Each mile they passed brought her closer to the precious rifles as well as new wonders to see in this wild land.

Marta rose from her bed and walked to the campfire, where the Indian guide was boiling coffee, and accepted a cup from him. The native regarded her with mild curiosity before turning back to his chores. He recognized her as being unlike the other whites he'd seen. Her accent and her manner held her out as different.

She sipped the scalding brew and studied the route ahead, shaking her head in disbelief. How had Dickinson been so wrong about this trip? It was as if he were blind. The mules would scarcely have lasted a week in this country, and their presence would have attracted the ever-prowling wolves that howled in the night and watched them with glowing eyes from the distant thickets and clumps of spruce.

Fortunately, the spy had recognized his errors at once. After clearing Thompson Pass, the three had pressed on foot past the Tonsina River to a trading post at the junction of the Klutina River with the Copper. They had emerged from the corkscrew mountain trail into a vast plain of rolling benches and thick forest that carpeted the floodplain of the mighty Copper River. To the shock of all, the Interior of Alaska was locked in winter. Boundless drifts of white snow, scarcely speckled with the dark green shoots of spruce trees, blanketed the benches.

At the post, Dickinson hired this native from the Ahtnas and two dog teams. Outfitted with caribou leggings, parkas, and bearskin mitts, the sergeant, spy, and Marta looked like natives themselves, a fact they hoped would aid their endeavor. The bemused trader pocketed the gold coin Dickinson handed him and took their unsuitable Valdez clothing and mules in trade. He remarked he could sell it all to those stampeders returning from the Forty Mile sick, broken, and wanting nothing more than to leave the land that had killed their hopes and so many of their friends. The trader was full of useful information, so Dickinson had spent a day pumping him for news.

Best news of all was that no one matching Beaufort's description had passed ahead of them. The trader assured them that no other route past his trading post was remotely practicable at this time of year. When Sergeant Sloan reminded him that a Lieutenant Schwatka had poled an expedition up the Copper a few years ago to explore the Interior, the trader pointed out that Schwatka and his men had nearly starved in the summer. This was winter. Besides, the man pointed to the frozen Copper River behind him. Nothing would have passed and escaped notice by him or the Ahtnas.

Dickinson shambled over to Marta's side and sat on a sack of flour. Their food for the ensuing weeks would be bacon and sourdough supplemented with whatever game they could catch. The Ahtna guide wryly suggested they get ready for a constant diet of rangy snowshoe hare.

Dickinson sipped his own coffee distastefully. "My apologies for this muck they foist off as coffee, my dear. It cannot compare with the fine roast you have in Colombia."

"Panama," she corrected him.

"Ah, yes, of course. Panama. I suppose you must find this food a bit spartan."

She grinned deviously. "My revolutionary army has no fancy uniforms. We fight with machetes and wear only the rags on our backs. Do you think we sit around in great houses and plan campaigns like Napoleon with coffee and cakes served on silver plates?"

"No?"

"No." She shook her head, and the ebony ringlets swirled around her face. "No, señor. We eat raw monkey and drink from muddy streams that carry yellow fever."

"Well," Dickinson sniffed. "I suspect you'll be right at home gnawing on a frozen hare, then." He turned to leave but her arm on his sleeve stopped him.

"Forgive me, Dickinson. I have a sharp tongue. I forget that your life is in as much danger as mine; that whatever hardships we face, both of us suffer the same. And for that I thank you for my Panama. It is just that all this is a great game to you where to me it is my life."

Dickinson smiled. "I try not to be too serious. Foreign intrigue can be rather boorish if you let it, what with all the diplomatic claptrap and all. But please believe me when I tell you that besting Sir Aubrey means a great deal to me, a very great deal."

"I take that to be an explanation of your flippant regard for this serious venture."

"The damned closest thing you'll get from me," he said. He looked at the mountains to their side and wrinkled his forehead. "We've been lucky so far."

"Do you call it luck to be reduced to three, to have your supplies tumble into the valley, and to be forced to send your mules back to the fort? I'd call it a disaster," she snapped.

"So far we're ahead of Beaufort if that fellow back at the trading post is to be believed. Hopefully, he bought our little charade and thinks I'm smashed to ruins at the bottom of Thompson Pass. But we can't count on that." He withdrew a piece of bannock bread from his pocket and turned the now frozen wad of grease-wrapped sourdough over in his hand to inspect it before throwing it away. A raven appeared from nowhere to snatch the cast-off morsel and fly away.

"No," he persisted. "Beaufort will be coming, but we've got the jump on him this time. One, two, maybe even three days at best, I'd wager. No time for him to set another ambush. We'll have to look over our shoulders, though. Yet that is the best I could hope for. It means we can still get to Dawson before that bastard, and that means the weapons are still within our grasp."

Her puzzled look caused him to stop.

"Don't you see," he resumed. "Even if Beaufort has sniffed out our little plan, he has no way of notifying the Mounties. There's no telegraph line from here to Dawson. According to Sloan, the only lines run along the Yukon River from Circle City and Eagle to the Canadian side, and those are mostly unreliable and far out of Beaufort's way. Beaufort would never opt to use them. No, to warn the constabulary he has to pass us. His other option is to overtake us and kill us on the trail. We must press onward as fast as we can."

Sergeant Sloan ambled over with two plates of bacon and sourdough bread in his hands. For all the hardship and danger, he was enjoying himself. Out here he was free of the mind-numbing boredom of Fort Liscum with its schedules and endless sick lists. Here, the air was fresh and clean, far different from that of Valdez, which the sergeant knew all too well would become a crucible of pestilence with the onset of winter. The fort and its town drew sick and diseased miners from along the Copper River like a magnet drew iron. The soldier reckoned by now the place would be filled with men coughing their lungs out with pneumonia and tuberculosis or lying in their own filth as dysentery drained their body's fluids. Out here, he might freeze, or lose a few toes, or stop a bullet, but he far preferred those options over what awaited back in town.

"A fine, lovely day it is," he remarked as a trace of his Old

Country heritage crept into his speech. "What would your orders be for today, General?"

Sloan had taken to calling Dickinson by grandiose titles as a sarcastic form of compliment. The spy, on the other hand, refused to rise to the bait now that he'd gathered the man's game. Instead, he responded by supplying himself with even greater appellations.

"Please, Sergeant, call me 'Your Highness' today. I'm feeling a bit regal."

Sloan guffawed, but Marta frowned.

"And what will this lady be," the agent continued, "after she has freed her country? A countess, perhaps? Or maybe a princess?"

He paused to stuff the cold, waxy bacon into his mouth and munch thoughtfully on it while he studied Marta. Clearly she was not amused by his suggestion, for she rose with her plate and walked over to the fire.

The Ahtna watched her coming, secretly hoping she would act like a woman for once and clean the dishes. But he made no suggestion and continued doing the woman's work while she passed without offering to help with the chores. Sloan had told him how she had killed the trooper back in the pass, so he avoided her as much as possible. Her action left no doubt in his mind that a forest demon had taken over her body. He'd heard of this happening once to a woman in the Taral Village near the narrows of the river, where the powerful tyone charged duty on all those who passed that place the whites called Woods Canyon. Chief Nicolai, the supreme leader of all the Copper River tribes, had told him the story himself, so it must be true. That woman had stumbled on the secret place where the men brought the bears they had killed. That place was taboo to females lest the bears' *inua* infect them. But this woman was noted for her curiosity. This bear's spirit was still strong in the animal's body, and he called to the woman as she passed. Foolishly, the woman had touched the bear's heart, and his spirit leapt into her body. Afterward she growled at all the men and killed her husband one night with his own spear. It took all the efforts of the shaman and the men to drive her off a high bluff into the river. She vanished screaming into a whirlpool. Even now none of the men would set their fish traps in that place, fearful the bear-woman would rise from the water and drag them to join her in her watery grave.

This strange woman from the far South was not possessed by the spirit of the bear, he was sure of that much. But she did carry a large knife and pistols and walked with the grace of a lynx. The three-stripe soldier Sloan mentioned she was called El Tigre after an animal much larger than a lynx, a great cat that killed men in her forests. That fit, the man reasoned. Her *inua* was much too powerful to be a lynx. He would be glad when this journey was finished. El Tigre made him uneasy. One thing he noticed that worried him greatly: even though her land was said to be warm, she was growing comfortable here in the Great Land and might decide to stay. The Ahtna shivered at the thought. The land already had enough wild spirits and crazy women.

★ ★ TWENTY-THREE ★ ★

"Well, I'll be goddamned!" Lem Sutter swore as he stared at the ice-coated heap blocking his doorway. The weatherworn trapper ducked his head to inspect the obstacle, squinting his narrow-set eyes and wiping the last of his supper of lynx guts from his fissured and stained fingers across his wool shirt.

Enfolded in ice-hardened layers of once wet clothing, the figure bore little resemblance to anything but an irregular pile of ice and snow. He bent close to the huddled figure and studied it for signs of life. Finding no evidence of breath coming from the blue-tinged lips or the tightly closed eyelids covered with hoarfrost, he stepped back and shook his head.

"Poor bastard, you almost made it," Lem muttered. "Got jus' to my door afore you froze solid as a rock. Piss poor luck to have that happen." He sighed, taking this rare opportunity in his humdrum existence of running a daily trapline to wax philosophical on the inequities of life in general and in the Arctic in particular. "Still, you musta been dumb as a stump to be traveling alone in this hard cold. A man by hisself ain't got no chance at all if he falls in. One minute you're warm and cocky, and the next minute you're froze solid as last week's moose turds."

The superstitious taint of Sutter's Welsh blood cautioned him to respect the dead lest they return to haunt him. He tipped his trapper's hat to the frozen body and gently proceeded to step around the dead man.

"Pardon me," he said, "but I gotta take a piss real bad. That's where I was headed when I opened my door and stumbled over you, mister. You near scared a year's growth out of me, I'll tell you that. Near pissed my pants when I saw you. Thought you was a grizzly or something. So if you'll excuse me, I'll be about my business real quick like, and then I'll be back to see if you got anything worth transferring to my pockets before I try to carve a grave for you outta this hardscrabble frozen dirt."

Sutter thrust his hand into his pants like a little boy caught with a full bladder and no tree in sight, torn between that urge and his attraction to the closest thing to a human he'd seen in a painfully long time.

"I'm sure sorry you ain't alive, mister. I haven't had a living soul to talk to since my squaw left me and went back to her people, and that's been over four months, I reckon. And it's damned lonely. I've taken to talking to my dogs, my coffeepot, even my hand ax, but it ain't no good. A man needs the comfort of another human voice."

"I ain't dead. . . ."

The voice was scarcely a whisper, and a rasping, unnatural one at that. It seemed to come from nowhere in particular, as the ice-coated lips never moved. Sutter jumped back three feet. He stood transfixed, with eyes wide as saucers and mouth agape. Almost a minute passed before his senses returned.

"You're alive?"

The encased head moved in a barely discernible nod. "I won't be for long if you leave me on your doorstep," the rasp continued, exhibiting the slightest tinge of exasperation.

That galvanized Sutter into action. He leapt forward to drag the body inside while his boot kicked the door shut. Hauling the figure before his cast-iron stove, Sutter stoked the furnace until its vents puffed noisily and the iron glowed cherry red. As the heat softened each stiffened layer of encrusted clothing, Sutter peeled it off like a dutiful squire removing armor plate from his knight, until his charge sat naked before the Yukon stove. Then Sutter rubbed the clammy skin with his roughened hands until a reddish color replaced the deadly blue pallor.

The trapper continued his vigorous ministrations until his charge began to shiver. So great was Sutter's fear of losing this other conversationalist that he forgot to talk during this treatment. Only when the shivering turned to severe tremors did Lem Sutter recall his own tongue.

"By golly, you're going to make it. Here, drink some of this hot tea. It'll warm your insides for sure while the stove toasts your hide." Sutter slopped a mugful of his homemade brew into a tin cup and poured a dose between the quivering lips of his patient. Half spilled down the man's front.

Nathan half choked on the blistering liquid, spitting it out as he sputtered. "For Christ's sake. I'm frozen. I don't need to be scalded as well!"

"Oh, beautiful!" Lem said. He stepped back, dropping the tin cup to the dirt floor, where it went spinning under his spruce frame bed. He clasped his hands together in joy. "Them's the first words I've heard in many months," he sighed. "You don't know how good they sound."

By now Nathan was gaining control of his quaking. He lifted a trembling hand to wipe the melting frost from his face. "I need your help," he chattered through clattering teeth. "I need it fast."

"And you'll git it, mister. You just keep on talking."

"No, no! Not for me. My friend . . ."

"You got friends out there? There are more of you?" Sutter could hardly contain his exultation. More people to listen to.

247

Nathan bobbed his head in spite of the pain it caused. "He's caught in a bear trap back down the river."

Lem straightened up and winced. "He's a dead man, then. But it ain't one of my traps. I don't trap grizzly. The fur's too stiff to my taste."

"We need to spring him free before he freezes to death," Nathan pleaded. "Please, mister, he's my friend."

Lem sighed. "I ain't got no jackscrews big enough to spring a grizzly trap. Best hack his leg off."

"He won't let us do that! Don't you have a hacksaw or something we can use to cut the trap?"

Sutter scratched his neck as he thought. "We'd be sawing for a month of Sundays. But I do have a splitting maul and a set of iron wedges. If he can stand the jarring on his leg, maybe we can wedge the jaws open enough to slip his leg free. Goddamn that will hurt—"

"He can take it," Nathan interrupted. "Get your wedges."

"But you're not fit to travel," Sutter protested. This sounded like a fool's errand, trying to spring a trapped man from a stout grizzly trap at fifty below zero. They would have to run back down the frozen river in the dark, and this lad might freeze up again, this time permanently. Then the speech-starved trapper would have no one to listen to. That thought drove him to despair.

"No," he said firmly. "I won't take you back. You're too sick to travel. You can't save your partner, best just face it. Nothing you can say or do would cause me to risk your life on this fool-ishness."

Sutter turned away to feed his stove, but the sound of ice chips clattering to his dirt floor reached his ear. Then he heard a ripping noise as frozen fabric and fur were forced to open their stiffened layers. Lem looked back over his shoulder at his thawing visitor just in time to see something shoved into his face.

The Wolf's Cub

The cold barrel of a pistol poked rudely up his right nostril. While Nathan's teeth still chattered, the hand holding the gun under Sutter's nose was rock steady. Nathan's eyes were harder and colder than anything inside the cabin.

"Care to hear what Mr. Colt has to say about that?" Nathan growled. "You won't like it."

Lem Sutter nodded his head carefully. "We'd best get packing. . . ."

Three hours later Lem Sutter's cabin was crowded with the shivering bodies of Nathan, Riley, Hennison, and Many Hats—more people than the trapper had seen since winter freeze-up of the river. The twelve-by-ten-foot chinked log cabin with its low ceiling forced the taller lad and Hennison to move about in a permanent stoop, and the entire lodging took on the semblance of a pickle barrel with the men sidestepping and twisting past the glowing Yukon stove and ducking its angled tube of hot galvanized stovepipe. Unfortunately for Lem, though, none of the men was talking much. From the looks on their faces none seemed ready to enter a civilized discourse, so the trapper held his tongue, hoping for someone to speak. He didn't have long to wait.

Hennison bent over Riley and flicked his fingers against the cold-hardened toes of Riley's left foot as one would do to test the ring of a fine wine goblet. The fingers striking the frozen flesh made the same sound as if they had snapped across a block of wood. Doc screwed up his face in a scowl. "Don't sound good," he said.

"So it don't sound like fancy crystal, Doc," Riley muttered between pulls on the limited reserves of Doctor Hennison's Magic Elixir. Many Hats was helping him with the bottle.

"Crystal!" Doc exclaimed incredulously. "Your last three toes sound like hard-frozen wood. They'll have to come off."

"Hell no! You ain't sawing no parts off me. You jus' got an

itching to carve on someone, that's all. I seen it festering inside you like a sore, Doc. Poisoning half of Alaska with yer rotgut ain't enough for you, is it? You sawbones ain't satisfied unless yer slicing something off of a man."

Hennison turned to Nathan in exasperation. "Nat, talk some sense into this lunkheaded goat, will you? He's damned lucky no bones are broken. That trap cracked the stock of his rifle, but not his leg. But his toes are frostbitten solid."

Riley aimed the bottle at Nathan before the lad could open his mouth. "Don't say nothin', Nat, my boy. My toes is my own property, so you've got no say in this matter."

"If gangrene sets in," Hennison continued, "he'll lose more than his toes."

"Screw you, Dr. Hennison. You can't whittle on my toes, froze or thawed. I'm taking all ten of them to the grave with me." The elixir was having its effect, and the gunman punctuated his statement by sending a glob of spittle sailing into the hot side of the stove. He grinned in satisfaction as the saliva crackled and vanished in a cloud of steam. "So there. What good's a man without all his . . . his appendages." He grinned wider on remembering that word from his reading. "Many Hats'll back me up, eh?"

But the Indian shook his head. He dropped to the dirt floor and pulled the mukluk from his own left foot. Riley started. Two smooth nubs projected where the man's great and second toes should have been. Many Hats removed his right boot with an equal flourish to reveal another three missing toes. While Riley and the others gaped at his deformity, the old man grabbed the bottle and took a long swallow.

"By God, Hats, yer down to only five!" Riley exclaimed. He wiped his hand over his sweating face in amazement.

Many Hats waggled his finger sagely at the gunfighter. "Toes, fingers, you can do without. Only one finger really matters." He jerked down the front of his caribou leggings to reveal that the inside of his crotch was well insulated by thick wads of downy white rabbit fur sewn carefully inside. "My woman takes good care of that finger for me," he said. "She would miss it as much as me if it froze. Your toes are nothing. Better look after what lives between your legs than worry about what stinks up the inside of your mukluks."

"If he'd caught his privates in that damned trap instead of his leg, we wouldn't have had to work so hard driving those wedges," Doc griped. "He could have easily slipped free without our help."

The thought sobered Riley somewhat, but he remained adamant. "Yer still not gitting no practice on my toes, Doc. That's final."

Many Hats shrugged. "No hurry. In two, three moons, they will fall off."

The weather conspired with the condition of Riley's leg to test Many Hats' prediction. The heavy cold that brought the temperatures to fifty below settled into the lowland lining the Yukon River like water filling a gorge. The entire valley that the river had carved from the rock was held prisoner within its killing grip. At night, the mercury thermometer that Doc carried to aid brewing his elixir dropped to seventy below zero.

Nothing moved along the riverbed, neither caribou nor moose. Even the hardy snowshoe hares kept burrowed in the snow, feeding on willow shoots within easy reach, while their natural enemy, the lynx, hunkered down to ignore his hunger pangs. Only the ravens, black as coal in the misty ice fog, danced about immune to the cold, warbling and cawing in delight whenever they spotted a fresh winter kill to feast upon. The black birds ruled the wretched day, such as it was, for the sun retreated hastily south, robbing minutes of precious daylight from each meager day until little more than a handful of hours filled the daylight. Instead, a lengthy twilight heralded a tepid sun that took forever to rise above the mountain rim in its abbreviated flight along the horizon. Never rising beyond that low vista, the sun would disappear, to be followed by a surreal twilight that filled the west with pastel shades of rose and pale purple. In fact, the sun served more as a nuisance since it offered up little warmth and merely turned the ice fog into a luminous shroud of gold that obscured all detail and made travel all the more hazardous.

While the ravens ruled the shrinking day, the night belonged to the wolves. Unseen, they announced their presence with long, chilling duets that filled the darkness. The dense air intensified and carried their howls until any call sounded just outside the cabin. Nathan's she-wolf paid little attention to these calls but the discreet swiveling of her tufted ears showed she followed every wail. In spite of the cold she refused to enter the trapper's cabin, choosing to burrow beneath the snow in a tight ball with her bushy tail wrapped across her muzzle. The two dog teams did likewise, uncoiling only when Nathan or Many Hats cut chunks of frozen salmon to feed them. Then the animals would shake off the layers of hoarfrost covering them, stretch, and begin the task of chewing the hard fish into pieces small enough to gulp down. The wolf refused this food, something that worried Nat. Although no one ever saw her hunt, she seemed to hold her weight.

All this time Jim Riley's left leg underwent myriad changes. Following extrication from the trap, the bruised lower leg swelled to three times its usual size. Then it turned a deep purple with bullae and blisters covering the stretched skin about the ankle and over the tops of his toes. Slowly, a reddish tinge replaced the purple hue, causing Doc Hennison to fret that blood poisoning was setting in. But Many Hats continued his treatment of padding the bulbous toes and leg with soft rabbit fur and coating the damaged skin with poultices of bark and reindeer moss. Whenever a blister would break and spill serum over the skin, the Athabascan would simply change the soaked fur and repair his cataplasm.

Nathan bridled at the delay that kept him from reaching Dawson and finding his son. To be within forty miles of the town and yet unable to look for the youngster tested his patience to the limit, but he checked his impulses, knowing it would be wrong to leave Riley before the man had time to heal. So he spent the scant daylight hours cleaning his pistol and hunting with the white wolf always at his side. In some ways he realized he was becoming more like her. On the cold, clear moonlit nights he would often leave the smoke-filled cabin to wrap himself in his caribou robe and lie in the snow beside the wolf. The two would stare at the burnished ivory disk as it floated through the night on its lazy passage across the blackness, or listen to the hiss of the Northern Lights as they snaked in bluish coils just out of arm's reach. The she-wolf's penetrating stare added to the disturbing thought that nagged increasingly at the far corners of Nathan's mind. She seemed to say: You are wild like me, with no place for you in the towns that men have built. You belong in the wilderness where the air is cold and clear and bites your lungs with its freshness, not breathing the stench of sweat, woodsmoke, and frightened men. The land has changed you, her eyes said. You no longer fit with your kind.

Nathan feared she was right. Most of all, he worried what he would do with his baby.

Hennison took the opportunity to rail about unorthodox medical practices and to repair the damage done to his wondrous elixir by his hasty escape from Circle City and the constant attacks by Riley, Many Hats, and Sutter. With the aid of his cure-all, the three men were fast becoming bosom buddies.

Sutter grumbled at first about Doc's extravagant use of the trapper's split wood to brew his potion, but a taste of the first products from the still silenced his objections. Soon he was a willing assistant, searching far from the cabin in forays for the moose nuggets and spruce cones that Doc now added to his drink. Many Hats contributed a few odds and ends from his medicine bag to the pot, and a partnership of three was formed.

By the third week every bottle that could hold anything was filled and corked with the latest version of Doctor Hennison's Wonder Elixir. The hard cold had lifted, and a warm Chinook wind from the south blew down the Yukon and scattered the veil of ice fog from the river's bed. As if on cue Riley's leg had lost its swelling and his two toes had shriveled to gnarled black talons. Tension grew in the hazy cabin as everyone sensed it was time for a decision. Nathan rehearsed arguments to convince his friend, and Doc made a special effort to appear more professional. But it was Riley who called the play.

"Well, at least we saved my leg and the other three toes," he said philosophically one morning as he attempted to twist off the mummified digits. "But these two has gone under. Best we whack 'em off and git on with it. But I'm sure gonna miss them two. We've trod many a dusty trail together."

"Why don't you save them, Jim?" Nathan added helpfully.

"Do you think I could? But won't they gits to smelling when things warm up? I knowed of a few Cheyenne who wore fingers and ears around their necks. I never got that close to them bucks for fear they'd take a hankering to add some of me to their finery. I suspect they was a bit ripe, though. I know they had a faithful following of flies that hung around them."

Nathan thought for a minute. He lifted a small medicine bottle from the table. The bottle was tightly corked and filled with elixir. "You could save your toes in this. It's got enough alcohol to preserve most anything."

Riley's eyes lighted. "Sure, Nat. I read about how the English preserved that big admiral of theirs, Nelson or something, in a cask of rum. We could store my toes for safekeeping. Then, when the time came to plant the rest of me, my toes could be included. I sort of like that idea."

"It's the dumbest thing I ever heard tell," Doc scoffed, looking up from pouring another batch of his potent brew into a string of bottles laid along the edge of Sutter's table. The trapper had proved to be an unexpectedly rich source of discarded bottles, something that reflected his years of battling loneliness on his isolated trapline.

"Dumb or not, if you want to git yer jollies whittling on my toes, I want to save them in yer snake oil. And that's my final word on the subject."

Hennison sniffed unconcernedly and returned to directing the distillate into his bottles. "Makes no never mind to me. Keep your mummified appendages for all I care. My partners and I are indisposed as it is. Besides, I don't expect you plan on paying me for my services."

"Paying you! Why, you—"

Before the epithets could fly, Nathan stepped in and soothed the two men's ruffled feelings. He thought it strange that these two who had seen so much horror in their lives could be so sensitive at times. Apparently the loss of his arm to a Union cannonball and the mountains of dead Hennison had encountered in the Civil War had not toughened him in a consistent manner. The same held true for Jim Riley. Forced to live by his wits and his pistol since he killed five men in the infamous General Massacre at Newton Station, Kansas, Riley had survived equal disasters. Apache and Comanche raids, range wars, and gunfights had filled his life since he turned eighteen. But Riley could be just as thin-skinned as Doc.

After much deliberation it was decided that each man could amputate a toe. One each, with Doc going first on the little toe to show Riley how a true professional would do it, and Riley to remove his fourth toe with the coaching of all present. Many Hats scratched his neck in mild amusement. Was it not just like these white men to make such a fuss over toes. He had removed all of his with little fanfare. Sutter, on the other hand, relished anything that led to more conversation.

With great dignity Hennison cleared the table of all his elixir but for three bottles. One would be used to sterilize the instruments, the smallest to hold the removed parts, and the third for all involved to drink as needed. The instrument, Jim's bowie knife, was rinsed with elixir as Riley laid his left leg across the table. Hennison opened the woodstove's door and thrust the blade inside. A greenish blue flame erupted along the length of the knife, accompanied by a loud pop of exploding elixir. Sutter swallowed hard and moved a few paces back from his stove.

Doc inspected the shimmering steel, turning it over slowly in his hand, and studying the greenish flame coiling along the blade like Saint Elmo's fire. "Ready," he announced with a flourish.

"Whack away," Riley replied while he snatched the drinking bottle from Sutter and took a long swallow.

"I shall."

"Don't look so gleeful," Riley cautioned, "and don't be slipping with yer drunken hand. I only plan on parting with two of my toes today."

Hennison waved the knife about in a wild flourish. "Only two?" he said in mock surprise. "Why for the same price I'll throw in a circumcision." The smoking blade dipped perilously close to the crotch of Riley's pants.

"The hell you will!" The gunman snatched his Colt from its holster.

"Easy, easy," Nathan cautioned. "Let's try to be professional about this."

"Yeah," Riley slurred, "let's be professional."

"Very well," Doc sighed. "This is all rather tiresome, but if professional is what you want, professional is what you'll get."

The bowie knife sliced down in a wide, flashing arc as Hennison's arm whipped across the gunman's exposed foot like the head of a striking rattlesnake. The other three men sucked in their breath sharply. Triumphantly, Hennison held up the knife in his solitary hand. Sutter started, and Many Hats clapped his hands together in glee.

Pinched tightly between the steel of the blade and Hennison's thumb were the withered remains of Riley's little toe. With one swoop Doc had amputated the toe and trapped the part with his thumb. He loosened his thumb to allow the wizened object to slide along the length of the blade, and then he circulated the blade with its object around like a serving dish for everyone's inspection.

"*My part* of the operation is complete, gentlemen," Doc announced grandly.

"Goddamn," Riley swore as he watched the bony stump of his former toe submerge in the blood that welled up from the freshly pared granulation tissue. "Goddamn . . ."

"Do it again, Doc," Sutter begged. "I blinked and missed the whole damned thing. Do it again, please."

Hennison laid the blade down flat on the table beside Riley's outstretched foot, taking great care not to dislodge the severed part. He stretched his hand out with fingers widespread in a grandiose gesture.

"No, no, friends," he began as if addressing a larger crowd. "Thank you, thank you, one and all. It is most gratifying for a true artist such as myself to be fully appreciated, but I cannot accept. Mr. Riley and I have an agreement. The second toe is his."

Riley looked sourly at the remaining frostbitten digit. But pride forced him to do his part. He gingerly picked up his former little toe and stuffed it down the neck of the bottle into the waiting alcohol. Next he retrieved his knife from the table and turned it over in his hand as if undecided. The heavy blade seemed to weigh a ton.

Riley turned an imploring face to Nathan, yet he was too stubborn to yield. "Tarnation, Nat, I dug many an arrowhead outta my hide and stitched up my scalp with saddle twine, but somehow this is different. Lopping off my own toes unsettles my craw."

Nathan came to his friend's aid. "Doc will be happy to finish the job, won't you, Doc?"

Hennison hung his head in false modesty. "If you say so, Nat." But he couldn't resist a final jab at Jim. "I'd feel forever responsible if Mr. Riley might slip and cut off something vital— like Mr. Hat's nose or the stovepipe."

Riley growled through his drunken fog and cursed himself for relinquishing the blade to the physician. But the damage was done.

The knife descended again and Riley's other toe went into the bottle with equal fanfare. This site bled more freely than the first, so blood seeped across the table and encircled the sample of elixir. Professional training got the better of Doc, prompting him to begin bandaging the stumps of Riley's toes. The gunman picked up the flask and turned it around slowly in his hand while he inspected the parts of his body that now floated about with a carefree indifference.

"Ain't you got no remorse?" Riley accused his toes as they drifted past his gaze.

No sooner had he uttered those words than a sharp voice penetrated the cabin walls. "This is the Mounties! You're surrounded! Throw out your weapons and come out with your hands up!"

"Christ!" Riley sobered considerably as he withdrew his bandaged foot and dove for cover.

Doc skidded to the floor a moment later, only to land on

top of Nathan, who already had his Winchester clasped in his hands. Sutter and Many Hats had not moved, but appeared rooted with their feet to the center of the room.

"This is your last chance," the deep bass voice boomed again. "You have one minute before I set fire to the cabin."

"How many are out there?" Doc gasped.

"One's too many if it's who I think it is," Sutter answered, still standing. "Is that you, Captain Steele?" he yelled.

"It is," the voice replied. "And I've been promoted to Commander."

"The Lion of the Yukon," Sutter whispered.

"Well, we outnumber you, Commander!" Hennison shouted.

"I've got Detachment E of the Yukon Field Force with me, my good man," Steele replied. His voice rolled through every moss-chinked crack in the cabin's walls.

"You're bluffing," Doc challenged.

In response a rifle bullet tore through the oiled-paper window at the back wall of the cabin, opposite from the direction of Steele's voice.

"I guess he ain't," Riley observed.

"Now come on out," Steele ordered.

A loud snarling reached their ears, followed by a yelping chorus of frightened sled dogs.

"Call off this wolf-dog," the Mountie commanded, "or I'll be forced to shoot her."

"Wait!" Nathan called back. "Wait, I'm coming out. Just don't shoot her!"

He leapt to his feet and rushed outside in his long johns. With the still working overtime, the cabin had become so steamy that Nathan had peeled down to his underwear for comfort. As the cold air hit him with the force of a fist, he staggered but managed to keep upright with his hands above his head. Blinking his eyes he stared about. The wolf was threatening a third dog team parked behind a clump of bare birch trees. Those dogs bucked and twisted in harness as the wolf circled them with her head held low to the ground. Every animal in that team knew wolves had no aversion to eating sled dogs if the fancy took them. Only the firmly set snow hook kept the skittish team from beating a hasty retreat from the menacing wolf.

"Keep your hands high," the officer cautioned as Nathan appeared.

The lad spoke a few words to the wolf, and she wagged her tail and settled back into the snow, but kept a wary eye on the proceedings. Nathan turned to the officer, who stepped out from behind a rock. Through the steam that poured from his exposed underwear, Nathan watched the man approach. A boxy, fox-fur trapper's hat sat squarely on the man's head, exposing a wide brow and broad-set blue eyes which regarded the unclothed lad with a mix of amusement and solemnity. The luxurious expanse of his mustache sported a thick covering of frost that made him appear like one of the Frost Giants of Norse legend. His look signaled a no-nonsense attitude.

With the fur hat and the unsheared beaver coat adding to the man's bulk, he could have been any square-set trapper, but the glint of his scarlet collar peeking through the wolverine trim of the parka's ruff, and the dark blue woolen trousers with their faded crimson stripe left no doubt that this man was a member of the North West Mounted Police. Surprisingly, the man's revolver was holstered under his parka. From a mile away, Nathan would have recognized the legendary Commander Sam Steele, whose firm but fair hand kept lawlessness under control in the Yukon.

"I'm not carrying a gun."

"So I can see, son. Best tell your associates to surrender before you freeze to death."

Nathan yelled to the cabin, and the door opened an instant later and Doc, Many Hats, and Sutter crowded into the opening with their hands grasping the icy air over their heads. "My friend Riley is hurt inside," Nathan added. "He can't stand."

"Is he shot?" Steele questioned.

"No, no, frostbitten toes. We just cut two off. He got caught in a bear trap downriver three weeks ago."

Steele nodded. "Nasty business, frostbite." He signaled to a thicket behind the cabin. "Come on in, Jenkins," he yelled.

The bushes moved, dumping their snow in a sudden cascade of whiteness, and another person appeared. This one carried one of the newly issued bolt-action Lee-Metford .303 caliber rifles with its smokeless powder rounds. The other Mountie jogged over to Steele's side and the two ushered the shivering Blaylock into the warmth of the cabin.

Riley looked up at the two Mounties from his position on the floor. His eyes settled on the trooper with the rifle. With his parka hood turned back he looked all of fifteen, certainly younger than Nathan. "Detachment E of the Yukon Field Force, eh?" he grumbled. "That's the oldest trick in the book. If I wasn't so befuddled from parting with my digits, I'd have never fallen for that. Where'd you git this pup from anyways? He ain't hardly old enough to shave, let alone be a Mountie. Things got so bad you resort to robbing the cradle for recruits, Commander?"

Steele glanced down at the blood-soaked bandage and smiled grimly. "Well, be thankful it worked. I'd feel bad about burning down Lem's cabin, but I'd do it if necessary."

He then proceeded to study his captives carefully, undisturbed by the awkward silence as he scrutinized the fidgeting men. He passed quickly over Many Hats and Lem Sutter but paused to inspect Nathan and Riley in detail. Finally he stepped back to where Trooper Jenkins stood at the ready with his rifle and blushing with rage. Jenkins's youthful age and the length of his weapon made him appear comical rather than threatening, but the force of Sam Steele's personality made up for whatever his aide lacked. The square-built man radiated power and authority. Looking at him, one could see how he was able to enforce the queen's laws on the thousands of stampeders that flooded Dawson. He was cut from the same bolt of cloth as the legendary Mountie who single-handedly rode into an Indian camp to arrest their warring chief.

"At ease, Jenkins," Steele ordered. "These aren't our men."

A general sigh of relief filled the cabin, but Riley cast a cautious look at Nathan. "Just who are you looking for, Commander?" the gunman asked.

"Two men who robbed the mail sled out of Dawson. Got away with ten thousand in gold. They were making a run for the American border, but we lost their trail a few miles back. I thought they might head for Lem's cabin, and when I saw your two dog teams outside, I thought I had them."

"Well," Doc spoke up, "we've been stuck in this hut for three weeks, Commander. So we couldn't be your robbers."

Steele cast a sharp look at Hennison. "Doc Hennison," he said. "No, I wouldn't peg you for having the courage to rob a Royal Mail sled." He stopped to pick up one of the bottles of elixir from the table to sniff it. He winced at what he smelled. "But I see you've not been idle, have you now? Still brewing your dreadful hooch."

"Only for medicinal purposes," Doc added defensively. "I am a physician, after all."

"God help those you treat with this poison," the Mountie snorted, "but you'd do better to remember your profession of medicine and abandon your efforts as a chemist. You were of great help during the influenza epidemic two years ago."

Hennison drew himself to his full height and ducked his head in a curt bow. "Thank you, Commander, for those most kind words. I know it must have pained you to utter them."

"You're a rascal and a rogue, Hennison, yet I must profess to a certain fondness for you." The officer then turned to look at Nathan and Riley. "These two have the look of gunmen, although no outlaw I ever saw would rush outside in his skivvies just to save his pet wolf."

Nathan smiled sheepishly.

"And," Steele continued, "Riley here was not likely to rob the mail with his foot looking like it does."

Riley started. "You remember us?" he asked in amazement.

"Jim Riley and Nathan Blaylock, I believe," the Mountie responded flatly. "Yes, I remember you two. You worked that mine on the outskirts." He paused to look intently at Nathan. "I was sorry to hear about the loss of your woman, young man. She was a very pretty Oriental girl as I recall. I was out of town when the fire happened, and you'd left by the time I got back."

His words stung Nathan more than the youth cared to show, causing him to turn away from the constable.

"A tragic loss." Hennison supplied the reply for Nathan.

"Tragic, indeed," Steele agreed.

At that moment Many Hats emitted an enormous hiccup which drew attention to his inebriated state. The Athabascan grinned sheepishly and fidgeted nervously under the scrutiny of the constable. Steele walked around the native like an admiral surveying a new ship. He removed his fur gauntlets and slapped them down onto the table.

"Selling liquor to an Indian is decidedly against the law. You all know that," he remarked.

"I didn't sell him any liquor, I gave it to him. And it's not liquor, Commander. It's medicine!" Hennison protested.

"Yes, medicine," Sutter agreed.

"Regardless, the man is drunk. That's as plain as the nose on my face," Steele countered.

"A slight side effect of the potion, I assure you, Commander. We would no more dream of giving liquor to this aborigine than we'd ply your maiden aunt with alcohol," Hennison interjected.

"My maiden aunt drank like a fish," Steele said, "and I say this man is drunk."

"Surely the law would not interfere with a doctor-patient relationship?" Hennison argued. "Mr. Many Hats is under my care for—"

Steele waved him silent. "I'll let the magistrate decide that. I'm afraid you'll have to accompany me to Dawson to stand trial. Consider yourself in my custody until this matter is resolved, Doctor."

Groans of protest rose from the others, but Steele silenced them with a hard look. "You'd do well not to provoke me, gentlemen. I also have received a bulletin from the American side about a certain dog team and sled stolen from Circle City. Your lack of cooperation would prompt me to look closely at your own animals, and I might not like what I would find if I did so. Now, Hennison has a good chance of convincing the magistrate of his case, given his silver tongue, but it's not up to me. So prepare to move. Jenkins will collect your weapons. Rest easy, they will be returned to you after we arrive in Dawson."

"Well, why do we all have to go?" Sutter asked.

"As material witnesses."

"But we got no material to speak of," Riley stammered.

"Well, your testimony will help set Doc free, then," Steele countered. "Beside, it wouldn't hurt for the doctor at the hospital to look at your foot."

Grumbling and muttering curses under their breath, the men handed over their revolvers and rifles to Jenkins and drew on their boots and parkas. Steele carefully collected all the bottles in a canvas sack—all, that is, except the bottle containing Riley's former toes. Riley slipped that one inside his parka for safekeeping. Then, bristling with the rifles like a porcupine, Jenkins led the way out the door to the waiting sleds. Many

Hats and Sutter followed while Doc and Nathan carried the protesting Riley to their sled. Commander Steele brought up the rear of the procession.

Riley was placed in Nathan's sled basket and covered with a bearskin robe. Sutter headed for Many Hats' sled, but Doc beat him into that basket, so the trapper was forced to ride the runners with the native. Jenkins, still clutching the weapons, waited for his superior to draw abreast as they headed for the Mounties' sled.

Without warning a shot rang out. Steele spun around, expecting to see a hidden pistol in the hands of his charges, but none of the other five men had one. He turned back in time to see Jenkins, arms still encumbered with rifles, pitch face forward into the snow. The young Mountie's mouth worked for a moment to form soundless words, but blood bubbled from his lungs instead to spill over the crystalline snow. Then his mouth stopped moving, and his head drooped into the drifts.

Another shot split the ear-shattering silence, and Steele staggered to one knee with blood gushing from an angry furrow above his right eyebrow. Cheers of elation rose from a snow-covered deadfall just beyond the farthest team, where a cloud of powder smoke hung motionless in the thick air. A third shot missed Steele altogether, raising a puff of snow by his knee. More eager voices followed the last shot as the assassins, sensing an easy kill, crowed again.

While the two Mounties had been caught off guard, the attack galvanized Nathan into action. Reacting more by instinct than anything else, he exploded forward in a blur of motion. Sprinting in the direction of the shots and past the fallen Jenkins, he snatched a Winchester from the dying Mountie. Dodging the hail of bullets that clipped the air around him, he rushed the breastwork of fallen spruce. Four bounds brought him to the snipers' nest.

The two bushwhackers lurched backward at this unexpected attack. Their rifles fired upward where they expected Nathan's momentum to carry him into a fatal intersection with their bullets. But the youth sprang into the air higher than the riflemen had anticipated, by kicking off on the fallen spruce log. Twisting in the air as the bullets harmlessly passed, he leveled the front sight of his own rifle on the center of the closest man. That man was furiously jacking another round into the chamber of his own rifle.

Both rifles fired as if pulled by the same finger, and the two antagonists vanished in an acrid cloud of gunsmoke. A hot slug sliced through the lapels of Nathan's parka and whined into the air to disappear. But Nathan's bullet caught the man in the throat, and he arched back in his death throes.

The second bushwhacker swiveled desperately to bring his rifle to bear. His efforts came too late. The thrust of Nathan's leap carried into the man, knocking the rifle barrel aside.

Heavier than Nathan, he hammered the butt of his rifle into the lad's side. Nathan felt two ribs crack. Worst of all, the blow caused his own rifle to fly from his grip. He fell heavily to earth. In spite of the pain in his side, Nathan scrambled to his knees just in time to look into the gaping barrel of the other man's rifle.

A twisted snarl spread across the man's face as he jacked another shell into the chamber. Something in his nature caused the man to pause for a split second, to gloat over his helpless prey. In that sliver of time another shot rent the air.

Surprise followed by puzzlement flooded over the man's face as he turned his gaze from his intended victim to the gaping hole in the front of his chest and to the blood stain that rapidly spread across the front of his parka. His confused look hardened into a death mask, and he sat back on his heels before crumpling onto his side in the broken branches of the downed tree.

Nathan rose slowly to his feet and looked past the corpse to see Commander Steele on one knee with his heavy Webley revolver clamped in both hands and braced against his leg. The officer had fired from a kneeling position, his bullet hitting true from a good fifty yards away.

Cautiously, Sam Steele got to his feet while he kept his pistol trained on the two fallen bodies. With blood freezing in his gray hair and congealing in streaks down the right side of his face, he advanced to Nathan's side.

Behind the men lay their team and sled. Steele satisfied himself that his attackers were dead before he walked to the sled, deliberately turning his back on Nathan, who clutched his rescued repeating rifle. Steele jerked back the sled blanket to reveal a wooden box with reinforced iron straps. Burned into the side of the box was HRMS ROYAL MAIL.

Without a word, Steele sprinted back to the side of his fallen fellow Mountie. But Trooper Jenkins was dead; his superior's fingers found no pulse at his neck. The officer gently rolled the body onto its back, closed the unseeing eyes, and arranged the man's tunic as if readying the body for parade inspection. Then he rose and drew himself to his full height. All this while his other unarmed charges stood with opened mouths at the suddenness of the attack and the equally rapid and deadly response by Nathan and Commander Steele—all except Jim Riley, who had managed to roll out of his sled and crawl on his hands and knees to Jenkins's side and retrieve his rifle. Now the sobered patient lay on his stomach clutching the Winchester while he watched the constable. The Mountie made no move to disarm Riley either.

"I knew his father," Steele said down to Riley, his voice heavy with undisguised emotion. "He was killed putting down Louis Riel's Uprising, shot by a drunken *metis*. The boy wanted to follow in his father's footsteps. I shall have to write to his mother now," he added sadly. "What a waste of a fine young man."

267

Steele walked back to the bodies of the robbers. "No one I recognize," he said. "Do you know them?" he asked Nathan.

"No."

"Better that way," Steele philosophized. "Killing an unknown man leaves the mind less encumbered than sending someone familiar to meet his Maker."

"They ain't going no place but to hell," Riley swore as he spit on one of the robber's bodies. "Dry-gulchers is the lowest form of varmint there is. They deserve nothing better than to be left out here. Might be the only good deed they ever done in their lives, feeding some hungry animal."

"Don't expect me to break a sweat with a shovel on this frozen ground," Doc chimed in. "I refuse to help bury the scum."

"No," Steele silenced their objections, "the bodies will have to be returned to Dawson. Jenkins warrants an official funeral, and these two will get a proper burial." He gave Nathan a sidelong glance. "You saved my life, Mr. Blaylock," he said slowly, as if weighing the consequences of his next action, "and for that, you may keep your firearms, but you are still under my custody until cleared by the magistrate. However, I shall put in a good word for you all when we reach Dawson, and I suspect the charges will be dropped."

Doc brightened as a thought entered his devious mind. "Do you suppose there is a reward for returning the stolen gold?" he asked shrewdly.

"I would not be suprised if there were one," Steele grumbled, "but would you have the gall to ask for your share, Doctor?" He dabbed his handkerchief at the wound in his forehead.

"Why not?" Hennison sniffed. "I could have been shot as easily as poor Jenkins. Besides, we are a team, after all. . . ."

TWENTY-FOUR

Not thirty miles out from the trading post at Copper Center, Marta clamped her mukluk down hard on the snow brake of her sled and stared into the shimmering haze directly north. Dickinson and the Indian guide pulled alongside and stopped. Studying her back, the spy fought back a surge of admiration for Marta. Standing tall and straight with her legs sheathed in caribou leggings, she struck him as unlike any woman he'd ever met before, or any other person for that matter. What other individual could adjust so easily to this biting cold and desolation when all her experiences were based on steamy jungles? Dickinson shook his head to clear his thoughts, yet his feelings remained.

The girl had shown a flair for handling a dog team, so much so that she now looked forward to the hours of silent running with only the soft padding of the dogs' feet and their panting to break the cold stillness as mile after mile fell behind. Sergeant Sloan had no objection to riding in the basket with supplies wedged around him, so Marta spent most of her waking days following the first sled or breaking trail when the Ahtna's team tired. Her eagerness to assume a man's role only served to confirm the Ahtna's initial diagnosis that an evil spirit possessed her.

"What's wrong?" the agent asked as he leaned from his own sled. He forced himself to concentrate on her eyes, but their bright green hue set in the wind-tanned brown of her skin left him distracted. He turned away from her and peered through the narrow slit carved in the wooden snow goggles he wore to prevent snow blindness. He could see nothing, so he stripped off the goggles like Marta had already done. His eyes rebelled at the sudden brightness, burning and flooding with tears. He quickly shaded his eyes with his mittened hand.

"Up ahead." she gestured with her head. "Someone's coming. I think it's a single sled, coming straight for us."

Dickinson sprang from the basket and fumbled in the layers of his parka for his binoculars. He found them and pressed the icy metal glasses to his eyes. The optics intensified the painfully bright day. "A lone man in a sled," he confirmed her pronouncement, feeling a twinge of resentment that her eyes were so much sharper than his.

"Sloan, get behind those rocks over there and cover us— just in case he's not really alone, and this is some sort of trap," Dickinson ordered. "I doubt seriously Beaufort is behind this, but I'm learning not to underestimate him. Besides, this fellow could be a bandit."

Sloan grabbed his rifle and hurried to his post, for the sled was closing the distance at an alarming rate on its downhill leg. Since the disaster at Thompson Pass, they had lived with the specter of Beaufort until his threat pervaded the night shadows and every blind curve on the trail ahead. Was he ahead or behind? Everyone wondered.

Marta eased her own rifle from its scabbard lashed to the willow frame of her sled as the unknown traveler bore directly down on them in a swirl of powdery spray. She studied the terrain.

They were in a wide floodplain of the Copper River where two rivers that the Ahtna called the Gulkana and the Gakona converged from the north in a broad wedge to join the Copper. Swinging to its right in a wide arc north and east, the Copper River unraveled into a dozen shallow, braided channels that now were frozen solid. Over thousands of years, the restless streams had flailed back and forth across the ground, seeking the path of least resistance to the sea. In doing their unsettled dance they had scoured the ground into a broad plain. Only the snowcapped Mount Drum rose far in the shimmering east above endless rolling benches of stunted and wind-savaged alder and spruce.

What she saw caused her to relax. This stranger would meet them in the center of the riverbed, where an ambush would be most unlikely.

The team limped to a halt fifty yards ahead, and the driver studied them with undisguised anxiety. He waved tentatively to them; and when Dickinson signaled back, he stumbled over. Marta watched him while her mitten rested on her rifle stock. The man looked half-dead. His clothing was torn and patched in places with scraps of fur wrapped around the worn knees and arms of his woolen clothing. A plaid scarf, frayed by the wind, encircled his face and kept his beaver hat from blowing away.

"God, am I glad to see you," the man exclaimed in a rasping voice. "I've not seen another white man for three months."

Dickinson looked knowingly at Marta on hearing this piece of information. What lay behind the man was little-known territory. He would have expected the man to be a busted miner fleeing from the Forty Mile claims or from Dawson along the Copper River. That he came from the black heart of the Interior puzzled him. "Where did you come from?" he asked.

"My name is Dan McCarty. I was a deck hand on the *Lavelle Young*, a paddle wheeler."

Dickinson frowned as he looked past the man at the flint-edged mountain range rising in defiance behind him. "A paddle wheeler? Up there?"

"On the other side," the man answered. "I've come from a

trading post on the Rock River just below Bates Rapids on the Tanana. My boss, Captain E. T. Barnette, sent me south to fetch his brother-in-law, Frank Cleary, back from Valdez. Am I getting close to Valdez?"

"Another hundred and fifty miles," Dickinson replied impatiently. "You say you haven't seen another white man? No Englishman?"

McCarty dropped to his knees in exhaustion. "No, mister," he sighed. "Not another white man, just Indians. And I haven't eaten in three days. I can answer your questions better if you could give me a bite to eat. I'd sure appreciate it. I've been chewing the frozen moosehide laces on my boots."

Marta gave Dickinson a stern look and dug a dented coffee can from her sled. McCarty's eyes misted at the prospect of a cup of hot coffee. He touched his battered hat to the girl, but he was too weak to help her. So he sat in silence while a cooking fire was started, and watched hungrily as a slab of bacon slid around the skillet in its own bubbling grease and strips of sourdough bread twisted on green willow sticks browned over the coals. All the while Dickinson stomped impatiently around the rest spot with his hands clasped behind his back.

Barnette's man was so busy eating he scarcely noticed Sloan return from his outpost. After half a pound of bacon, bread, and four cups of steaming coffee, McCarty burped appreciatively and juggled the last twist of hot bread into his mouth. "Okay," he said. "I got the energy to talk. Ask away."

"No Englishman on the trail, you say?" Dickinson pounced on the opportunity.

"I told you, not a living soul except thieving Indians." He cast a suspicious glance at the native. "They stole my watch and my pocketknife."

"But how did you get over those mountains?" Marta asked. She pointed to the daunting skyline behind him.

"It weren't easy, ma'am. But it can be done. We come up

272

the Yukon this fall, heading for the headwaters of the Tanana to build a trading post at Tanana Crossing. But the river dropped with the freeze, and Captain Barnette set up a trading post off the Tanana. We've built a small outpost there."

"But how did you get here?" Dickinson interrupted.

McCarty shot Dickinson a disgusted look and resumed explaining to Marta. He much preferred looking at her than this fop. "As I was saying, we come *up* the Yukon and the Tanana. But I heard of an army fellow, Allen was his name I think, who had come up the Copper River and crossed the mountains to reach the Tanana. He floated *down* the river to the Yukon. So I backtracked his route, hoping I'd find his pass through the mountains. And I did, I found it. But it's a devil of a trip." He paused to shake his head. "Once I find this Frank Cleary, I've got to go and head back with him to Captain Barnette's outpost. But this time, I'm going to bring a damned sight more provisions. The captain's brother-in-law is to run the outpost while I guide Captain Barnette and Mrs. Barnette down to Valdez. That'll make three damn trips over those mountains, something I'm not looking forward to. Anyway, the captain plans on raising more money to build a fleet of paddle wheelers, so he needs to get to Valdez. And personally, I think his wife won't let him leave unless she goes along—hardship or not."

"Amazing," Dickinson commented. He filed the knowledge away for later reference, cursing the fact that the War Office kept so many secrets from his superiors. He'd studied all the information given to him, but obviously that knowledge was incomplete and faulty. Was there a secret shortcut around this trail that Beaufort knew? he wondered. The thought disturbed him greatly.

"Any dangers you encountered that you could warn us about?" he asked as he parted with one of his precious cigars.

McCarty's face brightened as he drew in a mouthful of

273

smoke and savored its bite. "No sir. Only the ice storms and the overflow and the avalanches. But I suspect you've encountered them yourselves."

"Avalanches." Dickinson nodded grimly. "Yes, we met an avalanche. . . ." His words trailed off as he relived the swirling cloud of snow and rocks rushing down the narrow trail at Thompson Pass.

"Oh, yes. One other thing if you're thinking of two-legged varmints."

"Yes?"

"There was two men in our camp that we drove out this fall. Bad eggs both of them, professional gunfighters, killers no doubt about it. And one of them a rapist. I think he tried to have his way with the captain's wife."

"What were their names?" Marta asked sharply. Her intense and sudden interest caught both McCarty's and Dickinson's attention.

"Why, Nat—Nathan Blaylock and Jim Riley, ma'am. Riley's the older of the two, and Blaylock is the defiler, ma'am. Do you know them?"

Marta shook her head, and her swirling black hair gave all the men around the fire pause for impure thought.

"Well, if you should see them, I'd shoot them on sight if I were you. They're mighty dangerous with a gun, but the captain would consider it a great favor if you send them straight to hell."

"I will," Marta replied firmly.

McCarty blinked. His request had been directed to Dickinson and Sloan, the men. He hadn't expected the woman to answer him. That she was willing to kill two men left him uneasy.

"Do you think we might expect to encounter these criminals?" Dickinson asked.

"Hard to say, sir." The man puffed on his cigar as he answered. "But word has it they escaped in the direction of Circle City or Eagle or maybe even Dawson, so you might."

"Dawson!" The spy bristled. "Who said we were going to Dawson?"

"Why, you're heading in that direction, taking the Valdez to Eagle military trail, aren't you? They just cut it two or three years ago, I believe. Back in ninety-nine, I think it was."

"Yes," Dickinson hurried to cover his unfortunate blunder, "but we're going to Eagle. What do you know of this military trail?" he asked as he sought to divert the attention from Dawson.

"Not a whole lot, but miners I met in Rampart say it's not much of a trail."

"How so?" Sloan asked this time. Several of the men who worked on that route came from his squad. Both brought back horrifying tales of their experience.

"They said it's a backbreaking path, not more than five feet wide in spots, a horse trail at most that can trap a man with snowslides in the winter and mudslides in the summer. Last year five men got caught in a blizzard on the trail and froze to death. The last part over the spine of the mountains is the worst."

"Thank you, Mr. McCarty," Dickinson interjected. "Your description has been most helpful." The gloomy note of this conversation had gone far enough to suit him. "We intend to take every precaution possible. But you must agree that danger is ever-present on any trail."

"You got that right," the man agreed as he licked the inside of his plate. "Freezing don't bother me half as much as starving. The last hundred miles or so I was surviving on skinny rabbits. You don't suppose you could see yourself clear to sell me a bag of flour and a side of bacon, do you? I can pay for it."

"Of course," Marta replied before Dickinson could object.

Sloan broke camp, and both parties left within the hour.

Daylight was precious now and traveling in the night far too dangerous to contemplate, so the group pressed on while Mc-Carty raced for the safety of Valdez.

The rest of the day found them zigzagging across the braided fingers of the Copper past its junction with the similar icy threads of the Christochina River, and driving hard for the gap between the Wrangell Mountains with its majestic peaks to the south and the jumbled, broken tops of the Mentasta Range to the North. The Mentasta, dwarfed by the grandeur of the Wrangells, waited sullenly for these interlopers, for many passing through this range fell prey to the snowfalls and fierce storms that choked the narrow trail. What the Mentasta conceded in size to its southern brother, it made up in treachery. More than one unwary stampeder with his eye on the clouds encircling Mount Sanford ran headlong into his death on the military trail.

Two hours before dusk, the Ahtna turned his team up the narrow cut in the mountains that the frozen Porcupine River made and pushed them hard through Indian Pass. By nightfall, the weary teams crossed the overflow of the Slana River and reached the shores of Mentasta Lake. Earthen and log lodges dotted the lake like overgrown beaver lodges.

While Dickinson, Sloan, and Marta shivered and stamped their feet to shed their ice-encrusted layers, the Indian headed into the village to parlay with the village leaders. He returned with a disturbing message.

"These are Gwitchin from the Tanana, not Ahtna like my people. But they are gone."

"What!?" Dickinson sputtered. "Are you saying the place is deserted? Where did they all go?"

The Ahtna shrugged. "Who knows," he said with little feeling. "They follow the caribou. I had heard that the fall hunt was not good. They are very hungry and poor, for they have not seen the caribou pass this way for some time. We can stay the night if we agree to share our food with them."

"Damn," the spy swore. "I never bargained to feed half the bloody territory. But we really have no choice. It looks like a storm is brewing. All right. Agreed. Maybe I can trade some of Sergeant Sloan's medals instead of our stores."

The Ahtna snorted derisively. "Can they eat the Three Stripe's medals?" he taunted. "What comfort will ribbons bring to an empty belly?"

"Okay. How many are left in the village."

"Only two, an old woman and a baby."

"An old woman and an infant?" Marta repeated his words, not fully understanding. "Those are the only ones here?"

The Ahtna shivered as the gaze of the devil woman focused on him. He turned his back on her, hoping his medicine bag would provide protection, and looked to Dickinson for help. "Only those two," he said to the other man.

"I don't understand," Dickinson replied in a puzzled voice. "Why would the whole village move and leave a grandmother and a baby? It doesn't make sense."

Sloan stepped forward. "They left 'em to die, sir."

"Why?" the spy asked, but he already had comprehended the answer.

"Figured they couldn't make the trip, I guess," Sloan expounded. "Or not worth feeding, so they left them here to freeze or starve."

The Ahtna nodded sagely. "They are very weak. We can hit them on their heads, and then we won't have to waste any food on them at all."

Marta crossed the distance between her and the native in two strides. Her pistol poked hard into the neck of the startled Indian. "No, we won't hit them on their heads!" she shouted in his face. "This is their home. We'll feed them and offer them any aid we can. Is that clear?"

"Don't shoot him, my dear," Dickinson whispered sooth-ingly in her ear. "We need him as a guide."

Marta released her grip, and the Ahtna sprang back, in-creasing the distance from this crazy woman. Only his anger at being so rudely treated by a woman overcame his fear at an-gering this evil spirit inside her and caused him to speak. "Bet-ter to save your food for yourselves," he shouted, "than to waste it on the dead. You will wish you listened to me when your hunger drives you to chew your mukluks!" He spun on his heel and jerked his team into the empty village.

The rest followed. What Marta saw left her dazed and shaken. Wind-shredded scraps of hide torn from the lodges danced obscene jigs in the freshening wind, and piles of bro-ken baskets, birch poles, and frozen fishnets lay scattered about as if the people had left in great haste. Everywhere, signs of poverty and famine greeted her. The bones of a dog or wolf lay strewn inside the only lodge to exhibit any signs of life. The Ahtna contemptuously threw back the hide covering the en-trance to reveal an ancient woman propped against a lodge-pole with a small infant by her side. A single smoky fire of bent twigs struggled to provide the most meager warmth and illu-mination. The woman was too weak even to raise her head as they entered.

Marta knelt by the infant, opening the wrap. Her fingers touched the tiny forehead. A great sorrow filled her heart, and her shoulders sagged.

The forehead was cold. The infant had died.

Tears filled Marta's eyes as she replaced the cover. The old woman's head raised shakily to peer at Marta. Her face carried a thousand wrinkles, each etched into her skin by hardship or hard work, yet a glimmer of fire still flickered behind those rheumy lids.

Marta fanned the fire and added more twigs until the room

danced with their shadows. She boiled a thin broth from dried beef and spooned the liquid past those crinkled lips.

"Thank you," the woman whispered.

Marta drew back startled. "You . . . you speak English?"

The lips drew back in a weak smile, revealing stained teeth worn down to stubs from chewing hides to soften them. "From the Moravian missionaries . . ." Her sentence ended in a series of spasmodic coughs.

Marta ladled another spoonful into the woman, and was rewarded by another series of coughs. She feared she was doing more harm than good and started to withdraw, but the old woman raised one hand and feebly dropped it on the girl's sleeve. The curiously intense eyes, out of place in so worn a face, held the younger woman entranced. It appeared to Marta that this frail person was concentrating the entire sum of her vitality into the space of her eyes. The rest of her body certainly seemed beyond reviving.

"I have been waiting for you to come," the old one rasped. "I have a message for you—from the spirit world."

Marta stiffened. Chills unrelated to the clammy lodge ran down her spine. Logic told her this wreck was confused, delirious, mistaking her for a family member. "How could that be?" she asked. "I've never been here before."

But the dying speaker ignored her question. "We have suffered much, my child, but my vision is true. Your deepest wish will be granted."

"What?" Confusion reigned as Marta's head spun. The dimly lit space closed in around her.

The old woman nodded her head painfully, summoning the last ounce of her energy to speak. "The cub of the winter wolf will give you a child. . . ."

Marta dropped the spoon, spilling the broth in her lap. Her hand went instinctively to cover her mouth as she stifled a scream. But tears flooded her eyes instead.

"But . . . that is impossible . . . ," she gasped, but her words faded into silence as she gazed through her tears at the wizened face.

The light had gone out of the eyes. The old woman was dead.

"What did she mean 'The cub of the winter wolf will give you a child'?" Dickinson asked over her shoulder. Unnoticed by Marta he had slipped back into the lodge and stood half-cloaked in the shadows.

"Nothing," Marta snapped, ashamed of her weakness. She tossed her head flippantly. "She was dying and delirious—out of her head, that's all. I've never heard of a winter wolf person," she added defensively.

"But she sounded as if she were waiting for you, just to tell you about this wolf."

"There is nothing here but the confused ravings of a dying woman!" Marta said harshly. "Nothing!"

Dickinson watched her spring to her feet and turn her back on the two bodies. A grim smile crossed her face as she clapped her hands together as if knocking dust from them.

"Well, you won't have to worry about sharing our food with anyone now," she said as she strode out of the lodge.

Later that evening, Dickinson found her in another abandoned hogan. This one was smaller than the others but quite snug, with dirt and stout spruce logs forming the walls and close-packed poles chinked with caribou moss covering the roof. Marta had started a small fire and sat watching the tendrils of smoke waft up through the smoke hole in the ceiling. She sat alone, hugging her knees with a caribou robe covering her shoulders. Her pistol and rifle lay within easy reach.

He rapped lightly on the log doorway. "May I come in?" he asked.

She nodded without turning her face from the fire, but he could see her eyes were red from crying.

"I brought you some bannock bread," he said lamely. "It was warm . . . once."

"Thank you, but I'm not hungry. You should save it. We mustn't waste it. Some starving native might want it," she added caustically.

"Yes, I suppose I deserved that."

"No, I'm sorry. That was unfair."

"Most things are unfair." He shrugged. "Why be any different?" He moved closer, suddenly unsure of himself. Long-buried feelings seeped from beneath barriers he had thought were impenetrable. Suddenly he was back in London, awkward and roiled by mixed emotions. He reached out and lightly touched her shoulder. Surprisingly, she didn't flinch as he had expected. But she didn't rush into his arms as he had hoped.

"Marta," he began, "I . . . I've come to regard you with great affection."

She smiled at him sadly. "What of the mission? The Maxim gun?"

"Lord knows those things come first. I didn't intend this to happen, but you are a most remarkable person. I've never quite known anyone like you."

She turned to regard him with mocking eyes. "What? The great Yankee spy has never had a village girl? I'm surprised. There must be hundreds of peasant girls in my country eager to throw themselves at so handsome and wealthy a foreigner. Should I let you take me on this dirt floor, grateful that you consider me worthy of your interest?"

"I didn't mean that," he protested. "My intentions are honorable, Marta. When this task is ended, and it will be ended someday, I should like you to consider—"

"Marriage? A family?" She spit the words out with alarming bitterness. "Before you go further, you should know about me. *I am damaged goods.*"

"Damaged?"

"Yes." She turned to face him directly. "When the *federales* burned my village and killed my parents, they raped me."

"Raped?" Dickinson could hardly say the word. "That's why you reacted as you did when McCarty mentioned that outlaw, Blaylock. He is a rapist, too."

"Yes," she pressed on, "I was raped by the soldiers, many times." She paused to let her words have full impact and watched as Dickinson ran his fingers through his hair in disbelief. But she had more to tell him.

"When they were finished with me, they left me to die in the jungle. But I survived. I did not die as expected. The sisters cared for me. I was sick in my head and in my body for a long time."

"Sick?" he asked, not understanding.

"Sick," she replied coldly. "The soldiers gave me the French disease—syphilis."

"Syphilis?" He recoiled, withdrawing his hand from her shoulder.

She nodded gravely. "But I am cured. I no longer have the disease. The nuns treated me with mercury shots; and when I caught malaria, the fever of that illness destroyed the pox."

"Then . . . then it's all right then."

"No it's not all right. And that is why the old woman's prophecy is so wrong. I cannot have children. The syphilis and the cure saw to that. *I am sterile.*"

Now it was Marta's turn to be surprised. Dickinson knelt beside her and tenderly stroked her hair. "You poor dear," he said. "How terrible for you to receive so harsh a sentence when you are innocent. But my feelings for you are unchanged by this, except to be stronger. That you have revealed your darkest secret to me makes me hope you might have some feelings for me as well."

She was crying now, confused and shaken with long-pent-up tears of anguish pouring out of her. "I don't know. I need more time to think," she said after she could find words again.

A fresh snow fell all night as Dickinson rocked Marta in his arms until dawn. Sloan slept soundly in another lodge with their guide. In the morning, they awoke to a surprise. The Ahtna was gone, taking one of the dog teams and all of their food.

TWENTY-FIVE

Riley grimaced as he pressed his head between the cold iron bars to scowl across the narrow space into the jail cell opposite him.

"I told you not to smart-mouth that judge. I told you, I told you, and I begged you. But, oh no, you went right ahead and set him off anyway. I never saw such a stiff-necked, stubborn son of a bitch in all my born days. Why you ain't been shot dead yet is beyond me. I'd shoot you this very minute if'n I had the chance."

"Precisely why I'm in this cell and you're not, my good man," Hennison said as he grinned up maliciously at his detractor.

"I ain't yer 'good man,' nor nothing even close." Riley turned away in disgust. "He was going to let us go," he ranted to himself. "He was only looking for the chance. Some sign of—what's the damned word? Contrition! That's it. He was looking for you to make some sign of contrition, jus' say yer sorry or something like that, and he'd have sprung us sure as shooting. And you wouldn't do it!" Riley spun around in exasperation.

Doc merely snorted. He'd heard this lament at least a dozen times in the last five days. "He also wanted some community service, you forgot that, my gun-toting cretin."

"I ain't no cretin. I know what that word means, and I ain't one, so don't call me one. Just 'cause I didn't go to no fancy college for lopping off limbs don't mean I'm stupid." Riley paused for want of a correct word. "I'm ignorant, that's what I am, but I ain't stupid."

"Whatever you say, Professor," Hennison added. "But the only community I have any desire to service is the community of whores in this town." This conversation was boring him as always, but he tried once more to set the record straight, hoping to put an end to these tiresome tirades. Clearly Riley felt more uncomfortable being incarcerated than Doc did.

"Well, you didn't have to tell the judge that, did you? I never saw a judge turn so crimson in all my born days."

"That's because he's a hypocrite and a Canadian to boot. My guess is he feared my competition with the ladies of the night."

Riley shook his head in dismay. There was no changing Hennison. When all sensible men would back away from a fight, Doc would wade in with his tongue lashing away. "At least they let Nathan go free," Riley said as he tried to put a bright polish on their predicament. "Being locked up, unable to look for his son, and separated from his wolf would drive him crazy. Did you see how he paced his cell that one day before the trial? I swear he's taking on more of his she-wolf's nature instead of her getting tamed. It ain't natural, and it's damned spooky, besides."

The door to the cellblock opened, and a Mountie, smartly dressed in dark blue duty uniform, entered with two tin plates of meat and potatoes and thick slabs of bread. All spit and polish, he slipped the plates between the bars and left. A minute later he returned with two mugs of hot coffee. Then he stepped back to wait for the men to eat.

Riley raised his cup in salute. "You Mounties got the best feed in yer jails, I'll say that for you."

The Mountie touched the brim of his peaked service cap in

return. "Wouldn't want you Yanks to think badly of us, seeing as how you're our guests." His voice carried a strong brogue from the North Sea.

Absentmindedly, the trooper leaned up against a canvas-covered machine placed against the far wall. Only metal-spoke wheels were visible beneath the canvas. He drew back the cover and began to polish the shining brass cylinder.

"Irish are you?" Riley asked.

"That I am. And yourself?"

"I'm Irish, too," Riley replied.

"That's right. Riley, isn't it? What part of the dear old sod do you hail from, Mr. Riley?" the man questioned.

"Texas," Riley replied around his mouthful of potato.

"Ah, yes."

"Well, I'm Irish as well," Doc added. "With a name like Hennison, I'm as Hibernian as both of you. But I hail from the beautiful state of Tennessee."

"Tennessee, is it? Never been there."

"Well, it was beautiful—once. Before the Yankees got their filthy fingers on it. But it still makes the best sipping whiskey you ever tasted."

The trooper leaned forward in interest. "You don't say."

"I do. I swear it on my mother's grave. And I carry within my brain the recipe for that noble sour mash. Why, I could re-produce it in less than a day if I had the proper materials."

"Doc, don't start. . . ." Riley stopped eating to warn his as-sociate. He could only imagine the harsh punishment for run-ning a still under Sam Steele's nose. But the gleam was already set in Hennison's eye, so Riley sought desperately for some dis-traction. He settled on the object the Mountie was buffing with such affection. "Say, what is that contraption you got there?" he asked. "It looks like a cross between a stovepipe on wheels and a thrashing machine."

"Ah, this!" the trooper exclaimed proudly. He whipped the

rest of the cover aside to reveal a gleaming yellow machine with a polished wide brass barrel and frame astride heavy iron-rimmed wheels. A thick steel plate shielded the mechanism from the barrel, yet allowed the gleaming cylinder to protrude through an opening cut into the plate. The spoked wheels were wrapped with iron bands and could be detached from the axle simply by pulling a brass cotter pin at each well-greased hub.

"This, my friends, is the pride of the Yukon Field Force. This is Bertie."

"Bertie?"

"Aye, we named him after the late Prince Albert. He's too mean a thing to carry a woman's name."

"So what does it do?" Even Doc's curiosity was piqued.

"Well, you see, it's a Maxim gun. All brass plated and fancy to cut down corrosion from the salt air. Made originally for the Royal Marines, I'm told."

"A gun? It's too small for any respectable artillery piece." Hennison recalled his experience with cannon with distaste.

"No, it's not a field piece. It's a machine gun. It fires automatically."

"You don't say?" Riley guffawed. "A machine gun? Does it run on steam power or use electricity like them telephones I read about?" he joked. The image of men stoking a boiler or laying telegraph poles behind the gunner amused him.

"None of either," the trooper expounded proudly. He enjoyed having the leg up on these men. "It uses some of the recoil from each cartridge to operate the bolt and feed another round into the chamber. As long as you hold down the trigger and it has cartridges, it keeps on firing. Or so that's the conventional wisdom. But it gets itself jammed from time to time." He flipped back the upper half of the breech mechanism and swung the gun around so his prisoners could see the workings.

287

"It's dreadful wasteful on ammunition, it is. Simply dreadful. Fires at more than four hundred rounds a minute."

"Four hundred a minute!" Jim choked on another potato. "God Almighty, why would you shoot at something for four hundred times? There'd be nothing left."

But Hennison got the picture all too clearly. Union cannon could already reduce a human to a smoking spot, an image burned forever into his mind. He glared hatefully at the Maxim, and it appeared to return his hatred with equal malevolence. "Thank God they didn't have that work of the devil in the War between the States," he muttered. "Is there no end to man's efforts to destroy himself?"

Riley settled into an equally glum mood. Turning a weapon into a self-actuating machine only served to remind him of his impending extinction. With four hundred chances, anyone, even a green-eared whiskey drummer, could slay an opponent. What need was there for a gunman with his skills? Even here in the frozen Arctic, the fingers of progress were grasping at his coattails.

"I prefer my Winchester," he said gloomily. "It hits what I aim at with only one shot. But the new Marlin ain't a bad gun either."

"All old-fashioned lever-actions," the Mountie countered. "We've got the new .303 Lee-Metfords. Now those are sweet rifles. All bolt-action, they are."

"Are you expecting to go to war with the States?" Riley asked suspiciously.

"Not at all." The familiar bass voice of Commander Steele issued from the head of the steps. He nodded as his trooper snapped to attention before resuming his lecture. "You forget Canada only purchased the Yukon Territory from the Hudson's Bay Company in 1898. With such a dubious claim on the land at the onset of the Klondike gold rush, Ottawa had reason to fear that the thousands of Americans rushing across the border might wish to annex the Yukon. And then there was the possibility the stampeders might prove unruly like the late Soapy Smith in Skagway. We felt it wise to be prepared; after all, we only had twenty men in the field force when all the excitement began. This Maxim gun helped balance the sides. Fortunately, you Americans have proved more interested in digging for gold than causing trouble. Most of you that is." He ended his talk with a stern look at Doc Hennison.

The physician cast a halfhearted smile at his jailer. Secretly, he wondered if Sam Steele would have used that machine gun. Hennison thought him quite capable of pulling its deadly trigger.

"Be that as it may"—Steele clapped his hands together as he spoke, and the sound echoing in the corridor made Doc jump—"you two are free to go. Your friend Mr. Blaylock has paid your bail."

A wicked wind was blowing up the Yukon, and flakes of snow swirled along the frozen path as the men stood outside the Mounted Police stockade. Gray storm clouds, laden with snow, jostled each other in a low-level race to dump their load on the town. Riley cinched his gun belt and pulled his parka hood around his neck. Hennison shivered behind him. The jail had been cozy and well heated, and Doc wondered if he was better off incarcerated than freezing outside.

Nathan stood with them as his wolf studied the road into Dawson's downtown and sampled the air. With shoulders hunched and head bowed, Nathan presented a picture as gloomy and bleak as the developing weather.

"Did you find out about yer boy?" the old gunfighter asked tentatively. "The Gustafsons?"

"I found the Gustafson family," Nathan sighed.

"Well that's good, ain't it?" Riley said.

"No, it's not. I went up to the cemetery with Commander Steele when they buried those two bank robbers. People had seen them hanging around Dawson before the mail sled got robbed, but no one knew their names for sure. One barkeep thought he'd seen them in Skagway two years back with Soapy Smith, but he wasn't positive."

"So the headboards read 'Unknown Man Number One' and 'Unknown Man Number Two,' " Riley added. He'd seen too many of those weathered planks, and he held a growing fear he'd end up with a similar epitaph.

"Yes," Nathan continued, "and the Gustafson family was there, too."

"That was nice of them to come," Riley said, trying hard to find a bright spot in this cloud of depression. "I bet those two bushwhackers had a regular turning out. Probably more than they deserved."

"The Gustafson family was buried in the next plot, Jim. They all died of typhoid fever three months ago."

A nervous silence followed.

"The whole family?" Doc asked. In spite of the cold, Nathan's plight exceeded his own discomfort.

"The marker read 'The Gustafson Family.' That's all it said. And the date. Steele said there was a run of typhoid fever when they died."

"No mention of a little one, then?" Hennison grimaced. "Did you ask around, Nat?"

"I did, Doc, but this town has changed so fast no one even remembers who C. F. Gustafson ever was. And nobody knows whether he had an infant or if . . . if that little boy is buried in the Gustafson grave."

"I'll bet our old friend Arizona Charlie Meadows would know," Jim suggested brightly. All this gloom was weighing too heavily on him, and he acutely felt the need for a drink. "Lets head into town and pay the Grand Palace a visit."

The walk from the Mounted Police stockade along the bend of the Yukon proved puzzling as well as frightening to the three. Plainly the gold rush that had fueled the veritable eruption of this town on the muddy flats of the Yukon River was over. The thousands of gold-crazed men who once filled the streets and stood shoulder to shoulder by the riverside had vanished. Now, less than a tenth of that number moved about, and these men looked far different from their predecessors. Gone were the swaggering gaits and the boisterous, backslapping clusters of flush miners. Those the trio passed wore starched collars and ties and woolen trousers instead of muck-spattered coveralls, and bore the somber, worried looks of shopkeepers, bank tellers, and hired men rather than the feverish stare of men pushed to the limits of their endurance by the infection of gold lust.

"Company men," Riley muttered in disgust. "All these men are nothing but company men. They even smell like company men. What happened to the bravos? They can't all have left."

"Looks like they did," Hennison said.

He pointed across the river to the once booming town of Klondike. Now most of the shacks and huts lay fallen into snow-covered heaps that dotted the silent shore. Abandoned cables stretched across the river, and the battered white shapes of three stern-wheelers, the *Columbian,* the *Canadian,* and the *Victorian,* lay frozen in the ice like mausoleums to some Oriental potentate. Of the three ships, only the *Columbian* sported a single smokestack, making it appear all the more like some mournful marker to a dying era.

"Will you look at this place?" Riley asked in amazement. "It's gone civilized on us. Why, in less than a year it got tamed—just like the cattle towns when I was younger. I seen it time and time again. Next they'll be having church socials and taffy pulls and temperance marches. And they'll be no place for the likes of us."

They walked in awe past the giant Administration Building, the Court House, and the Commissioner's Residence with its flagpole and white picket fence half-buried in the snowdrifts. The copper-sheathed roofs and white board buildings appeared foreign and unsuited for their mud surroundings. But as they entered the main street, they found that milled lumber boards had replaced canvas and log on all but a rare shop. The familiar plumes of smoke still rose from the surrounding hills, but these no longer came from men stoking fires to thaw the muck atop their piece of frozen ground. Now the smoke poured forth from huge gold dredges whose buckets bit chunks of land that once took two men all week to move. Billowing tendrils trailed skyward from fields of steam-driven points now used to thaw the solid overburden with steam from company boilers. The lines of smoke rose like well-ordered fields of wheat. Where individuals once scraped and mucked for gold, now machines from conglomerated companies and interlocking trusts toiled.

Even the Palace Grand Theater was no more. Now it was called the Old Savoy. But its interior still sported the long, polished bar that had supported tens of thousands, and polished brass lamps still hung from the tiled ceiling. Yet, the gilded mirrors and the flocked wallpaper looked faded and tired.

"Charlie Meadows?" the bartender said as he smiled ruefully and poured three slugs of rye into shot glasses for the men. "Charlie sold out over a year ago. First he gave up the theater, got tired of shooting glass balls out of his wife's hands, I think. Maybe she was the one who got skitterish, I don't know. Then he sold the saloon. Truth is, I think this burg got too tame for him. Word has it he's got up some expedition to invade a cannibal island in the South Seas."

"That would be something Charlie would do," Riley agreed. He downed his drink and savored the sooty taste as it burned its way down his throat. Why in the world, he wondered, couldn't Doc make his poison taste this good?

"And Klondike Kate? Is she still here?" Doc asked hopefully. The generous-hipped brunette had been his favorite.

"Kate's on the lecture circuit, would you believe it?" the saloonkeeper answered. "Now she makes her living talking on her feet."

"A great pity. A major talent lost to this world," Hennison sighed as he swallowed another shot. He rolled the cut-glass tumbler between his fingers and studied the umber liquid inside the glass. Shoe polish, he thought. A dab of cordovan shoe polish added to his elixir would give it exactly the same color as this rye. But the nuance of this taste evaded him.

"Ain't no one left in town but Sam Steele?" Riley wondered.

"Ah, rumor has it the colonel is about to be transferred as well. He's stood in the way of the big mining companies, and they're pressuring Ottawa to recall him."

"A colonel? Is that what them pips on his collar was? I thought he was still a captain or a commander. That's what I called him, and he never said nothing to correct me. Ain't that something. First officer I ever met that didn't piss hisself 'cause you got his rank wrong. Leave it to the big companies to run out an honest officer," Riley philosophized. "I've seen the big cattle spreads do it in New Mexico to the honest marshals and the railroads to the town sheriffs in Kansas. At least those that was worth their salt."

"What of 'Big Alex' McDonald, the richest man in town? Surely the 'King of the Klondike' is still here?" Hennison asked.

The bartender looked sadly at his tattered dish towel. "He is. But Big Alex is flat broke. You'll see him wandering about. The mining companies got his claims away from him, and bad investments busted him. Such a pity, for all the millions he had, now he's a pauper. And his health is poor to boot."

Nathan looked up from his glass as a movement caught the corner of his vision. Many Hats was standing just outside the saloon doors. The beaver hat that once belonged to Doc Hennison sat proudly on his head, but now it was decorated with a thick, beaded hatband. He gestured to Nathan.

"That Indian can't come in here," the saloonkeeper said.

"Why not?" Nathan snapped. "Don't you think he's good enough for your place?"

"Easy, mister." The tavern man held up both of his hands to pacify Nathan. The boy's cold gray eyes, and the length of his pistol barrel, frightened the tradesman. "It's not that at all. No, sir, not at all. I'd love to have the extra business, but Commander Steele would close this place and clap us all in jail. Selling liquor to the natives isn't allowed."

"Don't seem proper to me," Doc observed. "Here we shove our so-called civilization down their throats, but we deny them one of the few pleasures available to a civilized man—fine whiskey. Perhaps the *only* thing we have to offer them of any worth."

"Well, it makes some of them mighty crazy, I'll grant you that," Riley noted.

"It makes some white men mighty crazy, too, but that never stopped us from selling to ourselves, did it? What better Christian thing could you do but share something you hold dear with a heathen? And I hold nothing so dear as a good drink."

"Somehow your logic is flawed, Doc," Nathan said as he muddled about in his friend's twisted theory. The fact that Doc made a thriving business of peddling his alcohol-laced elixir to half the natives from Dawson to Saint Michael gave Nathan good reason to believe his friend was biased on this matter. Secretly, he wondered if the harshness of his life had molded him to champion the underdog or whether he got his taste for justice from his father, Wyatt Earp. "Some men don't seem to thrive on drink like you do, Doc. I know I don't."

Hennison grinned expansively. Three shots served well to smooth the burrs off his rough-sawed edges. He opened his mouth to expound on another of his harebrained theories only to find he was looking at the back of young Blaylock's head. Riley, too, had turned to look at Many Hats. Doc followed their gaze, and what he saw caused even him to spill his drink.

Peeking out from behind Many Hat's legs was a small child. With one hand wrapped around the Athabascan's leg for security, the child gazed upon the trio inside with wide, dark eyes. His rabbit-trimmed parka hood was thrown back to reveal hair black as a raven's wing and cut straight across. He could pass for a native except that his serious eyes carried the trace of an upward slant at their corners, and his face was thin like his father's. The men were looking at the grave face of the dead Wei-Li save for Nathan's narrow jaw.

"Your son," Many Hats announced, but his words were unnecessary. No one held any doubts.

Nathan covered the distance between them in three bounds, but his rush startled the boy. So Nathan dropped to his knees to smile at the child, keeping what he felt was a safe distance. The boy hid his uncertainty with a mixed look of defiance and dubiousness. His grip on the Indian's leg tightened.

The she-wolf appeared from nowhere to stand beside Nathan on the boardwalk outside the saloon doors. She, too, studied the boy and sniffed his scent. Seeing the wolf, the boy's eyes grew even wider, but he held his ground. A thick silence filled the air.

Then, unexpectedly, the boy stepped forward and stroked the wolf's muzzle. The animal moved closer to lick the child's face instead of attacking him.

"Well, I'll be a sun-dried turtle!" Riley exclaimed. "She knows the shaver is your'n. She ain't never let no one touch her 'cept Nat, hisself. If that don't beat all."

Nathan slowly held out his arms and waited as the wolf led his child to him. He pressed the tiny body against him, marveling at how small it was until he realized this was the first child he had ever held as a grown man. The room erupted in cheers as the men crowded around the reunited father and his son.

"By damn," Hennison sniffed despite himself. "He looks more like Wei-Li and Nathan than when I left him. Of course he's got more hair now . . . and he smells a far piece sweeter than before. Guess he's learned to control his sphincters and not muss himself."

Many Hats felt a tug on his sleeve and turned to see the bartender slip a glass of whiskey into his hand. "I don't care if they do arrest me," the man bawled, wiping the tears from his beard. "This is the most beautiful thing I ever saw." He pumped the native's other hand before retreating behind the safety of his polished bar.

"Where in the hell did you find him?" Riley asked.

Many Hats chuckled. "In Moosehide."

"The Han Indian village?" Doc gasped. "Who'd have thought of looking there?"

"I did," Many Hats replied. "A good tracker has to look with both eyes. You only looked with your right eye at the white man's town, not your left one, because your mind closed the light tunnel from your left eye. But I saw Moosehide with my left eye, so I looked there. The son of the Winter Wolf's Son was there with a Han family. The Hans are not as strong as my people, the Gwitchin, but they took good care of the child."

Nathan looked up at Many Hats, his eyes shining with happiness. "I don't know what to call him. What's his name, Many Hats? What did the Hans call him?"

"The Silent One."

"The Silent One?" Riley sputtered. "What kind of a name is that to call a babe?"

"He does not speak," the native said flatly. "What else should they call him?"

"Not to nobody, he don't? Why he's almost three. His tongue should be growed enough to talk by now."

Many Hats shook his head.

"Well," Riley pondered, "that ain't natural." Instantly he regretted his words when he saw the hurt look that filled Nathan's face.

Nathan looked up at Doc for an answer.

Hennison stepped forward to lay his hand on Nathan's back. "Don't listen to this besotted cowhand. What does he know about infants. The closest thing this age he's ever dealt with were calves, and they don't ever talk. I tell you, some children are late starters."

"Maybe he's retarded," a miner piped up. He'd been watching the whole thing from his table nearby while he nursed a tepid beer that had long since lost its foam. "I had a sister who was slow like the lad."

Riley whirled to face this intruder, and his pistol threatened the miner. "Shut yer gob, you dirt driver, or I'll fill yer skull so full of holes you'll be ten steps below a gopher in wit. This here lad ain't retarded no way, and we'll hear no more talk of that." He raised his voice over the cowering miner and waved his revolver in the air. "That goes for everyone in this saloon."

"For once I agree with your uncouth assessment, Riley," Doc readily agreed. "Why, the kid's bright as paint. Just look at the gleam in his eyes, and how he follows what we say with interest. No, he's clever, all right. My guess is he's not had enough civilized conversation."

"Well, find Lem Sutter," Riley suggested. "That man would talk all day long to the side of a barn if he thought it might give him a decent reply. Where is Lem? Since they locked us up, he's not been around lately. Where's he been keeping himself?" As one of the self-appointed godfathers of the child, Riley felt a rising concern for the child's well-being, especially now that he'd seen the babe.

Nathan spoke over his son's head, as he'd raised the boy in his arms while he stood up. "Lem's been talking to the lady who runs the library. I suspect we'd find him there if we looked."

"Library!" Riley turned apoplectic. "Did you say library? This burg's got a library?"

"Yup, they've built one since we were here last. It's got a reading room and bookshelves," Nathan replied. He'd discovered it and the new public school in his searching.

"Damn! And me locked up for five days within spitting distance of those books, and not knowing about them."

"Watch your language around the boy," Doc cautioned. "We don't want him learning swear words or picking up that dreadful nasal twang of yours. We want him to speak like a proper gentleman, not some West Texas dust eater. As his godfather, I won't permit it."

Riley bristled at that last remark. "Godfather? Well, I'm here to tell you, I'm his godfather, too. And maybe more'n you are. He don't need no one-armed whiskey drummer for a patron. I shudder to think he might pick up that greasy Tennessee drawl you use for speech."

The two drew nose to nose with each one's fist gathering a handful of the other's coat until Nathan drew them apart. All the while the boy studied these men's curious reaction with his thoughtful dark eyes, safe and securely perched in his father's arms. Nathan explained his idea.

"We need to give him a proper name first. That'll help him to talk. No wonder he's not inclined to speak. No one calls him anything."

The godfathers released their hold on each other and acceded to Nathan's point. They retreated to the farthest table in the saloon and sat down to much mumbling and head scratching. Nathan kept his son on his knee, bouncing the child from time to time as he thought appropriate, but the action felt foreign to the young man. Being a father was going to take some adjusting to, he realized.

A protracted silence followed as each man sought the best name. At length Doc raised his head, adjusted his worn cravat, and beamed an expansive smile. "I have the perfect name for the young fellow. He should be called . . . Humphrey."

"Humphrey!" Riley's eyes filled with tears, and his face flushed a bright scarlet. He was lighting a cigar when this astonishing announcement caused him to drop the flaming lucifer match and the lighted cigar into his lap. With alacrity the gunman beat out the flames and retrieved the crumpled remains of his smoke. He jammed the shattered cigar between his teeth to control his mirth. "Humphrey? You can't be serious."

But Doc was. "Humphrey is my first name," he intoned with great solemnity. "And the name of my father and his father before him. In fact I'm actually Humphrey Stuart Hennison the third."

"Good Lord, Doc, you are serious." Riley blanched. "Humphrey the third, is it? They'd done best to stop at Humphrey the one. I can see why you shortened yer name to Doc when that bluebelly cannonball shortened yer frame to match." His teeth cut the remnants of his cigar in two as he ground his teeth in exasperation. "No way this shaver is going to be burdened down with the name of Humphrey. He'd have to fight every step of his way through life with a moniker like that."

"Have you a better suggestion?" Doc rankled at this rejection of his Christian name along with the fact he'd now informed his friends of something they could use to tease him.

Riley's face furrowed. "How about Buck?"

"Buck? Buck?" Now it was Hennison's turn. "Buck is the name you give to a horse."

Within an instant the two men were snarling and swearing at each other again. Many Hats used the opportunity to sweep up Riley's cigar into his pocket and empty the glass of whiskey Doc had set upon the table. It was times like this, when he watched the white men fighting over nothing, that he wondered why the Man Above had entrusted the whites with such powerful weapons. Perhaps, he reasoned, the Great Spirit expected the white men to kill each other in far greater numbers than could be hoped for by giving the terrible weapons to sensible people like the Gwitchin.

Nathan smoothed the jet-black hair of his son. "I'm partial to a biblical name like Jeremiah," he said.

"Jeremiah was a great prophet," Riley agreed. "I read about him in the Bible," he added proudly. "Jeremiah is a powerful name. You're his pappy, so you got the final word."

"Jeremiah." Doc nodded solemnly.

Nathan looked up at Many Hats for the final confirmation, but to his surprise the Indian was shaking his head. "What's wrong with that, Many Hats?" he asked. "Don't you like that name?"

"Jeremiah can be his white man's name," the old man added offhandedly. "But anyone with two eyes can see his real name."

"His real name?" Doc asked.

"Yes, his *real* name for the *real* thing in this world, the true things that matter. The wind, the mountains, the eagles, and the bear—they will know what his real name is just by looking at him, and they will call him by that name. So he, and all of you, should know what it is."

"Well, what in tarnation is his real name, Hats?" Riley wondered. "Would you be so kind as to inform us ignorant white folks?"

Mr. Many Hats Charlie smiled. His finger pointed to the she-wolf who crouched easily beside Nathan as she kept her yellow eyes fixed on the child.

"Wolf Cub."

"It's settled then," Doc chuckled. He offered a toast and waited as the other three men stood and raised their glasses. "Gentlemen, I give you Jeremiah Blaylock, son of Wei-Li and Nathan Blaylock and known to us *real* people as Wolf Cub."

TWENTY-SIX

Marta spent most of the morning piling rocks on the grave site of the old woman and the infant. With the ground too frozen to dig a grave, she resorted to covering the bodies with whatever rocks she could knock loose from winter's frozen hold. At first, Sloan watched in glum silence as she dragged the bodies to the edge of the abandoned huts and struggled to gather the necessary boulders to protect the bodies from the ravages of wolves and foxes. Her persistence finally shamed him, and he joined in until the corpses were well hidden beneath cold stone. Even Dickinson helped, but for another reason: he hoped Marta would be impressed by what might pass for sensitivity.

Then they huddled around a pitiful fire and evaluated their situation. Not more than a rucksack of flour and dried smoked moose meat remained to feed the three of them. Sloan had used the pack as a pillow, and the Ahtna had left without it. Ahead lay an equally treacherous road, and these supplies were far from sufficient. The weather did little to encourage any optimism. A fierce wind whipped across the frozen Mentasta Lake and sent cyclones of spiraling snow dancing through Mentasta Pass. Overhead, a dirty gray scud lowered until only the bases of the hills stood out from the threatening clouds that blanketed all.

"It'll be just as difficult to head back to Valdez as it will be to press on to Dawson," Dickinson argued. "We could starve either way. But Beaufort's not in front of us, that much is certain. If we head back, we run the risk of being ambushed by him."

"What'll we do for food, General?" Sloan asked. "What we have will only last a few days."

"We'll press on and hope to find game. Besides, I know for a fact there are a handful of mining shacks between here and Dawson. And Tanana Crossing should be just ahead. We'll find food there," he lied.

"Is that for certain?" Sloan asked.

"Absolutely," Dickinson lied more convincingly. "The trapper back at Copper Center told me so."

The sergeant trapped a flea between the rim of his long johns and his neck and ground it into a brown smudge. He mused that these pests who tormented him would freeze to death along with him if they failed to find food. It was small consolation. That and the fact that Dickinson would perish as well.

With the tardy sunrise showing only as a pink-and-crimson ribbon wrapping along the edges of the mountains, the three pushed their one sled and team through Mentasta Pass and hugged the side of the foothills that parted only enough to allow the passage of Station Creek. Following the creek's serpentine wanderings, the team skirted patches of treacherous overflow until they had covered thirty miles. Now the pass widened into a flat course of frozen brush and swampland that noted the origins of the Tok River.

By nightfall, the pinpoint lights of Tanana Crossing on the banks of the Tanana River glowed ahead. Dickinson rebuked himself for his fears, and even Sergeant Sloan flashed a toothy smile when he saw the camp. But their confidence shattered like the brittle ice that coated the rutted sled trail when they arrived in the village. Like the camp at Mentasta Pass, hunger and starvation greeted them.

Tanana Crossing was the place Captain E. T. Barnette had chosen for his trading post in anticipation of the Valdez-to-Eagle railroad promised by John Jerome Healy. But the iron rails existed only in Healy's head, and Barnette was stuck on the banks of the Chena River, with his hoard of precious supplies over two hundred miles downriver. The five men stationed at the army's outpost had retreated north to Eagle in the face of this grim winter. And worst of all, the caribou migration had not reached the Tanacross Indians who lived on the river's banks. Too exhausted to dwell on their misfortune, the trio found shelter in the army's empty shack and fell fast asleep on empty stomachs.

The next morning, crowds of starving natives clustered outside the cabin when the travelers awoke. To the shock of Dickinson and especially Marta, the villagers had come hoping to find food instead of trading what little they had. Not even Sloan's new ax or their rifles could coax the villagers to part with more than a handful of dried cranberries and a few stinking slabs of withered dog salmon, split and hung over drying racks last summer to feed their dogs. Dickinson rankled at the humiliation of being forced to eat the same brown, curled strips as his sled dogs.

With no hope of gathering more supplies and the specter of Beaufort rising in the back of his mind, Dickinson rode the runners of their one sled out of town the next morning with Marta in the basket and Sloan limping along. Every hour they stopped to trade places until they reached the wide marsh of Mosquito Flats by late day. Another thirty miles lay behind them. Mosquito Flats, a hellhole of swarming clouds of mosquitoes in the summer, lay locked in frozen silence. Marta brewed a hasty pot of tea, strengthened mainly by handfuls of Labrador tea leaves and spruce needles. Dickinson studied his tattered map.

"I estimate it's another hundred and thirty miles to Eagle

from here, but if we cut east when the military trail turns north to Eagle I think the distance is less than sixty to seventy miles to Dawson. Instead of going to Eagle and then down to Dawson we could cut straight for the city. We'd save time."

Marta watched him closely. The cocksure dandy of Valdez was unraveling with each step they traveled from civilization. Dickinson's air of confidence was worn thin, and the trek had shredded his bravado along with his clothing. She knew that for a proud man his loss of self-assurance was harder to take than the hunger they all endured, yet still the man pressed on. His actions spoke of more than mere devotion to duty. His hatred for Beaufort was driving him now, she realized. While that realization made him more human to her, she reasoned that such desperation of command could lead to fatal mistakes. And now she understood what feelings she might have for him were motivated by sympathy, not love. Wisely, she decided not to mention that to him. Whatever hopes or desires were propping him up at this time, he needed every one. So she smiled encouragingly.

Sloan peered closely at the map. The boundary trail that split off of the military trail to Eagle to cross into Canada looked suspiciously thin on paper. The Eagle-to-Valdez Route ran as a robust red line across the chart, but Sloan now knew from firsthand experience that this so-called road was little more than an animal trail in places. If the map showed the Eagle road as so thick a line, what disaster lay ahead if they followed this thin, anemic hairline labeled the "Boundary Trail"?

"It doesn't look like much of a path, General," he sighed. "Saving time won't count for much if we get lost and never make it to Dawson."

"I say we will make it," the spy insisted. Commanding others left him uneasy. He made a mental note never to engage in anything other than solitary espionage in the future. "What do you think, Marta?"

The girl pictured her fellow rebels, dying and enduring torture in the dungeons, while she suffered the discomforts of hunger and cold. The lush warmth of Panama seemed little more than a dream in her present surroundings, yet she knew real blood spilled there for the cause of freedom. Her sufferings were minor compared to theirs. For every day that passed, hundreds of her people perished.

"We must take the fastest route," she said with conviction. "If we take too long, the result will be as bad as if we failed."

"Good. I totally agree. See, Sloan, this woman's not afraid, why should you be?"

"Because, Your Honor, I'm only a soldier. I don't have a personal ax to grind or lofty aspirations of building a new country. My goals are limited to staying warm, alive, and fed the best I can while giving the United States their money's worth for the two dollars a day they pay me."

"Well, we're taking the shortcut," Dickinson huffed.

Sloan saluted and rolled out of the basket. It was his turn to run beside Marta as she drove the sled.

Sloan's instinct for survival proved right. Five more days passed while they struggled eastward, deeper and deeper into the grip of the unnamed hills and low mountains that separated the U.S. territory of Alaska from the Yukon Territory of Canada. Lower and less spectacular than the Wrangell and Alaska Ranges, this barrier proved to be just as treacherous. Twisting along a trail that seemed to rise and fall with the confused terrain, the party encountered smothering snowdrifts that hid patches of loose scree that could drag them all to their deaths in the narrow canyons and gullies, and barricades of splintered black spruce and stunted aspen that threatened to impale the unwary. This part of the country resembled a confused quilt of mountains heaped about in a design obvious only to a maddened mind.

Dickinson also underestimated the weather. The first four

days rose clear and cold as if to lure them into its trap. On the fifth day, with the Boundary Trail close at hand, a blizzard struck. With visibility down to ten yards and the hunger of four days gnawing at their bellies, the agent spotted a fork in the trail and turned their sled off to the right. With any luck, he reasoned, they'd reach the Yukon in a day—two at the most.

Four days later they were still struggling to break trail for their dog team as the storm piled foot after foot of fresh snow upon them. Visibility extended only as far as one's outstretched hand. Against this weather the team struggled to make five miles in the blinding whiteness of the shortened day. At night, they huddled together under a canvas lashed to the side of the sled and nursed their sickly fire of spruce cones and dead branches snapped from the exposed treetops.

The next morning the storm blew so fiercely that they clawed their way along, sensing the rise of the obscured land more than seeing it, until the dogs refused to go on. Marta caught a brief glimpse of a shadowy pass ahead. She shouted to Dickinson and Sloan while she dragged the lead dog forward into the relative shelter of the rocks.

Hastily, she overturned the sled, and the two men fought the flapping tarp into place. Rocks pinned the corners of the torn shelter down as the dogs dropped in harness and curled into tight balls to disappear under the snow. Marta strode back to the shelter.

Unexpectedly, her left foot caught on something, and she sprawled headlong into the snow. Cursing her clumsiness she got to her knees and tried to stand. But her foot was held fast, and the effort sent a jolt of pain running up her leg. Thoughts of broken bones and hidden bear traps flooded her mind, and she quickly felt her leg for a break. She found nothing until her fingers explored to the tip of her mukluk where it was held fast. No cold metal greeted her probing hand. Instead, her toes were wedged tightly into a hard, almost leathery-feeling vise of puzzling contour. Sharp points rose from the edges of this trap to fasten into her boot. Not hurt, but curious, Marta scooped the snow away, expecting to see a gnarled spruce root.

Her eyes started at what she saw, and she screamed. Her cry of alarm drew Dickinson. He raced to her side only to stare at what held her foot. Sloan approached and winced.

The trap stared up at them with unseeing eyes. Marta's boot was wedged into the open mouth of a human head.

Stiffened in shock and horror, Marta could only stand there unmoving with the macabre trap seizing her boot. Dickinson stood unmoving as well. Only Sloan recovered. With a savage blow he drove his rifle butt into the dead face, shattering the upper teeth that had snagged Marta's boot, and pulled her foot free. The death mask leered back at them with a grimace made all the more hideous by the gaping hole of its smashed smile.

"Poor bastard froze to death," Sloan remarked. He bent closer to inspect the exposed head. "Imagine that. Him buried up to his eyebrows with his last scream frozen on his open mouth, and you come along, missy, and stick your foot in it. Imagine that."

Marta shook violently and her teeth chattered. She wiped her boot repeatedly in the snow as if to remove any stigmata, but no blood issued from the solidly frozen corpse. His skin appeared pink and living except for the scattered darkened scabs on his cheeks and the glazed and forlorn eyes. Involuntarily, her fingers ran across the frostbitten scabs on her own lips, and her mind pictured herself in this cadaver's place. Calming herself with great effort, she remembered to cross herself. Sloan broke her trance.

"Can't have happened too long ago," he observed. "The foxes and ravens haven't got to him yet."

Dickinson dropped to his knees, digging with both hands around the head. He uncovered the neck wrapped in a threadbare scarf and both shoulders covered by a coarse woolen coat. One hand emerged from the snow a short distance away from the head, the fingers curled and the wrist bent as if taken with a palsy. The hand and shoulders twisted about the head in an unnatural way.

"He looks like a miner to me," the agent said.

"What do you suppose happened to him to twist him so?" Marta asked. She forced her mind to analyze the scene, hoping her momentary panic was forgotten by the others.

Dickinson shrugged. "Rigor mortis, I suppose. Maybe his muscles contracted as he froze. Maybe he died with a seizure." He looked up at the wall of whiteness that engulfed them. "Best we start a fire before we end up like this poor devil."

The three turned away from the body to kindle what fire they could. With nothing more to eat, each person rolled in his caribou robes and tried to sleep. The aching of her stomach awoke Marta, and she looked about. The storm continued with no sign of slacking its fury. Darkness had replaced the light, so the blowing snow whirled about them in a darkened cloud that confused all senses. The girl crept from her bed to crawl away from the lean-to to relieve herself.

On the way back she passed the head, now almost reburied by the falling snow. A pang of sadness struck her: in another hour this body would disappear beneath the snow, lost forever save for a few scattered and gnawed bones that might emerge in the spring. His identity never would be known. The same fate awaited her if they failed to find the Yukon River. She felt her strength dropping with each day without food. The land would win simply by delaying them. She reckoned they had two more days before they too disappeared.

Marta frowned at the outstretched hand of the corpse. The snow had been scraped away from the forearm, and a thick hunk of the arm muscle was missing. Damn the sled dogs, she swore to herself. But a chill ran down her spine at what she saw.

The dogs had not eaten the arm. The muscle had been cut cleanly away as a butcher would dress out a joint of beef. One of her companions had eaten part of the dead man's flesh!

Shaken, she crawled back into her bed. Beside her, both Dickinson and Sergeant Sloan slept undisturbed.

During the night the storm died. When morning came Marta awoke to an unearthly silence. Days of hearing the howling wind caused her ears to ring with the thunder of the silence. No wind ruffled even a single branch nor stirred the tumbled snow. It was as if the entire air had hardened into the clearest, unseen crystal, and that solidification of the world trapped all sound and movement and held it in an uneasy grip waiting for some cataclysmic event to shatter the bonds and loose all matter in a single rush of madness.

Cautiously she moved her legs and watched the blanket of snow ripple over her caribou hide. A good six inches covered their camp. The dogs existed only as vague mounds with scuffed black patent-leather noses thrust upward to the air. For an hour, the girl lay in bed watching the dawn suffuse this eerie world with flashes and shadows of pink and mauve and a thousand shades of purple until the sun peered over the mountains as a fiery orange ball. The ball climbed into the lower part of the sky and proceeded on its abbreviated trek along the horizon. Meanwhile the sky ignited into an eye-watering, intense blue. She raised her head to study the sheltering rocks that encircled their camp like two cupped hands. Capping the tops of these ridges were thick layers of snow and ice. The wind and storm had shaped each snow cornice into a smooth covering that arched overhead, extending beyond its rocky base like the foamy crest of a titanic wave. These two waves hung over them in ominous silence.

Dickinson stirred, poking his head from beneath his robe. He squinted at the intensity of the light and sat upright. A cloud of snow fell from his fur hat. He exhaled carefully, watching his breath turn to crystalline steam. He forced his eyes wide against their protests.

"By God!" he exclaimed. "We may make it yet. Look down there!"

Marta scrambled to her knees at the excited tone of his voice. She followed the direction he pointed to, and her heart leapt. They were camped within a bowl formed by two jagged peaks that framed the pass. Below them, the unmistakably flat course of a broad, winding river lay frozen like the rest of the ivory landscape. Wind-carved bluffs and steep banks rose on both sides of this icebound course. Only one river in the Interior boasted such size. Below them ran the Yukon River.

And threading its way along the ice was a dog team with a single musher.

Dickinson jumped to his feet and shouted, but his voice quaked and croaked from weakness. The rider continued unchecked. Beside him Sloan yelled as well, with equally poor results. The sergeant dug his rifle out from his blankets, jacked a round into the chamber, and fired into the air. The explosion rent the silence like a close-by bolt of lightning. This time the musher stopped and looked up in their direction. Sloan fired again. . . .

The fragile crystal that held the land ripped apart with a gut-wrenching crack overhead that sounded as if the azure fabric of the sky had torn in two. Marta's head jerked up in the direction of the sound. A deep, thundering rumble greeted her, increasing in strength until it swallowed all other sound and continued to build while the ground beneath her knees trembled. Above her, cracks appeared in the smooth snow cornices and widened into gaping fissures. Powdery surface snow raced ahead of the shifting mass and sifted down onto the camp like hunting dogs in search of their prey. The sunlight ignited these millions of minuscule ice crystals into prisms of red and blue.

A moment of frightful clarity struck Marta. Now she knew how the poor unfortunate in the trail had died. Now she knew what had twisted his limbs so grotesquely. Her mouth formed the word of warning as she watched the tons of snow sliding down.

"Avalanche!" she screamed.

TWENTY-SEVEN

Nathan halted his sled and turned his head in the direction of the shots. He'd ranged a good thirty miles from Dawson in search of game. For the last week he had seen few tracks other than those of the snowshoe hares and the foxes that hunted them. The sudden winter storm caught him miles from Dawson, forcing him to seek cover until it passed. For the last four days he and his animals had weathered out the blow in a small cave beside the river. To amuse himself and to feed his team, he set rabbit snares close to the cave. He caught three rabbits while his constant companion, the she-wolf, brought back five on her own. As he fed his catch to his dogs and chewed thoughtfully on a stringy hind leg, she smugly swallowed all of her rabbits.

Pinned down by the storm, Nathan reflected on his luck at finding his son. The boy's curiosity and eagerness rekindled the child in the man. Each day he changed, yet a part of him constantly reminded Nathan of Wei-Li. One thing Nathan swore as he watched the shadows of his fire paint colors along the walls of the cave: his son would never grow up in an orphanage.

He and Riley supported their "family" by supplying meat to the mining camps and the restaurants in town. Most large game had been slaughtered or driven far away during the gold rush, so most game hunters returned empty-handed, but

Riley's savvy and Nathan's skill raised their success rate until they were in great demand. And while supplies of food brought in by the new railroad link with White Pass reduced the risk of another famine like that of '98–'99, men grew tired of eating salted pork and lusted after fresh meat.

The two hunters took turns, one watching the child while the other was away. Many Hats shared their table, but baby-sitting was beneath him. His contribution to the cooperative came in the form of tales and legends he taught the boy and from finding a cabin for the party. Doc Hennison, on the other hand, relied on his mystical gift to separate gullible men from their money. By day he brewed his elixir, singing and cursing over the fumes like a deranged chemist, and each evening he would slip from their cabin with a moosehide parfleche filled with bottles cradled lovingly in his arms. Away he would go, clinking into the night, only to return at daybreak with gold coins and gold dust filling his pockets, his bottles empty. Where he went and what he did, he refused to say.

Now Nathan found himself searching for the fool whose shots had spooked the moose he'd been trailing along the river. No bullets clipped the snow around him or snapped through the frigid air, he noted, so they weren't shooting at him. Obviously some cheechako, new to the land, who couldn't hit the side of a barn from the inside. If they were shooting at him his best chance for safety was to proceed as normal, since their shots were way off the mark. No wonder game was so hard to find with these fools muddling about, he grumbled.

A flash of light, sunlight glinting off a rifle barrel, caught his eye. There it was again off to the left near the old Boundary Trail. The shooting stopped, but another, more ominous sound reached his ears: the freight-train rumbling of a mountain of moving snow. He looked hard in that direction. Three figures were standing on the sled route. What else he saw raised the hairs on his neck.

The narrow pass where the shots came from became a living, dangerous creature as the snow from both slopes rushed down into the pass like the jaws of a trap springing shut. Clouds of lighter flakes roiled into the sky above the sliding tons of snow. Like an enormous white volcano erupting with frozen death, the avalanche poured its compacted snow into the pass while a milky plume of ice crystals billowed overhead.

Whoever fired those shots lay in the center of that white whirlwind, and fool or not, no man deserved to die like that. Nathan raced his team toward the pass. If they were buried, every second counted. The wolf sensed his urgency and harried the team.

In ten minutes, Nathan's sled reached the pass—what was left of it. Splintered trees, overturned rocks, and uprooted bushes dotted the fringes of the snow pile blocking the gorge. Scattered remnants of a camp littered the snow. Miraculously, the dog team had bolted with the first tremor and now stood to one side with the sled still hitched. The force of falling from so great a height had packed the snow as hard as concrete. Nathan could actually run across this fresh surface without sinking beyond his boots. He spun about, searching for survivors.

A man was buried to his knees, clothing torn and face already swelling from angry bruises. Caught like a fly in molasses, he looked about in bewilderment while his fingers scrabbled at the snow that bound him.

Dickinson blinked in confusion before his senses returned. He pointed to a patch of beaver fur just visible beneath a layer of snow.

"Marta! She's in there!" he croaked. "She's buried in there!" Cruelly, the snow held him fast beyond reach of the spot where the girl was entombed.

Nathan rushed past the spy and dropped to his knees, mittened hands scooping at the surface. The back of a beaver parka emerged, and he dug harder. Next he unearthed the hood. Pulling it back he gasped at the head that came into view.

The ebony hair was thick and black like a raven's wing—like Wei-Li's. His first thought was that an Athabascan woman had been trapped; but when he brushed the hair aside, he found himself staring at the pale face of a beautiful woman. Her eyes were closed as if asleep, and her full lips slightly parted to expose straight white teeth. Her nose was thin and straight, but her cheekbones were too prominent to be purely European. He hunched over her face to check for breathing and the smell of her hair assailed his nostrils. But no breath issued from her lips.

A burst of fury stabbed at his heart that so rare a creature should be so heedlessly crushed. Like Wei-Li, the fates hungered for beauty, especially taking delight in robbing the world of whatever loveliness they could find. With Wei-Li he had been too late to help. But here he might have that precious time that he had been denied less than three years ago. Here he could make a difference! That fury turned to energy, and he stripped his mittens off to dig his fingers into the snow that held her. Mindless of the bleeding from his broken and torn nails, Nathan dug like a madman to release the upper half of Marta's body. He ripped up her parka to press his ear against her bare chest. Her skin was still warm and a faint heartbeat reached his ear.

The young man jumped to his feet and grasped her beneath the arms and pulled. Marta's body refused to budge. The tightly packed snow spurned all attempts to break its grip. He renewed his digging, working in a frenzy.

By the time Dickinson had released himself, Nathan had freed the girl down to her thighs. But the snow continued to lower her temperature. In desperation, Nathan wrestled the girl free from her tomb. Using all his strength he pulled her atop the snow pack. Still, no air came from her lungs and her heartbeat grew more distant.

First, Nathan tried levering her arms back and forth over her head as Frenchy, a Portuguese sealer, had once taught him to do for drowning seamen. The lad cursed the lack of a barrel to roll the woman over. His efforts had no effect.

Then he remembered seeing a Koyukon shaman blowing smoke into the lungs of a dying native. Of course, he reasoned, this woman isn't like a drowned person. No water or snow needs to be pushed from her lungs. The parka hood protected her face and kept snow from her nose and mouth. She needs air pushed back into her lungs.

Quickly he knelt over Marta, fastened his mouth over hers, and blew until her chest rose. He repeated the process. Nothing happened. He blew again, and he continued to fill her lungs with his breath until his head swam and he thought he would pass out. Nothing. Still something made him press on, even though his breathing broke down into painful gasps.

Marta jerked once and coughed weakly. Then she gasped. Her eyelids fluttered, and she breathed on her own. Dickinson stood over the two, still dazed. Nathan ran to his sled and laid out his caribou robe. The spy blinked in astonishment when this stranger stripped Marta naked, then threw off his own clothes beside the furs and slipped under the covers with the unconscious girl. Dickinson fairly choked as the furs moved from the rhythmic action of their two bodies.

"Here now," he stammered. "Stop that! Good God, man, have you no decency? You may have saved her life, but you've no cause to take liberties with the poor girl!"

His words having no effect, Dickinson sprang at the couple, but Nathan's one arm pushed him away with surprising ease.

"Get away," the young man ordered.

The spy rushed for the rifle on Nathan's sled. The wolf growled a warning before he could jerk it free of its beaded moosehide scabbard.

"I wouldn't try that, mister," Nathan warned.

Dickinson turned to face the long barrel of Nathan's Colt leveled at his chest. The caribou hide lay partially displaced, exposing the couple. Nathan held the pistol steady with his right hand while his left hand continued to vigorously rub Marta's naked back.

"I'm trying to warm her up, not make love to her, you damned fool!" he shouted. "But I doubt you'd know the difference. Now, if you want to save her life, get a fire started and boil some strong tea. You'll find the fixings in that pouch tied to the right side of the sled."

Dickinson stood fixedly, bristling at these orders.

Nathan's anxiety over saving the girl turned to rage, and he boiled over. "Jump to it quick before I'm tempted to shoot you and feed her your liver to warm her up!" he snarled.

Marta awoke inside a cramped cabin. The single room of the log shack hove into view as she forced her eyes to focus. An oil lamp burned on the table beside her bed of spruce poles, casting its pale yellow glow over the room. The light failed to reach the farthest corners, where shadows silently lurked. All in all, the place was dark and gloomy, a fitting backdrop for her mood.

The reality of what had happened flooded back into her thoughts. The shots, the avalanche, all returned with frightening clarity. In her thoughts she relived the terror of that white flood, engulfing her and sweeping her away as if she were a leaf, the cold snow rolling her body and tossing her until it chose to bury her. For a few frightening moments she had experienced being buried alive. Then there was nothing.

Slowly, she tested her body, moving first one limb then the

next, until she satisfied herself that no bones were broken. Each movement was painful, but she'd been hurt worse in the past. Marta tightened each group of muscles to sample their discomfort until she'd mapped out her injuries. Only bruises, she realized. She'd been lucky. Again.

Suddenly a pair of deadly yellow eyes rose above the level of her covers. Marta froze. A wolf was calmly examining her from the bedside. How had this wolf gotten inside the cabin? The amber eyes bored into her very soul for a moment before the head vanished as stealthily as it had come.

Another pair of eyes raised above the level of her bed to study her. These eyes were coal black with a curious upward tilt and belonged to a small child. The child studied her just as intently as the wolf had, and Marta felt as if the boy and the wolf were related. But the boy extended a pudgy hand to lightly touch her face. Marta smiled at the contact of his warm fingers. Instantly, the hand withdrew. Then the child dropped below her line of sight and disappeared like the animal.

From the shadows, a tall, lean man emerged to stand over her. Marta startled at his extraordinary eyes. They were pale as the wolf's yet of a different color—gray and clear as the glacial ice. Is this a place of magic eyes? she wondered. Primal superstitions from her native land filled her thoughts. Was this a family of half humans and forest beasts? She shook her head to clear that nonsense, and that act made the room spin.

"Awake, eh?" Nathan said. "You're lucky to be alive. Not too many people can claim they tangled with an avalanche and survived."

Marta forced her head to turn. Her focus improved with this movement, and she saw an empty cabin except for the man and the boy holding the wolf beside him. The place was a mess, cluttered with wads of clothing and tools in a way only men living without a woman could accomplish. The air was stale as well, and she doubted that the room had ever been aired out.

"Where am I?" she asked.

"Dawson. We brought you here three days ago. You've been delirious at times. Doc thought you might have hit your head."

"Doc?"

She sat up and the robe fell from her, revealing her naked-ness. She blushed as his eyes darted over her breasts, and her hand went to her throat, where she felt a hard object hanging about her neck. A surge of anger flooded over her, not be-cause this man had seen her naked, but because she had blushed like a schoolgirl. She wondered why she should care.

Slipping back beneath the caribou robe, her fingers caught the thing at her neck and held it up. It was a carved stone dragon, shimmering in its milky green opalescence, tied about her neck with a rawhide thong. She recognized it as jade. A jade dragon in a house of wolves and a pale-eyed man. Sud-denly, the image of the dying Indian woman at Mentasta Lake filled her mind. Son of the Wolf, the woman had whispered be-fore she died. Had her fading mind glimpsed the future? Marta drove that disturbing picture away.

"What doctor?" she asked again.

"Doc Hennison. He lives here with Riley, Many Hats, and the two of us," Nathan answered. He reached out to pat the boy on his head. "What's your name?"

"Marta Kelly. Where are the two other men I traveled with?" She answered in clipped tones. Her hunch about no woman was right.

"That Dickinson is an odd one. He's in town, acting like a fellow who's planning to rob the Canadian Bank of Com-merce." He watched her closely, oblivious of the fact that his scrutiny made her nervous. "He paced around you like a caged marten until Doc assured him you'd be okay, then he took off like a shot. Is he your husband?"

"No." Strangely, Marta felt slighted that the spy was not at her side waiting for her to regain consciousness, although she knew that feeling was unreasonable. To Dickinson, his rivalry with Beaufort came first and foremost.

"I didn't think so."

"What makes you say that?" she bristled. "Don't you think I could have a husband?" She hated herself for her outburst, but the words were out.

"He just doesn't seem the marrying type, that's all. But you could have any man in Dawson . . . from what I've seen of you," he said with a grin.

Marta felt her face burn. Furious with this man's ability to make her blush, she turned her head aside.

Nathan noted the discomfort his words had caused. Beneath her prickly facade, he sensed she had been deeply hurt in the past. While something in her reminded him of Wei-Li, this girl lacked the stony fatalism of his lost love, and thankfully she showed no traces of the greedy hunger of Mrs. Barnette.

"What about Ser . . . Mr. Sloan?" she asked, regaining her poise.

"Never found him. I only dug you out, and Dickinson worked himself free."

Marta bowed her head into her hands. Sloan now, too. This scheme left a trail of blood. The robe fell from her back, but she no longer cared. Obviously, this pale-eyed man had seen all of her. She stiffened slightly as a small hand pulled the covers over her back. She looked up to see the boy standing beside her. She smiled at his enormous eyes. He looked like the children that populated her village in an age that seemed a thousand years ago. For an instant her home flashed before her eyes, the smell of the flowers after the rain, the soft grass, and the dark-eyed children—just like this little boy.

"What's your name?" she asked him directly.

"He doesn't talk," Nathan interrupted. "But he's my son, Je-

321

remiah. Everyone calls him Wolf or Cub, because Sweetness has adopted him."

"Sweetness?" she asked incredulously. "The wolf is called Sweetness? She looks anything but sweet." The absurdity of her situation caused her to break into giggles. Suddenly Nathan was laughing just as hard.

When Marta finally caught her breath, she wiped the tears from her eyes and fondled the jade dragon absentmindedly. "Where did this come from?" she asked.

Nathan sat on his haunches like he'd learned from Riley. The old gunman preferred to squat whenever possible, a throwback to his early years as a cowpoke. Nathan had picked up the habit. His face drew level with Marta's.

"That belonged to my wife, Jeremiah's mother. She was Chinese and put great stock in its magic powers. It's kept me alive, I think. When you looked like you might not make it at first, I took it off and tied it around your neck." He smiled self-consciously at his boyish foolishness. "You can't say it didn't work. You woke up, didn't you?"

"Belonged? Where is she?" she questioned him.

"She died almost three years ago. Right after the squirt was born."

"How did it happen?" she asked.

Suddenly, the tragedy of Wei-Li's burning and death poured out of Nathan like ice blocks surging free of a spring breakup. In all that time, he'd told no one. Riley and Doc knew the details all too well, and there had been no others worth sharing his grief. Yet, this stranger's simple question broke his heart open. All the hurt, recrimination, and anguish drained out. Head bent, his voice low and level, he told her the story. Only the nervous action of his hands, alternately smoothing and ruffling his son's hair, betrayed his deep feelings. When he finished, he looked up, not knowing what to expect. He found the girl watching him closely, tears brimming in her eyes.

The Wolf's Cub

The young man's openness, added to his evident anguish, caught Marta off guard. Something about him compelled her to explain her own sorrowful past, but she held back, wavering with indecision. Before she could decide, the front door burst open, and two bizarre creatures stomped inside. One wore a tattered wool logger's cap jammed tightly on his head, and lacked a right shoulder and arm. The other looked every inch the hunter with his thick beaver parka and greasy Stetson lashed about his ears with a red woolen scarf. Marta noted the long-barreled Sharps rifle slung over his shoulder and the bulges over his hip where his pistols pressed against the insides of his coat. The men's arguing ceased when they saw the girl.

"Am I a good physician, or am I not," Doc said as he preened. "See! I told you she'd be all right."

"Leave it to you to take credit for something you had nothing to do with, Doc," Riley muttered. He planted the rifle's butt heavily on the dirt floor.

"Any luck, Jim?" Nathan asked.

"None whatsoever, lad. Didn't see hide nor hair of nothing worth ventilating with a bullet. We're in big trouble. We ain't shot no game to sell since you dug up this pretty thing, and our credit ain't up there with the Bank of England. No offense, ma'am," he said as he touched the brim of his hat, spilling a cloud of snow onto Marta's bed.

"Where are your manners, sir?" Hennison demanded. "Introduce us to this fair damsel, Nathan. You'd think we never taught you proper manners."

"Well, we ain't no proper gents, Doc, so put off them fancy airs," Riley interrupted. "And we never did teach the boy nothing proper."

"Miss Marta Kelly, may I introduce my friends, Doc Hennison and Jim Riley," Nathan said. "Their bark is less than their bite, I must warn you."

"Charmed, my dear." Doc bowed low and kissed her hand.

"I gather you are a visitor from a climate far warmer than this stink hole. Mexico or the Central Americas, I'd wager a guess."

"How did you know that?" Marta asked in alarm, quickly withdrawing her hand.

"Be not disturbed, Miss Kelly. It is my business to know those things."

"You was mumbling in Spanish while you was delirious, ma'am," Riley answered. "Doc ain't that savvy."

He shucked his hefty coat and threw it into one corner before squatting on his heels as if he were beside a campfire. Doc dropped into the one chair beside a splintered table of two-by-fours and propped his muddy boots on the table.

"Cheer up, my lads," Hennison said. "I'm still tapping the townsmen's pockets with my special drink. Tonight ought to be good for a few more coin of the realm or a pinch or two of color. I'll get right on it after supper. By the way, what is for supper?"

"The usual. Stew," Nathan replied.

He got out four bowls and a loaf of frozen bread, which he proceeded to divide into slabs with an ax. Three of those pieces he laid atop the woodstove to thaw. Filling two bowls with the thick mix, he handed one to Marta and one to the Cub. The girl's stomach growled loudly at this first food in many days. Hennison took another bowl, but Marta noticed his portion was decidedly less than hers. Riley peered into the pot, then turned away to resume his squat in the corner.

The stew and the second slice of warm bread tasted more glorious to her than any meal she could remember. Marta stopped after she gulped down all her stew and the second piece of bread. She looked around in confusion. Riley and the young father weren't eating.

"What's wrong?" she asked. "Why aren't you two eating?"

"I'm not hungry," Nathan answered.

"I ain't either," Riley added, smiling.

The realization struck Marta like a slap across her face. "It's because there isn't any more, is there? That's it, isn't it? I ate what you'd saved for both of you."

"Don't fret, ma'am, Nathan and I really ain't hungry," Riley reassured her.

"Nathan, is that your name?" she asked. "You didn't tell me."

"Yes, Nathan Blaylock."

"Nathan Blaylock . . . the rapist!" The words flew from her mouth like darts.

His face blanched, and he jumped to his feet. "I'm no rapist!" he cried. "Who told you that?"

"A man we met on the trail near Copper Center. McCarty, I think his name was. He said you'd forced your attentions on his captain's wife," she replied defiantly.

"Barnette's man," Nathan spat venomously. "That's his side of the story, and it's a lie!" He snatched his coat from the pile and rushed out into the night. Riley grabbed his parka and followed him.

Hennison wiped the last spot of grease from the inside of his bowl and licked it carefully off his finger. He regarded the door sadly. "Nathan's many things, young lady," he said slowly. "He's killed men, but none that didn't need it. One thing for certain, he's no rapist. He's saved my life more than once, and I count myself a lucky man to call him a friend. You just ate what he and Riley were saving for the rest of the week. I've also watched them scrimp on their victuals so the baby could eat." The physician paused to release a deep sigh. "I wish I were that principled, but I'm not."

Marta watched in silence as Doc got to his feet, rebuttoned his coat, and dug his parfleche from a corner pile. Looking stealthily at the closed door, Hennison crossed quickly to the other side of the room and located a glass bottle containing two darkened objects floating in its liquid. He slipped the bottle into his bag and opened the door.

He turned to announce grandly, "Time to make my appearance. My clients await. Would you be so kind as to look after young Jeremiah? I won't be long. Get some more rest, my dear, and, believe me, your virtue is quite safe with my friends."

Hennison paused with his face half in the shadows to glance back at her. "One thing you might consider, miss. It was Nat, your so-called defiler of women, who nursed you back to health, and not your friend Dickinson."

With that he vanished into the night.

Marta hugged her knees in silence while she struggled with the confusing thoughts in her mind. This frozen land was full of contradictions. Safe shelters became death traps in a moment's notice, good acted in evil ways, and the so-called bad did good. It made her head spin, and she emitted a long, heartfelt sigh before placing her head on her knees.

A small hand touched her hair. Carefully it ran light fingers over the ebony strands like one would caress a frightened bird. She turned her head to look at the small boy who patted her. His saucer-sized eyes matched the blackness of her hair. Beside him the wolf studied her with its own golden glare. Marta reached out and encircled the child with her arms. Willingly, he snuggled against her.

"Am I softer than the others here?" she asked him. "I think so. Riley bristles like a prickly pear cactus, and, I fear, Doc Hennison would sell you for a dollar if he could. Even your father who loves you is not as warm, for he's a man. A little child needs the hug of a woman, eh?"

She raised her head to focus on the solemn face. "You have a right to look that way, *niño*. It is a hard life for little ones. Hard for the innocent."

She hugged him tightly. "If I could have a son, I would like him to smile more than you, but that will never happen. Still, I *can* make you smile more." She dug her fingers under his jacket and tickled his ribs.

The boy twitched, then burst into a fit of squeals. The wolf cocked one ear, but made no move to charge. Marta tickled the boy again. Another round of giggles followed. Soon both boy and woman were laughing and acting silly. This continued until both crashed exhausted back onto the bed.

"Jeremiah," Marta said as she patted his small back. "Such an impressive name for a little *niño*. Did you know you're named after a saint? But you don't talk, do you?" She pointed her slender finger at the tip of his nose. "Can you say 'Jeremiah'?"

The boys lips moved without making a sound.

"Perhaps not. Jeremiah is too hard? What was the other name they called you? Cub? Yes, that's what you're called. Cub. This wolf thinks you belong to her, so Cub is a good name. Can you say 'Cub,' then?"

"Cug," came his tentative reply.

Marta started. "You can talk! I'll bet these men never took the time to work with you. They look like the kind that would order you to talk and then go away, expecting you to practice on your own. Am I correct, Cub?"

"Cug," he answered, this time with more assurance.

"Very good, but you must say 'Cub.' 'Cub.' You are not a 'cug.' You are a wolf cub. That handsome man with the short temper is your father, and this wolf is your mother."

After a half hour, the boy finally got it right. Marta clapped her hands together and hugged him. The child mimicked her clapping. Excited, he wriggled away and danced around the room reciting his name. Marta beat time on her blanket and laughed as the word bubbled out of the child. A cold draft struck her face, and she turned in its direction.

Nathan was standing in the doorway watching.

Jeremiah crashed into his father's legs, clasping the knees, and shouted up at him: "Cub!"

Nathan reached down and swung his son high into the air. Jeremiah reiterated his one-word vocabulary again and again. The man turned a grateful face to Marta. "You got him to talk. That's his first word," he stammered. "I don't know how to thank you."

Marta watched him guardedly. "Apparently, you already have. The doctor says I owe my life to you, that you cared for me after the avalanche. Why didn't you take me to the hospital?"

Nathan shrugged. "That Dickinson fellow got real nervous when we suggested it. Doc figured the guy was hiding something, and when he found a scrap of paper in your pocket, he knew his hunch was right."

"Paper? What paper?"

"A note about the Lee-Metford rifles that the Mounties have stockpiled. Colonel Steele told us about those new bolt-action rifles. I doubt more than a handful of men in the Yukon know they even exist. All of us use lever-action rifles, or the old falling-block types like Riley's Sharps. Lee-Metfords use a .303 caliber bullet. Only army types use that round up here. It's too new for the rest of us, and not powerful enough to stop a bear or drop a moose reliably." He paused to watch her reaction at his next sentence. "Army types or revolutionaries," he said.

Marta stiffened, just as he expected she would. Part of her reaction was shock, though. *She'd written no note about the rifles!* Dickinson must have stuffed the paper into her coat in case they were discovered or turned over to the police. Maybe he'd expected her to die, and was using her to cover his trail. The thought left her shaken and uncertain.

"I don't guess you want those rifles to take over the Yukon,"

Nathan continued, "and you were talking in Spanish while unconscious. I figure you want them for south of the border."

The girl struggled to regain her composure. This young man with the icy eyes disturbed her. Standing with his son in his arms he sent conflicting signals—warmth and love for his child mixed with an undercurrent of unpredictability, of danger, like the jaguar of her homeland. He also had an unnerving way of talking as if he could read her mind.

"I misjudged you," she countered, hoping to change the topic. "Hennison told me you nursed me back to health. I apologize for what I called you. You obviously are a gentleman."

Nathan grunted in distaste. "No, I'm no gentleman, leastways not what passes for a gentleman around here—and I don't care to be one. But in my dealings with women, just say I've had bad luck."

"All women?"

"Some women . . . The ones that count." Now it was Nathan's turn to feel uneasy. "But the captain's wife chased after me."

"And you let her catch you, didn't you?" Marta asked slyly.

He grinned. "I told you I wasn't a gentleman."

Their eyes met, and they both blushed. Her hand played with the jade dragon around her neck. Before more could be said, the cabin door flew open. Marta blinked at the solidly built Indian encased in a caribou anorak and sporting a splendidly beaded beaver fedora. With each trip to Moosehide, the Han village, the hat that formerly belonged to Doc Hennison acquired a new load of beads. Many Hats stepped inside, prudently removing his hat to protect it from the low doorframe. Holding it before him in his two hands, he gave the couple a curt bow before sitting on the only chair.

"Many Hats Charlie," Nathan introduced his friend. "This is Marta Kelly from . . . someplace south."

"Cub!" Jeremiah chirped proudly.

The seamed face of Many Hats rearranged its lines until they draped around his broad smile like a waterfall of wrinkles. "So, the wolf cub wags his tongue," he grunted.

"Marta got him started," Nathan said.

The Athabascan shook his head. "Leave it to a woman to release more words into this world," he snorted, but his gruffness failed to conceal a note of pride. The old man then sat there waiting expectantly.

After an awkward silence, Nathan finally asked, "What brings you back so early, Many Hats? I thought you planned on going to Moosehide."

Charlie bobbed his head. "There is a big fight in the singing house. I thought you should know."

"The Palace, er, the Savoy, they call it? Where you brought Cub?"

"Yes, Hennison and Riley are in the middle of it. You best go help them."

Nathan turned to Marta. "Will you look after Jeremiah?" he asked. "I don't know what happened, but I've got to help my friends."

She nodded, holding her arms out to the boy. Nathan rebuttoned his parka and left. Many Hats rose with great solemnity, still protecting his hat with both hands, and exited after Nathan.

"Well, *niño*," Marta pouted, "as usual, the men have left us to fend for ourselves. We'll just have to entertain ourselves."

She picked up a scrap of smoked hide and began to braid a cord while Jeremiah watched intently. Scarcely more than a few minutes passed when the door slowly opened. Marta raised her head from her task, expecting to see one of the four men returning. What she saw instead sent chills down her spine.

Standing in the doorway was a man she had never seen before. The light from the oil lamp cast flickering yellow fingers

330

over the man's face, but nothing the lamp could offer added warmth to the face that scrutinized her in minute detail.

While the features were long and angular, the flesh was soft and puffy, almost effeminate for a man, as if the person was accustomed to being pampered. The long aquiline nose shadowed a pair of pouting drawn lips that curved downward at the edges in a heartless smirk of superiority. That curve reminded Marta of the tree boas that lived in Panama. She half expected a forked tongue to flick at her.

Thick eyebrows arched smugly over heavy-lidded eyes. But it was the eyes themselves that dominated this haughty face. Cold, lifeless like a dead fish, they absorbed warmth like a chunk of ice. Only the reflected glow of the lamp in those blue eyes hinted of immense cruelty, not from heat of passion or moral conviction, but from a clinical sense of preeminence— as one might feel while squashing an annoying mosquito or cracking the neck of a snared and hapless rabbit.

Such eyes belonged to a hangman, and their gaze sweeping over Marta made her feel unclean and violated all over again. She had seen that look before, on the faces of the hidalgos whose heel ground her people's faces into the dirt. The *federal* officer who raped her had such a look.

The eyes flickered apathetically, reminding her of a weasel, before the man bowed. All the while he kept her fixed with his stare like a snake mesmerizing a trapped bird.

"Pardon the intrusion, m'dear," he said. For his size, the voice was disturbingly high-pitched. "I must have the wrong address. . . ."

The door closed just as silently, leaving Marta hugging little Jeremiah while a deadly fear knotted her stomach. Without having met him, she recognized the man. He could be no other. Here was Dickinson's nemesis, the one who haunted his dreams and dwelt amid his shadows. Beaufort was in Dawson.

★ ★ TWENTY-EIGHT ★ ★

"I . . . I never expected it to happen," Doc Hennison stammered, his face white and drawn. "It wasn't supposed to happen, believe me."

"Wasn't supposed to happen? That jus' don't cut it, Doc!" Jim Riley turned his head to snarl over his shoulder at the physician, who tugged at his arm. That same arm held his Colt Peacemaker, the barrel firmly pressed into the center of the forehead of a deathly frightened whiskey drummer. His other arm held the quaking man in a vicelike hammerlock. The man tottered on the edge of fainting dead away. What degree of drunkenness he'd enjoyed evaporated when Riley's revolver screwed into his head. His bowler hat lay trampled in the soggy sawdust on the barroom floor.

"Please," the man pleaded. "I didn't mean to . . . Please, don't shoot me. I've a wife and three children."

"Well, they're about to become a widow and orphans," Riley replied. " 'Cause I'm going to shoot yer lights out, then I'm going to kill this fool quack—something I should have done a long time ago."

"You can't be serious," Hennison countered. "You'd kill us over a trivial thing like this?"

"It ain't trivial to me, Doc. I told you not to mess around with them, but—no, you had to go right ahead. Now look what happened."

"Very well, if your mind is made up," Hennison sighed. "Shoot him first. He is the culprit, after all." He released his grip on Riley and gave the nearest exit a sidelong glance. Dodging among the gathered onlookers, Doc figured he had an even chance of escaping once the smoke from the first round clouded the air.

"What . . . ?" The drummer fainted at that news; but while his body sagged limply, his head remained trapped between the pincers of Riley's gun barrel and his steely hug.

"Hold on, Jim!" It was Nathan's voice cutting through the confusion. "What's going on here?"

Riley looked disgustedly at the flaccid figure in his grasp. "This fool swallowed my toes!"

"Your toes?"

"My damned toes. The ones I frostbit, that I keep in that bottle."

"How'd he get your toes?" Nathan asked, puzzled. He forced back a smile. The situation was humorous until you saw the fury on his friend's face; then it became no laughing matter.

Riley's only reply was a venomous glance at Doc.

"I'm afraid it's my fault," Doc confessed. "I should explain."

"I think you'd better, and quickly, too, before Jim shoots this fellow."

"Well, I came up with the idea two weeks ago. I was looking for a . . . something novel to boost sales of my tonic. And—"

"And—," Riley snarled.

"And I hit upon the idea of concocting a drink with Riley's frostbitten toes." Hennison mopped his brow with a faded red handkerchief. "Sort of like using olives in a martini. I called it a 'sourtoe,' a rather clever play on words, don't you think? Sourdough, sourtoe, do you get it?"

"You're gonna get it, Doc!" Riley moved his pistol to point it at Doc. The drummer's head flopped to one side.

"They were never supposed to be eaten, believe me. Your toes don't float. They stayed safely on the bottom of the glass. Even the most macho man I'd dare to drink the sourtoe left them untouched. It's worked without hitch for these last two weeks, and I got a dollar a drink." Hennison pointed his finger at Riley. "That money kept us going when you failed as a meat hunter. It put bread in our mouths. Don't forget that! And each night I'd return your precious withered toes, safe and sound."

"What went wrong, then?" Nathan asked incredulously.

Hennison shot a disgusted look at the unconscious salesman. "This fool was too drunk to notice, I guess. Before I could stop him, he swallowed them both. Now, Riley wants to shoot him and cut him open to reclaim his lost digits."

"Doc, you should have asked Jim before you took his toes," Nathan admonished his friend. "How would you feel if someone did that to you?" As soon as the words slipped out Nathan realized his mistake. War had taken Doc's right arm without his permission.

"Someone's got my whole right side," Hennison rebutted the argument. "It wouldn't surprise me if it's hanging in some Yankee medical school, but you don't find me sniveling about it. A real man wouldn't think twice about donating a few odd toes to further the cause of mankind!"

"How does making a goddamned fool drink advance mankind?" Riley swore. "All you did was point up what we already know: there's a heap of stupidity circulating in the guise of humanity. And I aim to reduce that number by two."

Nathan rubbed the back of his neck. "What Doc did was wrong, Jim, plain and simple. But whatever his faults, he's saved both our lives. You can't forget that. We've been down many a long trail together."

Riley ignored that logic and looked back at the man in his

arms. "I don't know this jasper from Adam, and he's got my toes," he said sullenly.

Hennison had moved behind Nathan for added protection, and from this position he rebuilt his confidence. "Shooting him won't help. His stomach's already got your toe half digested."

"Jim," the young man added, "you taught me how to use a gun, and it was you who said how easy it was to let loose a bullet and how nothing in the world could ever get that same bullet back—so I should be damned sure what I shot. This man's a drunken fool, and he swallowed your toes without even knowing it. Are you going to kill him for being a fool? If you do, then everything you taught me you don't truly believe, and you'll deserve to be hanged for his murder."

Riley loosed his grip and let the man drop. "I'm gonna miss them toes," he sighed.

The crowd, sensing the bloodlust was gone and no gunplay was forthcoming, shuffled back to scattered clusters and separate tables. Without bloodshed, no one bothered to call the Mounties, so the saloon drifted back into its monotonous undertone of muffled conversation mixed with the clink of whiskey glasses and poker chips. The scent of killing receded as well, to be replaced by the usual pungent tang of stale sawdust and sweat, woodsmoke and old tobacco.

Nathan gave Hennison a hard look, and the physician parted with one of his coins to buy Riley a bottle of rye. After three drinks, the gunman looked up at his two companions.

"Well, got any other plans?" he asked forlornly. "We got no money. Game's been driven out of the country, and my toes—our only moneymakers—are et. What do we do now?"

The clink of metal on the bar beside them drew their attention. A handful of gold coins, all double-eagle twenty-dollar gold pieces, rattled about on the polished mahogany surface.

Dickinson smiled across at the astonished men. "You men have done me a favor. Now perhaps I can be of some service to you."

"I ain't giving up no more toes," Riley grunted.

"No, nothing like that," Dickinson replied as he bent closer and lowered his voice to a whisper. "You have a fast sled, you know the trails, and you're skilled with weapons. Those are all skills I need."

"You want us to rob the bank, is that it?" Hennison said.

"No, no, nothing so prosaic as that, but it's worth five thousand in gold. Are you interested?"

"For five thousand, I might part with another toe," Riley said to no one in particular. "But I'd like to keep the big toes."

"He doesn't want your stinking toes," Hennison growled. "He wants something else. Just what is it?"

"First I want your word that what I ask remains a secret between us. These gold coins on the bar are payment for your silence. If you refuse, you take the coins and forget what was discussed. Do you agree?"

All three nodded their heads.

"I want you to steal four crates of rifles and a special weapon from the Mounties." To Dickinson's surprise, none of the three even blinked. In fact Doc rubbed his hands together in glee.

"I'd love to, especially after that smarmy magistrate threw me in their stinking jail," Hennison chortled. "What's this secret weapon you mentioned?"

"It's called a Maxim gun," the spy said slowly.

"Oh, yes, that Maxim gun," Hennison added offhandedly.

"You know about their Maxim gun?" Dickinson asked in astonishment. "You know where it is?"

"Sure." It was Riley's turn to elaborate. "They keep it in the back of the jail where they locked us up. It's all wrapped up and polished to a shine. We seen how it works, too. Sort of like a

Gatling gun, only better. Feeds the cartridges on a long belt."

Dickinson scarcely could contain his excitement. These men actually knew the location of his elusive prize. All the while Marta had lain unconscious, Dickinson had sought out the hidden whereabouts of the Maxim—with no success. The crates of Lee-Metford rifles resided in the storehouse inside the Mounties' stockade on the edge of town. No one could tell him of the machine gun, not even the one or two policemen he'd plied with liquor on their off-duty hours. Here, these three could pinpoint the exact location for him. It was an unbelievable stroke of luck.

Only Nathan held some reservation. "This has to do with the girl, Marta, doesn't it?" he said.

Dickinson looked at him sharply. He'd underestimated this one, he realized. On the spur of the moment he decided truth was his best ally with this Blaylock. "Yes. Her people are oppressed by a foreign power, and she needs the weapons to fight for freedom." Sadly, he found he couldn't tell the whole truth. Too many years of hiding from it had crippled his tongue.

But his statement struck a resonant chord with all three. No sooner were the words out of his mouth than each was reliving his past bid for freedom, Doc with his failed Second War for Independence against the North, Riley with his chaotic cattle wars, and even Nathan with his burning desire to escape the orphanage.

"When do we get started?" Riley spoke for all of them.

But Dickinson gazed past him to the farthest corner of the long bar. Color drained from his face as if he'd seen a ghost, and his hand started to shake so violently that the whiskey glass spilled large droplets onto the gleaming wood. The others turned to look.

A large, heavyset man raised his drink to salute them. Shadows half cloaked his features but his clothing tagged him as a dandy. He swaggered slowly into the light and toward them.

337

"You know that flash?" Doc asked Dickinson, but the man could only stammer.

Riley winced when the light exposed the stranger's features. "Christ Almighty, he looks like a sidewinder!" he exclaimed.

The man slid near and tipped his hat with a mocking salute. "My dear Dickinson, how good to see you," he hissed in a thin voice. His lips parted to reveal tiny white teeth with a wide gap between the middle two, causing them to resemble fangs.

"Aubrey . . ." Dickinson found his tongue, yet his words were forced and high-pitched.

"Surely you'll introduce me to your friends?" The man appeared to be playing with the spy, enjoying his discomfort, stalking him like prey.

"This is Sir Aubrey Beaufort of Her Majesty's Foreign Office." Dickinson deliberately omitted revealing the names of his associates. But it was to no avail.

"And these three are Hennison, Riley, and Blaylock from the American side." Beaufort shocked them with a glimpse of his knowledge. "I've already paid a call on the charming Miss Kelly," he added.

"You know us?" Hennison asked.

Beaufort nodded. His eyes flicked from one to the other. "And I believe I can even read your minds." His eyes grew even colder, something none of the others thought possible until they saw the change. "Gentlemen, a word of advice. Forgo any enticements Dickinson might offer you. They will only lead to your deaths."

With that he turned and walked away. A silence enveloped the group as they watched him exit the doors. But his warning had the opposite effect on one.

"Forgo any enticements! Who the hell does he think he is,

telling me that?" Doc sputtered. "By God, what I'm told to forgo or not to forgo is my own goddamned decision."

Riley stroked his chin. Ever the professional in these matters, he didn't like what he'd just heard. If this Beaufort already knew about the rifles and the machine gun, he held all the cards. He sighed in resignation. Even against all odds they needed Dickinson's money. The gunman saw little choice.

"If this dude is onto us, we ain't got much time," he said. "Obviously his move was to throw us off balance. He'll be expecting us to regroup or formulate a new plan. So we've got to move tonight, if we're going to move at all."

"Tonight!" Hennison's face flushed in triumph. "He won't be expecting that."

"Yes, by God!" Dickinson smacked his fist into his palm. "You're right. He'll expect me to hesitate like I've always done. Tonight is our best chance. We'll grab the weapons and race across to the American side. With a good head start, we'll be back in Valdez before Aubrey can catch up, and we'll place Marta and the guns on the next boat south."

Nathan interrupted. "Marta . . . Miss Kelly won't be strong enough."

"Let her decide that," Dickinson cut him off. Nathan's attention to the girl had not gone unnoticed by the spy.

He ushered the men to the most isolated table in the part of the theater, away from the teeming bar. Since Arizona Charlie Meadows's sale of the Savoy, only the saloon ran consistently. Nightly shows no longer enlivened the attached theater. In the shadows, the group formulated a plan of attack.

"Steele's still out of town, so the post will be on a more relaxed footing," Riley informed them. "One of the Mounties let that slip when I was talking to him yesterday. Nat, you're good at planning. What do you suggest?"

Riley's question was more than academic. He'd noticed the

lad's misgivings. Being a father fettered Nathan's normal exuberance, but Riley knew the young man was essential for any success. Drawing Nathan into the planning would insure his involvement.

"We'll need three sleds," Nathan answered. "One for the rifles, one for the Maxim gun—it must weigh over three hundred pounds with all its parts—and one to carry our supplies and Marta. We'll need to set a hot pace, and she won't be able to keep up for another few days. That means Many Hats and his sled." He stopped to give Dickinson a hard look. "Hats gets paid the same as the rest of us, agreed?"

"Agreed."

"Five thousand divides evenly by four," Doc added craftily.

"Five thousand it is. One thousand two hundred fifty apiece."

"All right," Nathan said. "We need a diversion. Just inside the stockade of Fort Herchmer is the storage barn. It's filled with hay for the Mounties' horses, and it's right next to the barracks for the Yukon Field Force." Nathan had learned from Colonel Steele that the Field Force had been attached to the Mounted Police since 1900, boosting the strength of the police force to over three hundred men—a far cry from the twenty North West Mounted Police who first faced the tide of gold seekers in 1897.

"Many Hats will hold the teams with Marta down by the river, hiding among the frozen stern-wheelers. On our signal they'll come a-running."

"And the signal?" Dickinson asked.

"I'll set fire to the barn. That dry straw and hay should go up in an instant. The fire will keep the Mounties busy, not only to save their feed but to keep it from spreading to the barracks. When the alarm is sounded Dickinson will break open the shed with the rifles while Doc and Jim pound on the back door of the jail. The guard will think they're calling him to help with the fire, and open the door—I hope. Leastways he won't be expecting a break into the jail. I'll help Dickinson load the rifles while you two wheel out that Maxim. Don't shoot a Mountie whatever you do, is that clear? If we kill one of them, they'll follow us across the border for sure or ask the U.S. Army to help. Stealing their guns will only sting their pride, and I'm hoping they'll want to cover up the fact that they can't guard their own weapons. Once out of town we head for Alaska, follow the rivers, and cut across the glacier to Valdez."

Dickinson's face lighted with obvious joy. The plan was well thought out. He withdrew his pocket watch to steady his trembling fingers and studied the timepiece. "Darkness obviously is no problem. Is two hours enough time to pack the sleds?"

"Hell, most of our stuff is packed," Riley explained. "We ain't got a whole lot."

Twenty minutes past midnight found Nathan lying on his belly behind a pile of snow just ten feet from the doors to the fodder barn. A tattered white sheet, "borrowed" from one of the prostitute's cribs in the Whitecastle District, covered his parka like a poncho and helped him blend with the snow that covered everything. The preparations had taken four hours rather than the two they'd planned, but now Marta and Many Hats waited in the shadows of the ice-locked steamers a mere two hundred yards away, and Doc and Riley were in position behind the jail. Dickinson was nowhere to be seen, a fact that made Nathan uneasy, but he took some solace in knowing Jeremiah was safely hidden with his old Han family in Moosehide. With the money from this, Nathan resolved to take his son to Alaska and settle down for good. That notion, more than anything, had caused him to undertake this job. This money would buy him time for his son.

Nathan froze in place. The barn doors parted and a beam of yellow light spilled over the snow. Two shadows appeared

341

within the light and stopped just outside to shut the doors. One Mountie carried a hay bale in his arms while the other walked beside him with a lantern. Before closing the door, the one extinguished the lamp and hung it on a nail just inside the barn. The sounds of laughter reached Nathan's hiding site as the men approached. They were walking directly toward him, he realized. Reversing his heavy Colt to use as a blackjack if necessary, Nathan burrowed deeper into the snowbank. The voices grew louder until they sounded directly overhead. Then they stopped.

" 'Ere, wot's this?" one of the Mounties said.

"What's the matter, Jack?"

"Look at that," his companion exclaimed. "That's not bloody right."

"What are you gaffing about, Jack? I don't see nothing."

Nathan tensed, ready to spring.

"Over there, I tell you," Jack persisted. "Some sod went and dropped the boot brush from his kit in the snow over there. Sar'n Major MacAslan'll give the poor sod what for if'n he sees that. Pick it up, will you, Ned? I gots me arms wrapped around this bloody great wad of hay."

Nathan cracked one eye open to see their polished boots standing inches from his face. The man with the bale stepped closer and his boot crushed down on Nathan's hand, the one without the revolver. Pain shot up Nathan's arm, but only the tightening of his eyelids betrayed the agony he felt. At this moment the half-moon chose to peek from an edge of cloud. Nathan prayed the men would move on before the moon became totally exposed.

"I don't see nothing. No brush, nothing."

"Take me load, and I'll fetch it," Jack said. "It's right over there."

"I will not. This is one of your tricks to pass that bale off to me, Jack. Get on with you. I'm freezing my arse off out here.

342

That brush ain't none of our concern." With that, the other hurried in the direction of the stables. Jack sighed and struggled after him with the hay threatening to upend him at any moment.

Nathan resumed his breathing and kneaded his hand to relieve the pain. Raising up for an instant to glance at the receding men, he scurried between the barn doors.

The lamp was still warm to the touch. Nathan opened its fill cap and sloshed oil across the lower bales of hay. Holstering his pistol, he cupped his hands, mindful of the swollen left one, and struck a lucifer match to an oil-soaked patch. The sulfur tip blazed into life. Fire leapt along the ribbon of coal oil.

In seconds, the hay was wildly ablaze. Nathan dashed back out the doors and raced around to the shadows of the building.

"Fire! Fire!" he yelled.

Lights appeared in the barracks windows and the door opened. By now, flames flickered through the cracks in the board walls, causing the entire storage barn to glow like a jack-o'-lantern. Shouts of alarm echoed through the night, and the metallic clanking of an alarm bell added to the confusion.

Nathan raced around the back of the barn, running low to the ground to reduce his silhouette against the burning building. He collided heavily with a figure in the shadows, and the two bodies flew into the snow from the impact. Nathan's pistol butt rose above the other person even before the two hit the ground.

"Don't! It's me!" Dickinson hissed. His arms flailed protectively before his face.

"About time you showed up," Nathan grunted. "Where are the rifles?"

Before Dickinson could answer, Nathan clamped a gloved hand across his mouth. Noise outside the stockade wall to their backs drew his attention. Releasing his hold on the spy, Nathan sprang to the low parapet and cautiously raised his head to look over the wall.

The grinning face of Many Hats stared up at him. The Indian held both his and Nathan's dog teams while Marta waited farther in the shadows with the third sled. Wisely, the Athabascan had muzzled the dogs to keep them from barking. Many Hats raised his hand in salute. Nathan pointed to the small sally port in the back wall less than ten feet away.

Leaping down to the ground, Nathan raced to the portal, raised the bar, and threw his weight against it. The door failed to budge. Snow and ice blocked the door. Furiously, the young man used both his hands to dig the opening free. He hit it again with all his weight and it creaked partly open.

By now the fire was raging beyond control, casting frightening shadows across the compound. An organized bucket brigade of Mounties stretched from the front of the building all the way out the front gates and down to the river, where men were chopping furiously at their holes in the river ice to keep them from freezing closed. Ice-rimmed buckets passed up and down the lines of men, but the Mounties were fighting a losing battle.

Dickinson had located the rifle shed and dragged three crates to the back portal in the time Nathan took to break the gate free. The frozen air bit into their lungs as they skidded the boxes into two of the waiting sleds. Nathan glimpsed Marta's face framed by her fur parka hood and flushed with excitement. Many Hats waited with arms hanging loosely at his sides, imperturbable as ever.

"What's keeping the others?" Dickinson hissed as he helped Nathan load the crates into Marta's and Many Hats' sleds.

Miraculously, the Canadians were gaining control of the fire. While the front half of the barn lay in smoldering ruins, more steam and smoke billowed from the remainder of the structure than flames, signifying the water brigade was winning. And more worrisome were the figures splitting off of the bucket lines to move away from the fire. Any minute someone would stumble upon them.

"Push harder, damn you," came Riley's voice from the shadows.

"Go to hell!" Hennison answered back. "I'm pushing as hard as I can."

Out of the darkness the two men appeared grappling with the wheeled Maxim gun. Were it not for the seriousness of their situation, Nathan might have laughed out loud at this comical scene. Riley struggled ahead in the deep snow like a draft horse, almost on his knees, in a harness the two had concocted out of bedsheets from the jail's bunks. Doc pushed from behind with his one shoulder set against the metal carriage. The metal-rimmed wheels dug into the ruts and snow, and all the while the two men sputtered at each other.

With one great groan, Doc shoved the gun carriage into a deep rut, where it remained fixed. Quickly, Nathan brought his sled up to the Maxim since it would no longer move. The great wheels stared defiantly at the youth. Obviously it was too large for the basket.

"Goddamned piece of shit won't fit in the sled," Doc swore. "What do we do now?"

Nathan studied the gun carriage and the fluted barrel. His eyes rested on the hitch pins holding the wheels to the undercarriage. The oversized wheels had been built to overcome rugged terrain, but not snow and ice. Here, their size only added to the gun's lack of maneuverability. But the quick-release pins enabled the wheels to be rapidly removed for deployment by pack mule like a mountain howitzer.

"Pull the pins and leave the damned wheels here," Nathan advised. He turned his gaze on Marta. "Surely your country can find a pair of wheels to put on this thing."

She nodded grimly. The wheels were separated, and the machine gun rolled heavily into the basket of Nathan's sled. Without further hesitation, Nathan whistled softly to his team and the she-wolf led them off at a quick sprint. Riley just had time to jump aboard as the sled raced past. Marta followed suit, with Doc Hennison sprawled halfway across the rifle crates. Many Hats' team brought up the rear, with Dickinson standing on one runner.

At that moment a warning shout sounded; the half-moon now clearly illuminated the three fleeing teams. A rifle cracked, and a bullet whipped up a plume of snow where the group had been a second ago. With little more than the whisper of the sled runners over the frozen ground, the arms thieves vanished over a furrow and disappeared in the darkness of a drainage ditch running obliquely to the river.

Ahead lay the wide, moonlit expanse of the frozen Yukon. Crossing it would leave them exposed for a half mile, but there was no other way. The three teams broke from the cover of the ditch and leapt across the shore ice. Nathan urged his team on as his back muscles knotted in anticipation of a bullet strike. More shots echoed through the darkness, but the bullets went high. Just when it looked grim, a whirlwind spiraled the snow cover on the Yukon into a covering cloak of frozen dust. The same wind fanned the embers of the storehouse, forcing the Mounties to beat back more flames. Fifteen minutes later, the teams reached the shadowy banks of the far side and jumped the frozen overflow to disappear amid the hoarfrost and powdery brush.

Dickinson tipped his face to the moon and crowed with glee. "Yahoo, we did it boys. We caught his highness, Sir God-damned Aubrey, flat-footed and asleep in his bed or wrapped around some whore in Whitecastle."

Riley looked up from his place in the basket at Nathan and

shook his head. "We ain't in the clear yet," he said flatly. "Not by no long shot, we ain't. The hairs on the back of my head are still tingling. I ain't lived this long not to heed them warnings."

The teams raced on in silence, the soft footfall of the dogs and their low panting being the only sounds to fill the night. Not even the owl's hoot sounded. To Nathan it was all magical and dreamlike—speeding along noiselessly while the moon's shadows licked over them in tongues of indigo and burnished pewter. The soft padding and surreal landscape lulled him by its hypnotic tempo. Only the bite of the frigid air seemed real. His eyelids drooped and his head bobbled on his shoulders as the trance overtook him. The sled ran downhill, gathering momentum, before the trail hooked to the left. Automatically, Blaylock shifted his weight to the inner sled runner as the sled entered the curve.

"Jesus!" Riley screamed.

Instantly, Nathan awoke. A freshly cut spruce tree blocked the narrow pass, crossing the trail like a toll gate and resting on splintered limbs which supported it at waist height. Moonlight glinted off the rifle barrels of four men behind the barricade. The downed tree was meant to stop their sleds, Nathan realized. But to stop would be suicidal. The sled route threaded among rock ledges at this point and narrowed into a funnel. Once stopped, they would be easy targets for gunmen, fish to be shot in this barrel. Yet the tree blocked their way.

"Hold on Jim!" Nathan yelled to Riley, who already clutched a .45-70 Marlin lever-action in both hands. "Hold on! We're going through!"

Nathan cracked his whip and screamed at his dogs. The she-wolf bolted forward even before the words left his lips as if she'd read his mind. "Hike! Hike!" he cried.

The surge of the sled caught their ambushers off guard. Expecting Nathan to slow or stop, the men held their fire in hopes of a better shot, but they quickly recovered. Flashes of flame erupted from the roadblock, and Nathan heard bullets flying past him with their distinctive snapping sound.

The fallen tree lay less than ten yards ahead. Another second would find them crashing into the bristling trunk. Riley wedged his knees against the birch sides of the sled and braced himself for the impact. He planned to get one good shot in at least.

But Nathan had no intention of doing what these assassins expected. Five yards from the trap, he flipped the sled on its side. Crashing onto his right shoulder, Nathan felt the wind knocked from his lungs, but he held on. The racing dogs burst under the waist high tree and dragged the overturned sled along with them. Evergreen branches snapped and spruce needles filled the air with the violent passage. Riley flew into a snowdrift behind the barricade while Nathan slid on his stomach under the death trap, dragged along with his team and sled. The startled men manning the trap spun in confusion as their would-be prey darted past to land behind them. Desperately, these men struggled to bring their rifles to bear.

But Nathan was already sliding away on his back with his Colt spitting death and smoke at them. His first shot caught the closest rifleman square in the chest. The impact jerked him off his feet and caused his shot to go wild. His fingers fumbled with his rifle while he struggled to his knees. Nathan's second shot split the man's forehead. He fell forward like a marionette whose strings had been cut. A third shot hit the second bushwhacker in the belly. He hunched to one side, but his rifle fired, and Nathan felt the bone-jarring slap of a bullet striking his left hip.

Riley's .45-70 roared from the snowbank to tumble the third man off his perch with its heavy lead slug. The old gunman calmly levered another round into the chamber and finished off the staggering man Nathan had gutshot.

In less than a breath's time, Nathan's unexpected action had turned the ambush into a death trap for the others. Three men lay dead, their blood turning the snow around them into misshapen puddles that gleamed darkly in the moonglow.

Riley scanned the edge of the woods for any others. A fleeting glimpse of an escaping man prompted him to send a shot in that direction, but he knew he'd missed.

"Damnation!" Dickinson choked as he hurdled the tree and landed near Nathan. His pistol was drawn and his hat twisted oddly on his head by the excitement so that one earflap half covered his left eye. "Damnation," he repeated. "I never saw anything so slick in all my life. I thought we were finished, but you pulled that trick off. You're amazing. Have you done that before?"

"Once is enough," Nathan responded weakly. Fiery pain was replacing the numbness in his left side, and a warm wetness spread inside his parka.

"Well, I'd like to shake your hand, Mr. Blaylock. Wait until Teddy Roosevelt hears what you did. He'll personally invite you to the White House, I'm sure." Dickinson held out his hand.

Riley called back from where he was checking the dead men. "Hey, Nat, we know this one. Royce, I think was his handle. He was in old Soapy Smith's Skagway gang. The other two look likewise familiar. I'll bet that English Bob we met in the saloon hired them to bushwhack us." Riley calmly ransacked the men's pockets, keeping their tobacco, one watch, and the fifty-dollar gold piece each man had. He whistled softly. "Fifty bucks each. We're worth more dead to that Beaufort than we are alive."

"I think it was Beaufort who got away," Dickinson said. "You missed him, Riley."

The old gunman's head snapped up at that reproach. "Well, pardon me, yer highness, but I didn't see you doing nothing but playing with yer gun. Nathan and me could've used some help."

"You were in my line of fire," Dickinson responded coldly. "I couldn't shoot for fear of hitting one of you."

"I was scared you'd shoot one of us if you ever shot at all," Riley snorted. "What you really mean is none of these men here had their backs turned to you. That's where your experience lies: back-shooting!"

Dickinson was about to reply when Marta rushed past the two of them. Her shoulder struck the spy and spun him to one side.

"Stop it, the two of you!" she shouted. "Can't you see Nathan is hurt?"

Both men turned from their argument to find Nathan slumped against the fallen tree. The leg of his pants shone dark and wet. Marta grabbed his arms and helped him to the ground. She deftly unbuttoned his parka and pulled his shirt up. An angry furrow plowed across the top of his left hipbone, where the bullet had struck. The flesh lay back, bruised and bloodied. She glimpsed a splinter of whitish bone in the depths of the welling blood. Thankfully she noted no bowel protruding into the wound.

He grinned weakly at her.

Riley's head appeared behind her, wearing a worried look. He squinted at the injury. Doc Hennison slid to his knees beside his new patient to inspect the damage. His fingers reached forward to probe the wound only to have them stopped by Marta's grasp.

"Wash your hands, you pig," she commanded. "They're filthy."

Doc cast an astonished look at her. "Who's the doctor here?" he demanded. He paused to turn his hands over in the moonlight to check them. "They're clean. I washed them yesterday."

Marta response was to fling a handful of snow on his outstretched hands. "Scrub them with snow. You're dirty."

"We're not into U.S. territory yet," Nathan said while being examined. For some strange reason lying wounded before this girl made him feel weak and vulnerable. He found talking helped keep up his facade. "We've got to keep going. It's another four hours."

The bullet had missed Nathan's vital organs, but had shot a chip off the crest of his hipbone, and that kept up troublesome bleeding. Doc packed the groove with clean flannel, and ordered Nathan to hold pressure on the dressing.

"Your luck continues, my boy. Nothing vital damaged, just a notch in your iliac crest. Something interesting for the ladies to hold on to when you take them for a ride," Doc joked lewdly.

He'd expected Nathan to blush, which was why he'd made the joke. And the lad did as expected, but to Doc's surprise, the girl blushed just as fiercely.

Despite his protests that he could still mush, they packed Nathan into his own basket and manhandled the Maxim gun onto Marta's sled. Without asking, the girl took command of Nathan's sled, leaving Dickinson and Riley to fuss with hers. The she-wolf accepted her new boss without comment, and the team resumed its journey.

Dawn found them past boundary on the Alaskan side and camped near Chicken Creek. Miners scrabbling about the creek in search of gold lived in a few scattered shacks while they waited out the winter. Half the residents wished to give their settlement the elegant name of Ptarmigan after the snowy white birds, but no one could spell that word. So sentiment was running high to calling the place Chicken after the nearby creek. Chicken, they could spell.

On Riley's advice they hid in a string of abandoned shacks as remote from the settlement as possible. The wary gunfighter's neck hairs still prickled, leading him to continue his constant vigilance. They stayed there for three days while the weather turned clear as Nathan recovered from his wound. Doc and Many Hats lost no time in setting up their portable still while Dickinson fumed over the delay. His two brushes with Beaufort he reckoned successes, and that gave him a false confidence. Besides, only a blind man could fail to notice Marta's attraction to Nathan. Feeling jilted only heightened the spy's resolve to deliver the Maxim gun to Panama. The mission and mastering his archrival Beaufort grew to an obsession.

On the fourth evening, Dickinson checked on the patient and his nurse, something he did at least twice a day. Marta stood by while Nathan assured the spy he was recovered.

She watched Dickinson stomp out and slam the rickety door. His actions over these days had grown more imperial and abrasive. The fact that Marta had moved into the shack to nurse Nathan while the others shared another hovel irritated him all the more.

"Why did you say you could travel tomorrow?" she asked her patient with exasperation. "You're still weak."

Nathan sat up from his caribou robes. He winced imperceptibly. "I'd rather be on the trail than have Dickinson poking around me all day."

"He's changed," she said sadly. "This mission turned out to be more than he expected, and he's unsure of himself. He's wealthy and pampered, an American hidalgo. He's not used to sleeping on the trail or eating cold food with his fingers. Everything is strange to him here, and his wealth is of no use—that frightens him more than anything else."

"I suppose," Nathan agreed. "Alaska is too new a land to have hidalgos—just us rawboned and stiff-necked peasants. And the land doesn't care much for us, either. We have to fit in and make do with whatever bone she chooses to toss us."

Marta's hand reached out to touch his. "I never got to thank you for saving my life," she said, her voice soft.

Nathan smiled wryly. "No, you never did. All you did was call me a violator of helpless women."

She sat back. "Are you sorry you did?"

"No. When I thought about it I figured your country needed a sharp tongue like yours. Throwing off Colombia will require more than bullets."

Marta looked hurt. "It must be my Irish blood—from my father," she stammered. "Joined with the Miskito blood of my mother, it's an explosive mix."

Her look, so much like a scolded little girl, touched Nat. He regretted his blunt words. "Can you imagine what Jeremiah will be like—half Chinese and half bastard?" he joked.

"You should not criticize yourself for something that was not your doing," Marta said sternly. "You are a fine man, a good man, and your son will be a good man, too."

"I wonder. What kind of a life can I offer him, drifting from place to place? The kind of work I do is risky. One day I might not come back. Then what would become of my son?" He looked up at her, and she saw the fear and dilemma that filled his eyes. "But I can't stand the thought of placing him in an orphanage. It would kill me if he thought I didn't care for him. That was the worst part of all when I was with the Sisters of Charity—believing that my real father and mother never cared for me. That's a terrible cross to place on a little child."

Marta slipped onto the bed beside him and placed her arm around him. "God plays ironic tricks on us," she mused. Her other hand smoothed his hair. She had meant to console him, but his closeness stirred different feelings in her, feelings she had discounted in the past as weakness. What men had done to her, she would never forget, but this man made her heart beat fast. . . .

Nathan felt the fluttering of her breast. "Don't be frightened," he said. "What Dan McCarty told you was a lie. I never hurt a woman in my life."

She looked down at him, unsettled by the passion that engulfed her, yet unwilling to retreat. "I'm not afraid," she replied, her voice husky with emotion.

To his surprise, she kissed him. Her lips touched his, tentatively at first, yet soft and warm and full of promise. He kissed her back just as carefully. Nathan remembered Dickinson's tale of how Marta stabbed the soldier that tried to molest her.

She drew back as if sampling the effect. Her heart was threatening to jump from her chest now, but this was a new feeling. She worried he might leap at her, rip off her clothing, grasp at her with heavy hands, and force himself on her. But he did none of those things. Instead, he simply returned her favor with equal measure, no more, no less. To Marta, this was a new event: sharing. It gave her added courage.

She unbuttoned his shirt and ran her trembling hands over his chest. The touch of his muscled chest sent bolts of electricity through her arms. Her hands dragged her onward, searching, exploring, while her mind reeled in confusion.

Marta broke away, struggling in one last effort to escape this trap, but her will was halfhearted, and his eyes summoned her back. With a sob, she loosened her belt and let her clothing fall to the floor.

Nathan watched her with widening eyes. Stepping from her heavy shirt and pants, she emerged like a butterfly from an unadorned cocoon. She still wore his jade dragon around her neck.

There was no comparison between his lost love and this woman. Where Wei-Li had been slender and willowy, Marta was broad shouldered with full breasts and generous hips. Her creamy café au lait skin contrasted sharply with Wei-Li's pale tones. If one could compare Wei-Li to a graceful swallow, then Marta Kelly was a swan.

She shivered in front of him, enjoying the obvious approval

of her naked body mirrored in his eyes. Then she slipped beneath the caribou robe and into his arms. . . .

Later that evening, exhausted by their passion, the two lovers lay in each other's arms and dreamed hopeless dreams. Each rebuilt the past and changed the present to create an impossible future. Marta built a world where she could present Nathan with children, a place of peace and sense where the world would leave them alone to raise their family. But always her mind drew back to her scarred and barren womb, and her hopes shattered like hoarfrost in the wind.

Nathan recalled the pirates and shining knights of his childhood and all his plans to change the world. Ironically, he was the long lost son of a great man just like his fantasy, he noted. But all he had to show for it was Wyatt's long-barreled Colt revolver and the embrace from his father that still burned in his mind. Now he had a son of his own, one that he treated just as shabbily. But with Marta, things would be different.

He started to speak, but her finger pressed to his lips stopped him.

"Before you ask, my love, you must know something about me—something terrible."

"I don't care what it is," he protested.

"You must know. I . . . I am not a whole woman."

"You look good to me," he tried to joke, to ease the tension he sensed in her. "In fact"—he touched his throbbing wound—"I doubt if I could have survived making love with any more of a woman."

"I cannot have children," she said bluntly.

"Something about what happened with those *soldados* in Panama?" he asked. "Dickinson mentioned it."

She bowed her head and nodded. Her cheeks burned with anger that the spy would bandy about so private a confidence.

A wave of fury surged over Nathan. "I'll go back with you and kill every son of a bitch that touched you," he vowed.

She kissed him sweetly. "No need to, my love. I already have."

He looked deeply into her eyes. "Don't worry about having children," he whispered. "I come with an instant family, and the little Cub sure took a shine to you. Besides, the doctors could be wrong."

She looked at him and smiled. "We won't know if we don't try again, will we?" she said as she pulled him over to her.

TWENTY-NINE

The weather cleared and Nathan's wound healed as if the two were linked together. On the fifth day, as he moved about his dog team, a glorious day greeted him. The sun fairly shot into the cloudless sky, turning the land into stark contrasts of dazzling white with a painfully blue sky.

Marta and Nathan smiled a lot while the sleds were packed. No one questioned their decision to sled together except Dickinson, but he was ignored. The new arrangement found Dickinson and Doc traveling together and Riley riding shotgun for Many Hats. Both their sleds carried the crates of Lee-Metford rifles while Marta and Nathan hauled the precious Maxim gun.

With the two lovers setting a blistering pace, the caravan made remarkable time. Dickinson's worries about Beaufort lessened when no counterattacks came from behind them. With each mile, they drove deeper and deeper into the heart of Alaska. While his pride still stung from Marta's rejection, the spy now focused all his attention on delivering the machine gun to the Panamanian rebels. That the girl preferred this unpolished killer to him was her misfortune, he reasoned. The loss was far more hers.

Three days of fine weather found them past the Forty Mile River, across the Mosquito Flats, and into Tanana Crossing. The change in the village astonished Marta. The village no longer tottered on the edge of starvation and ruin. In the short weeks since her party had left, the caribou migration had arrived. The population of the place appeared to be tripled, and smiles and laughter greeted them everywhere. Racks of frozen caribou meat dotted the landscape, as did dogs barking and fighting over scraps of hides and scattered bones. Alder-fed smoking fires filled the air until the whole village wavered beneath the gray tendrils of smoke that rose above the river. The smell of roasting steaks and chops left Riley and Hennison in a perpetual state of salivation.

Many Hats insisted on bartering for fresh meat, claiming that the Tanacross Athabascans were worse thieves than the Han and would rob an innocent like Nathan. When Doc volunteered to accompany Many Hats Charlie on their provisioning forays, Nathan's suspicions were aroused. But the two men enjoyed haggling, and their sales of Doc's Magic Elixir added meat without depleting what little flour and tea the party possessed. Hennison's ability to manufacture his walloping medicine out of almost thin air amazed the young man. Still, he welcomed whatever gave him more time to spend with Marta. Even the happy natives remarked on the time the two lovers spent in bed.

The second evening, the couple encountered Many Hats and Doc returning from a successful transaction. Their stagger suggested the two salesmen had also sampled their own wares.

"Nathan, my boy," Doc hailed them, "and the charming Miss Kelly. A fine evening, is it not?" He touched the peak of his woodchopper's hat.

"It is, indeed, Doc," Nathan replied. With his arm around Marta and his belly full, he felt grand.

Doc turned to slap Many Hats on the back. "Capital. Mr. Hats has just proved once again that he is the most shrewd salesman I have ever met. I don't know why I wasted my time trying to teach you the trade, Nat, my boy. And, God knows, Riley is beyond instruction. All the while this natural-born genius was wasting away in that mudhole called Eagle, without my knowledge."

Marta smiled while Doc paused to wrestle a half-filled bottle of his elixir from his partner to wet his lips.

Doc continued. "The man is phenomenal. I cannot praise him too highly. We have formed a partnership, the two of us. I shall endeavor to keep production up to match Mr. Hats' prodigious salesmanship."

Both men belched appreciatively and patted one another.

"That's great, Doc. You've been looking for a partner, and I'm happy Many Hats fills the bill."

Hennison peered closely at his young friend. "You won't be disappointed, will you, Nat? You are still my good friend, of course. Nothing will ever change that, but—if you don't mind my saying so—you never showed the true aptitude to do my product full justice."

"No offense taken, Doc. I guess I never could elaborate on the magical properties of your hooch."

"Please. Elixir, not hooch, Nat. You make me sound like a moonshiner rather than a pioneer of modern medicine."

Hennison looked past Nathan at the scowling figure of Dickinson approaching. "Here comes the slave driver," he remarked. "Time for Mr. Hats and me to make ourselves scarce. I feel too good to have my mood soured by Mr. Dickinson."

The two amateur chemists staggered off. Nathan thought about hiding, but not fast enough. Dickinson flagged them down.

"I've just come from checking the Maxim gun," he said rather gruffly. "I found two native children poking about the sled. We really should post a guard." When his suggestion was met with blank stares, he added, "To protect the gun. Someone might steal it."

Nathan looked at his boots in embarrassment. What would these Indians do with a three-hundred-pound machine gun that they didn't know how to operate? Dickinson was showing signs of unraveling. His coat and jacket, while torn and rumpled like the others, were now carelessly buttoned, and he'd taken to not shaving.

Marta smiled gently at the spy. "We'll be leaving tomorrow," she said. "I'm sure the gun will be safe until morning."

Dickinson pursed his lips as if to answer before tramping off, but said nothing. Instead he withdrew his tattered map from inside his coat and wandered away while rechecking their route. The two watched him until he turned down a row of lodges and vanished from sight.

"The guns mean a lot to him," Nathan noted.

"And to my people," Marta added. "I feel guilty for each day they go without these weapons. My people are fighting with machetes and shovels for their freedom—against soldiers with rifles and cannon. Some even fight with rocks and their bare hands. The machine gun itself will help so much. It will save many lives. The sooner it arrives, the better."

Nathan's heart ached at the thought of Marta leaving. He pulled her close to him. Somehow he hoped he could convince her to stay with him. He had to think of something.

"Funny," he said. "I never considered a gun saving lives. Truthfully, I'm not looking forward to tomorrow. Each mile we make takes us closer to Valdez and your leaving. It makes me want to drag my feet."

Marta pressed her fingers to his lips. "Think only of tonight, not tomorrow. Tonight is only for us, a time to be selfish, to think only of ourselves."

Morning came all too soon.

Dickinson hurried them out of their warm beds into the blackness before dawn. Following the military trail by the light of a three-quarter moon, the sleds hugged the dark shadows of the Alaska Range and followed the sinuous origins of the Tok

River, then turned west to follow Station Creek as it wrapped along the eastern edge of the range through Mentasta Pass.

The village showed renewed signs of life, with twinkling fires. With the return of the caribou herds, the exiled Ahtnas and Copper River tribes emerged from their places of hiding to rebuild their tenuous existence. But Dickinson had no plans to stop. The teams swept past the lake and slipped into the narrow Indian Pass without being noticed.

The image of the dead infant and the dying woman came to Marta as she rode in the sled. The old woman's prophecy rang in her ears. Son of the Winter Wolf, the old one had said, would give her a son. . . .

"No, it's not possible!" Marta cried into whistling wind that cut her face like a razor.

A gust swallowed her cry so that her words echoed only in her own mind. But to her amazement, both Nathan running beside the sled and his she-wolf leading the team sensed her anguish. Without breaking stride both turned their heads to look back at her. The moonlight reflecting off the snow flashed across their two sets of eyes.

Marta shivered. The pale gray of Nathan's eyes matched his wolf's yellow eyes. Two sets of ghostly orbs stared at her from the darkness, delving within her soul for an instant, before they turned back to follow the dimly lit trail. In that instant Marta knew the Son of the Winter Wolf truly ran beside her sled!

The push continued even as the east lightened at their backs. The serrated peaks of the Wrangells on their left and the Alaskas to their right blazed with a fiery ribbon of dawn dancing along their knifelike edges. The speed and silence of the dog teams made the onset of morning all the more ethereal to Marta, and her heart kept beat with the rapid pace of the animals.

Ahead, the broad floodplain of the Copper River beckoned with its islands of stunted trees struggling amidst the braided channels that scoured the land. Now they were retracing their earlier route. But the Ahtna guide was gone, as was the stalwart Sergeant Sloan. A note of anguish clutched Marta's throat as she remembered his face. A real trooper, a professional soldier—he would be proud to be remembered as such, she realized. Yet, veteran that he was, the land still killed him as quickly and as easily as it would the tiny voles that burrowed under the snow.

This was the route they had taken less than three weeks before, but Marta saw nothing she could recognize other than the white-crested dome of Mount Drum far to the south. Despair clutched at her heart, for she realized now what plagued Dickinson even more than his fear of Beaufort: this wild territory of Alaska was too much for him—or for her. Only a rare creature like Nathan Blaylock belonged here. All others were unwelcome trespassers, interlopers to be dealt with harshly by the country.

At the junction of the Gakona with the Copper, Nathan drew to a halt. Immediately, Dickinson pulled his sled alongside.

"Why are we stopping?" he demanded. "We should push on to Copper Center Trading Post."

Nathan held up his hand. "We have to wait. Listen."

Both Dickinson and Marta swiveled their heads in search of some noise, but they heard nothing.

"Is this some silly trick? Something to make you look good and impress the young lady?" he asked impatiently.

"Listen again."

Marta heard it first. It began almost as a sensation within her head rather than a sound. But then it grew to the point that none could miss it. A clicking, faint at first, scattered and disorganized, meandered across the frozen riverbed as if thousands of knuckles were being cracked with without regard for design. Soon the sound filled the air.

"What is it?" she asked Nat.

"Caribou. A large herd." As he spoke thousands of slate-colored dots poured out of a hidden gully like army ants on the march. "They're crossing the river, and we have to wait for them to pass. The cows will attack our sled dogs if they get near their yearling calves. From here on we'll be seeing the scattered followers and stragglers until we get to Valdez." He kept his voice even when he mentioned the town that would test their love.

The she-wolf looked at him expectantly as if to say: Let's leave these humans and hunt with our brother and sister wolves that even now follow the herd, silently dogging the group, and killing the stragglers. The hunting will be good, and the caribou are still thick with winter fat. Nathan could read her mind, but he only smiled sadly at the animal and hoped she could read his thoughts as well.

Nathan's predictions of stragglers proved accurate. After brewing tea and sitting on their haunches around the fire like cattle drovers, they waited for the bulk of the herd to pass. This took over three hours, and even then solitary animals dotted hills and gullies alongside their trail ahead. To Dickinson's chagrin, the rest of the day was lost. Their party hardly reached Copper Center before nightfall.

The storekeeper was surprised to see them alive, for their treacherous Ahtna guide had passed through with the story that all the whites had died in a storm. The trader's curiosity peaked when Dickinson blocked his looking at the contents of the sled, but he figured the teams held contraband. Nathan and Marta volunteered to sleep beside the sleds at the edge of the trading post to keep the curious away.

That night, the Northern Lights entertained the lovers as they lay in each other's arms. Naked beneath their caribou robes, they kept warm and watched the hissing bands of light snake across the black velvet sky. Their lovemaking grew more urgent as each realized Valdez was no more than three days away. There, both would have to make a decision, and not an easy one.

The distressing news from the storekeeper that strange men were prowling along the narrow passes that followed the cut of the Tsina River into Keystone Canyon forced Dickinson to ask Nathan if another route existed. On his advice, the teams left the military trail where it crossed Stewart Creek and headed along the foothills to the base of the Tonsina Glacier. The plan was to follow it onto the Valdez Glacier, using that ice field to enter Valdez without passing through any of the many canyons that might hold another ambush. Dickinson insisted on this way in spite of Nathan's warnings of the danger of glacier travel in the winter.

"It's all ice, isn't it?" the spy retorted. "Winter or summer, what's the difference? Just a matter of more of it in the winter."

"The difference is in the winter the snow doesn't melt away to reveal the crevasses and drop-offs," Nathan argued. "The Valdez Glacier Route is filled with unmarked graves of all the miners who died up there. Most froze to death, but just as many dropped out of sight into some bottomless pit."

"You're being melodramatic," the spy scoffed. "I'd rather take my chances out in the open on an ice field than be bush-whacked again by Beaufort. Surely you must see his predilection is for ambush. No, we're safer out in the open."

But the glacier bore no resemblance to what Dickinson expected. Driving to the foot of the Tonsina they encountered something far different than the smooth block of ice the agent imagined. Instead of an even sheet of progressing ice, they came upon irregular blocks of shattered ice and heaps of slimy gravel gouged from the glacier's moraine by the enormous weight of the frozen water. Pulverized rock in the form of glacial flour dusted everything that snow failed to cover.

The going was awful. Pulling and pushing the sleds by hand over this tumbled landscape took all day. By dusk, they had only reached the roof of the Tonsina. With bleeding hands and scraped knees the travelers stopped to make camp.

"Don't unpack the sleds," Dickinson ordered. "We'll stay long enough to eat, that's all. I want to press on."

"In the dark?" Riley stammered. "Are you crazy?"

Dickinson pointed to the full moon rising over the land of ice. Its light shone on the vast white field, causing it to glow with the illumination of a thousand lamps. "Look! We'll have plenty of light. See how bright the moon is?"

"You're asking for trouble, Dickinson," Nathan added. "Moon or no moon, the shadows will hide the snow bridges and the crevasses. You risk everything crossing in the dark. Best to wait until morning."

"I'm in charge here," Dickinson snapped. "And you're in my pay, so you'll do as I say—unless you want to back out. But there'll be no pay for a coward. The deal was to get these sleds to Valdez, nothing less."

Nathan turned to Doc for support, but none was forthcoming. "We've come this far, Nat," Hennison muttered. "Valdez is just a day or two away."

The youth looked at Marta, but Dickinson blocked his view. "She goes along with me, in my sled," he said. "She's important to the success of this operation—almost as much as the Maxim gun. All you can do is bed her, but I'll get her to Valdez."

Riley saw his friend tense like a wolf ready to spring, and he stepped between the two, turning his back to the agent while his hand grasped Nathan's arm.

"Won't do no good to kill this ignorant son of a bitch," he whispered. "Just hurt your chances with the girl. She might not realize you was doing it to protect her. Best go along and keep an eye on her to keep her out of harm."

Jim's steely grip on his gun arm steadied Nathan until

he felt the rage draining from his body. He shook his head in disgust and walked to where Many Hats was starting a fire from sticks he'd collected before they mounted the face of the glacier.

Dinner was eaten in silence while the moon climbed over the mountain peaks. The dogs gulped snow and gnawed at the frozen hunks of salmon and caribou meat tossed to them. Without a word, the group scoured their tin plates with snow, smothered the pitiful fire, and pulled their snow hooks. At the last minute Marta broke away from Dickinson to jump into Nathan's sled. Before she did, she kissed Nathan fiercely on the lips.

"I'll ride with you while you break trail," she said.

Nathan scowled. "We shouldn't let him push us. There's no reason to take this risk."

Marta smiled knowingly at him. "Let's just cross this damned glacier and get it done."

The crack of Nathan's whip in the air provided his reply. The team lurched forward, and the sled sped away.

Crossing the back of the glacier called for new skills. What looked like rolling swells of ice turned out to hide deep fracture lines and sharp walls of ice thrusting upward where the surface was broken. Nathan was right about the moon's shadows, too. It took all his concentration to keep his eyes focused on the unending whiteness. The snowy blanket covering parts of the glacier ran unbroken forever in hypnotic constancy only to open suddenly into a yawning chasm that would swallow them. Once, twice, thrice, Nathan swerved at the last moment to keep from riding into empty space. More than once his foot felt the snow crumble beneath it and vanish as he skirted a drop-off.

Concentrating so hard took all his effort, so Nathan scarcely noticed when they crossed the Tonsina Glacier and began the steady winding climb up to the plateau of the Valdez

Glacier. By this time he was dripping with sweat and shaking from the combined mental and physical effort.

Half a mile onto the Valdez sweep he realized where they were. They had reached the crest. Guiding his team to a level plain, he stopped. Ahead, miles of unblemished snow stretched to the horizon and off to both sides, bending with the curvature of the earth like a vast ocean as it vanished.

Dickinson drew his sled to a stop behind them. "See," the agent crowed, "I told you there was nothing to fear."

He spoke too soon.

A forbidding crack sounded beneath their feet. The snow shifted, then stopped. Nathan stared down into a widening slit that yawned between his boots. Dickinson gaped in disbelief.

"We've stopped atop an ice bridge!" Nathan shouted.

At that moment, the fragile crust of ice gave way. Moaning in an almost human way, chunks of snow and ice dropped away and tumbled into the inky blackness of a chasm. The collapse threw Nathan and his team to one side while the sled with Marta and the Maxim gun slewed toward the precipice. To his horror, the girl and the sled slid over the edge.

In desperation, Nathan screamed at his team and dove across the traces to the sled. The lunge of the animals and his weight pinned the lines to the edge with only the nose of the sled projecting above the icy lip. Marta had vanished from sight.

Painfully, Nathan inched along the lines toward the rim. His heart soared at what he saw. Marta was hanging in space, holding on for her life with her fingers entwined in the lacing of the swinging sled basket. Dickinson remained frozen in place. Riley and Many Hats rushed to help, but their weight caused the crust that still supported Nathan and his dogs to buckle.

"*Get back!*" Nathan yelled. He watched them retreat before turning his attention back to the girl. Even that movement caused the sled ropes to slip another inch over the edge. Any minute, Nathan realized, and the entire outfit would slide from beneath him and vanish into the rift.

"Cut the Maxim free!" he commanded Marta. "Use your knife!"

"No! No!" Dickinson screamed from his fixed location. "Don't! We need the gun!"

Marta looked up at Nathan, her eyes shining brightly with fear and uncertainty. "He's right!" she cried. "Save the gun! It's more important than me!"

"No!"

"Yes, listen to her," Dickinson babbled. "Without her weight we can pull the sled back up. We can save the gun!"

"Shut up, you shit!" Nathan snarled. "Cut the goddamned machine gun loose, Marta, now!"

"Don't do it—," Dickinson yelled, but his voice cut short when Riley's rifle butt crashed into his head. He slumped onto his back.

"You jus' go right ahead, boy, and pull that pretty gal up here like you planned," came Riley's even voice. For all its indifference he could be leaning against a bar in downtown Dawson.

Nathan thanked the coolness of his friend. "Jim," he whispered, "get ready to grab for my ankles."

"Right."

Marta's eyes filled with tears. "Good-bye, my love," she whispered.

Her fingers opened and she slipped out of the harness.

Nathan launched himself into the emptiness. His fingers locked on Marta's wrists, and the two lovers plummeted down. Just then, Riley's hands clamped like vises onto his friend's ankles. The youth and the girl dropped a foot before snapping to a halt. There they swung, engulfed by the blackness of the hole below them. The sled raced past them, dragging the tethered dogs to their doom. Their yelps and cries of terror seemed to last forever before they smashed to their deaths a thousand feet below.

Slowly, painfully, inch by inch, Riley, with the help of Many Hats and Doc Hennison, dragged the couple back to safety. Just as the two were safely back from the edge, the remnant of the collapsed ice bridge gave way and vanished into the void.

Riley rolled onto his back and rubbed his grizzled chin. "A bit too close for my tastes," he sighed. He raised his head and looked at the unconscious Dickinson. "What kind of a lowlife would let a person die to save a hunk of steel?" he wondered out loud. "If he's a prime example, I'm damned glad I ain't civilized."

Marta lay sobbing in Nathan's arms. Her entire body quivered, and this weakness made her ashamed. Since that terrible day in the jungle, she'd forged an iron purpose: to overthrow the tyrannical government that allowed such injustices to happen. She had dedicated her life to that aim and denied all else.

Now this gentle killer with the pale, wild eyes had opened her heart and showed her the power of a sharing love, and her life had split into two conflicting camps. Nathan owned her heart, but her mind and will, whether by sheer momentum or sheer stubbornness, pressed on for her original intent. Torn between the two, she was prepared to die to save the machine gun that would so greatly help her beleaguered cause. But deep inside she wanted desperately to live and love.

Many Hats crawled cautiously on his stomach to the edge of the abyss. Struggling to see into the darkness, he finally inched back and made his pronouncement. "All gone," he said.

"Yup," Riley agreed. "Might as well hole up until morning. No sense losing the rest of the sleds."

He and Many Hats started a fire while Nathan helped Doc rig a makeshift shelter of the two remaining sleds and a canvas

tarp. They dragged Dickinson inside to recover. Marta an
Nathan wrapped themselves in a robe and huddled togethe
awaiting the dawn.

Their tiny fire shone like a miniature beacon on the va
whiteness of the ice field. Unknown to them, their light wa
being watched.

THIRTY

Nathan awoke to a tongue licking the side of his face. Instantly he was awake. The golden eyes of the she-wolf stared unblinking at him. At her feet lay two snowy white ptarmigan. The wolf gave him one more lick before picking up one of the birds and retreating a few paces, where she lay down to eat her catch.

"Where you find these things amazes me," he said. "Thank you. Marta and I could use a good breakfast." For the hundredth time he thanked his lucky stars that the wolf refused to run in harness. Otherwise, he would have lost her with the rest of his dog team.

Nathan plucked the bird and cooked it while he watched the birth of a new day. Marta still slept, but the others were moving about the camp. Dickinson sported a dirty handkerchief on his head for a dressing. While he squatted by the fire, Nathan studied their surroundings. By some trick of shadow the moonlight had concealed a barrier over three hundred yards from their camp which the sunlight now exposed. Directly between them and Valdez lay an ice face which rose to a height of some sixty feet. A split in this facade created a narrow pass which they could squeeze through. This ice wall ran for miles. A detour around this natural barrier would take days.

Nathan nodded in the direction of the ice ridge as Riley crouched beside him to pour a cup of watery coffee. "Funny I never saw that last night," Nathan remarked.

"Well, it might have slipped up while we was sleeping, Nat, but I kinda doubt it. Light and dark sure can play tricks on a fellow out here." He paused to rub the back of his neck. "I got that prickly feeling again. Keep a sharp lookout, will you. That notch there is a perfect place for an ambush."

Many Hats swooped the coffee cup from Riley's hand and trudged past the fire until he stood between them and the ice rise. He squinted against the glare that rose increasingly from the snow as the sun climbed higher.

A slapping sound broke the stillness. It resembled a hand thumped against a leather coat, to be followed a second later by a distant crack coming from the ice wall. Both Riley's and Nathan's heads snapped up at the chilling sound. It was all too familiar to them: the sound of a bullet solidly striking flesh. A puff of smoke from the rim of the barrier confirmed the long range shot.

Many Hats turned slowly on stiffening legs. A ragged hole appeared in the center of his parka to match an exit site between his shoulder blades. The impact knocked his beaver hat with its beaded hatband off his head, but he remained standing. Bright red blood pumped onto the front of his coat to freeze into scarlet ice. He half fell to his knees while his hand groped for his prized hat. With one final effort the old Indian retrieved his hat and placed it on his head before he sank onto his left side. By the time Hennison got to his side he was dead.

"Git down, Doc!" Riley shouted.

Mindless of any danger, Doc cradled his late partner. He looked bewilderedly at his friends crouched behind the sleds. "They killed the best salesman I ever knew," Doc stuttered. "Why would they do that?"

Dickinson fumbled in his sled for his binoculars, only to have Riley rip them from his hands when he found them. To Nathan's sharp eye a minuscule figure stood waving on the top

372

of the wall where the puff of smoke hung motionless in the still air.

"Goddamned fellow's got one of them newfangled glass telescopes for a sight on his rifle," Riley announced as he studied the figure through the binoculars.

"Hello! Hello!" came the distant shout from the assassin manning the glacial rampart. "Have I got your attention, Dickinson?" The voice was high-pitched, with a distinctly English accent.

Dickinson's face drained of color. "Beaufort!" he cried.

"Precisely!" came the shouted reply.

"How did you get past us?" Dickinson cried in dismay.

"Poor Dickinson," Beaufort shouted, "always out of your league. I had no need to overtake you on the trail after you escaped my little reception. You've forgotten about the railroad. The White Pass and Yukon now connects to the edge of Dawson. I simply rode the train, then took a packet steamer to Valdez. I've been waiting for you in the comfort of the hotel. I positioned my men in Keystone Canyon, but I knew you'd come over the glacier. When one of my scouts spotted your fire last night, I hurried out to greet you with my surprise."

"What do you want?" Dickinson asked.

Nathan covered Marta with his body, mindful that Beaufort's high-powered rifle could easily punch through their flimsy cover. They were out in the open with no protection.

"Can you get a clear shot at him, Jim?" Nathan asked.

"No, he's moving about too much. If I try a shot and miss, he'll set back and pick us off one at a time."

"Can we make a deal?" Dickinson yelled. "What do you want? Me and the rifles? Is that it?"

"The rifles, yes. But not you, Dickinson. You're worthless. I want the other one, the real man. Nathan Blaylock."

The others looked puzzled. Why would he want Nathan?

The English agent answered their question. "I've taken
dislike to Mr. Blaylock. He vexes me."

"Go to hell!" Nathan shouted at the distant figure. "Yo
can rot up there. I'm not giving you a clear shot, you bush
whacker!"

"I think you will!" Beaufort laughed. He vanished behind
an outcropping of ice to emerge holding something aloft in hi
left hand. He shook it violently.

"Cub! Cub!" squealed a child's voice in terror.

"Sweet Jesus!" Riley swore. "He's got little Jeremiah!"

But all in the camp recognized the baby's cries. Nathar
eyes wide in panic, struggled to his knees. "He's got my sor
I've got to go—"

Dickinson's fist caught him off guard. The blow struck fu
force on his chin, knocking him unconscious. Under cover c
the tarp, Dickinson quickly stripped off Nathan's jacket and ha
and pulled them on.

"What the hell are you doing?" Riley asked. "That man ou
there is a cold-blooded killer. You don't think he'll let you gc
do you? You don't stand a chance."

"Shut up and listen," Dickinson commanded. "I'm going t
draw him out. He'll think I'm Nathan until I get close. Then I'
rush him and grab the baby. You get that Sharps ready an
wait for a clear shot."

Before Riley could answer, Dickinson stood up and wave
his arms. He kept Nathan's fur hat low on his forehead to hid
his face. "Okay, I'm coming," he shouted, doing his best to in
itate Nathan's voice.

As he stepped into the open, Beaufort watched hin
through his scope, unconvinced. The assassin centered th
crosshairs on Dickinson, and his finger took up the slack in th
trigger of his custom-made hunting rifle.

Marta lunged from behind the shelter and grasped Dicl

inson's leg. Her face and eyes contained too many unanswerable questions.

Dickinson gently broke off her grip. "I'm doing this for myself, Marta. I realized I'd gone too far yesterday. Nothing is so important that it supersedes our humanity. I stooped to eating the flesh from that poor frozen corpse to maintain my strength, and yesterday I even planned on sacrificing you to save the Maxim gun. Let me go now. I've got to redeem my soul."

She hung her head in acceptance, and her hands dropped away. This gesture of despair caused Beaufort not to shoot. Surely the girl was imploring the man he imagined to be Nathan not to go. Now he would have that troublesome pest who had wrecked his ambush where he wanted him. He lowered his rifle and raised the screaming child in front of him as a shield. That old gunman, Riley, had a dangerous reputation with his buffalo rifle. Unseen by Beaufort, Dickinson took that moment to slip his revolver into Nathan's oversized coat sleeve.

Riley slipped his .50 caliber Sharps from its moosehide scabbard and wriggled into position. Ever so slowly he lifted a corner of the tarp to permit a clear field of fire. With infinite care he adjusted the vernier scale on the rear peep sight to four hundred yards. Better to overestimate and aim high than to have the heavy bullet drop too low and miss, he reasoned. Any solid hit with that lead slug would put Beaufort down, if not kill him. One good shot was all he'd have. He wet his fingers and pinched the front sight to clean it and remove any glare.

Dickinson's walk of over three hundred yards of open ground took forever. Taking advantage of the sun at his back, the agent kept his chin down and his face in shadow. Beaufort watched him come, always holding the frightened child between him and his adversaries.

Fifty feet from him, Beaufort ordered a halt. "That's far

enough," he snarled. "I know about your reputation with a gun, Blaylock. You've caused me endless trouble, but I'm about to rectify that." He shifted the rifle in his one hand, holding it like a pistol with his finger on the trigger. "Never play by the rules is my motto."

"Wait!" Dickinson jerked his arms higher and in doing so pulled his pistol from hiding. But Beaufort still used the child as a shield, blocking any clear shot.

"Dickinson!" Beaufort erupted in fury. "I should have known you'd try something stupid!"

The sporting rifle barked in his hand and Dickinson doubled over from the impact of the high-powered bullet. Beaufort shifted the child to reload his rifle.

A snarling blur of white fur sprang at the rifleman's throat. The she-wolf, undetected, had stalked this killer who threatened her adopted cub. Her charge drove him off balance, and he dropped the young boy. Instead of pressing her attack, she broke off and raced for the child, snatched him by the scruff of his neck, and dragged him in the direction of a protective outcropping of rock and ice.

Her decision to rescue the child cost her dearly. Beaufort reloaded and fired at the retreating pair. The wolf yelped in pain as the bullet struck her, but she maintained her hold on the child and pulled him to safety before Beaufort could fire again. Behind the rock she covered the child with her dying body to protect him.

The wolf's action stripped Beaufort of his human armor. In that split second Riley squeezed the set trigger of his Sharps and felt the heavy gun buck against his shoulder. Dickinson, too, fired his pistol although his blood made his grip slippery.

Riley heard the solid smack of his round hitting home and saw Beaufort spin around from the impact. Dickinson's shot went wide. Momentary elation died as Riley saw Beaufort stagger to his feet with his pistol in hand and vanish behind the ridge. The assassin was going to finish young Jeremiah and his protecting wolf. Riley lurched to his feet only to be passed by a whirlwind.

Nathan dashed over the open ground, pistol in hand, heedless of any danger as he sprinted toward his son. Each stride carried him closer while he prayed he would arrive in time.

A pistol shot echoed across the glacier.

Beaufort smirked in satisfaction as another bleeding hole appeared in the wolf's side. Still she snarled at him, guarding her cub.

"Want another one, you bitch?" Beaufort gloated. "And then one for that brat." He cocked his pistol and steadied his aim.

Suddenly, a shadow fell across his line of sight. He raised his head from the pistol to see the shape of Nathan Blaylock rising above him, threatening, and outlined by the sun like the image of death itself. Both hands were clamped on Wyatt Earp's revolver that aimed directly at him.

"No . . ." Beaufort held his hands up.

He never finished his plea.

When Marta and Riley reached the spot, they found Nathan cradling his son and his wolf. Beaufort lay dead with a bullet through his left eye. Dickinson lay dead not far away. Marta approached Nathan and held out her arms for the shivering Jeremiah. To her surprise the she-wolf raised her head and licked her hand instead of growling. Then the light faded from those yellow eyes, and the wolf's head dropped into Nathan's lap.

Jeremiah held out his chubby hands to Marta and sniffled. Carefully, she took him from Nathan's arms and began to rock him.

"Cub," the child said, happy to be held and comforted once more.

THIRTY-ONE

The journey into Valdez took all day. Less than a handful of words passed their lips during the entire trip, and most came from Jeremiah and Doc Hennison. Behind them, on the plain of the Valdez Glacier, the party left two burial scaffolds rising above the immutable ice. One contained the carefully wrapped body of Many Hats Charlie, offered to his gods with his prized beaver hat laced on his chest. The second, smaller, but just as carefully wrapped body held the remains of the she-wolf. At their feet for the ravens and foxes to eat was sprawled the body of Sir Aubrey Beaufort, late of Her Majesty's Foreign Office.

Arriving in Valdez with the body of Dickinson and the crate of rifles, the travelers caused quite a stir. While Nathan slumped against the sled and Marta held his son, Riley and Doc pushed their way through the crowd and sought the nearest army post.

Half an hour later they returned with a sergeant who gaped at the sleds before rushing off to summon help. He returned in ten minutes with a squad of soldiers who posted the area and kept the onlookers at bay. The sergeant also brought a bottle of rye from the saloon for them.

Raising his head Nathan was startled to recognize two faces among the curious crowd. Standing apart from the rest, a couple inspected him fixedly. Defiantly Nathan raised his chin and stared back into the faces of Isabelle and E. T. Barnette.

Bundled in stylishly long beaver coats, the captain and his lady watched him intently. Isabelle clutched her throat as she chewed her lip and blinked in confusion. Her face was pale as if she viewed a ghostly apparition. Captain Barnette glared at him with a look of pure hatred. The fire in his eyes and the grinding muscles of his jaw left no doubt his vendetta was not over.

Long before dark, Captain Abercrombie arrived by motor launch from Fort Liscum. He examined the dead agent, then the rifles.

"I was afraid it would come to this," he said sadly. "Sergeant Sloan is dead as well? What a waste. Well, two of my men will escort you to the hotel. I suspect you'll feel more human after a good meal and a bath."

"We need to take the rifles with us," Nathan said. "Too many good men died for them."

Abercrombie shook his head. "Sorry, we'll take possession of the Lee-Metfords. I've orders to return them to the Canadians although I'd just as soon keep them for my own men since we've not received the new Springfields we were promised. Washington is smoothing over this affair with our neighbors."

"No!" Marta protested. "These guns are for my people. To free them from Colombia!"

Captain Abercrombie saluted her. "No longer necessary, my dear. I've just received an important cable that might interest you. While you were . . . er, engaged in this misadventure, the United States has signed a treaty recognizing Panama as a sovereign state and guaranteeing its independence from Colombia. You already have your country, Miss Kelly. May I congratulate you, miss, and welcome you to the United States territory of Alaska. You are the first Panamanian citizen I've met."

Tears filled Marta's eyes as she stood there speechless. An embarrassed Abercrombie removed himself. His men dispersed the crowd, taking with them the precious rifles and the body of the man who had died for those guns.

Nathan wrapped her in his arms, and the three of them walked down to the beach. The setting sun backlit the mountains surrounding the Valdez Narrows until the sky and the water glowed as if afire.

"Now you can stay here, with us," Nathan suggested. "You don't have to go back to fight. The fighting is over."

Marta looked up at him with eyes brimming with tears. Her heart was breaking. "All the more reason I must go, now, my love. I must help build my new country."

Nathan sighed and looked at his son asleep on his shoulder. "I guess I understand, but I hoped . . . Well, remember what I said about having bad luck with the women that mattered to me?"

She kissed him fiercely. "We still have tonight."

The steamship's horn blew a farewell blast as the vessel pulled away from the dock. The usual crowd of well-wishers jostled along the plank wharf and waved hats and handkerchiefs. To one side, three men waved at a beautiful dark-haired woman who signaled back at them from the ship's railing.

Doc Hennison patted Nathan paternally. "It's better this way, Nat," he said.

"I know, Doc, but that doesn't make it any easier," Nathan replied. He was sandwiched between his friends, and he appreciated their support.

The woman lifted a small child to the rail. "Wave to your father, Jeremiah," she said with quivering voice. "He loves us both very much, and someday we will be together again."

The child waved until the figures on the dock were too small to see. And his father watched until the ship vanished into a low fog bank just opposite Shoup Glacier.